Old Land, New Tales

Old Land, New Tales

20 SHORT STORIES BY WRITERS
of the SHAANXI REGION IN CHINA

EDITED BY

Lei Tao and
Jia Pingwa

amazon crossing

Old Land, New Tales was first published in 2011 by China Intercontinental Press as 陕西作家短篇小说集. Translated from Chinese by Zhang Min, Nan Jianchong, Hu Zongfeng, Liu Xiaofeng, Wen Hui, Du Lixia, Wang Hongyin, Zhang Yujin, Qin Quan'an, Yang Narang, Liu Danling, Zhang Yihong, Li Meng, Ren Huilian, Ji Wenkai, Xiaohui Xue, Chen Yi, Zhang Yating, Yang Jinmei, Liu Yuan, and Guo Yingjie as a work for hire, copyright China Intercontinental Press. Published by AmazonCrossing in 2014.

Published by AmazonCrossing, Seattle

ISBN-13: 9781477823705
ISBN-10: 1477823700

Library of Congress Control Number: 2014900610

Members

Li Guoping, Vice-Chairman

Wang Fangwen, Secretary General and Director of Creative &
Liaison Department

Wang Peng, Vice-Chairman

Ye Guangqin, Vice-Chairman

Bai Aying, Vice-Chairman

Feng Jiqi, Vice-Chairman

Gao Jianqun, Vice-Chairman

Zhu Hong, Vice-Chairman

Mo Shen, Vice-Chairman

Li Kangmei, Vice-Chairman

Leng Meng, Vice-Chairman

Hong Ke, Vice-Chairman

Zhang Hong, Vice-Chairman

Yan An, Vice-Chairman

Qin Quan'an, Deputy Secretary General, Shaanxi Translation
Association

Wang Xiaowei, Vice-Director of Creative & Liaison Department

Hu Zongfeng, Deputy Dean, School of Foreign Languages,
Northwest University

Li Hao, Vice President and Dean of the School of the Arts,
Northwest University

Yang Dafu, Former Dean of English Studies School, Xi'an
International Studies University

Li Xijian, Dean of Chinese Language and Literature School,
Shaanxi Normal University

Zhang Yujin, Associate Professor of International Studies, Xi'an
Jiaotong University and Deputy Secretary General, Shaanxi
Translation Association

Kong Baoer, Chief Reporter of Xi'an TV Station and Board
Member, Shaanxi Translation Association

Advisors

Allison Adair, Audrae Coury, Robert Farnsworth, Robin
Gilbank, Buffy Gilfoil, Andy Gross Green, Darlene Kunze,
Sonya Lason, Michael Lestz, Myrtis Mixon, Julia Phillips, Vicky
Tangi, Mary Warpeha

Contents

Old Land, New Tales

Lei Tao

Let Literature Fly through the Blue Sky and White Clouds

As the spiritual secret history of a nation, literature (especially novels and short fiction) is the product of many communications and collisions. This evidence of spiritual life is valuable not only to a particular nation, but to the civilized society of the whole of humanity. From the May Fourth Movement to today, many international literary works have been translated and introduced into China, resulting in an evolution in Chinese literary aesthetics. Beyond style, readers discover the world's diverse visions and virtues through literature. Meanwhile, works of many Chinese writers have now been translated into a wealth of other languages, helping readers around the world understand the current diverse spiritual and ethical pursuits of the Chinese nation. This mutual exchange is a pillar of the international community.

The reforms of new China have opened the country's borders to many new and diverse channels for cultural exchange. Chinese writers are now finding broader aesthetic communities through translation—and, with this exposure, finding confidence to explore new territory.

Seated in central China, the Shaanxi region is one of the cradles of Chinese civilization. The province's principal city and current capital, Xi'an, is the eastern terminus of the Silk Road, which leads to Europe, the Arabian Peninsula, and Africa—making Shaanxi a longtime hub of cultural exchange, both within China and overseas. With the reform of new China as its inspiration, the Shaanxi Writers Association of China's Literature Translation Special Committee started the SLIP program in 2008 to introduce and popularize outstanding works by Shaanxi authors.

The members of the Shaanxi Writers Association and Provincial Translation Association reached out to local literature and translation circles, seeking stories that reflect Shaanxi writing in all its diversity and richness. The twenty tales selected for this book represent the standard and style of contemporary writers from the old but civilized land of Shaanxi. This community of writers, defining Shaanxi literature as a unified school, includes many winners of national awards, including the Mao Dun Literature Award, the Lu Xun Literature Award, the Bing Xin Literature Award, and the Stallion Award.

The sky of literature is vast and blue, and it is a realm full of hope and fantasy. Writers dream of adding wings to their works, to watch them fly through the blue sky and white clouds of the heavens. It is my hope that through reading these stories by conscientious writers and lovers of life, we might help drive forward the peaceful development of the world, linking human progress across cultures from the ancient perspective of this province in the heart of China.

We are under the same blue sky, and we have the same destination. This is the home to literature and also the source of our strength.

Lu Yao (1949–1992)

Lu Yao, formerly known as Wang Weiguo, of the Han nationality, was a contemporary Chinese writer. He was born into a peasant family in Yulin City, Qingjian County, Shaanxi Province. His family was too poor to raise him, so at age seven he was adopted by his uncle in a village of Yanchuan County. After middle school, he returned home to work as a farmer in 1969.

He graduated from the Department of Chinese Language and Literature at Yan'an University, which launched his writing career, and after graduation he edited the literary magazine *Shaanxi Literature*. His first novella, *A Suspenseful Scene*, was published in 1980 and won the country's first National Award for Best Novella. He won the award again in 1982 for *Life*; the film adaptation won the Hundred Flowers Award for Best Feature Film and was a hit across the country. That year, Lu Yao joined the Chinese Writers Association and his novel *In the Difficult Days* won the Novel Prize in Contemporary Literature.

In 1988 Lu Yao completed his thirteen-volume, million-word masterpiece *Ordinary World*, which won the third Mao Dun Literature Award. Before the book was even finished, it was broadcasted as a radio play on China National Radio. Lu Yao passed away in 1992, at the age of 42, at the height of his career.

LU YAO
Elder Sister

My twenty-seven-year-old sister should have been married a long time ago. In rural areas, it is a disgrace for a girl of that age to continue her unmarried life in her parents' home. Embarrassing rumors have been circulating in the village, which sting more than the severest slap to our faces.

Papa has become a man of few words. Ever since Mama died, he has simply kept his mouth shut, busying himself with all sorts of farmwork. Neither Sister's marital prospects nor other family affairs can arouse his slightest interest.

I love my sister. Pure, tender, and kind, she is a white cloud in the azure sky. Villagers say she is good-looking, and what they say is true. Every village here, no matter how remote or backward, boasts at least a few stunningly beautiful young ladies who, like the local produce—dates and daylilies—are known across the region, from the provincial capital to the neighboring towns and villages. Why, don't you believe it? Go and ask whoever is on the road.

I am not bragging when I tell you that my sister is one of these beautiful women. She has been my idol since childhood, when I developed a love for art and a taste for beauty. Mama once told me that a provincial singing and dancing troupe had intended to recruit Sister as an actress when she was still a little girl; however, Mama and Papa refused, on the grounds that she was too small and that they would not like to be parted from her.

Several years have passed since Sister graduated from high school. She took entrance examinations for higher education but failed each time, only a few points short of the admissions criteria. Sister went to high school in a time when the Cultural Revolution was seething with enthusiasm—so she didn't learn much. On the foreign-language section of the entrance exam, she didn't even know the twenty-six letters of the alphabet; it seems that her hopes of becoming a college student are gone forever.

There's no way for her to become a worker, either, for the security of that kind of career can be had only through a back door. And even when a back door is opened for her, there's never a current vacancy to be filled. It seems she is destined to labor her whole life away in the fields. However, Sister doesn't seem to mind at all being a farmer. Since she was brought up in this barren area, not even the toughest farm tasks deter her. Everyone in the village says she equals a man in doing farmwork.

The feet of matchmakers have worn thin the threshold of our house over the years. Among the candidates they sought for my sister, most were cadres or workers from bigger cities, but none has ever struck her fancy. Villagers feel sorry for her to have missed so many golden chances; they wonder why a twenty-seven-year-old girl is not the least bit worried about an event as important as her own marriage.

But in fact, Sister has had a sweetheart. This is a secret kept from everyone in the whole world but me.

The boy Sister loved was Gao Limin, an educated young man from the provincial capital. People say his father was a deputy governor of our province, his mother the director of a certain bureau.

Accused of heading a spy organization, they were arrested and imprisoned soon after the Cultural Revolution broke out.

Of the dozen young people who came to our village with Gao Limin, some were recommended to study in universities and others were taken on as workers. All of them returned to the cities eventually—except for Gao Limin. He was detained because of his parents' case. Not only couldn't he get away from our village, he couldn't even lead an easy life as a farmer; wherever he went, from the commune to the county, he'd be given a dressing-down.

Those years found him a most wretched dog, for in the eyes of the masses, being the son of spies was worse than being a reactionary. Most villagers dared not associate with him for fear of courting unexpected disasters. So Gao Limin, like a lamb alienated from the herd, could keep only his own company. His clothes were too shabby even for a beggar; he ate only raw food, as he didn't know how to cook, and as a result he often suffered from stomachaches that would send him rolling about on the muddy ground.

My sister couldn't bear to see him suffering like that, so she often went to help him with cooking, sewing and mending, and washing. On holidays, Sister would bring him home and give him the best food we could offer. Sometimes I doubted I was her younger brother, because she seemed to care more for Limin than she did for me.

My parents never uttered a word against Sister for doing it. They were both kindhearted farmers just like her. However, some folks in the village began making up stories; they said my sister and Gao Limin had an improper relationship. They didn't dare spread such rumors in the presence of my sister or my parents, but they often repeated them to me when I was a little boy. And each time I would protest.

"Sister's just being kind to Limin," I'd say furiously. "How can you guys ruin their good names?"

They would always burst out laughing.

Everyone knew that Gao Limin was the son of spies. Why should Sister treat him so kindly? I kept turning this question over in my mind.

Once, out of earshot of my parents, I asked her. "Sister, Limin is the son of spies; why don't you just steer clear of him like everybody else does? Aren't you afraid people will say you're politically naive and can't tell a friend from an enemy?"

My sister smiled, pressing her finger on my nose. "Baowa, you are more radical than Secretary Liu of the commune. Limin's only fallen on bad days. He is no class enemy, so we need not make a clean break with him. Don't you remember Grandma's instructions? Grandma—may she rest in peace—used to say we should try our best to help those who are down. She said that if we do something evil, we'll be struck dead by lightning. Look, here in our village he has no friends, no family to depend on. Can we bear to see him suffer to death? Let them talk bullshit—there is nothing to be afraid of!"

All of a sudden I was enlightened.

To rumors and slander Sister just turned a deaf ear, and when all the other educated youths left the village, she cared for Limin more tenderly than ever.

I still remember the day Limin fell sick. Sister spent a whole day looking after him. She took flour, sesame, and pickled leek flowers from home and made him a meal of noodles. Noodles! What a rare meal! Keep in mind, we were rationed to no more than fifteen jin of wheat per head per year.

It was late afternoon. My sister remained in Limin's cave dwelling because a high fever had beset him. By the time it was dark enough to light a lamp, Mama grew worried and went over to have a look. Instead of bringing Sister back, she herself stayed and joined in the watch for the whole night.

How nice the relationship between Sister and Limin! Who could say their relationship was improper?

However, it was not long before I came to understand what the gossipers actually meant by "improper."

One late summer afternoon, the clouds in the western sky burned crimson like fire for a moment before they changed into ash gray. As daylight lingered, I snatched a few clothes and went to the river in front of the village. The clothes to be washed were not so dirty, but I am a boy who greatly loves cleanliness and beauty.

As I walked along the path above the threshing ground, I suddenly heard two people talking behind a pile of wheat straw. They were the voices of a man and a woman.

Driven by childish curiosity, I stooped down and sneaked to the back of the wheat stack. My goodness! The sight almost scared me out of my wits. The man and woman were none other than Limin and my sister. Limin was holding my sister in his arms and kissing her madly on the cheek! I shivered, stumbling and scrambling all the way back to the path.

I stood there, my heart beating violently as if it would leap out of my mouth. I wanted to run away at once—but then their voices came again, and I had to hear what they were saying.

"You're a kind person, Xing'er. I love you. I'll never leave you. I can't live without you. Tell me that you love me, too. Promise to love me, OK? But no, for what . . . My parents have been in prison for six or seven years. It seems I'll be marked as the son of spies for the rest of my life. Of course you'll be afraid . . ."

"No, I'm not afraid. I can wait, even if you are jailed."

Limin wept. Soon he spoke to my sister again.

"Xing'er, I'll give you all I have! I'll never forget it's your love that comes to my rescue under these circumstances. But I lived in clover as a child; I am not sure I'll make a good farmer in the future. You'll be implicated . . ."

"I'm not afraid, Limin! I love you. You'll always find me at your side—even if you become a beggar."

Limin wept again, sobbing like a baby. My sister joined him—and obviously not out of sadness.

Oddly enough, tears welled up in my own eyes, and I wept too.

I fumbled my tearful way to the quiet riverside. In the dusk I stood motionless, eyes gazing at the distant, somber outline of mountains. Ages passed before I could really figure out what had moved me to tears. My dear sister! Limin was such a rotten piece of meat that even a fly wouldn't take a second look. While everyone shunned him like a plague, you fell in love with him! Despite my vague understanding of the love between man and woman, my innocent, childish heart told me that my sister had done something right.

That evening, Sister invited Limin home and took the liberty of making *jiaozi* dumplings for supper. My parents, always thrifty, kept asking my sister: why eat such good food when it's neither a festival nor a New Year's Day?

Sister and Limin might have been laughing up their sleeves. Yet they did not know there was still another who was just like them, laughing up his own little sleeve.

———

Years later, great changes took place. After the downfall of the Gang of Four—Jiang Qing, Zhang Chunqiao, Wang Hongwen, and Yao Wenyuan, the leaders of the sect of ultraleftists during the Cultural Revolution—Limin's parents were set free, their unjust cases having been redressed. The following year, my sister encouraged Limin to register for the college entrance examination. They both took the exam, but with utterly different results. Limin was enrolled in a university in Beijing. My sister, a few points short of the admissions criteria, failed again.

Limin left. All the villagers talked about him, their enthusiasm lasting several days. They said that now that everything had changed—now that he had turned from a blackbird to a phoenix—ten to one he would spread his wings and fly away.

My sister was feeling a most complicated mixture of happiness and sadness. She was pleased for Limin's success on the entrance examination but upset because it would mean several years of separation from him.

I, an older boy by now—I'd be attending junior high school in two years—had learned something about the secret of love. I knew that my sister would feel sad and lonely. She loved Limin so much that even a moment's separation would upset her. And when my sister was upset, I was upset.

Still, I didn't expect there would be any solution.

I found that my sister had been regularly frequenting the road opposite the village. There she collected Limin's letters from the hand of Uncle Li, the town postman, and in return gave him letters to be sent to Beijing. It looked as if my sister had reached some agreement with Uncle Li; perhaps she had asked him to keep the whole matter a secret. So far, no one in the village knew except me.

Sister was loath to let the cat out of the bag. The villagers' tongues had finally stopped wagging; if they discovered this new secret, they would make bawdy jokes to embarrass a shy girl like my sister.

Papa appeared to be ignorant—or was he just pretending that he cared only about his land and crops? Sometimes I saw him gazing at Sister's back in a pitiful, melancholy way. He said nothing, but he'd usually heave a deep sigh.

I always knew when Sister received a letter from Limin. She would hide herself and read it behind the wheat stack on the threshing ground (the thought of the place still makes my cheeks burn and my heart pound). Back home again, her face ablaze with joy, Sister would sing cheerful songs. She has a sweet voice, and she can sing as well as the people on the radio.

Seeing Sister in high spirits, Papa would knit his brows. Fretting, he'd interrupt her to plead in a mournful tone, "My dear child, please stop singing. It hurts my heart."

Every time Papa said that, I would silently blame him for spoiling Sister's good mood. Still, I loved him and sympathized with him. Look, his hair had turned gray after Mama passed away. What a pitiful man he was!

When my sister was happy, I felt lighthearted. Outwardly feigning ignorance, in private I was humming songs. I am not a good singer; to be frank, I'm more of a painter. However, under such circumstances I simply couldn't help but sing to bless my sister. Any boy with a sister would agree: although to all appearances he has no interest in her marital state, at heart, how much loving care he harbors for her welfare!

———

It is New Year's Day again.

We rural folks don't normally celebrate New Year's Day; we regard it as a city-dweller's festival. We celebrate only the Spring Festival—a special day that we mark by eating special foods. Yet today, as other households in the village pay no attention and serve their simple, everyday food, our family, like a household of city dwellers, prepares for this foreign festival.

In fact, it is Sister who wanted to celebrate New Year's Day. Sister has been in charge of the family affairs since Mama died. Papa never interferes. As usual, he said nothing and went to the mountain after daybreak to chop firewood.

I know Sister is happy. Yesterday she received a letter from Limin. However, I still silently wonder: Aren't you making too much of this, Sister? Isn't it going too far to feast on a meal of jiaozi? Just for receiving a letter from Limin? Don't you know there isn't much flour left in the vat?

But I don't want to oppose Sister's decision. I have always supported her in whatever she wanted to do.

Early in the morning, Sister goes to the vegetable cellar to dig carrots for the jiaozi fillings. She washes them clean and rubs them on an iron grater into shreds, which are later thrown into a boiling pot, scooped out, and kneaded into a ball. This she places in a white porcelain bowl. Then she begins to pound garlic and peppers, peel scallions, and get many other things ready. When all these preparations are finished, she gives me two yuan and sends me to town to buy two jin of mutton.

I am very glad to run this errand for her. With a plastic bag in my hand, I set out at once.

No sooner have I rushed out the door than Sister runs out after me. For some reason, she throws her arms around my shoulders, smiling. I can feel her arms tremble slightly.

My sister, cheeks red like a morning cloud, hesitates for a moment and then whispers in my ear: "Don't play on the way. Buy the meat, and come back quickly. Sister needs the mutton for the jiaozi. Today we have an important guest coming from afar. Guess who? It's Gao Limin, the cadre who once lived and worked in our village! He came back to our province last month and is now doing his internship in a local factory. He said in yesterday's letter that he would return to our village."

I feel a fiery passion transferred to my body from the arms of my sister. I look up and see shining tears in her eyes. Not until this moment do I notice that my sister has had her hair cut and that she is so beautiful, with her neck white as snow, her face pink as peach blossom, and her hair black as pitch—like a nymph who has just stepped down from a picture. I am so astounded that I'm unable to say a word. Nodding to her, I dart toward the town.

At last I understand why Sister wants to make jiaozi today. Once, on the Dragon Boat Festival, I saw her get out the dates and glutinous rice for making zongzi. And on the Double Sixth Festival, she prepared ground buckwheat to dry in the sun for making liangfen, and the shelled peanuts, sunflower seeds, and the like to winnow in the wind. She wouldn't let me touch these precious treats in normal times. It turns out that she has kept them for Limin.

The sky is overcast, and there are snowflakes drifting in the air. The snow, which must have started some time ago, cascades down heavily as I head for the town. Silence reigns over the fields. Not a sound can be heard except for the quiet rustling of the snow. A few distant mountaintops looming in the mist begin to turn white.

In the snow, I run, dance, and shout like a little lunatic. I feel excited because the young man Sister has missed day and night will soon be back. He was looked down upon in the village, but this time he will come back as a proud college student. A college student from Beijing! Beijing . . . is it a place you can easily reach? I have been there, too—in dreams. I will ask Limin to tell me all about Beijing. My heart is filled with affection and longing for him because he is going to be my sister's husband, my brother-in-law. I even imagine that he, like other brothers-in-law, will hold an engagement ceremony and entertain the whole village so that my twenty-seven-year-old sister will no longer be ridiculed for being single. An older, unmarried girl is often mercilessly belittled, and Sister has been suffering a lot for that.

Indulging in wild fancies as I run, I arrive at the town.

Mutton has been sold out in the state-owned meat shop, so I get it from the free market at the flood land outside of town. With meat in hand I turn around, stride onto the road, and make for home at once.

Someone calls me from behind.

I stop to look back. It is Uncle Li, the town postman. He knows everyone—far and near, young and old—for he has been carrying letters along the road in the vale for so long.

Uncle Li catches up with me, snow on his fur hat and shoulders. Passing a letter to me, he pats me on the shoulder, smiling. "Give it to your sister!"

Then he goes away.

I look at the words on the envelope. The letter is, indeed, addressed to Sister, from some chemical factory in the provincial capital. Sister said that Limin had come back for an internship in a local factory. Is this letter from him? But then more questions bewilder me: Isn't Limin coming to visit us today? Didn't Sister receive his announcement only yesterday? We have no acquaintances or relatives in the capital; who else can have sent this letter? No one but Limin! But why? Is something wrong?

Worried, I open the letter without further consideration.

The salutation "Dear Xing'er" scares me into a shower of cold sweat. I dare not go on. Good heavens, what an absurd thing I have done! I can't read my sister's love letter without her permission!

But now that I've opened the letter, will Sister even believe me if I say I didn't read it? Besides, it's almost impossible for a little boy who has never read a love letter to withstand the temptation. I decide to read on, thinking Sister so dotes on me that she will certainly forgive me. Anyway, I am a tight-lipped boy. I won't tell anybody—not even Papa. Sister doesn't know how well I've kept her secret about what she and Limin did that day behind the wheat stack.

By the roadside I find a spot away from wind and people, and I start reading.

Dear Xing'er,

How are you?

I think I'd better get straight to the point and get everything clarified.

Unfortunately, I can't write you a longer letter. I suppose on the eve of the New Year you will have received the letter I sent you yesterday.

I intended to return on New Year's Day. I would like to tell you the whole story in your presence, but I don't think either of us could stand that face-to-face torture. Therefore, I've decided not to return. I think it might be easier to have things settled in a letter.

I have to tell you that my parents do not approve of our marriage. You may have seen in the provincial newspaper that my father has resumed his post as deputy governor. They disapprove mainly because you are a farmer; they say it would be impossible for us to ever live under the same roof. When I asked them to help find a job for you in the city, they refused, saying that they must not violate the Principles and abuse their power.

My parents have found me a girlfriend—a college student whose parents and mine, old comrades in arms, have been through thick and thin together.

Dear Xing'er, I love you as far as feelings are concerned, but since my parents suffered all kinds of hardships in the previous years and are now getting older, I cannot stand to see them continue to worry about me. Besides, a long-term view shows that our marriage involves not only the problem of separation, but also the practical disparities between job and occupation, commodity grain and rural grain—all of which would pose great difficulties in our life. Out of these reasons, dear Xing'er, I have yielded to my parents after a painful struggle—or rather, I have yielded to another side of myself. I am a selfish person. Forget me, please! Oh God! How terrible these words are.

This is nothing less than a thunderbolt from above! Although some of the sentences in the letter are beyond my understanding, the main idea is clear enough: Limin wants my sister no more!

I feel a swarm of mosquitoes droning in my head, sky and earth revolving, snow falling the other way round. Tucking the letter into my pocket, I take to my heels.

Arriving home, I rush into the courtyard but stop momentarily.

A song seeps out from inside the room, hot as red pepper, melting away in the snow. It is Sister, singing, "Honey, do you know a heart is burning for you? This heart will follow you no matter where you go, rain or shine . . ."

It is one of Sister's favorite movie songs. Tears flood down my face. Under a sky filled with whirling snowflakes, the earth keeps me still company and listens to Sister singing. I remain in the courtyard for a while. Then, wiping tears with my sleeves, I edge my way, step by step, into the room, my legs heavy, leaden.

Sister is frying shelled peanuts beside the kitchen range. Smoke rises. Peanuts crackle.

Perhaps the expression on my face betrays me. Sister comes out, casts a surprised glance at me, and asks me abruptly, "Baowa, where is the mutton?"

I look at my empty hands. A light dawns upon me: I left the meat back where I read the letter.

I make no reply, just take out the letter and hand it over. As I can bear it no longer, I throw myself onto the edge of the kang bed and cry out loud.

It must be a long time before I stop crying; when I raise my head to look for Sister, she is not in the room. Scattered on the ground are the leaves of the letter, and the whole room is permeated with the choking smell of burnt peanuts.

Where is Sister? My heart pounding, I rush out of the room in desperation.

Outside, the wind and the snow are coming even harder. There is already a thick blanket of snow on the ground. As far as the eye can reach, everything is white: mountains, valleys, frozen rivers, and all. Everything ugly on the ground is covered by the white snow.

Sister, where have you gone?

I try my luck along the path above the threshing ground, moving out of the village, across a vast, open vale, and, blindly, toward the riverside. In the teeth of wind and snow, I slip and fall from time to time, in search of my dear sister.

I've barely made it to the riverside when I spot a figure seated on a boulder; like a snowwoman, the figure is white from top to toe. Is that my sister?

It is. Knees wrapped in arms, she stares perplexedly into the blurry distance, her eyes devoid of their normal liveliness. It looks as if she has ceased breathing, lost vitality, and turned into a beautiful marble statue.

I sit quietly by her side, resting my head gently on her shoulder. I begin to sob again. As dusk closes in, the wind begins to ease off, while the snow, heavy as before, continues sending down its silent flakes. A flock of sheep streams down the slope opposite, moving slowly toward the village.

Sister extends a hand to caress my head. Her hand, ice-cold, is shaking slightly. I look up and see, faintly, a few fine wrinkles on her forehead and at the corners of her eyes. She seems to have aged many years all at once. Oh, my dear ill-fated sister!

Papa appears before us, as if from nowhere. There are lines of sweat on his face, snowflakes on his head, and dusty plateau mud on his clothes. His hair looks pure white.

Papa stoops down, brushes snowflakes off Sister's and my clothes, and takes out from under his elbow a fur hat to put on my head and a red scarf for Sister's neck. Then, with his big, callous palm, he begins to remove the snowflakes from Sister's head—and in so doing he caresses Sister gently and affectionately. Now I know, Papa, that you love not only your land and crops, but also Sister and me so dearly as well.

Sister stands up, leans her head against Papa's chest, and bursts into tears.

Papa heaves a deep sigh, saying, "Ah, I know, I know all . . . I knew it, I knew! Papa didn't tell you because I was afraid you'd be upset. I knew he'd desert us someday. It's getting dark; let's go home . . ."

In the darkness, large snowflakes still soundlessly descend into this world.

As in the old days, Papa, with one hand taking Sister's and the other mine, leads us through the fields and toward the village. Treading on the mat of soft, loose snow, he mumbles, "Good snow, what a good snow . . . Hope it can help grow good crops, then we'll be better off next year . . . Ah, at least the land won't desert us . . ."

Dear sister, did you hear that? Papa said the land won't desert us. Yes, on this promised land, we will finally harvest our own happiness with toil and sweat.

Translated by Zhang Min

Chen Zhongshi

Chen Zhongshi was born in 1942 in the Baqiao District of Xi'an City, Shaanxi Province. He began writing in 1965. Since 1979, when he joined the Chinese Writers Association, he has published nine novellas, over eighty short stories, and more than fifty pieces of reportage, prose, and essays. He has published collections of short stories, including *The Village* and *Going Back to the Old Poplar*; literary criticism collected as *My Creation Experience*; a collection of essays; and several collections of novellas and novels, including *Early Summer* and *Fourth Younger Sister*.

Chen Zhongshi's short story "Trust" was awarded the National Outstanding Works prize in 1979. In the years since, his novels and other works have won many awards, including the Contemporary Literature Prize, the National Reportage Prize, the Shaanxi Double-Five Literature Prize, and the Mao Dun Literature Award. His piece "A Willow on Qinghai Plateau" was included in one of China's primary literature textbooks.

2

Chen Zhongshi

A Tale of Li Shisan and the Millstone

"Myyyy . . . sonnnn . . ."

Whenever he created an especially good and satisfying line for his opera, Li Shisan would sing it out with great feeling. Actually, he sang out every line. He even recited each line of the spoken parts, hearing in his head the drumbeats and stringed instruments. Then, after considering and scrutinizing the lines, he would write them down on cheap linen paper with his half-bald writing brush, the second one he'd gone through already. He was too poor to buy the finer Xuan paper favored by painters and calligraphers. But though the linen paper was coarse and rough, it was as tough as leather, holding together no matter how often it traveled from hand to hand and was flipped from front to back by the shadow-play actors while memorizing their parts. Linen paper might not be fine, but it stood its ground the way the soft, thin Xuan paper never could.

"Myyyy . . . motherrrr . . ."

As he sang and wrote, Li Shisan felt exulted and content. Suddenly, he heard a loud, angry voice from the yard.

"Listen! Just listen; what's that old madman singing? His voice has shaken the tiles off of the walls."

Mrs. Li was scolding, and it was not the first time. The problem was that Li Shisan's singing was intoxicating. His voice flowed out through the door and windows of his house into his neighbors' houses and out into the streets and lanes. People dared not enter his yard for fear of interrupting his work; however, his singing was so irresistible to one and all—grown men and women, lads and lasses—that they quietly climbed up the wall around his yard and elbowed for space, their heads appearing along the gray tiles. When Li's wife scolded, their heads would disappear down the other side of the wall; when she went back inside to her spinning and weaving, the heads would reappear.

Li Shisan's wife often decreed that he could write operas at will, but had better not sing or murmur while writing. Each time, he would promise not to sing ecstatically again—but once he started writing, he couldn't help himself. A few pieces of tile lost could not stop him. Even if the wall toppled over, he would never quit.

He mimicked a woman's soft voice: "Son . . ." Now he took on a husky male voice: "Mother . . ."

He sang out the lines about the mother's and son's deaths, unaware that his wife had barged in. Suddenly he heard her angry chiding: "Damn your singing!"

Li Shisan turned back to stare at his wife's unpredictable face. It took a while for him to drag his attention from the world of his opera. "What's the matter?" he asked. "What happened?"

"Do you want to eat lunch?"

"Of course!"

"What do you want to eat?"

She was a genial and prudent wife. When she'd married Li Shisan, she had started consulting her mother-in-law for advice on cooking every meal. After the death of her parents-in-law, naturally she turned to her husband for help.

Out of habit, Li blurted out distractedly, "A bowl of dry noodles."

"You can't eat dry noodles."

"Then noodles in soup."

"Can't do that either."

"Why not?"

"No flour."

"Oh. Then boil a bowl of millet porridge."

"No millet, either."

Then Li Shisan came to realize the seriousness of the situation. He grew entirely clearheaded, and his thoughts snapped from the scene of that mother's and son's deaths and separation, in their house in the opera, to the scene there in Li Shisan's own house.

While he considered their plight, his wife said, "Only a basin of grits left—but your stomach can't take them anymore."

Indeed, he could no longer eat grits porridge. He had eaten it almost all his life; his stomach couldn't bear it anymore. Less than half an hour after eating it, he would vomit acidic bile, regurgitating into his mouth and suffering terrible stomach pains. Thinking of the grits, he said angrily, "Why didn't you tell me sooner that we're out of flour?"

"I told you three days ago, the day before yesterday, and even yesterday. I asked you to borrow wheat to grind. You forgot—and now you cast the blame on me."

Li Shisan backed down. "Now," he said, "you go and borrow a bowl of flour from our neighbors."

"I've already borrowed three bowls from three of our neighbors."

"Borrow one more time—and be embarrassed just one more time."

Displeasure flickered across Mrs. Li's face, but she didn't reply. As she turned to go, they both heard a clangorous yelling outside.

"Elder Brother Shisan!"

No other voice was so familiar and so melodious; no other voice could make people feel so happy from top to toe. It was Tian Shewa! At that discouraging moment, hearing Tian Shewa's voice not only recovered his happiness, but also made Li Shisan forget about lunch.

Tian Shewa was the famous master of several shadow-play troupes in the area north of the Weihe River. His theatrical company was known as the Double Excellent Troupe: excellent in singing and excellent in shadow puppetry. So whenever a new opera script was finished, Li Shisan always gave it first to Tian's troupe to be rehearsed and performed. As soon as rehearsals began, he would stay with Tian Shewa and several others in the troupe to help them get to know the characters and the intricate relationships among them, as well as the lightness and heaviness of gong, drum, and cymbal. Li Shisan would not allow the company to bring the performance to the stage until he felt satisfied with the rehearsal. In front of an audience, Tian Shewa took the characters from Li Shisan's bald writing brush and turned them into living people. He held an important position in Li Shisan's heart.

"Shewa! Come in here!"

While Li Shisan stood shouting, Tian Shewa had already come into the room, almost running into Li Shisan's wife. Oof! Mrs. Li staggered but steadied her feet; Tian Shewa lost his balance and fell down heavily on the wood threshold. Coming over quickly to help Tian Shewa up, Li Shisan saw a cloth bag fall to the floor with a resonant, heavy sound. He asked, "What is that bag?"

"I brought two dous of wheat for you," Tian Shewa said, patting the dust off his coat and trouser legs.

"That you come to my home is fine, because I have missed you! But why do you bring me wheat?" asked Li Shisan.

"For you to eat!"

"But I have food! We have plenty of wheat, peas, millet, and corn."

Tian Shewa didn't want to talk about the grain; his expression changed to one of both sympathy and reproach. "Alas, my elder brother! I fell head over heels at the door. Won't you invite me to sit down?"

Li Shisan hurriedly brought a stool. When Tian Shewa sat down, Mrs. Li placed a bowl of cool, boiled water into his hands. Tian Shewa dramatically sighed, "Ah! Sister Li treats me well—she knows that I am thirsty after walking so long a distance."

Li Shisan turned to his wife. "Hurry up! Make noodles now! Shewa must be hungry after walking several dozen lis. This afternoon we'll eat dry noodles."

Mrs. Li turned and left the study. She had been sure she'd have to borrow flour from the neighbors once again. Now she felt relieved by Tian Shewa's two dous of wheat; after grinding it into flour, she'd be able to pay back the many bowls of flour borrowed from neighbors in recent days.

"Brother Li," Tian Shewa asked, "what new play are you planning?"

Li Shisan answered, "You know I'm never idle. I am planning something, but nothing is definite yet."

"Please recite a scene or sing a few lines. Let my ears enjoy it first," urged Tian Shewa.

"Sorry, I can't. An unfinished opera mustn't be sung to others," Li Shisan replied. "If you lift the lid from the pot and let the steam out before the buns are done, the buns will be cooked into stiff paste."

Tian Shewa knew well Li Shisan's habit of secrecy while writing operas, and he knew the answer even before he asked—but he needed something to chat about to keep Li Shisan from returning to the topic of the wheat.

"Brother Li," Tian Shewa said happily, "these days the theater's business is going very well. My throat can hardly bear it—but I can't rest. We haven't seen business like this for many years; we have performances almost every night! Only when there are operas to sing can we carry wheat home and have dry noodles in our bowls."

Li Shisan enjoyed Tian Shewa's cheerful laughter. It was the carefree time of year when the wheat had been harvested, the seeds hoed, and the autumn seedlings fertilized; all along the Weihe River on the central Shaanxi plain, every large town and tiny village would be holding "work is done" festivals. Families and friends would be coming together to celebrate the bumper harvest and relax after the summer's busy harvest season. A shadow-play troupe would be invited to each village to perform; each family of the village would contribute a liter or half liter of wheat as payment. This time of year offered even more work for the acting troupes than during the Spring Festival.

As soon as Tian Shewa stopped laughing, Li Shisan's brows wrinkled and his eyes focused. He said, "But the drought has lasted a long time this year. It hasn't rained a drop in the area north of the Weihe River, and the wheat crops are poor. How is your theater still doing so well?"

"The performances are good! Our acting is marvelous, and your plays are so well written! *The Match of Spring and Autumn* and *A Flame-Foal* have been shown in one village after another. The villagers aren't satisfied seeing them eight or ten times in their own villages—they hurry to see them in the neighboring towns as well!"

"Oh!" His brow smooth again, Li Shisan felt gratified.

"Tell you what, my brother Shisan: your Huang Guiying, the heroine of *A Flame-Foal*, has fascinated all the country folk, rich and poor, old and young, men and women. Someone even wrote a folk song about her: 'Even if you haven't got a lit' of wheat, seeing Huang Guiying is a special treat.' It seems that people care less about their crops than about getting a chance to enjoy the play!"

While the two men talked cheerfully, Mrs. Li came in and asked for help. "Have you finished your conversation? I've rolled out the dough into sheets. Shall I cut and cook them right now?"

"Yes, do it now," said Li Shisan.

"Cook the noodles only for my brother," said Tian Shewa. "I already ate before coming here." He stood up, lifted the bag he had brought, and asked, "Where's the grain vat? Let me pour this wheat into it."

Dragging Tian Shewa by the arm, Li Shisan insisted on his staying until after the meal; Mrs. Li also muttered a request for him to stay. With a strong and healthy body, Tian Shewa was at his prime. But Li Shisan had already suffered from chronic stomachaches and now was hit again with shortness of breath from his asthma. Thus, after pulling on his friend to entreat him to stay, Li Shisan was out of breath and coughed severely.

Tian Shewa brought the bag into the next room, lifted the wooden lid of a chest-high porcelain urn, and was shocked. It was empty! He lifted the bag onto his shoulder and unfastened the rope. Crash! Two dous of wheat poured into the urn. He turned to the couple behind him and dropped onto his knees before them.

"My brother! I should have come earlier! It never occurred to me that you might already have run out of food. Yesterday I heard from a traveler who'd come through your village that your life was very hard, so today I brought the two dous of wheat to see if . . ." Tears began rolling down his cheeks.

Moved and ashamed, Li Shisan helped Tian Shewa up. "It is because I am not good at farmwork, and there is a shortage of rain this year, so my wheat seedlings are as thin as a monkey's hairs. The stone roller has got nothing to grind, and the wheat has all been eaten . . ." He shrugged and laughed uneasily at himself.

Mrs. Li defended her husband: "Shewa, why are you crying? Your brother is singing and happy all day without the slightest worry about his situation."

Tian Shewa wiped tears from his face. With wide-open eyes, he said resolutely, "As long as I, the obscure actor, have something to eat, I will not let my brother, the great playwright, go hungry! If I have dry noodles to eat, I will not let you eat noodles in soup."

Turning to Mrs. Li, he added: "Sister Li, you let my brother decide whether to eat dry noodles or noodle soup. I will bring some more wheat in a few days."

With his hands cupped, Tian Shewa bowed three times and then smiled. "Brother, I have to go. I have a performance tonight." He headed to the yard and then turned back again. "Brother Li, I know you've been planning a new play. I'll be waiting for it!"

"I'll tell you as soon as it's finished," Li Shisan promised. Speaking of the play helped him forget his troubles. "Having wheat, I have nothing to worry about."

———

Li Shisan and his wife toiled away at the grinding. Two millstones, each more than a foot thick, were fit tightly together. There was a drilled hole as big as a child's fist in the upper piece, into which the grains of wheat were poured. The wheat was ground over and over again between the rotating millstones; finally the flour flew out through the mouth.

To rotate the millstones, a thick wooden rod was fastened to the upper stone and usually tied with a rope to livestock. Wealthy families often used a mule or horse to drag the millstone; those animals moved with the greatest speed. In families of commoners, domestic cows or bulls were a practical choice; their strength made the work easy. But the families too poor to afford even a dog had to drive the family members themselves to work the millstone. Then the millstone was pushed rather than pulled. It was often said that the three hardest kinds of farmwork were drawing a plow, striking adobe, and pushing a millstone. Only the strongest men were capable of doing it. And only those who were too poor to keep cattle or hire assistants found themselves forced to exert all their bodily strength just to sustain their families.

Sixty-two years old, Li Shisan now held the rod to his chest, both hands grasping the end of the stick from below. He positioned it between his chest and belly and leaned forward, feet pressing down on the ground. In this way he could gather enough strength and momentum to rotate the heavy millstone, which weighed several hundred jin. Li stood by the harness at the outer end of the rod—the part that would be fastened to a bull or horse, if he had one. His wife stood close to the inside end, next to the millstones. She, too, held the rod at the place between her chest and belly, but she held it against her with her right hand, while with the other hand she continually poked the grains of wheat into the hole. When the crushed fragments flew out and gathered on top of the millstone, she swept them with a small dustpan. Then, leaving the grinding, she took the crushed grains to a nearby shelf, where she opened the lid of a yellow wicker basket and poured the particles inside. When she shook the grinding handle to settle the grains, the wicker basket rattled loudly; it was the habitual sound of grinding wheat.

"You'd better have a rest," said Mrs. Li.

At her loving words, Li glanced at his wife; she was shaking the handle, her slim shoulder swaying slightly. He raised his arm to wipe his sweaty face with his sleeve. He didn't stop his work, but hummed, "Mother's . . . son . . ." Halfway through the sentence, he seemed to be stifled and couldn't utter another word. Panting huskily, he pushed the mill slowly and began mocking himself. "Alas, my wife! I should have become a county magistrate. Why, now I'm reduced to working like livestock at a millstone. I'm a horse—and not even a swift one. I can't even match a crippled cow. Alas, my ancestors must have put the incense in the wrong censer."

"It is what we call Destiny," his wife replied. She stopped shaking the handle, fetched the wicker basket, and poured the wheat bran in. Returning to the millstone, she grasped the rod and again murmured, "Destiny."

Reluctantly Li muttered, "Right, it is Destiny."

Li Shisan continued to push the millstone. To grind a dou of wheat, he had to turn the millstone thousands of times; he thought of the saying, "The road ahead will be long."

Li's civil-service career had been as tortuous as the grinding work. At the young age of nineteen he had passed the county level of the imperial examinations and become a xiucai—a scholar-official—to the joy of his family and the admiration of his neighbors. He passed the provincial exam and became a juren two decades later at thirty-nine; he'd scored in the top twenty among all who took the exam in Shaanxi Province.

Beijing seemed within easy reach; after working hard for another thirteen years, he advanced to the capital to take the triennial general examination, traveling with food on the back of a mule. After a certain number of top scorers were recruited, another sixty-four examinees were kept in reserve as official candidates. Li Shisan's name was on that list. These candidates were allowed to take the title of the county official, but without salary; it was only an honorary title. One had to wait a long time to take a real position—there was no telling exactly how long. When finally there was a vacancy and it was your turn, then you might assume the post and get the salary of a county official.

Li knew how the bureaucracy worked. During that period of tedious waiting for his turn, he felt a tremendous fear; anxiety and disappointment enveloped him, and eventually his long-held desire for an official post vanished. That was when he made the most crucial decision of his life. Li believed that the glorious official title should be attained through learning and ability. Paired with money, the title would add no glory but only humiliation to his ancestors' reputations.

He began to write plays. He started out by imitating the musical scores of Wanwan Tone, local plays that had been popular in Weibei Plateau. Li's first play, *The Match of Spring and Autumn*, was performed by Tian Shewa's shadow-play troupe. With Tian's good voice and ingenious ability at "stringing the shadow," the play was an immediate success and was performed in all the villages north of the Weihe River.

From that point on, Li Shisan was immersed in the great joy of composing plays. He wrote eight plays and two playlets, all of which were performed by the shadow-play troupes.

And yet, here were the playwright and his wife, laboring to turn the millstone and grind the wheat that Tian Shewa had brought the day before. Once the wheat was ground into flour, they would no longer have to worry about conjuring up meals with no noodles to cook.

"Brother Shisan!" a voice yelled.

It was Tian Shewa. Why was he here again today? He burst into the mill breathlessly even before his hasty shout had faded away. He stopped abruptly, face-to-face with Li Shisan, who had just turned from the grinding to greet him. Panic and terror hung on Tian's face. "My brother," he said, "things look pretty bad."

Panting heavily from his labors, Li Shisan didn't ask. It never occurred to him that disaster could befall him in his own house. The millstone could not be pushed out of its track by any means. For an instant, Li even considered that Tian might be bluffing on purpose. After all, storytelling and exaggerating were the professional habits of these shadow players.

"My brother," Tian Shewa shouted, "the emperor has given an order to arrest you!"

"Hey," Li Shisan said calmly, "you're a grown-up. Why would you spread groundless rumors like this?"

Seeing Li Shisan's nonchalance, Tian Shewa turned pale. He slammed his fist loudly into his palm and spoke hurriedly as if he were reciting his lines in an opera: "Emperor Jiaqing sent an official to the county. My housekeeper's third son is the cook in the county government. As soon as he heard about the message, he sent someone to tell me. I ran all the way here to let you know. And yet to my surprise, you don't believe a single word I've said—"

Li Shisan interrupted: "Did they say which law I violated?"

"Obscene tongue and foul tune," Tian Shewa replied. "The emperor said that, like overgrown weeds, your plays have spread into several provinces. The emperor was so irritated that he sent officials to Weinan to escort you to Beijing. Even those shadow players who've cooperated with you—including me—are to be punished . . ."

Tian Shewa paused and grew silent. As he considered their grim fate, Tian Shewa set his swallowtail-shaped eyes on the face of his beloved brother. He spared no glance at his sister-in-law, who was still holding the mill rod.

Li Shisan was dumbfounded. His face turned from grayish yellow to grayish white—whether from anger or from fear, it was hard to tell, but Tian Shewa was scared speechless.

All of a sudden Li Shisan stood up, threw his head backward and then forward, and gave a loud cry; a spray of blood erupted from his mouth. A beam of red light, as crimson as sunshine, flashed through, and the whole mill was suffused with red flame. Like a flying blood waterfall, rushing and whirling with a resonant sound, the blood splashed and spattered onto the crushed wheat and the carved angular millstones, reddening everything it touched. Tian Shewa froze in terror.

Li Shisan squared his shoulder again. He faced upward first and then forward with a jerk, as another stream of bloody flame spouted out. Finally he tumbled onto the mill pan, one hand limp.

For a moment, Tian Shewa was at a loss. Then he snapped out of his panic. He carried Li Shisan in his arms and laid him gently on his back on the floor. Frightened, Mrs. Li squatted and rubbed her husband's chest and forehead, wailing, "Please don't go . . . you can't leave me alone . . ." She firmly pinched the bridge of her husband's nose.

Eventually, Li Shisan opened his eyes. He pushed away his wife's hand still pinching his nose. After a moment he struggled to sit up, both hands pressed on the floor. Mrs. Li and Tian Shewa stepped forward quickly to help him from either side. Li Shisan sat slowly up. He heard Tian Shewa's cry and Mrs. Li's. Taking a breath, Li asked Tian, "Why don't you run away?"

"Look at you!" Tian Shewa replied. "How can I bear to leave you suffering and run away alone? Let them arrest both of us so that I can take care of you."

Shaking his head, Li said, "It is better that we both run and disappear."

"That is what I was waiting to hear. Now, be quick."

Standing up, Li tried a few steps and found he was able to walk. He said to his wife, "Don't worry about me. If the emperor wants my life, there's nothing you can do about it. You can't be of any help. If there's any way to escape, I will manage to send you a message and get my play back. My writing is just moving to its climax. Keep the play safe for me."

Trying to act natural, the two men walked out through the gate, crossed the lane of the village, and even politely said hello to the villagers they passed. A neighbor asked them where they'd be performing that night. Tian replied that they'd be in a remote village on the north plateau. Hearing this, the man said with great pity that it was too far for them to go.

Once out of the village, they turned from the main road onto a one-foot-wide footpath with corn plants as tall as a man on either side. Vanishing into the vast green sea of overgrowth, they felt a sheltered safety. Soon, as if by prior agreement, they both stepped out onto another footpath. The path was covered with grass and smelled of mint.

They crossed over a ditch. The flowing stream and the white poplars on either side had once been a source of inspiration for Li Shisan; he would stop to wash his face in the limpid water and absorb the poetic beauty of the scene. Now, neither man found poetry in the trees or water; nothing was left but panic, terror, and desperation. When Li Shisan gathered his strength and jumped over the ditch, he suddenly felt faint; his vision blurred. As he steadied his feet on the other side of the ditch, blood again spewed from his mouth.

After a short rest, the men resumed their escape. The path was still lined with stretches of thick emerald crops like a dense green fog, hot and suffocating. A ridge divided the end of the path into another fork. There, Li Shisan stopped and said, "It is time to say good-bye now."

Tian Shewa shook his head, startled. "Good-bye? To whom? To me? But I'll never part with you, even to death!"

Li Shisan replied, "We should not be so stupid to be caught together and killed! You, who can sing and act and bring shadow puppets to life—you should have a chance to live!"

"No, no, no!" Tian Shewa shook his head more quickly. "Anybody can play with puppets. A troupe of my fellow actors would take my place if I died. But nobody but you, Brother Shisan, can compose such brilliant plays. You must not be the one to die."

"Neither of us should die," said Li Shisan. "Of course it is good for both of us to be alive. But now we have a slim chance of escape. We have to run in different directions if either of us is to live. Perhaps we will both get out. But we must not be caught together and killed."

Tian Shewa was not convinced. "You are ill. If I left you alone, I would be the same as the ungrateful wretches in your plays."

Li Shisan thought for a moment before speaking. "You have all my original play manuscripts in your box. I have no regrets, because I composed all those plays. But if you were killed, your house would be confiscated and the plays would be burnt into ashes. They would be lost. So you should get the chance to live."

This moved Tian Shewa into silence.

"In fact," said Li Shisan, "that you live means I'm still alive."

Tian Shewa gasped. Tears fell from his eyes.

"Your life is now more valuable than mine," Li Shisan continued. "Hurry, hurry up; all my scripts depend on you."

Li turned and walked away.

Tian Shewa quickened his step to catch up. He fell to his knees, kowtowed to Li Shisan three times, got up, folded his hands, and made deep bows, swearing, "My dear elder brother, set your mind at ease: as long as I'm alive, not one of your scripts will be lost!"

Li turned and spoke over his shoulder. "Even if you do lose your life, the scripts can be protected," he said resolutely. "Hide them before you flee."

"I will," replied Tian Shewa. He ran into a field of corn and then cursed aloud to the sloping land: "You're no longer my emperor, Jiaqing!"

All was silent.

Li Shisan walked along the gently inclined path. It occurred to him that he should turn and walk in a different direction, since nobody was stupid enough to flee along the official thoroughfare on the Weibei Plateau. But he didn't feel like running away. On one hand, he was quite sure that his life would come to an end in a few hours. On the other hand, he did not like the idea of getting caught by the running dogs of Jiaqing, nor that of dying in Beijing. Still, now he wouldn't die by the millstone or on the kang bed at home, which would have caused his wife terrible pain. Though he hadn't given her a comfortable life while he was alive, he could die knowing he had not driven her into misery. And, of course, he didn't want to die in front of Tian Shewa. The closer the two had become, the farther they wanted to keep from each other when death beckoned.

The vast Weibei Plateau, then, was the best possible final resting place for Li Shisan.

Facing the plateau against the Weihe River plain, Li Shisan tottered step by step and spat out a mouthful of blood, moistening the dry, trodden earth beneath his feet with an undignified mixture of water and blood.

He spat another mouthful of blood as he struggled upon a field ridge.

When he felt yet another spray of blood welling up, Li Shisan knew it would be his last. Twenty lis away from the village, he turned around, gazing at the green central Guanzhong Plain across which the Weihe River flows, and spat out his last mouthful of blood onto the earth road, no longer seeing the sun and clouds over the Weibei Plateau.

About the Story

It was the late 1950s. One Saturday, I was coming home from school to get food for the next week. On the road I saw people of all ages, carrying their small wood stools in their hands and steamed buns in their handkerchiefs, hurrying to Ma Jia village to see the movie *Huoyan Ju*—the first Shaanxi opera to be put on the big screen. By sunset, the space in front of the stage was filled with people who'd traveled from neighboring villages, carrying their stools and their food. Back in my village, I'd hurried to finish my meal and join my friends to go see the film. Huoyan Ju, the play's legendary horse who could walk a thousand li in the daytime and eight hundred li at night, was undoubtedly miraculous—but it was Huang Guiying, the beautiful heroine, who left a deep impression on me. In the play, Huang Guiying was unswervingly faithful to her love, having compassion for the poor and eschewing the rich; only under duress did she resolutely marry the son of a high official. The image of Huang Guiying offered the hope for a bright future to the poor young men in the countryside as well as the better-off youth in the towns.

Fifty years later, I learned that the composer of *Huoyan Ju* was Li Shisan.

Li Shisan (1748–1810) came from a small town in Weinan County; his birth name was Li Fanggui. Li studied very hard, hoping to do well on the imperial examinations for civil servants. He worked his way up in rank until he earned the "empty" title of an official candidate for a vacancy. Suddenly, at age fifty-two, he woke up from the disappointments of bureaucracy and had no more interest in fame and honor.

At that time, shadow plays were very popular in the area north of the Weihe River. The shadow-play troupes were anxious to find good scripts, so they turned their expectations to this learned man. Li Shisan could not resist the enticement; he promised to give playwriting a try. Thus his first play, *Chunqiu Pei*, came into being. In the two hundred years since, it has been adapted by many opera companies, from the Shaanxi Opera to the Peking Opera and beyond. When this play began to bring him great fame, he decided to take the name of his home village as his pen name. His playwriting career really began when the name of Li Fanggui fell into oblivion.

In order to prove Li Shisan's identity as the first productive playwright of Wanwan Tone, a branch of the local Qin Opera in Shaanxi Province, I went to consult with Chen Yan, a contemporary playwright. My assertion was proved true. Only ten years passed between Li abandoning his official career in favor of playwriting and his death at age sixty-two under the terror of threats from Emperor Jiaqing. (Various accounts claim that Li was frightened to death or enraged to death.) In that brief decade, Li Shisan wrote eight plays and two playlets, collectively known as his Ten Great Plays. Most of them have been adapted by nearly all the major Chinese opera companies and have held their appeal to audiences for more than two centuries.

I can't help imagining how amazed Li Shisan would be to hear his plays, the work of a Shaanxi composer, performed in all the different dialects of China. Imagine if Li, unable to speak Mandarin and never having even heard the different southern dialects, had a chance to appreciate one of his plays performed by Hunan Opera or Peking Opera. I believe it would have given him the courage to face down the threats of Emperor Jiaqing, not to mention redeeming all his labors both in writing the plays and pushing that heavy millstone.

When he was frightened enough to spit blood at the grinding work, and then again before dying on the dusty road of the Weibei Plateau, Li Shisan never knew that, 150 years later, his play *Wanfu Lian* would be adapted into the opera *Nuxun An* and become an immediate success.

Later, the well-known playwright Tian Han (1898–1968) adapted *Nuxun An* into *Xie Yaohuan*, which created a great stir. Its success lasted for a while, and then suddenly *Xie Yaohuan* was met with a severe attack from almost every corner of the country. But time has marched on, and the past is history; in this case, Tian Han had the courage and safety to confront the attack and did not have to spit blood.

When I first read the details of Li Shisan's life in an article by Chen Yan, I was too excited to fall asleep. I felt a bit pleased with myself, for his tale corroborated what I had believed about Li: that literary merit was determined by a writer's artistry with words—not by what the writer lived on (steamed buns or stale bread), where he slept (Simmons or adobe kang), or what was hung on his wall (paintings or hoes). The tale of Li Shisan and his millstone convinced me that it was his sensitivity to words that compelled him in his art, despite his miseries and hardships. Even reduced to working his old legs at the millstone at the age of sixty-two merely for a bowl of noodles, Li Shisan still enchanted us with his creations. Grinding the wheat, putting aside the rod, and then creeping into a humble little room, furnished with only a square table, a chair, and a bench, he held his writing brush, opened the inkstone, and became absorbed in his writing.

In his lifetime, the only material benefits Li received for his writing were those two buckets of wheat from Tian Shewa.

Still, it was that exquisite sensitivity to words that frightened and enraged Li Shisan to death at hearing Emperor Jiaqing's menacing threats. Thus his writing brush was stilled forever. That is why I chose to bring Li Shisan to life in my story.

Translated by Nan Jianchong

Jia Pingwa

Jia Pingwa, a prominent and celebrated writer and essayist, was born in 1952 into a farming family in Danfeng County, Shaanxi Province. He began to write while studying in the Chinese department of Northwest University in Xi'an. Jia Pingwa first achieved fame in the 1970s and 1980s with his award-winning short stories and novellas, the majority of which are set in Jia's rural homeland in Shangzhou Prefecture.

Jia is known for his realistic depiction of the culture and life of Shaanxi Province. His writing often focuses on peasant life during China's reforms and urbanization since 1978. His works include *Shang Zhou, White Nights, Earth Gate, Old Gao Village, Remembering Wolves, Happy*, and the autobiographical novel *I Am a Farmer*.

He has won many prizes for his work, including the Third National Novellas Award, the National Short Story Award, the Prix Femina (for *Abandoned Capital*), the Pegasus Prize for Literature, and the French Arts and Literature Prize conferred by the French Ministry of Culture and Communication. In November 2008, Jia Pingwa won the seventh Mao Dun Literary Prize for his twelfth novel *Shaanxi Opera*.

Jia Pingwa

The Country Wife

1

Darky was older than her husband. She did all the work at home. She fed the pigs, rounded up the sheep, and went to the Black Cliffs to cut and collect firewood. When evening came, her small husband would pester her. He was a short, monkeylike man, but well read. He would use all the tricks he had learned from books to fuck with her. It made Darky angry. She came to hate him. At night she was tempted to push him off of her.

"You're my land," he would say, claiming the right to plow any way he pleased.

The evening was dark; stars lit the sky and coldness crept in from the window. Her husband was on top of her, crying out the names of other women. She recognized those of the young and beautiful in the village. When her husband rolled off, he fell asleep beside her as if seriously ill.

Hearing her sobs, her father-in-law scolded from the next room, "Sigh and choke on shit! You're too full of yourself to sleep." The old man's temper grew worse and worse. Darky couldn't contain her sobs; her father-in-law continued to scold, "What did you eat and wear in your mother's home? Are you not satisfied with this happy nest you fell into?" Then came the sounds of the abacus.

Her father-in-law was the credit agent of the town. His skill with the abacus was well known throughout the nearby villages. In recent years, as the family's wealth increased, the other family members began to pull long faces at Darky and chide her for being ugly, dark, and fat.

At first, Darky tried to console herself. Her mother's home in the deep mountains was poor; her food here was indeed better than what she'd grown up with. Back home, her elder brother's face was always sallow. He came to the town every couple of weeks with mountain produce. After a meal with her, he would say, "My sister is a real lucky bird!"

This only made her more bitter; she would reply, "Good Brother, is a bird lucky with only good food?"

She had no one to talk to. She badly wanted a baby—but the goddess of children did not send her one.

Disturbed, she lay in the dark with her eyes wide open. The stars outside the window faded, and the rain began to fall. If it rained for a whole night, the sweet-potato vines on the slope would spring new roots, and she would have to hoe them again.

There was a heavy knock on the gate, followed by three clicks. Her father-in-law quickly called out, "Coming, coming!" He hurried to the gate, his shoes half-on.

A man's voice asked, "Are you drinking with someone?"

Her father-in-law answered, "No, just waiting for you." The two men went inside, cursing the rain. Their chatter sounded like ghosts chanting scriptures.

Darky's mother-in-law knocked at Darky's door with her bamboo pipe. "Darky, get up. Your dad is drinking with his guests; cook something for them. Don't pretend you're sound asleep!"

Darky was used to this. Still, she didn't understand why these visitors arrived in the middle of the night. They carried mysterious objects in wooden boxes or in sacks. Her father-in-law never allowed anyone to touch them. Darky noticed but never asked about them.

She got out of bed. In the kitchen, she prepared plates of fried eggs, thousand-year eggs, tofu, and smoked pork, carrying them all on a platter to her father-in-law's room.

The visitor was a playboy. He pushed a bundle of money toward her father-in-law and said, "This is yours. What do you think about it, as long as—"

As Darky entered, her father-in-law stepped on the guest's foot and slapped his hat down over the money on the table. Darky was quick to pretend she'd seen nothing. She murmured shyly, "It is midnight and dark; I cannot cook anything good." The visitor gazed at her with bold, queer eyes. Darky hurriedly felt her coat buttons in case they were buttoned wrong. Her gesture made the visitor laugh.

"Go and sleep," said her father-in-law. "There's nothing else for you to do here."

Darky went to her room with impunity and sat on the mud-brick bed. Her small husband was already awake. "Who is it," he asked, "the mayor?"

"No, the mayor has a big nose. This guy looks like a large fish."

"It must be Wang of the east village," her small husband said. "He's made a killing in the transportation business, so he's rich enough to marry a country girl with a face as tender as water."

Darky's face grew dim. She said nothing.

Her husband added, "Dad made a tidy sum, too."

"If Wang is doing the business," Darky asked, "how could your dad make anything from it?"

"Dad has a share in the business."

Suspicious about the family's income, Darky persisted. "Where did he get the money to invest?"

Her small husband's eyes shone. "You think you've married an ordinary guy? My dad may not be an official, but do you know what he deals with? You may be ugly, but you have an ugly duckling's fortune."

"I don't care about the money. When I married you, you were just a poor bachelor."

"I know you're afraid of our fortune. You fear you can't be a good match for me."

Darky shut up. She heard her father-in-law inviting his guest to drink more. The sounds of plates hitting the floor suggested they were already a bit high. Her husband asked, "Why so silent?"

"I'm not worried about me," she said, "but about you. Blood money will make you bloody. You're really not so wealthy—why did your mother ask me for the money for her coffin when we married?"

Her small husband answered, "The money of the guy next door is not bloody; why don't you go and live with him?"

Darky got into bed, pulling up the quilt to cover her body from head to toe. Her eyes had closed, but her heart could not. A stream of black blood was boiling inside. She hated the poverty of the life she had come from and her failure to make herself a good match for her husband. She hated her husband for having money and, therefore, thinking himself better than her.

When the cock crowed three times in the early morning, she fumbled for her clothes. It was time to boil feed for the pigs. The courtyard was bright with water, for the rain had not stopped.

Suddenly, the sky above the courtyard next door flashed red. She was so surprised that she climbed the wall for a look. There was a bonfire on the neighbor's step, and a man squatted beside the fire. A new carrying pole stood with one end under the threshold and the other end over the fire. The man bent the carrying pole with his hands, and it sprang like a bow.

"Early bird Mu Du," Darky shouted, "we seldom have good rain. Why don't you sleep for a while longer?"

Mu Du, startled, turned his head. The fire made his face look as red as pig's blood. Seeing it was Darky, he just grinned.

She shouted again. "It's only a carrying pole. No need to care about it too much!"

"If I don't make it soft, it chafes."

"It is still a burden for a man," she said. "Are you going to the Southern Mountain to carry alpine rush?"

"Let Bald-Head in the southern courtyard do that. He makes a return trip in three days and makes no more than three yuan. I'm much stronger than he is."

"Some guys go out to do big things," Darky said. "They make thousands of yuan."

Mu Du replied, "I don't have a pull cart. Even if I could afford one, I don't have the guts."

Darky gave a long sigh. She felt sorry for him, for he was poor and clumsy. He lived with his dad. He was over thirty but not married yet. There was no woman in his family to do needlework. When Mu Du's pants wore out, one could see black-and-white thread twisted around the patch.

Darky wanted to ask, "How could Bald-Head be as clever as you are? Besides, to carry alpine rush you have to walk mountain paths. A clumsy guy like you must be very careful." But she swallowed the words.

As she was about to go back down the ladder, Mu Du called out, "Darky, here's a hot one for you." His hands fumbled in the ashes and picked out something blackish. He tossed it from hand to hand with a loud exhale. He quickly stepped to the wall below her and, on his tiptoes, offered her the object. It was a fist-sized potato.

Darky said, "No eating, I haven't washed my face." She went down one step but came up again and found Mu Du, with a different hand, working hard to pass the potato to her, his dark belly open to her view. She caught the potato; it was hot as a piece of charcoal. She broke it in two. Hot steam rushed out, the two halves shining in the dawn. She took a bite.

"Isn't it good?" Mu Du asked with a satisfied grin.

Darky was already down from the ladder. Her hair, after the rain shower on the wall, was dripping wet.

2

Winter came. Mu Du had worn out two carrying poles. Nasty bumps grew on his shoulder. But even if nipped, the bumps did not hurt. His family remained steady and could afford the essential things—cooking oil, salt, soy sauce, and vinegar. He made a set of new winter cotton-padded clothes for his father. Their life was neither too rich nor too humble.

November 6 was a bright day. The father and son made a new and longer carrying pole. They scorched it over the fire and rubbed it repeatedly with soybean oil. Like a mirror, the carrying pole reflected the two men's disheveled hair and unclean faces.

In the courtyard at high noon, they set up an altar with an incense burner and laid the new carrying pole, with red ribbons on both ends, horizontally upon it. Mu Du knelt down in the dust, piously kowtowing to worship the god of the carrying pole. He felt indebted to the carrying pole for providing his family pocket money and therefore freeing him from carrying alpine rush.

Since the weather was growing cold, Mu Du planned to get charcoal from deep in the mountains. After their worship, his father tied a bag of food at one end of the carrying pole and six pairs of straw shoes to the back of Mu Du's belt to send Mu Du on his journey. Mu Du walked backward to the courtyard gate and then turned around and stood at attention. He bit his teeth thirty-six times, and then he drew four horizontal lines on the ground with his right thumb and five vertical lines across those four. He began his incantation, "Four Horizontal Lines and Five Vertical Lines":

Today I begin my working life.
King Yu protects me on my way.
King Chu You drives bandits away.
Thieves dare not creep into my yard.
Tigers and wolves avoid me and my home.
It is a long journey from my home.
A man on my way might almost die.
In such a hurry and moment of haste,
The protection of the goddess is sent to me.

After the incantation, Mu Du strode out without turning back.

Watching his son step out of sight, Mu Du's father picked up a clump of mud and placed it on the Four-Five Lines. He leaned on the gate, tears blurring his eyes. The sound of firecrackers came from the courtyard of his neighbor.

———

In the twelfth lunar month, Darky's father-in-law, the credit agent, bought a share of a mushroom farm in the town. With ample capital, the farm purchased mushroom spores and built many workshops; after successful cultivation, its earnings doubled several times. The credit agent received money like running water. Darky's father-in-law sold his house and built a courtyard in the downtown area, all brick from top to bottom and as grand as a lord's temple. The villagers were surprised by the family's sudden wealth. Darky, too, was stunned.

When it was time for the family to pack their belongings and move to the grand new home, many people came to lend a hand. On the trailer Darky placed a stone pillow she had taken from her parents' home, but her small husband threw it away.

"That's my pillow!" Darky shouted.

Her husband replied, "You now live in the town; must you act like a savage?"

"I've been used to it from childhood," she protested. "Without it, my head fills with fever."

Her small husband cursed, "Miserable wretch!" and then deliberately left the stone pillow behind.

Panic-stricken, Darky just stood there for a while. Neighbors eyed her, but she did not talk back, nor did she weep. Picking up the greasy pillow, she hugged it and then gave it to Mu Du's father. "Uncle," she said, "we are leaving. I give this to you. It is a star fallen from the sky. All his life, my grandpa used it and passed it down to my dad. When I got married, my mum gave it to me as dowry. The pillow is quiet and cool. When your head touches it, it will soothe your eyes."

From then on, Darky lived in the town. Her life became busier; now not only did she do all the cooking for the family, but she was also put in charge of domestic tasks like feeding the chickens, the pig, the dog, and the cat. All the daily fieldwork fell to her. Moreover, her parents-in-law insisted that not even a tiny mote of dust or single speck of wheat straw could be left in the courtyard each day. Darky slept less than ever.

Her small husband complained of her gluttony and demanded she keep slim. He called her "Black Soybean," for as her body grew slender, her skin darkened.

At the end of the year, Darky's husband bought her a pair of leatherette shoes. Each market day, Darky was asked to wear the shoes, but they made her large feet ache. By the time she came back from the market and took off the shoes, her eyes brimmed with tears. She knew her small husband was not fond of her and thought her ugly. She was born plain. How could a pair of leatherette shoes change that?

Her husband beat her and threatened her with a knife. Finally, Darky grabbed her husband, whose arms and legs seemed to be frozen, and threw him onto the kang as if it were a manure basket, saying, "I'm showing you my strength!"

When outsiders heard about this incident, they joked about it. As Darky worked in the fields, someone would ask, "So, Darky, have you taught your man a lesson again?" Darky kept silent. The questioner would needle a little more: "Darky, why not wear your leather shoes? Your family is so well-off, why don't you ask your father-in-law for a wristwatch?"

After hearing these jokes too many times, Darky began to wonder: How did the family become so rich? Many households do business in the town, and no others have made money so easily.

When her small husband returned home that evening, she asked him about the secret to his father's wealth. Her husband answered, "I've been hearing the jokes and gossip, too; they all envy us. If anyone asks again, just say, 'We're not breaking any laws, so what's the problem?'"

Darky's father-in-law continued to have frequent late-night visitors. Whenever she would enter the room, they'd stop talking. In the daytime, her father-in-law would invite town officials to drink and eat. One time the mayor, drunk, pointed his finger in her father-in-law's face and shouted, "You motherfucker! You just run a credit cooperative, but you live a better life than me, the mayor. I warn you, I've gotten anonymous letters claiming that you were sticky-fingered with the loans."

Her father-in-law turned pale and hurried to help the mayor onto Darky's kang, serving him tea and vinegar. Soon the mayor threw up all over the bed.

Shortly afterward, rumors circulated around town that her father-in-law had pledged to contribute 30,000 yuan to enlarge the local elementary school and improve education in the town. Darky wondered where so much money was tucked away and how much her family had in total.

School officials from the county came to make a public announcement; her father-in-law stood on the rostrum, his face glowing with excitement, red silk draped over his shoulders and a big red flower pinned on his breast. From then on, the red silk banner awarded to him hung in the main room at home. When the gate to their yard was wide open, passersby could see a stretch of brilliant red from the street.

After the school was renovated and expanded, her father-in-law became the honorary schoolmaster, and Darky's small husband was hired as a gym teacher. He became an important man in the school, leading his students to play basketball happily every day.

At first, Darky did not understand how her father-in-law, such a stingy person at home, could become so generous in public—but now she understood. At night her small husband tormented her in bed, telling her that now she was not the wife of a farmer but the wife of a government official. Darky did not feel the benefit of his being a cadre; on the contrary, she suffered more. In the darkness he called out the name of the prettiest maiden in the town and forced Darky to answer his cry. Darky was livid: "She is herself, and I am myself. Go and fuck her, if you dare!"

Eventually her angry challenge was accepted. One night her husband did not return home. Two days later, Darky went to the school; in her husband's room she saw the prettiest woman in the town. Her husband claimed that they were discussing education.

Maybe these two really are learning together, Darky thought. Maybe I shouldn't interrupt. On leaving, she said to her husband, "You've been here for several days. The room is damp—you should buy some charcoal to keep it warm it at night."

For a month or two, her husband stayed away. At first she felt relieved, relaxed; she enjoyed getting a good night's sleep. But eventually she began to feel lonely. When she saw her husband she noted that, like a lamp burning too much oil, he was getting thinner day by day. She started to feel upset. She went to the school again, only to find that her husband and the beautiful woman were still "learning" together. With no hard evidence, Darky returned home in low spirits.

At the school there was a workman from West Plain who cooked lunch for the teachers in the daytime and guarded the doors in the evening after the teachers left. Sitting on a stool at the school entrance, he listened to a radio at the maximum volume, his cigarette twinkling in the darkness. Darky became acquainted with him during her frequent visits to the school. His name was Lai Shun. He had a mole between his brows and appeared honest and well behaved but miserably poor. On his feet were a pair of yellow rubber sandals that sloshed as if filled with water.

Whenever Darky came to the school, Lai Shun would shout, "Come here!" He'd offer her his low stool and let her enjoy the music on his radio.

On one visit, Darky said, "Lai Shun, you're good at making ends meet. You earn a state salary. But you wear these rubber shoes all the time. Don't they hurt your feet?"

As shy as a cat, Lai Shun drew his feet back. "It's not that I don't want to be decently dressed. I earn only twenty-eight yuan each month, and I have an eighty-year-old, muddleheaded grandpa, a mum who's an invalid, and three younger sisters in school. I'm not as lucky and happy as your husband!"

"Oh, your grandpa's still alive?" With three elders in the family, Lai Shun would be in debt for half his lifetime in order to afford three coffins. To change the subject, she asked about his wife.

Lai Shun snorted. "How can I get a wife? The year before last, I was engaged to a girl, but then she broke it off and married a cripple whose father suddenly became rich. I left home in a fury and came here to work."

Darky heaved a sigh for him.

Three days later, Darky took a pair of cloth shoes from the bottom of a chest and brought them to Lai Shun. He took it as a joke, speaking favorably of her neat stitches but not daring to sincerely accept them.

"You have high taste, Lai Shun!" Darky said. "Do you mind that they're not made from corduroy? I made them for my husband, who wore them for a day and then put on leather shoes the next day. Try them on. Do they fit?"

After washing his feet in a basin, Lai Shun squeezed his long, thick feet into the shoes. Darky laughed heartily, suggesting he could make do with them by cutting the buckle with scissors. Lai Shun agreed but didn't follow her suggestion. After work, he put on the new shoes and skipped around like he was doing a folk dance.

On hearing that Darky had given his new shoes to Lai Shun, her small husband shrugged. "Lai Shun is unlucky," he said. "He's over thirty years old, but still a virgin."

Darky frowned. The single man longs for a wife, she thought, while the married man leaves the wife alone at home for two months!

Her small husband added, "Since you have given him shoes, why not offer him something rarer?"

Darky spat out, "What rubbish!"

However, her small husband continued seriously, "No, it makes sense. Let's not mind each other's affairs."

"Do you want me to loosen the halter for you?" Darky asked. "I know what you're doing at the school. Those women don't come there to play basketball."

They began to quarrel. He raised his hand to strike. Not strong but nimble, he punched Darky in the stomach and went back to school.

After a severe tongue-lashing from her parents-in-law, Darky endured a sleepless night. When she rose at daybreak, she had pitch-black circles beneath her eyes.

Darky set out for the school, planning to make a scene. But as she neared the entrance, she had second thoughts. Her small husband had behaved badly, but he was now a teacher. What a disgrace for him if she made a scene at his workplace!

Lai Shun spotted her and greeted her warmly. When he asked about the dark circles under her eyes, Darky pulled him into a private corner and said tearfully, "Lai Shun, you're an honest man. Tell me, does my husband behave himself here? Please tell me the truth!"

Her words startled Lai Shun; for a little while he was speechless. When she pressed him for an answer, he replied, "I don't know for certain! I haven't actually seen them. You're a handsome woman; how could your husband behave disgracefully?"

"You stay at school day and night; please keep an eye on him," Darky urged. "This is a secret between you and me. Don't mention it to anyone—I don't want to become a laughingstock."

Lai Shun nodded and watched her leave, sighing sadly.

After supper one evening, as Darky was turning to carry water from the river, she met Lai Shun squatting on the bank, washing clothes. He seemed to have something to tell her but swallowed it.

"Are you keeping me in the dark about something?" she asked.

Lai Shun looked sheepish; he opened and then closed his mouth.

Darky said, "As the saying goes, you can see only skin, but not bone. I didn't expect that you were that kind of guy, too!"

Finally, lowering his head, Lai Shun told her how her small husband had had a fling for a long time with a woman in the town. After that woman turned her back on him, he'd recently picked up the mayor's youngest daughter. That very evening the girl had come to the school again and had not even tried to be discreet. Lai Shun had seen her enter the gym teacher's well-lit office and soon after had seen the light go out.

Darky's body recoiled. She felt dizzy.

"I shouldn't have told you," Lai Shun said. "But my conscience wouldn't let me keep quiet. Never mind. After all, he is your husband—and that girl's father is the mayor. They wouldn't dare go too far."

Darky silently carried her water home.

At the village gate, she drew the carrying pole off her shoulder and spilled the water into the buckets, then fell to the ground, sobbing.

Darky had always suspected it—but now that she knew for certain, she couldn't contain her anger. She rushed to the school alone; Lai Shun was not back yet. The school appeared pitch dark.

Darky felt a little scared. True, her husband and the girl were acting most shamefully. But if she walked in on them together, the girl might be so disgraced that she'd hang or drown herself. I shouldn't rush in, Darky thought. As long as I can split them up, that will be enough. My man is so timid, and the girl will be ashamed; we'd still be able to live together as a couple.

Standing in the school yard, she called to her small husband. He called back that he'd already gone to bed and she should talk to him the next day. So Darky made up a story: "Your dad sent me to tell you he needs you urgently. Get up quickly! I'll wait in the outhouse." She wanted to give the girl a chance to flee unnoticed, so she walked straight to the backyard toilet.

When she returned to the yard, the light in her husband's room was on. She entered and found her small husband smoking on the bed; the quilts were rumpled, and sweet incense was burning. He asked frostily, "What the hell is so urgent? Can't you wait till daybreak?"

Darky replied, "Can't I even come here to see you? You haven't been home for days. Aren't we still a couple?"

"You came here just to say that? Are you finished? Go home."

As Darky got up to leave, she heard something behind the cabinet. She looked down and saw two feet, small and exquisite. With a snort, Darky sat back down and stared fixedly at her husband. "Tonight, I will not leave. Fetch me a glass of water."

Her husband understood her intention and put a glass of water before her. She asked for another, and again he obeyed. Then she said calmly, in the direction of the cabinet, "Come out, drink some water. A little hot water won't hurt you."

A girl with a bewitchingly beautiful face sauntered out from behind the cabinet. She had disheveled hair and pink underwear.

Darky could not restrain a flash of admiration. "Such a knockout!"

The woman did not blush. Sitting beside the bed, she fixed her eyes on the ceiling without a trace of shame. Darky, on the other hand, turned pale. "You're awfully bold!" Rage boiled up within her, but she calmed herself, saying, "I won't beat you two, nor will I curse you. I only beg you not to destroy our family. If this affair were to be exposed, it wouldn't do any of us any good. So drink the water and go!"

The woman dressed and started to walk out. At the doorway she turned back to pick up a small jar of face cream from the table. Then she was gone.

But Darky's husband and his mistress did not change their ways. They stuck to each other like glue and continued their wrongful behavior. Darky came to regret the tolerance she'd shown that night.

She fought repeatedly with her husband about it. Backed by his father's financial resources and the mayor's power and authority, Darky's small husband now carried on flagrantly. It was agonizing for Darky. She tearfully turned to Lai Shun for comfort, and Lai Shun in return shed tears for her suffering.

One market day, the weather was cold, the ground frozen. While Darky, shivering, was buying some charcoal, she ran into Mu Du. He was jet black all over, looking like a hungry devil. "Darky," he said, surprised to see her. "You are so skinny—are you OK?"

Remembering when Mu Du had given her a hot potato beside the wall, Darky softened and began to cry. Mu Du said kindly, "So what the villagers are saying is true. Your man has bullied and humiliated you?" He asked for details. It took some time before Darky could give voice to what had happened.

That afternoon, Mu Du found Lai Shun and let loose a stream of abuse, saying that Lai Shun should not have told Darky about her husband's affair. Lai Shun felt wrongly attacked; he complained that his conscience wouldn't allow him to keep quiet.

Mu Du replied, "Your conscience? The credit agent's son was born a bad guy. Can a leopard change its spots? You told Darky everything and made her live like neither a human being nor a devil. Look how thin she has become. Is your conscience at ease now?"

Lai Shun was speechless. The two men racked their brains but could not come up with an idea to lift Darky out of her misery.

Mu Du cursed the credit agent and his son for being blind in their eyes and their hearts. However, they were in the mayor's good graces. Who knew how much ill-gotten money the credit agent had sent him.

Lai Shun had an idea: "We can take the firewood from under the cauldron just by settling with the girl! If she's too ashamed to go to the school, Darky's man will no longer be a problem."

That night, Lai Shun and Mu Du wore masks and took their positions near the school—Lai Shun on sentry duty and Mu Du lying still beside the road. As the mayor's daughter approached, Mu Du tackled her, grabbed her tightly, and punched her. Finally, he scratched her delicate face, saying, "Since you don't want to save this face, let me take the skin off!"

The mayor's daughter had been attacked, but only she and the small husband knew why. They could not speak about it in public. The girl told her father that a man had blocked her path and tried to rape her. The mayor ordered the local police to investigate.

When questioned, the girl said she thought the criminal's voice sounded like Mu Du's. Mu Du was promptly taken into custody. He confessed to the charge but revealed his reason for jumping the girl. As a result, the local police station did not pass the case up to the county bureau, nor did they release Mu Du right away. Under the mayor's orders, Mu Du was kept behind bars for fifteen days.

3

Before long, the small man divorced Darky and married the mayor's daughter.

Though she was no longer a part of the upstart family, Darky did not move away. She gathered her pride and refused to accept a single thing from her former husband. She returned to the village and bunked in a cowshed in the fields. Hearing the news, her elder brother came to her and lamented, "My poor sister!"

Darky asked, "Why do you cry? Have I done anything shameful?" At that, her brother's tears stopped. Instead he complained that she had exchanged her comfortable life for a life of misery. He wanted to bring her back to their parents' home. Darky refused. "I would rather stay to see what other tricks they might play!"

In the daytime, Darky cultivated with great care the field assigned to her. She became a jack-of-all-trades in farmwork and a match even for a strong man. In the evening, she tended the kitchen fire and cooked for herself. Despite her brother's laments, Darky lived a comfortable and carefree life. She swept the withered grass dust beside the road and burned this fuel to heat the kang; lying in bed was like lying in a pan upon the stove. She used to think that without a man, a woman was like a vine that had no sturdy tree to lean on or a kite without a string. But it turned out that a woman was also human and could live vigorously on her own!

Lai Shun often came over and helped her chop wood and fetch water or simply chatted with her. Darky would offer him a meal or a cup of tea. At dusk, she would always say, "You'd better go. Rumors cluster around a divorcée's door!" But Lai Shun didn't care.

One day he'd dropped in as usual. He told Darky that her former husband's family had just made a great deal of money when the credit agent bought a share of a straw-bag factory. They both sighed over the unfairness of life.

Darky asked, "Is the new couple living a happy life?"

Lai Shun answered, "Money makes the mare go! The woman is pregnant; they'll have a baby within the year."

Darky stared blankly at the mountains on the other side of the river, but she was unaware of the clouds in the sky and the smog above the faraway village. Lai Shun couldn't tell what was on her mind; Darky wasn't sure herself. When she finally sent Lai Shun away, a thin, faint smile played around the corners of her mouth.

In the village, rumor had it that Lai Shun was making a move on Darky. When Darky eventually heard the idle chatter, it made her heart heavy. Combing her hair in the morning, she looked in the mirror and saw just a face—dark, but smoother than before. Surprised to find herself neither old nor ugly, Darky said to herself, can't I be left alone and single? At this thought, her cheeks flushed. She felt something unspeakable in her heart.

When Lai Shun came again, Darky paid special attention to his face. His voice made her ears itch.

However, it was Mu Du who appeared in her mind and stubbornly stayed there. During Mu Du's fifteen days in jail, his old father brought him meals. Once, on his way to visit his son, the old man had stumbled over a stone and fallen. The food pot was broken, and the porridge spilled on the ground. Knowing that an old man of his age had sat on the ground crying, Darky felt like a knife had stabbed into her heart.

On the day Mu Du was released, she went to see him and was startled at his thick beard and pale face. He told her, "Darky, I didn't mean to do you any harm."

But since she'd moved into the cowshed, Mu Du had not visited. Did he still feel that he had let her down and felt too ashamed to visit? Or had he begun gathering alpine rush from the deep mountain instead of carrying charcoal?

During one of Lai Shun's visits, while Darky was lost in her thoughts, he cleverly heaved a sigh and said, "That heartless bastard abandoned you; he is blind in his eyes and his heart! He said you were ugly, but he was wrong; you are a wonderful woman. You needn't worry about forming a new family."

Darky's face changed. She smiled but cut Lai Shun short. He left soon after, indulging in fantasy. Lai Shun wore old and shabby clothes, but he was always washed and clean-shaven. He'd even chatted and traded jokes with Darky's ex-husband a few times.

As the autumn rain fell, Darky's newfound vigor began to wilt. Sitting on the edge of the kang, she watched bubbles appearing and vanishing in the puddles outside. Darky pictured, farther away, the river and then the range upon range of mountains. She had just a smattering of education and no knowledge of things like poetry, but there was a touch of poetry in her heart. A gloomy mood consumed her. It made her nostalgic for the autumn rains of her childhood at her parents' house, and even for the days she'd spent in her small husband's home. Thinking about how wretched and miserable her life was now, she buried her face in her hands and sat that way for some time as dusk fell.

Listening to the harsh sound of raindrops falling relentlessly on the roof, she recalled what had happened after her divorce. She remembered all the matchmakers and so many men, including Lai Shun. At the time they had all been just illusions, nuisances she hoped would not return.

In the rain, Darky ventured out to check on a plot of land near the river that she'd just begun to cultivate. She had planted radishes there; would the seedlings be washed away by the flooding river? The rain was letting up, but the wind was still strong.

Darky looked carefully. The radishes were well rooted, and the river had not risen too much. But the surging water flew by shiny and rapid. Suddenly, in the distance, a fire glittered and then extinguished in a wink. Darky stared and saw a light-reddish spot on the other side of the river. It looked like a fox's eye, appearing one second and disappearing the next. She heard the rushing of the water and, after a moment of silence, a slight creaking sound over the sands.

Fearing a ghost, Darky held her breath. She watched a shadow approaching, and she could eventually make out a man wading across the river, carrying alpine rush on his shoulders. From the sturdy build and clumsy steps, Darky recognized him and shouted, "Mu Du!"

Mu Du, startled, nearly fell. The cigarette butt between his lips streaked dark red and disappeared. Once he saw it was Darky, Mu Du laughed while he put on his trousers. But his laugh had a strange ripping sound.

"You brave the river on such a stormy day?" Darky asked. "The current could sweep you away!"

Mu Du replied, "I've collected a full load of alpine rush. I have to hurry home through the night—otherwise I'd be trapped and starve to death in the mountains. How daring you are to come here at night by yourself! Why don't you stay safely at home?"

"I've come to check on the radishes, to make sure they aren't washed away by the flood."

"Come to my house for radishes," Mu Du said. "This year, our radishes are growing well—white and long. You can have as much as you can eat!"

"Why should I take yours?" Her question confused Mu Du. Realizing he was facing a young divorcée, his warmth seemed to sink into the water and could not resurface. He asked roughly, "So, Darky, you haven't found a man yet? How can you keep it up, living alone all this time? Be sharp-eyed and marry a man who really cares for you!"

Darky felt her face grow warm. Her body seemed deliciously tired. She leaned against a willow tree on the bank.

They fell into an awkward silence, each focusing on the river, the willows, the opposite bank, with occasional furtive glances at each other. The yapping of a wild hound in the distance cleared Darky's mind. She said, "Let's go back." The way home was equally silent, and Mu Du felt the load on his shoulders grow heavier.

Ten days later, a matchmaker found Darky. A man had offered 300 yuan as a betrothal gift to marry her. When Darky asked who the man was, the matchmaker told her it was Lai Shun.

Darky noted to herself, he has the guts to do it! But she was alarmed and confused. The matchmaker argued, "Indeed he is poor, but he looks presentable. More importantly, he's not from around here—so after the wedding the two of you can leave this place. When you're out of sight of your ex-husband's family, then your ex-husband will be out of your mind!"

"I'm the daughter of a poor family," Darky replied. "So I mind his poverty. Anyway, I intend to stay here. I'll try to make my own living and keep up with my ex-husband's family."

Annoyed, the matchmaker said, "You talk nonsense! That family has now joined with the rich and powerful mayor. What can you do to them?"

"I won't do anything to them—but justice will!"

"How stupid you are," said the matchmaker. "No wonder your life is unhappy. Do you know what justice is? Justice is a baked potato: if you're familiar with it, it will be soft; if not, it will be hard."

"Is there no fairness in the world?" Darky asked.

The matchmaker returned to the topic at hand. "So, you are not pleased with Lai Shun? But there's clearly chemistry between you when you're together. Why the reluctance to marry him?"

Darky said, "What connection do I have with Lai Shun?" Finding no common ground, the matchmaker left. Darky was full of pent-up anger.

Soon after, another go-between came to Darky's house and proposed a marriage with Mu Du. Darky snorted with laughter: "All the bachelors are coming to me!"

The go-between said she had been approached by Mu Du's old father. Mu Du said that Darky was perfect, but he was too shy to tell her how he felt. The go-between had planned to bring Mu Du along, but halfway there he had wrapped his arms around a tree and refused to let go no matter how hard she pulled.

Hearing that, Darky could not help giggling—but then tears appeared in her eyes. Her voice choked. She lay on the kang with a heavy heart. Thinking Darky was against the idea, the go-between said, "You know Mu Du's family. Admittedly he is poor, but he is good-hearted. Besides, you came to grief on account of a wealthy family. Granted, his appearance is not outstanding—but he is sincere and kindly. If a man is handsome, he may have a wild heart and never be satisfied."

The go-between continued to make her case. "I heard that Lai Shun offered three hundred yuan as a betrothal gift, so Mu Du will give three hundred fifty yuan! I'll just leave it here on the cabinet." And the go-between left. Darky grabbed the money and ran after her but failed to catch up. She returned home and sat in a daze till midnight.

Darky married Mu Du after the wheat sowing. On their wedding day, Mu Du sported a newly shaved head and chin, and he wore a length of red silk around his waist and a brand-new cap. He invited relatives and neighbors to enjoy the wedding feast and drink in the courtyard. After several drinks with his guests, Mu Du grew unsteady. He was not a good drinker. He wildly urged his guests to eat and drink more, shouting, "How can three bowls be enough? I take two bowls for a snack! Have some more!"

Darky, sitting as custom demanded inside on the kang, could do nothing but wait, listening to the noisy feast in the yard and the cheerful chatter and hearty laughter of the guests teasing Mu Du. Looking out through the window lattice, she saw the wall that reminded her that she had once been part of the neighboring family. Mu Du had handed her a hot potato over that wall. She thought of the strange meanderings of human lives.

She scanned the group of guests, but did not see Lai Shun. Her heart grew heavy. Mu Du came inside, muttered, "Headache," and fell onto the bed and immediately into drunken sleep.

Soon Mu Du's hunchbacked father came in and repeatedly called his son, trying to wake him. "You should take care of your guests!" he said loudly. "How could you get so drunk while everyone's still here?" He left and came back with a pillow for his son. Darky was amazed to see that it was the stone pillow she had given the father many years ago.

When night fell, Mu Du woke and saw Darky in her bridal clothes sitting under the light. His heart was filled with the passion of a new bridegroom. Shyly he spoke her name, but could find no other words. Too timid to approach her, he just rubbed his hands restlessly like a bashful, naughty boy.

Darky took pity on him; Mu Du was plain looking, poor, inarticulate, inexperienced, and still a virgin. Today I marry him, she told herself, and I will be his woman from now on. So she combed her smooth, bright hair and pretended to be a bit shy, but a seductive passion showed in her eyes. Mu Du blew out the candle and pounced like a hungry tiger.

When Darky awoke at dawn, the scene looked completely different. The arm around her body was as strong and hard as an iron stick, with protruding veins and muscles and overgrown yellow hair. Her eyes fell on the shiny mulberry carrying pole leaning against the bedroom gate. That pole had had to feed two mouths in the family, and now there was a third. Her husband, strong as an ox, would exert his energy and life with her body as with the carrying pole—day in and day out, year in and year out. Her body tingled.

When Mu Du finally awoke, he spoke vehemently about new experiences and feelings. About how he would love her and dote on her. He could kill a dog with a punch, but he would never lay his fist on her; he would live only with her, perfectly content for the whole of his life, never even looking at other women. He also spoke of the loneliness he'd felt, as a bachelor, when he saw two dogs in heat in a cornfield.

Darky asked, "Mu Du, why didn't you invite Lai Shun to the feast yesterday?"

"I did," Mu Du replied. "He promised to come, but he never showed up."

"He's a nice guy; don't appear too proud in front of him. Find an opportunity, and treat him to a hearty drink."

"Sure," Mu Du agreed.

On the third day after the wedding, as Mu Du was passing by a wheat field after selling his alpine rush, Lai Shun popped out from behind a wheat stack. He had grown thinner, his eyes bleary. He said to Mu Du, "You're living a happy life now! With a wife, you are a somebody!"

Mu Du cupped his hand in salute and complained that he had missed Lai Shun on his wedding day.

"Since I didn't go that day," Lai Shun said, "would you make up for it today?"

"Absolutely! I just sold some alpine rush, so I have money in my pocket. You just wait here—I'll fetch the wine!"

Mu Du rushed into town and back like a gust of wind, returning to Lai Shun with a bottle of wine. Mu Du suggested they go to his home, where they could drink out of glasses, but Lai Shun said, "No need. It's OK to drink here without any dishes." So the two went behind the wheat stack and started drinking.

Mu Du was not a good drinker; after several swigs he began to see double. Lai Shun continued to drink and persuaded Mu Du to drink more. Sipping his wine, at first he congratulated Mu Du on his marriage. But soon he whimpered, "Mu Du, you are my friend—you can take my clothes, but you shouldn't have taken my wife!"

Startled by Lai Shun's words, Mu Du said that he would never do such a dirty thing; he was not an animal.

Lai Shun persisted. "Darky should've been my wife; I proposed to her first. I offered three hundred yuan, while you gave three hundred fifty. You won Darky's hand in marriage only because I'm poor!"

Mu Du replied sharply, "Lai Shun, you wrong me as well as Darky. She didn't refuse you because you offered less money. She didn't even accept my betrothal money."

For a long while Lai Shun sat in a daze. "Really?" he said finally, with a boozy hiccup.

Mu Du swore to it, pointing toward heaven. Lai Shun raised the bottle and said, "Then I wronged her. I fall behind you. Come, let's drink. I drink . . . and you drink, too!"

Because Mu Du felt so guilty for putting Lai Shun down, he forced himself to keep drinking. Soon the earth and sky were spinning around him, and his body felt as soft as ooze. A child nearby, viewing the scene, hurried off to report to Mu Du's hunchbacked father.

When the old man arrived, Lai Shun was trying to pour more wine into Mu Du, who was so drunk he had passed out. The hunchback wrested the bottle from Lai Shun and smashed it to pieces, cursing: "Lai Shun, you are disgusting; you hate my son because you didn't get Darky! You know Mu Du is honest and simpleminded. How dare you try to drown him with alcohol!"

Lai Shun, who was almost drunk, hastened to insist that he had no evil intent. The hunchback couldn't restrain his anger and hit Lai Shun on the head. Grumbling and swearing, the old man carried Mu Du home on his back.

4

No one was sure how much fire was beneath the smoke. Lai Shun earned wide infamy and dared not call at Darky's home for a long time.

As for Darky, she did not believe that Lai Shun bore such ill will, and she remained concerned for him. When she explained to Mu Du how she felt, he didn't know what to say; it was hard to separate right from wrong. However, the hunchbacked one, like an owl, would curse Lai Shun whenever he spotted him, even from far away. At home with his son and daughter-in-law, he would proclaim, "Our home is poor, but a humble family still has pride. No wildcat would dare bully us."

Mu Du didn't understand his father's anger, but Darky knew he was speaking to her. Mu Du might not be a good match for you, he was saying, but since you are now his wife, you must keep the fences intact. You cannot be a woman of two minds.

Darky's face might have shown divided feelings, but her heart did not. She remembered the suffering her former husband had caused her when he'd brought another woman into the family. She understood clearly how to behave as a good wife.

The town school bell always woke Darky at dawn. The drawn-out peals rang through the house and into her ears, reminding her of the pale-faced bell ringer. She could not imagine him sleeping soundly at night. After ringing the bell, what must he think about while sitting at the school gate by himself?

Mu Du usually awoke after the bell. He went to the fields and dug the ground hard, stripped to the waist, sweat wriggling like earthworms down his dusty back. Or he would carry alpine rush or charcoal on his shoulder pole from deep in the mountains. He would trudge the saw-toothed mountain ridges, black all over, eyes wide as a newly wrought porcelain jug. Exhausted by his heavy labor, he was hardly aware of the sweet wife waiting for him on the kang and would fall quickly into a deep sleep.

With Darky in the family, father and son no longer wore ragged clothes. Darky cared for their things and cooked them delicious meals. Nevertheless, the poverty-stricken home still seemed a bottomless pit. The family worried deeply about their failure to keep up with their neighbors, let alone surpass them.

Darky spoke to her husband. "You carry your shoulder pole all over the mountains to the point of exhaustion, while the credit agent's family earns money so easily. Let's think about other things we might do."

Mu Du asked, a little suspiciously, "So, you're missing that family again?"

"Why would I miss them? Do you think I'm that shameless? It's just that others make a killing through business; why not us? I don't expect us to get rich quick, but we don't have to remain poor all our lives."

As for what kind of business they could take up, Mu Du, like a tiger, wanted to swallow the sky but did not know where to take his first bite. Darky was equally at a loss. One day, when Mu Du went to town and passed the straw-bag factory in which the credit agent owned stock, he saw an imposing scene: an even expanse of straw-twisting and bag-sewing machines in the yard, and men and women in a flurry of work. Unable to resist, Mu Du stepped admiringly into the yard, watching and touching here and there. Suddenly a bold idea struck. Seeing the credit agent come through the front gate, he asked warmly, "Uncle, does your factory still want hands?"

The credit agent looked down, examining Mu Du over the top of his spectacles, and said, "Absolutely we want hands!"

Without hesitation, Mu Du asked, "Would you hire me? I'd like to sew straw bags, too!"

The agent laughed in front of the workers. "Do you see that stone pestle in the corner? Show us how many times you can lift and tamp it!"

Mu Du pulled off his shirt and took a deep breath. He raised the stone pestle and brought it down hard. One, two, three . . . he tamped forty-eight blows, sweat streaming from his face. He stood up and said, "I'm hungry. But after four bowls of noodles, I can manage sixty blows in a row!"

The workers, watching, laughed up their sleeves. The creditor said, "That's enough. You were born for this. Go find a family building a wall and work for them!" Mu Du realized that he had been made fun of and became purple with anger.

When Mu Du came home and told Darky what had happened, she snapped, "Why did you turn to him for help? I'd rather we starve to death than beg at his door!"

"Since he has refused me work in his factory," Mu Du replied, "I won't ask for help again. Instead I'll ask for a loan from the credit cooperative. With capital we could do business in town."

Darky protested, "Never ask him for anything! Do you think he'll grant you an honest loan? Whoever borrows from him must send him secret bribes. I would rather throw a gift into the river than offer it to him!" The couple argued for a long time before finally sitting face-to-face in silence.

The following day, Mu Du left gloomily—but at noon he came back all smiles. He told Darky that he had come across the seventh son of the Wang family, a young man who was honest but footloose. As he had neither capital nor business acumen, he had gone to work in the coal mines at Tong Guan, beyond the mountains. Digging coal in the pits was as dangerous as dealing with ghosts or visiting the Palace of the Devil, but the lad had returned home safe and sound after earning 1,300 yuan in three months. And now he was buying rafters and bricks to build a new house.

Darky had never been to Tong Guan and little understood the conditions of the coal mines. But she was delighted to find a way to earn a lot of money through hard labor. So the couple immediately began to collect expenses, clothing, and other things Mu Du would need for traveling. However, when Mu Du's hunchbacked father heard their plan, he shook his head like a rattle-drum and said, "I went to Tong Guan in the old days; you had to exchange your life for money. I learned that good girls refuse to marry men in Tong Guan, because once married there they would make black water for three years and eventually become widows."

As soon as he mentioned widows, the father knew he'd made a slip of the tongue; when her former husband had left, Darky became what was known in the village as "a living widow."

Darky, undeterred, suggested, "It is really difficult to make money with hard labor. Why not invite the seventh son of the Wang family and ask him what it's really like there?"

So they invited the Wang son home and questioned him closely about the situation at Tong Guan. He told them, "Indeed, it is hard, but not as horrible as your dad has said. You can make a lot of money—if you were born lucky."

Mu Du was convinced. "I got married in my thirties. Ain't I a lucky dog?" Once he had made up his mind to go to Tong Guan, neither his wife nor his father tried to stop him.

On the day Mu Du was to go, his family invited the seventh son of the Wang family to dinner. They urged him to guide and support Mu Du throughout the journey. Mu Du, slow-witted and dim eyed, would have to depend wholly on Wang away from home. The seventh son stroked Mu Du's chest in a gesture of reassurance.

So the elderly father again set up an incense burner and asked Mu Du to kowtow to heaven, the earth, and successive generations of ancestors. Then Mu Du walked backward to the courtyard gate and turned around to stand in the doorway. Once more he murmured the incantation for going out and drew four horizontal lines and then five vertical lines across them as a protective talisman. The family tearfully saw him off on his journey.

After Mu Du left, Darky had to sleep on the big earthen kang alone. Mu Du's snoring had always invited her to tuck herself into a deep sleep. Now, without his thundering roar, she awakened frequently during the night. Looking out the window, she saw the night sky where the moon was bright and the stars sparse. As the silvery moonbeams poured over the bed, she prayed thousands and thousands of times for her husband. Nevertheless, the school bell ringing at daybreak sounded like a drearily weeping chant.

Darky shouldered all the work in the field. She hoed the ground, carried manure, and reaped the wheat. When others had finished autumn sowing, she was still busy digging the ground. In the moonlit night, the hunchbacked father helped her in the field—but at his advanced age, he grew so exhausted that he coughed blood and had to lie down. She had to send for a traditional doctor and boil the prescribed medicinal herbs on the stove.

When Darky returned to the field, she found that the area she'd left unworked two days before had grown smaller. She was suspicious. Steamed buns left out might be stolen, but work left undone? Who on earth would be so kind?

It was the end of the month, when dark clouds swallowed the moon at night. Getting ready to take up her digging, she saw a shadow bending and rising at the border of the field. She sneaked up and, to her surprise, found it was Lai Shun.

Standing behind him, short of breath, she said nothing. Lai Shun turned around at the sound of her breathing, and his eyes gave off an astonished gleam in the dark.

Burning with rage, Darky asked, "Who allowed you to dig for me?"

Lai Shun replied, "I can't go to your home; can't I at least come to your field?"

Darky didn't know what to say. After a long silence, she raised her pickax to dig the ground, and Lai Shun followed suit. Though they stood side by side, they were separated by the panic of one and the grief of the other.

At night the sky seemed painted with charcoal. There was not a single soul in the fields, not even a wandering dog. A marmot scratched the earth nearby, oblivious to human affairs. Darky and Lai Shun continued digging till the cock crowed. Though the newly hoed soil was not virgin land, it gave off a rich and delicate fragrance from the quiet night's humidity. They sat on the edge of the field. Their strenuous labor had quelled the tension between them, and their excitement dispelled their exhaustion.

Darky tried to tamp down her arousal. She said, "Lai Shun, thank you so much. You'd better hurry back home and sleep."

Her words, uttered gently and full of tenderness, filtered through the dim night air. Lai Shun replied, "I wouldn't be able to asleep if I tried."

"Well," Darky said, "then come to my house, and I'll cook something for you."

"You'd dare?"

Darky knew he was right; she did not dare. Though the hunch-backed father was ill, he was neither deaf nor blind. Her husband was away; she couldn't lead a robust man into her home in the dead of night, even if no one else was around to see and spread rumors. She lowered her head and said, "Lai Shun, don't come and don't help me any more."

In a righteous rage, Lai Shun jumped to his feet, shouting, "I will help you! I can't watch you living such a miserable life!" He smelled strongly of tobacco smoke and sour male sweat. He approached her in the darkness. She felt two hands—burning, rough, but trembling—grasping her own. She jumped back as if from an electric shock. Then, waving her hands aimlessly in the air, she ran home.

The following noon, the town postman delivered a letter written by Mu Du from his dark underground world thousands of miles away. Mu Du was still as uneducated as Darky was. The letter was written on a sheet of cigarette paper; it consisted of only one short sentence:

"It gets colder now, I can't sleep well at night, bring me my hairy ¤¤."

Darky read the letter three times and failed to understand the meaning of ¤¤. Was he talking about what they did together in the dark? She was a little annoyed at Mu Du's one-track mind, but she knew that he missed her. She pictured his ugly but lovely face and mentally scolded him with a sullen look. You shameless man!

Mu Du's hunchbacked father searched her face as she read the letter and then happily pinched the fifty yuan from the envelope and asked what his son had said. Darky, flustered and bashful, read the letter out loud. Her father-in-law said, "Oh! He wants us to take his hairy lambskin coat to him. He doesn't know how to write 'lambskin,' so he drew circles instead." Darky's face turned red with embarrassment.

Alone, Darky laughed at her own ridiculous assumption. Her husband barely knew how to write and only did so when it was absolutely necessary. Writing a letter was as difficult as working in the pits. How could he be carefree enough to flirt with her on paper?

She exhaled a deep breath and began worrying about her simple and honest husband, away from home and family. How did he get his meals? Where did he sleep? What was it like to crawl through the dark pits, hauling coal, where the eyes were useless and one had to be alert to terrible danger with all one's senses? She counted herself lucky that she had escaped the hands of Lai Shun the night before and that she had not betrayed her husband, who risked his life to make money for her.

Remembering that moment with Lai Shun, Darky felt intensely loyal to her husband. She would remain vigilant against the temptation of Lai Shun. But however beneficial her resolve was for Mu Du, thousands of miles away, for Darky, a young married woman with normal sexual needs, spending the night on a huge, empty bed by herself seemed unbearable and unfair.

She began to feel bad for rebuffing Lai Shun. He was a nice guy, after all. When she had considered remarrying, she could have married him. Marriage is unpredictable, she thought. A woman gives her heart and soul to one man or another. Once she marries, her husband can enjoy her at home to his heart's content, while other men cannot possess her, even when her husband is gone. Is this what fate means?

The next time Darky saw Lai Shun, she was picking wild herbs on the ridges of the fields. She saw him at a distance and took the initiative to greet him. Lai Shun cheerfully returned her friendly greeting, and the two stood under the warm, early winter sun and talked at length. Lai Shun drew her attention to the briskly flowing water in the river beyond the fields: a myriad of blue flamelike points of mist soaring from the cliff on the other side of the river and the shimmering arc upon the mountains far away, barely visible through the sunshine and rain clouds. She felt part of a sweet dream, as if it were the first time she'd encountered the glorious scenery of the nearby mountains, though she had been born and raised there.

In time, Darky grew increasingly plump and smooth skinned. Her dark, solid muscle now turned delicate and soft. Very fine wrinkles appeared around the corners of her mouth like a Chinese pearleafed crab apple. With the fifty yuan Mu Du sent each month, Darky bought a felt hat for her old father-in-law. She made herself a pullover with white flowers on a blue background, in which she looked graceful and poised. When she combed her hair smooth and went to the river with a basket of radishes, she would show a smidgen of her charms. Once, when she was strolling hastily along a path with her back to the golden rays of the sunrise, somebody watching her on the road called out, "Knockout!" She was so embarrassed that she instantly squatted down and froze. It was Lai Shun, and he continued his praise. He said that as she came over the hill, the morning rays magically surrounded her with a layer of red radiance, like fine fur around her body. "It was just like the divine light around the Bodhisattva!"

Her heaviest load became her father-in-law's illness, which worsened day by day. They had plain food but no luxuries like meat, so she went barefoot to the ditch to dredge up river snails—the villagers called them "sea cows." She scalded them in boiling water, gouged out a bit of flesh into a bronze spoon, and stir-fried it for her father-in-law.

One day, after lunch, the hunchback napped on the kang while Darky prepared pig swill by pounding the dried sweet-potato vines that grew atop the yard wall. Suddenly she heard Lai Shun calling her softly from the door.

She looked up to see him pouting his lips at the main room. He whispered, "Your old dad at home?"

Darky whispered back, "He's taking a nap."

Lai Shun leaped onto the threshold, stood under a grape trellis that crisscrossed a corner of the yard, and said, "That's good. Or he'd treat me like a threatening tiger or leopard!"

"What's up?" Darky asked.

Lai Shun gave no reply but wore a weird smile. The sunbeams peeping through the grapevines covered him with spotted shadows; he looked as naughty and funny as a little boy. From beneath his shirt he pulled out a frosted sack made from a scarlet castor leaf. "Today the school canteen gave us something special to eat—four cubes of this. I saw you scraping sea cows from the ditch and knew that you both needed a bit of fat in your guts. So I only ate one."

Inside the castor leaf were three fat cubes of marinated pork.

Darky felt a warm current rushing through her heart. She received the gift with both hands, saying, "You're just like a kid. I'm not hungry. You take them—I won't."

"Why not!"

"I'm already so plump," Darky said. "The more I eat, the fatter I get. Take them for yourself. Don't let the villagers see them and become envious!"

Lai Shun replied, "Then I'll take one and you take two."

Darky took one cube—a mouthful of grease—and wrapped the other up with the castor leaf, saying, "I will keep this for old Dad." She'd hardly finished speaking when the hunchback stepped out from the doorway, eyes burning with fury. He let loose a torrent of abuse.

"I don't care about one cube of meat! Mu Du's woman, aren't you afraid that the meat will be poisoned? Chuck it out!" He staggered over, seized the meat, and threw it to the ground, trampling it into a scrap of oily sludge. Then he jabbed his skinny forefinger in Lai Shun's face and roared, "Lai Shun, you're an indecent and despicable creature! Her poverty and starvation have nothing to do with you! And you have the nerve to come here and offer her meat when Mu Du is away? You dare to take advantage of my family? If you're so shameless, go and take liberties with the mayor's daughter!"

Lai Shun was blinded by the flood of abuse. He forced open the door and rushed out, frightened, while the old man continued to curse him angrily.

Returning to the room, Mu Du's father sat feebly on the threshold, sweating heavily, his mouth full of foam.

Darky quickly bolted the yard gate in case the neighbors had overheard. After helping her father-in-law sit down on the bed, she tried to explain but soon returned to her room and sat in a trance. She blamed the hunchbacked old man for being oversensitive and making trouble out of nothing. She reexamined Lai Shun's behavior closely and felt even sorrier to have made him go through all that.

A woman is blessed with a tender sense of pity, and she is pleased by affection and adoration from men; their sympathetic actions or considerate words often win her gratitude. On the other hand, if a man acts aggressively, like a rascal, the woman's gratitude will soon vanish. But then a clever man pretends to have been wronged and humiliated—and then the woman's tenderness returns as deep as the overflowing sea. Lai Shun was one of those clever men.

The following day, Darky purposefully went to the school gatehouse after school and comforted Lai Shun with a few words. Lai Shun wore a bitter look, so Darky stayed awhile and helped him scrub the clothes that were soaking in a basin.

That night proved a golden opportunity for Lai Shun's cultivated sulk. It was neither cold nor damp; the moon shone brightly and the crickets chirped. Seeing that Darky treated him with sincere feeling, Lai Shun's melancholy faded from his heart. He chatted freely with her, his words tiptoeing on the borderline between proper and improper. As he watched Darky scrubbing the clothes, the hair on her temples rising and drifting, creating a sweet and charming look, he couldn't help himself; he gripped Darky's waist with his two hungry paws.

Darky vainly struggled in alarm and cried, "Lai Shun! Lai Shun! Are you crazy?" Then she quietly fainted. Lai Shun laid her down on the small bed.

Sympathy is a woman's strength and also her greatest weakness. That night, Darky's sympathetic nature pushed her into a pit of grief.

When Darky became clearheaded, she watched the lamp in the room as its tiny wick went dim and nearly out; only a small blue flame glimmered faintly. She remembered that when her body had been laid down, this robust man did not treat her rudely like Mu Du; instead he handled her patiently, with tenderness. So she knew that he was either an old hand in dealing with women or a novice who had learned without a teacher—which proved him wiser than Mu Du either way. With a blank face, she rose from the bed and, without casting a glance upon Lai Shun, quietly left the room.

Lai Shun had no idea what Darky was thinking. Since he couldn't find any proper words to comfort her, he watched her leave without a word.

On her way home, she heard the sound of his radio at high volume.

5

In April, Mu Du came home. He had always been dark in the face, but now he had become darker, like a ghost or a devil, the rough pores of his skin inlaid with coal dust that could not be rinsed away. His lambskin jacket had worn down to the cotton lining and had been left in that other world underground. However, on his cotton bag there was an extra large pocket. He put 2,120 yuan into the pocket, sewed it up tightly, and did not take off his clothes for several days on the train. From the train station he hitched a ride in a car and slept in an inn over a thousand miles away. Finally home, he carefully took out the money; after days of soaking in his sweat, it stank.

The villagers regarded Mu Du as a homecoming hero; he had earned a small fortune within a few months. He spoke grandly about his adventures in Tong Guan, as if he'd just come back from abroad. While money had made the credit agent's son sink further into degeneracy, it made Mu Du crazy with excitement.

Only at night did Mu Du give a true account of what a dark and terrible underground world the coal mine was. A shift lasted for a whole day. He'd had to take thirty-two pancakes with him, chewing them like a wolf down in the pits. When he'd emerge from the mine, a crowd of coal miners' relatives would be waiting at the entrance, staring expectantly for their loved ones; nobody ever awaited him. At first, the bright sunshine offended his eyes. He'd be unable to move and would have to squat there like a black spider or a blind bear, waiting for his pupils to adapt to the dizzying rays.

Mu Du learned to worship gods and bought a protective peach-wood talisman. One time, the pits caved in. He had watched as a boulder fell and crushed one of his workmates to death. The blood burst out from the man's head like spurting water.

All these details made Darky's hair stand on end. Covering Mu Du's mouth with her hand, she threw herself at her husband, embracing and gently warming his stinking breast, arms, and head, her face bathed in tears. She said not a single word about Lai Shun.

One day Mu Du came across the credit agent at the town fair. The agent asked jovially: "Mu Du, you made a fortune?"

Mu Du answered humbly: "Comparing me with you is like comparing a man's lean pinky to his waist!"

The agent roared with laughter. "I didn't hire you in my factory, nor would I lend you money. I wanted you to work on your own. Now you've really made a killing! How will you manage your two thousand yuan? Would you like to invest it in our credit cooperative and have your money produce sons and grandsons?"

When Mu Du told Darky about the creditor's suggestion, Darky insisted that the money should be neither saved nor spent extravagantly. They should start a business with the capital.

Eventually they decided to start a restaurant. They began modestly, since Mu Du was good at nothing but hard labor. They found a small storefront at the eastern end of town with a rent of only forty yuan a month. A big willow tree stood in front of the restaurant. During the day, a signboard flapped like a flag amid the bright green of the thousands of thin branches dancing in the breeze.

The locals were not used to eating outside their homes in the daytime. However, the town was a hub of communications—so businessmen, workers, and passersby, coming and going from all directions, came to eat at the restaurant. The customers were gods. Darky and Mu Du would greet them with smiles, letting them take a seat on the stone stool beneath the willow and offering them a pot of tea while they awaited their meals.

The couple would light the fire and make noodles. Darky, her large, full breasts trembling beside the kneading board, rolled the dough as thin as paper. Before Mu Du brought the water to a boil, she would lean over the windowsill and chat with the customers.

The customers were well traveled and had wide experience. They liked to chat with women. They would make up fabulous stories—a mouse that gained human wit, or a wedding between a woman and a ghost. Darky was a good listener; her rich facial expressions showed interest, surprise, and joy. Her captivating face left a deep impression on the diners, and they talked about her everywhere they went. The restaurant's business was booming every day.

The town's nighttime culture centered on drinking, so the restaurant bustled with noise and excitement after dark. Liquor changed those men of the mountains into a different race. They cursed wantonly and drew Mu Du to join them in drink. Since Mu Du was not a good drinker, he would turn and shout to Darky for help—and thus Darky would join the company of men with strong arms, while Mu Du, tittering and smirking, urged her to imbibe. The drunkards would curse Mu Du, calling him a lucky dog for marrying such a good-looking and competent wife. Their envious taunts made Mu Du feel proud and vain; he'd boast about his macho prowess.

The restaurant became well known near and far. Many people had heard about Darky, and soon some of those good-for-nothings began to make a move on her.

One day, after the restaurant's rush hour, Mu Du went home to look after his hunchbacked dad. Darky rinsed the noodle board and had just sat down to rest for a moment when her small ex-husband peeped into the restaurant from the gate. When Darky saw him, he assumed a mock-serious manner, pretending to nonchalantly scrape his fingernails with a nail file.

"What are you doing here?" Darky said. "Service is finished."

The small man replied, "Don't turn against me—I was your man once! So, you're getting along quite well?"

Darky shrugged. "I won't wave the stick." She lowered her head and cleaned the board again. She thought he had left, but when she raised her head she saw that he was still there.

Halfway over the threshold, he looked attentively at something in his hand, asking, "What's this?"

Without thinking, she replied, "What?"

The small man stepped in and opened his hand. It was a blue quartz digital watch; two black dots flashed continuously on its screen. "Want it?" the small man asked. "Take it!"

"Pooh." Darky pushed him out of the gate, spat, and then closed the gate tightly.

Nevertheless, the credit agent often came to the restaurant and ordered meals to entertain his guests. Darky treated him in a professional manner—business was business. As for Mu Du, he would offer the agent a seat and some tea with a flattering demeanor. After dinner, Mu Du would put his own tobacco casket on the table and invite the agent to smoke. When the credit agent asked about their business, Mu Du would describe everything in detail, stressing that his small business was nothing compared to the agent's income from his factories. Darky found Mu Du's flattery contemptible and told him so. Mu Du replied, "After all, he is a big shot in our area!" Hearing that, for the first time in her life Darky spat in his face.

Mu Du and Darky continued to run their business successfully, and soon they were making a good profit. Unfortunately, the hunchbacked father's illness became serious. After lying in bed for half a month without food, he came to the end of his time in this human world. The couple closed the restaurant for ten days, had a decent cry in mourning, and buried the dead man. Although the hunchbacked father had been impoverished, he'd been upright and unyielding in temperament throughout his life, and he'd died a clean death. He left no family obligations, except that now one of them had to watch the restaurant and the other the old house. Gradually Mu Du became indifferent to bedroom things.

Lai Shun continued to do odd jobs at the school—heating up the water, doing the cooking, ringing the bell. Whenever he saw the small man and the mayor's daughter, happily hugging and kissing each other with soft murmurs, he suffered pains and itches as if he had a grain of sand in his eyes. (When the couple was on bad terms, they overturned desks and chairs and hurled things like pillows, teapots, and underpants out the window.)

The couple reminded Lai Shun of his affair with Darky. He was unable to stop thinking about her. When Mu Du's father passed away,

Lai Shun heaved a deep sigh in his innermost heart. He bought some touch papers and burned them in front of the dead man, weeping bitterly. Seeing him crying, Mu Du was deeply moved and wanted to help him up. But Darky stopped him, saying, "Let him alone—he needs to get it out of his system."

Henceforth, Mu Du's aversion to Lai Shun disappeared. When Lai Shun stepped into the restaurant in his spare time, Mu Du treated him warmly, offering food and drink at mealtimes. Lai Shun was a bright, changed, and nimble man who helped the couple with the washing; he'd greet guests and offer them the menu. He was much better at attracting customers than Mu Du was.

However, Darky knew Lai Shun's heart. The more solicitous he was, the more uneasy she felt. She delicately asked him to hold back from his busy activities at their restaurant. But the more Darky tried to restrain Lai Shun, the more Mu Du felt Lai Shun was a good guy, which in turn made Lai Shun work harder to please Darky.

In private, Darky told Mu Du, "This is our restaurant; we don't need his help. Next time he comes, let him do nothing!"

But Mu Du replied, "He is so good-hearted to help us. If we dismiss him like that, it would create a rift and hurt his warm heart!" Darky had to keep her silence.

One hazy moonlit night, Darky hurried home from the restaurant, eager to go to sleep. With the yard door open, she could see new seedlings swaying in the breeze, shining darkly under the old Chinese scholar-trees outside the courtyard. As Darky sat in the yard, she heard a soft sound like that of a crawling snake. She looked around suspiciously and saw a dim, smoky light, red like a firefly. She rose with fright, asking, "Who's there?" Lai Shun approached.

"You are sneaking around," Darky said. "I thought it was a thief!"

Lai Shun said, "So you stay at home while Mu Du sleeps at the restaurant?"

"We have shifts, and he has to chop meat tonight. Where have you been? Are you just passing by?"

Lai Shun answered, "I've come from school especially to see you!"

"Take a seat. Tonight the moon is so beautiful. Have you been to your hometown recently? Do the cuckoos chirp?"

"Last night they chirped, and four days later the winter wheat will be filling out its ears. After that people will talk big about the coming harvest—the wheat this year is better than the last. But in my hometown up in the mountains, the wheat is just flowering; it ripens twenty days later than on the plain. So I can help you like a migratory farmer until it's time to go harvest wheat!"

Darky smiled softly and said, "So you do, help me to do everything . . ."

"Darky," said Lai Shun, "I know I shouldn't come to your home. But I dream of you and feel empty-hearted when I wake up."

"What's your dream?"

"Sometimes in my dream, you're dressed in a new suit of clothes and look like a girl of seventeen or eighteen. You go to town and sing opera while many people play musical instruments for you. And in other dreams, you're sobbing under the weeping willow in front of the restaurant. When I have good dreams I worry: dreams are the opposite of reality, so isn't this a bad omen? And when I have bad dreams, I worry that they might come true. So tonight I came over to take a look at you. It's ridiculous, isn't it?"

Darky was amused. "Lai Shun, you have a sweet tongue and your words are too pleasant to my ear!"

Lai Shun, adopting a stern expression, said, "It's true! If I'm telling a lie, let the devil take my soul away."

Then Darky looked into Lai Shun's face, thin and shining white. He did not evade her glance but returned it boldly. His mind flew high into the clouds.

Afterward, Darky tilted her head and watched the bright moon in the sky and a pair of birds perching in a willow at the foot of the yard. She could tell that the birds were a couple; they balanced their bodies together on a thin twig with their small talons, one sleeping soundly, the other lightly dozing and waking. They reminded Darky that human beings, like birds, pair off wing-to-wing during the daytime, while at night they sleep together, leaning closely against each other. That is how life should be, she thought. And yet Lai Shun led a pitiable life, dreaming of another man's wife every night. Thinking about that, she felt dejected and sighed for him.

"Lai Shun, at your age, why don't you find a wife?"

Her words touched a tender spot in Lai Shun's heart. But instead of shedding tears, he laughed.

Darky asked, "Why are you laughing?"

"It serves me right to be a bachelor! Had I been more persistent in proposing to you, we would have been a couple. It's a pity that I didn't. Mu Du has had a better fate."

Darky kept quiet.

Lai Shun said, "Darky, does Mu Du treat you well? It's good to run a restaurant, but it's hard work, so you need to take care of yourself. During your period, you're not supposed to touch cold water—but you continue to fetch two full buckets of water on a shoulder pole from the river!"

Darky was surprised; how could he know such things? From her complexion? Mu Du—who ate, drank, and slept with her—had no idea about that, while Lai Shun had discovered it! It dawned on Darky that this pale-faced man truly cared for her well-being, and she was deeply moved.

She replied, "He is a silly man, but he does what I ask."

The two chatted away about many things, and Lai Shun forgot about the time. So did Darky, who had never conversed that way with her ex-husband when she left the deep mountain for marriage on the plain. And then there was Mu Du, who never offended or beat her but was not particularly considerate—and it never occurred to him that his wife might be lonely. Humans want not only respect but also love. A woman can be as strong as a tiger, but sometimes she also feels as weak as a puppy or a kitten.

As they talked, naturally and comfortably, Lai Shun took Darky's hands, licked them with his soft tongue, and bit them gently with his teeth. She said nothing. Afterward, she saw him to the door.

The moon was bright in a star-studded sky, and the night was deepening. The golden wheat encircling the village rippled in the cool breeze; the moonlight on the stalks made the fields look like ocean waves. The dense, intoxicating fragrance of the April fields swelled in Darky's breast.

The restaurant opened every day and did not close even during the busy period of the wheat harvest. Mu Du, like a strong ox, bore the heavy burden of reaping wheat at night, threshing grain, plowing the fields, and sowing seeds, while still selling meals during the day. When his work was done he was exhausted and instantly fell into a sound sleep. He lay on the kang like a dead snake fallen from a treetop.

When Darky woke up at midnight, she could not rouse him. She could only wait for the school bell to ring at daybreak.

Their family was no longer poor. Indeed, they'd become respectably well-off. Now when Darky came across the credit agent and his small son, she would walk past them without a glance rather than step aside or keep a distance. One market day, she was in a private clothes shop when the small man came in with the mayor's daughter. He asked the price of a silk scarf. As he and the shopkeeper bargained noisily, Darky approached and asked brusquely, "How much is it?"

When the shop assistant replied, "Thirteen yuan," Darky said, "I'll take it!" She drew the money from her pocket and swaggered off with the scarf hanging from her hand. Her behavior embarrassed the small man and his young wife, and they blushed profusely. Darky never wore that scarf, not even in the cold winter.

Mu Du once asked her, "Why did you buy it if you don't wear it?"

Darky replied, "Can't you understand?"

Seeing Darky spend money freely, Mu Du himself gradually followed suit. Others often played tricks on him and made bets with him; naturally he was the loser and had to buy wine or cigarettes as a penalty. Sometimes, the winner would gnaw some pig's feet or take two bowls of noodles instead.

Eventually Mu Du began gambling at card games. When he was in a good mood he would play all night, unaware of Darky asleep on their big and lonely bed.

At meals, Darky set out two dishes on the table, with two chairs and place settings, so they could eat together. However, after filling a bowl and garnishing the rice, Mu Du would stride out the door, bowl in hand, to eat and chat with others. After supper, when Darky asked Mu Du to sit and talk with her for a while, Mu Du would say, "You take care of all the things in the restaurant! Just tell me if you have anything that needs doing."

Darky asked, "Can't you talk about anything else?"

"Anything else?" Mu Du would reply. "Nothing! Let's go to bed." He would fall into a wheezy sleep as soon as he lay down.

That was always the moment when Lai Shun would arrive. Darky would not let him go, asking him about this and that, prolonging their time together.

One night, Mu Du went out to gamble, and Lai Shun and Darky chatted at her home deep into the night. Darky complained about Mu Du, her eyes brimming with tears. Lai Shun soothed her, but the more he comforted her, the more brokenhearted she felt. She laid her head in his lap and sobbed.

As the cock crowed a second time, Mu Du came home, pushing the door open and entering the room. The light was out. He saw a shadow at the rear window and asked, "Darky, is there someone outside the window?"

Darky was terrified but covered her fear, saying, "What? A ghost?"

After he undressed and lay on the kang, Mu Du said, "My eyesight is getting poor. I thought something was moving outside the window! It's said that ghosts do exist. Even if we haven't seen one, it's better to shut the window in the evening."

Darky replied, "Let the ghost come and keep me company, since you don't stay at home."

Mu Du said, "I hope it isn't true that when you talk of a ghost it's sure to come! Let's go to sleep." Almost immediately he began to snore.

6

Sometimes events surprise us, changing the fate of those involved as well as innocent spectators. Overnight, the credit agent found himself in a tight spot: arrested, tried, and convicted, he was sentenced to prison for fifteen years. He had violated the law: over three years he had embezzled a total of 33,000 yuan from public funds to buy shares in private enterprises and had taken 6,600 yuan through public or private blackmail. The police had hotly pursued and fiercely investigated his crimes.

The investigation squad from the county stayed in the town for ten days. On the early morning of the tenth day, Darky, sleeping soundly in the back room of the restaurant, was awakened by ear-piercing bursts from a motor horn. Looking out through the window lattice, she saw a prison van at the gate of the agent's family. Shocked and frightened, she kicked Mu Du, sleeping on the other side of the kang, and said loudly, "Wake up, the cops are arresting somebody!" When they opened the door, the street was filled with chattering people.

Darky stepped out and asked, "Who was arrested?"

A man said, "Didn't you hear? Good will be rewarded with good and evil with evil—and now it's time for the credit agent to eat what he has been cooking for himself!"

Darky was taken aback. When she was the agent's daughter-in-law, she had feared that he was doing something against the law, but since she left that family she never put her nose in their business. Though she'd expected the day would come when he received his due punishment, her heart softened as she saw a pair of shining handcuffs on the agent's wrists and his short son, chasing after the prison van, half-dead with weeping. She said to herself, all is over for this family. All is over!

When Darky returned looking pale, Mu Du asked, "Did you give any evidence to the cops?"

"They didn't come to me," she replied. "Even if they had, what could I tell them?"

"People are saying you accused the agent of illegal acts in poison-pen letters, that you regarded the family as a deadly enemy and wanted to trap the agent!"

What that man in the street had said to her began to sink in. Darky said, "They're just making a bullshit guess! The agent has aroused the wrath of both God and men; naturally somebody would take action against him, even if we wouldn't!"

Mu Du sighed. "Life is really unpredictable. Just a short time ago he was a man on the rise, the honorary schoolmaster with red silk draped over his shoulders and a big red flower pinned to his breast. Now he's a criminal!"

"You are so innocent," Darky said, "you would have no idea even if somebody were to hoodwink and eat you. He sponsored the school so as to give himself more leeway. But heaven does not pardon evil men like him!"

"In that case, his son can't teach at the school any longer?"

"Probably not," Darky replied. She fell silent.

As expected, the small man was dismissed from the school and once again had to live like a peasant. No longer could he lead students in a basketball game or flit to and fro between parallel bars. He looked like a vegetable blighted by frost, living with disheveled hair and a dirty face. And he had to pay for his father's crimes. He sold half of the newly built brick building but still owed 800 yuan. It was said he was so depressed that he whimpered in his home all night.

Lai Shun told Darky about the small man's recent woes. Darky in turn spoke to Mu Du. "Since his family abused public property, he had to give every penny of it back. But now he is penniless, which is indeed miserable."

Mu Du clapped his hands and shouted, "Great, that's great—he should hang himself!"

But Darky said, "We can feel good seeing his family get their due punishment, but we are better off now, and he is young and has to support his old mother and wife. Why don't we send him some money to fill his pit? What do you think?"

"What's wrong with you?" Mu Du asked. "You want to invite the mockery of others?"

Darky said, "Why would others sneer at me? When I got divorced, they laughed at me. Today, if I relieve his distress, they should sneer at his family, not at me!" She was determined, so Mu Du yielded to her.

Darky called on her former husband. His mother felt so ashamed that she dared not meet Darky and hid in the inner room. The little man sat alone in his own room, where he had nothing but bare walls. All the wardrobes and suitcases were gone. When Darky took out money, he threw himself on the floor to kowtow to her.

Darky learned that after the credit agent had been caught, the mayor was given a grave disciplinary warning from the Party. He was removed from office and sent to another town government as a minor secretary. Meanwhile, his daughter, the small man's second wife, bagged all the valuables from their home and went to live with her parents. Before long, there was gossip about the small man's marriage to the mayor's daughter. The story was that in the beginning the newlyweds were not only inseparable, but couldn't keep their hands off each other. Sometimes they even did their bedroom work during the day and were spied on by the students. Later, the woman became fed up and often spent the night elsewhere. Someone saw her hugging and kissing a handsome young stranger at the corner of the wall. This was well known in the town, secret only to the small man. When his wife would not sleep with him, he beat her. After that they slept together, sharing the same bed, but with different minds. Eventually, they supposedly agreed to an animal-like arrangement on Sunday nights. His wife would swallow three sleeping pills after supper and let him do as he pleased while she gradually lost consciousness.

When Darky heard this story, on the one hand, she took pleasure in the small man's misfortune; on the other, she was repulsed by his wife's crudeness.

The small man did not ask for a divorce—but since his wife never came home, he lived the life of a divorced man. One day, when Mu Du and Darky were busy kneading dough in their restaurant, the small man, sitting under the willow by the restaurant, called timidly, "Brother Mu Du!"

Mu Du invited him to come in and made tea for him. Soon Lai Shun arrived. The three men started chatting, but each with his own mind. The small man said, "Brother Mu Du, I'd like to work in the coal pit at Tong Guan beyond the mountains. Could you show me the way?"

Lai Shun said, "You want to work in the coal pit! Can you stand the hardships?"

The small man sighed. "I need money badly."

Mu Du replied, "It may not be a bad idea to go there, but your life will be at risk at all times. If you're lucky and shed sweat there for several months, you'll have enough to start a proper business after you come back."

Standing motionless in the dim shadows, Darky thought that if the small man had had such ambitions sooner, he would not have fallen into such dire straits. Recalling her own bitter experiences with him, she could not help shedding tears.

He had been enslaved by money all his life: money was the devil he had to pursue.

The small man eventually left for Tong Guan. Unfortunately, within two months, a telegram came: he had been smashed to death by a landslide in the coal pit.

When her ex-husband's corpse arrived, Darky saw that he was headless, but the flayed and empty skin of his face remained. She fell into a heap and burst into tears. After pulling herself together, she fetched a dry gourd from the restaurant, fit it on the head of the corpse, and pinned the facial skin to it so it resembled a head.

In the autumn, as social reforms became more and more popular, people from factories in the big cities would come to the town, promoting the sale of goods and purchasing some mountain products. Two new streets were added in the town. The women who had sat on the sides of the street, doing needlework and gossiping, were now running a store where they installed a plank door and slanting windows larger than the door. They arranged shelves full of goods for sale.

Darky's restaurant was expanded from one to three rooms, now reaching close to the huge willow in front. They served not only noodles but also a variety of stir-fried meat dishes. They hired a chef, an old man invited from outside the city limits with a salary of one hundred yuan a month.

Mu Du still wore the same clothes, neither shabby nor neat, and did the heavy manual labor. Darky, with smooth hair and a delicate face, was neatly dressed and in charge of greeting the guests, while an ample and wide-hipped girl washed the dishes and bowls. The girl had no parents and lived with her brother's family. Darky paid her thirty yuan a month, with meals provided in the restaurant.

Darky was fond of the fat girl and shared with her good food and drinks. After the restaurant closed at night, Darky would invite her to share the bed, and the two would talk at length about relations between men and women. The girl was a rough diamond who had already learned about sex between men and women. She asked Darky why she had not seen her employers sleep together since she'd started to work there. Darky would always change the subject.

Lai Shun often came to the restaurant, chatting and laughing with the boss and workers. But after three cups of liquor, he would become fish-eyed. His blank eyes would fix on the oblique beam of light shining through a hole in the roof. The fat girl could never understand what he was staring at. She saw only innumerable insects sinking and rising in the light. Darky just said, "Do your washing up." She then seated herself at the table and drank silently.

At nightfall, Darky asked the fat girl to rest with her at home while Mu Du stayed at the restaurant.

The old chef asked, "Mu Du, why don't you go home to sleep with your wife? Don't you trust me here?"

Mu Du said, "What's the difference between sleeping at home or here?"

"If you stay here, who will warm your wife's feet?"

Mu Du chuckled. "We're a seasoned couple and no longer young!"

The old man replied, "How old are you? Are you older than me? When I was your age, I wouldn't go out every night."

Mu Du laughed. "Sometimes I go home—and so what? Once or twice a month is enough."

"What a man!" The old chef shook his head. "You're supposed to have pillow talk with your wife. Every evening, couples out in the country go for a walk shoulder-to-shoulder on the riverbank." Then he sighed. "But I guess there are differences between town and country."

One night when Mu Du was sleeping in the restaurant, Darky sent the fat girl to fetch something from the restaurant at midnight. The fat girl came back from the restaurant feeling wronged, but Darky paid no attention.

On the night of the Midautumn Festival, the moon was bright and round. Families were enjoying their reunion moon cakes, peanuts, and chestnuts at home. There were few customers at the restaurant. That afternoon, after the old chef returned to his home in the town, the fat girl closed the restaurant early and arranged some drinks and refreshments on the stone table before the gate. When she called the couple to come to the table, Darky was nowhere to be found.

Mu Du said, "She probably went to the school to invite Lai Shun, who is all alone tonight." They waited a long time, but Darky did not return. Mu Du sent the girl to the school to look for his wife. When the girl returned, she reported that the school gate was locked. There was not a single soul there.

Meanwhile, in a small hamlet fifty miles deep in the mountains, something extraordinary happened. A child shouted shrilly at the hamlet's entrance, "Hurry up and have a look! The village head has tied them up with a rope!" Those enjoying moon cakes in their homes thought somebody from beyond the mountain might be putting on a monkey show to liven things up for the holiday, or maybe a village hunter had caught a rare and precious bird or beast from the mountain deeps. They rushed out to see the fun. As they crossed the old single-log bridge across the mountain stream at the village entrance, they saw an abandoned thatched shed in a melon patch. Inside it, a naked man and woman were bound with rope. Only a bedsheet covered their bodies.

The village head questioned them. "Where are you from?"

"From Western Plain Village."

"Why do you come here?"

"We were on our way home, but it's hard to walk at night, so we stayed here overnight."

"What's your relationship?"

"We're husband and wife."

"Any proof? Did you bring your marriage license? You're not a couple of eloping sluts? Or are you human traffickers?"

"No, no. Look, we brought a luggage roll along with us. We went out to do manual labor and wanted to make a dash home for the family reunion, but . . ."

Their story seemed plausible, so the village head untied them, berated those who'd gathered to watch the scene, and gave back their clothes. However, some villagers thought that even though they were a couple, their actions, outdoors on such a beautiful night at the entrance to their village, despoiled the festival atmosphere. So the villagers brought a pail of cold water and poured it over the couple from head to toe as a punishment.

The man and woman stifled their reactions and rushed down the road, the woman stumbling and crying out repeatedly. The man helped her up and urged, "Run, run until you are sweating all over. Otherwise the chilly air will sink into your bones!"

Raising her head, the woman was encouraged to run, although she did not know how long the road ahead was or what awaited them at its end: bitterness or sweetness, sorrow or happiness?

Translated by Hu Zongfeng and Liu Xiaofeng

Zou Zhian

Zou Zhian, born in Liquan County, Shaanxi Province, graduated from the Normal School in 1966. He served as a teacher of the Liquan Primary School; a staff member of Liquan County's cultural center; and director of the Chinese Writers Association, Shaanxi Branch. He made his literary debut in 1972, and his works include the novel *Psychological Exploration of Love*, short story collections *Nostalgia* and *Oh, Little Stallion*, and the collection of novellas *Why My Heart Is Fluttering*. Both "Oh, Little Stallion" and "Village Branch Secretary Falling from Office" won the National Award for Best Story in consecutive years, marking Zou Zhian's place in the literary canon. His style reflects the emotions and ideals of Chinese farmers as well as the changes in rural China. His work records the development and spiritual journey of Chinese farmers during the reform period, keeping an agrarian focus in the ever-urbanizing culture.

ZHOU ZHIAN

Oh, a Colt!

1

Feeling tired and fretful, and knowing he was on the verge of making careless mistakes in his work, he walked out of the county Party
Committee compound and strolled into the fields on the edge of
town, where the lush green expanse of wheat and the yellow fields
of rapeseed flowers were radiant and beautiful. The cold, clear air
had grown mild and moist shortly after sunrise. The remote mountain range to the north had been enveloped in a thin mist all month.
Butterflies and swallows, so vital, so full of life and energy, foretold
the coming spring.

Zheng Quanzhang—nothing special about his name—was, at
twenty-nine years old, now in charge of the personnel affairs of the
whole county. He used to be secretary of the County Youth League,
after training for three years in the cadre school. When the reforms
started across China, he was appointed director of personnel for the
county. To qualify for an appointment or promotion in the county

Party Committee, each local candidate had been examined with a stiff test. Zheng was now on the examination board himself.

Zheng's thin lips were always tightly shut, as if he knew too many secrets. He looked like a man in his forties, with sunken eyes and a sallow face resulting from his overtaxed mind. Sauntering along the country roads in his shabby and inappropriate clothes, fording the ditches and ridges between fields, he might be mistaken for an unhappy middle-aged farmer with a throng of children to raise and the threat of fines for exceeding the birth quota. Only his flashing eyes—bright, tough, and stubborn—showed his youth. His eyes still radiated vigor even after a whole night of meetings where yawns were frequent.

He had no appetite for breakfast; he forced down some bites of steaming bread and then walked to the fields in search of temporary peace and rest, refreshing himself. Then he returned quickly to his office, walking along the wall to avoid people, oblivious to the calls behind his back.

Back at the office, Secretary Bai of the county Party Committee came over. In contrast to the shabbily attired personnel director, the newly transferred, fair-complexioned Secretary Bai, gentle and cultivated, was always dressed well. He was still making up his mind about Zheng Quanzhang. To his eye, Zheng was an unconventional and uninhibited young man, proud and unyielding.

Smiling, Secretary Bai gave Zheng an exploring look. "Vice-Secretary Tang of the Party Committee has just arrived," he said.

Zheng Quanzhang said nothing, but looked into Secretary Bai's friendly, thoughtful eyes.

"He is concerned about Ma Zhankui . . ."

"Why is he only concerned with Ma Zhankui?" asked Zheng Quanzhang scornfully. "Tang and Ma are relatives by marriage! A vice-secretary of the Party Committee should understand the importance of avoiding suspicion and unfairness. What kind of a model nominates close relatives to key positions?"

"He said that Ma Zhankui lodged a complaint with the Party Committee, claiming that the restructuring group failed its duty by leaving him half-examined. He's demanding a conclusion."

"He has no right to demand that," Zheng Quanzhang said. "During the violent crash in the great Cultural Revolution, Ma Zhankui stayed in a fortified area for half a year. He was witnessed carrying a rifle, even though we had no evidence to prove it. And then there's the construction project: the four mu of land he purchased for the Fertilizer Bureau. The Bureau paid forty grand, but the seller, Nanguan II Village, only received twenty grand. Where did the rest of the money go? A villager testified that he overheard Ma Zhankui—the mayor of the village!—discussing with his accountant how to divide the twenty grand. We've got the written proof." Zheng Quanzhang pointed to his safe.

"And moreover," he continued, "he is not a good candidate because his work for the Fertilizer Bureau was a complete mess. Think also about his old age and his lack of education. We're short on time for this restructuring; we can't offer him an evaluation right now."

"But Vice-Secretary Tang said—"

Zheng Quanzhang interrupted with a smile. "Drop it!" he ordered. "No matter what anyone says, we followed the clear instructions of the central government." He spoke with an unyielding tone, a youth's firmness and indignation, unsympathetic to Vice-Secretary Tang's defense of Ma Zhankui.

"Secretary," he said, looking at Bai with a smile, "do you want a party that's effective and powerful, or one that's out of date, good for nothing, and full of flaws?"

Secretary Bai laughed, but his long, thin eyebrows remained creased.

Zheng Quanzhang thought for a moment. "Look," he said, "trust me with this, and let me handle it. If Vice-Secretary Tang asks you again, tell him that you've handed it over to me and he can consult me directly."

Secretary Bai gratefully threw him a you-are-clever look—but out loud he insisted, "Still, you'd better reconsider Ma's case. I don't think it's proper for you to ignore the vice-secretary's orders."

Zheng Quanzhang knew well what Bai meant. If Zheng didn't follow the vice-secretary's instructions and do as he was told, he'd find himself in some other kind of trouble. Since Vice-Secretary Tang had come there to deliver the message in person, who knew what else he was capable of? Reexamining Ma Zhankui's case would be no problem—but was that all Tang wanted? No, it was Tang's hidden unreasonable demands that Zheng Quanzhang objected to.

The moment Zheng had been appointed director, he'd resolved to seize the opportunity for institutional reform and make it fair and square at its roots. Previously, they could do nothing about the unfair power structure but curse and complain. But now the central government was giving them a great chance, a strategic chance, to wipe out corruption and repair the flaws. Ignoring that opportunity would be a sin—a sin more serious than any that ten evil cadres could commit.

"All right," Zheng relented, "I'll muster the manpower to have the case reexamined. But we must respect the facts."

"That's for sure," said Secretary Bai.

"But we're short of hands—almost everyone's on assignment. I don't know how we can spare anyone."

"Try to think of a way, fellow comrade. Think of a way."

Secretary Bai left with the awkward relief that comes from completing a thorny task.

Zheng Quanzhang thought to himself, a good guy, but a little soft. He shouldn't accept these unreasonable orders; he should've silenced Tang by bringing up Ma Zhankui's obvious problems. His softness might cause trouble in the future. Why is it that the longer they're in government positions, the weaker people become in front of their superiors?

Before lunch, in search of the proper staff to reexamine Ma Zhankui's case, he was surprised to run into Ma Zhankui himself coming out of the men's restroom. It was odd for Ma to come here to relieve himself; the Fertilizer Bureau was not in the county Party compound. Ma Zhankui hurried out of the restroom with his pants half-belted to catch Zheng Quanzhang by his hand. Apparently he had heard Zheng passing by.

Ma Zhankui, director of the Fertilizer Bureau, was short, stout, and swarthy. He loved to wear sunglasses and had short but strong fat fingers. No one knew how he'd managed to marry off his daughter, who worked in the county medicine plant, to the son of Vice-Secretary Tang. The valuable marriage connection now presented itself to Zheng Quanzhang.

"Hello, Director!" Ma Zhankui grasped Zheng's hand tightly, as a policeman would an escaped criminal, and pulled him aside. "It has been hard to get to see you!"

Zheng Quanzhang paid special attention to the thick eyebrows over the shades and the watery eyes behind them.

"You really ought to get something decent to wear," Ma continued, his tone warm and casual, as if he'd come just for this chat. "You're losing weight," he added, pulling Zheng's hand firmly downward and inward, toward his embrace. "Take care of your health! Joking is joking, but one thing is serious: be healthy. You should pour some boiling hot milk over two eggs—otherwise your wife will not be satisfied."

"Rest assured," said Zheng Quanzhang, also in a mock-serious tone, "she is quite satisfied with me!"

Suddenly Ma Zhankui's tone changed, and he implored, "Please don't be too hard on me. Let me off!"

Zheng Quanzhang forced a smile and continued to hold Ma Zhankui's hand tightly, to assure him and put his mind at rest—and, more importantly, to get away from Ma Zhankui.

The rumors about Ma Zhankui's sunglasses went like this: He wore them not according to the weather, but according to the political climate. At the very beginning of the reforms, when candidates from the mass recommendation were preferred, he took off his shades. When he was being examined for a position, he wore them. When the investigation was over, he took the shades off again, and when he learned that his evaluation was complete, he put them back on.

Strangely, he isn't even embarrassed about it! Zheng Quanzhang thought to himself, amused.

2

Reporting and listening to reports; reading material and writing material; listening to and giving instructions; being surrounded by and breaking up a crowd; telling the truth, lies, half-truths, or half lies; neither eating nor sleeping in peace—these were all now part of Zheng Quanzhang's life. At this kind of crucial moment, a person's soul might reveal itself through all kinds of faces: happy, flattering, pathetically smiling, forced smiling, bitter, furious, indignant, stupefied . . . It was very difficult, but inspiring, to stick to truth and principles.

Every Saturday after dark, his wife—a strong, good-looking peasant woman who managed their farmlands—would leave their child at his parents' house and ride her bike to join him. Only then could he escape all the complexities and be forced to enjoy a temporary quiet and rest. She alone brought him real warmth, with her intelligence and her understanding of his career; she was like a frontline supplier in a tough battle.

"That's enough," she'd say. "Let's go home. You're dead tired every day and still you earn only forty-five yuan a month. You are not a premier, are you?"

"Right, let's got home," he'd agree. "We won't drink such dirty water."

But they could grab only occasional sweet nights, or sometimes only a few sweet hours, for he often came back to work at two o'clock in the morning.

In their brief refuge, his wife always warmed him with her hot breasts, for his whole body was as cold as ice; his long, skinny fingers trembled, and his socks stuck to his feet.

"Don't value power too much," she'd say gently.

"I know."

"Meng, the last county magistrate—when he retired and came back to his hometown, he walked with a stick and wet his pants. His daughter-in-law had to take care of him."

"The Party and the people trust me," he said. "I'm such a humble man, and they entrust me with such an important task. I have to do something good for them. Every man has his moment when he emits light and heat, and my moment is now."

"All lights have to turn off sometimes."

"Yes, or walk with a stick and wet one's pants without being cared for."

After some silence, in the soothing, bright moonlight of the spring night, his wife updated him on the health of his parents and their child, and then caught him up on the main family affairs.

"Altogether twelve people came to visit our house: seven strangers, three colleagues, and two relatives, all with presents, which included nine packs of cigarettes, two articles of clothing, twelve boxes of snacks, a pair of chairs, and five bottles of alcohol. As you requested, I kept an account book and put away the things that could be stored. I brought the perishables to sell in the cooperative, and I kept the money and food coupons."

"How much did we get?"

"Well, I had to take my clothes out of the suitcase to make room for so many presents. I left my clothes out on the kang."

"And beginning tomorrow, you send them back, one by one."

"Why? Didn't we come to an agreement that you would send them back after the structural reform?"

"No! Whoever receives them should send them back!"

"You can't eat your words," his wife protested. "I tried everything I could to turn the visitors away—raising a racket, pushing and pulling, trying to ward them off. But they were too strenuous. They left the gifts on the kang and dashed away, hardly finishing their words. How could I possibly catch up with them?"

"All right, you go to Brother San Bao's and ask him to send them back for us. Tell him to hush things up—he should just send the presents back and say nothing."

"San Bao can't be counted on. He smokes like a chimney. What if he sneaks a pack of cigarettes?"

"Fine, then you keep the presents and I'll send them back later."

"You've got a stubbly beard growing! And I can feel your bones now . . ."

"If you're not satisfied with me, you shouldn't come here."

"You call this dissatisfied?"

They often got up at dawn when the whole courtyard was still in slumber. After they washed and dressed, Zheng escorted her to the outskirts of town. In the cold late-spring dawn, a chill arose from the glittering dewdrops on the wheat stalks, small flowers, and grass. The damp fields were fresh, peaceful, and misty in the morning. They held a sense of solemn purity.

Beyond an outcropping, the red sun was trying its best to rise over the green horizon, making the dew sparkle brilliantly.

3

Zheng Quanzhang grabbed a clerk to help him reexamine Ma Zhankui's case. It was true, the decision should have been handed down much earlier. Ma didn't grasp the problems of his own limited knowledge, abilities, and attitude, not to mention his old age—he was nearly fifty. All those liabilities indicated that he was no longer suitable to be the director of the Fertilizer Bureau. The committee had already warned Ma several times, refusing to consider his credentials for the post, because he overindulged in games of majiang, playing all night and sleeping all day after he had built his two-story, eight-room house. There was nothing wrong with reexamining him, Zheng realized, for the second examination guaranteed an even more solid conclusion.

Wearing a tired and cold expression, Zheng Quanzhang, too modest to put on new clothes, went with the clerk to find their witness, the villager on the Nan Guan production team.

Frightened and restless, the whole family of the middle-aged villager treated the investigators strangely. The wife bustled in and out, hands sticky with flour paste, their daughter following her mother in confusion. The villager himself showed up with a flushed face; he smoked hissingly on a long-stemmed Chinese pipe, his trembling fingers unable to strike a match.

Zheng Quanzhang suddenly had a certain premonition.

"Well, it was not true. Not true . . ." the villager said, his long face turning red. "I was mistaken . . . mistaken . . ." He trailed off, staring at Zheng and the clerk and then casting his eyes down, his thumb pressing the pipe bowl.

He resumed his testimony. "The other day I went to find the team leader. I wanted to contract for some Chinese parasol trees. When I came to the office window, I heard Director Ma say to the team leader and the accountant, 'You two each get five days according to the Bureau's decision.' I mistook it as 'You two each get five grand, the same as the Bureau's payments.'"

"How do you know you were wrong?"

"They came to my house to correct it." His wife blinked rapidly, and he revised his story. "No, wait, they didn't come to me. Instead, I was afraid that I wronged them, so I went to them to correct it. Not only they themselves, but also their wives and children, agreed that I'd gotten it wrong."

Zheng Quanzhang sank into silence and smiled coldly. He couldn't be cross with the peasant; he should try to persuade him.

"I was a countryman too," Zheng began. "I know how important money is to a peasant. The four mu of land was sold for forty thousand yuan, and only twenty thousand appeared in your team's account. If we find the rest of the money, then each household on your team would get an average of six or seven hundred yuan." The man was listening attentively. Zheng continued, "Old Brother, beat out the evil and tell us the truth—don't let the whole team down. You know that the government and the law will protect you. You mustn't be frightened." The villager nodded his head again and again, blushing to the base of his neck.

But his wife spoke up: "He was telling the truth, the whole truth!"

"Right," the man echoed weakly, "I was telling you the whole truth."

Saying nothing more, Zheng and the clerk left the poor family.

"They certainly corrected themselves suddenly," Zheng Quanzhang declared.

They went to find the team leader and the accountant.

Apparently mistaking the neatly dressed and broadly built clerk as an important figure, and Zheng Quanzhang, young and poorly dressed, as a follower, the team leader and the accountant spoke directly to the clerk.

"Nothing wrong! There is nothing wrong," said the team leader, a sincere expression on his round face.

"Well then, where are the twenty thousand yuan?" asked Zheng Quanzhang.

The team leader finally noticed him. He looked into Zheng's eyes and then quickly looked away. He smiled to his accountant.

"This is an affair of our production team." He avoided Zheng Quanzhang's gaze.

"I would like to know where the money is today."

The team leader hung his head, smiling coldly, and then suddenly his expression changed, and he looked up. "Who do you think you are, with your shabby salaries and all your concern!" he shouted loudly. "I won't tell you."

"Then I might have to resort to the law."

The team leader was huffing and puffing. Zheng's words finally sunk in. He made as if to open the cash drawer, but then stopped and flipped the clasp of the lock. "OK, I'll tell you," he said, looking pale. "We contacted Tibet to buy cattle for our production team, with each household receiving one head. If we had entered it in the accounts, the production brigade would get all the money and we would have no cows. We didn't tell the villagers for fear that the information would be leaked."

What he said sounded reasonable. But Zheng Quanzhang returned quickly, "Who in Tibet got the money? I want to have a look at the receipt."

The team leader refused to take out the receipt. He pulled the accountant away and insisted that Zheng and the clerk leave the office, complaining repeatedly that Zheng might turn their operation into a bad situation.

Zheng considered his position. If what they said was the truth, it would be only slightly inappropriate with the financial formalities. If they were lying, they were looking at a serious embezzlement of public funds. But when it became public, the embezzlement would fail and they'd have to return the money.

Next they went to visit the man who'd witnessed Ma Zhankui carrying a rifle in a fortified area during the Cultural Revolution. He too refused to stand by his original testimony. He said that he later realized that the person he'd seen was another man who looked like Ma Zhankui, but was not Ma Zhankui. He claimed he'd been mistaken. He pulled out a new written testimony he had prepared.

The situation became complicated.

Zheng Quanzhang was coming to understand that Ma possessed unusual powers and remarkable abilities. How crafty he was! What meticulous preparations! Shame on him, such a devious scoundrel!

Rage poured out from the bottom of Zheng's heart. He began to blame himself for his lack of preparation and experience. He should have investigated more thoroughly and gathered enough evidence to build an airtight case. He'd jeopardized the investigation by acting in such a rush. We must find a way to make everything clear, he thought. One has to face many difficulties . . .

He returned to his office, annoyed, and gave Secretary Bai a truthful account of what had happened.

In the evening, Vice-Secretary Tang came to the county compound. After speaking with Secretary Bai, he paid a special visit to Zheng Quanzhang, who was at home discussing affairs with some visitors.

Secretary Bai shouted outside Zheng Quanzhang's door: "Quanzhang, Vice-Secretary Tang comes to visit you!"

Zheng felt a special kind of resentment well up in him, driving him to prepare for a confrontation with the vice-secretary. He wanted to let Tang know that not all the party members and cadres were cowards, worthless wretches, soft in sticking to the truth. He would find a way to make Vice-Secretary Tang respect the cadres and masses and to remind Tang of his own responsibilities. Adrenaline made Zheng eager for the provocation and careless about courtesy and formalities. Not until Vice-Secretary Tang held his hand did he realize that he had behaved with complete indiscretion as the others were leaving the house.

"You might take a seat," Vice-Secretary Tang said.

He was a leader in his fifties; he had an elderly, generous, kind face with a wrinkled forehead. He was an ordinary old man wearing an old blue, fur-collared overcoat. His breath smelled of cigarettes, and he was missing some teeth. These observations, together with Tang's elderly and feeble hands, suddenly evoked in Zheng Quanzhang sympathy and reverence.

The confrontation dissipated.

"You are so young!" said Vice-Secretary Tang. "I thought you were in your forties, but Secretary Bai just told me that you're only twenty-nine years old." He sounded friendly and genial. He looked at Zheng Quanzhang lovingly, obviously recalling his own youth. "You have accomplished a lot."

Secretary Bai smiled. "Comrade Quanzhang is indeed very hardworking."

"Young and promising," Vice-Secretary Tang concurred. "The prefecture committee knows about you. Your position on this problem—in my view, it is not big." He didn't make it clear whether the position was not big or the problem was not big.

His last sentence destroyed Zheng Quanzhang's goodwill for the man. Was that a deal or a threat? Suddenly he despised the old man. Vice-Secretary Tang was like the complaining old Ninth Grandpa in his village or an old bureau chief who would rather die than retire from his position, insisting he still had some suggestions to offer and demanding that his overage son take his position. The adrenaline was returning to Zheng Quanzhang . . . but Vice-Secretary Tang had already begun to take his leave.

After the leader had gone, Secretary Bai asked anxiously and reproachfully, "What's the matter?"

"I was in a bad mood."

"Business is business. You shouldn't behave that way. Remember, he visited you specially."

"He was performing the sword dance while planning an attempt on my life. He was acting with covert, wicked motives."

"Forget it. Report what you have about Ma Zhankui to the leader, and let the whole thing pass. When Ma has other problems, we'll get him examined again. After all, he's only a powerless Fertilizer Bureau chief!"

"Fertilizer is one of the lifelines of the rural people. You could downgrade the power of such a chief," Zheng Quanzhang said. "Did you promise something to Vice-Secretary Tang?"

"No, I didn't."

"I did tell you that if there was any problem, you could pass the buck to me."

"But I didn't do so."

"Then how did you reply?"

"I said we might consider it."

"Then have it be considered by the standing committee!" Zheng said indignantly. "If a suspicious character like Ma were nominated for a new leadership position, you'd report it immediately!"

Secretary Bai's smooth, pale face blushed. He was rubbing his hands and looking into Zheng Quanzhang's eyes blandly, calmly, and wisely.

"Comrade Quanzhang," said Secretary Bai, "we haven't gotten along with each other for a long time, but what I've heard and seen have told me the same thing: you are upright, intelligent, and capable. You are a good comrade who is determined to carry out reforms. You are young and have brains and a bright future. I don't worry about myself, for I hold my position, and they could not shake me off. But I'm afraid you might spoil the ship for a halfpenny-worth of tar."

"I'm not afraid," Zheng Quanzhang said. "At worst, he might not approve of my appointment as the minister of organization. If so, he should give me a reason. Besides, I believe that in the prefecture committee, everything doesn't hinge on one man!" He felt confident that he was honest and upright and strong enough.

That night, he had his supper quite late and fell into a sound sleep with his hands under his head, fingers in his thick, black hair, oblivious to the entire world.

4

County Party Committee Secretary Bai didn't tell lies; he was truly worried about Zheng Quanzhang. The fair-complexioned leader, with his flaccid wrinkled cheeks and strong forehead, was by no means unwise. He was different from those foolish leaders who expected their subordinates to be more foolish than they. Ambitious in his career, he hoped to make a change during his term of office. He desired all his cadres to be upright, intelligent, and capable. Although he was new in his position, he was quite satisfied with the standing committee members provided by the former county Party Committee secretary and other Reform bodies.

Bai was especially satisfied with Zheng Quanzhang, the personnel director of the Organization Reform Group. When Bai had first arrived, he hadn't believed that Zheng was only twenty-nine, so he consulted Zheng's personnel files to confirm it. Zheng was born in 1955. After high school he did physical labor at a people's commune and then joined the Party one year later. Making unremitting efforts to improve himself, Zheng was appointed vice-secretary of the commune, earning his salary from the commune-run enterprises. Later on, he became a registered cadre and was promoted to secretary. When the cadre school enrolled new students, Zheng was enrolled with an average score of 96; he graduated three years later to do service for the county Organization Committee. During his three years in the cadre school, he learned a lot of obscure information in courses such as philosophy, political economics, the international Communist Party movement, literature, aesthetics, psychology, Chinese history, world history, and management. His ideas and talents were far beyond his age, yet his character and mettle were like unpolished rocks. In his daily duties, he showed sophisticated clear-sightedness and maturity; but with his wife, he was still a young man.

Secretary Bai had once come upon evidence of the man's youth. Zheng was sitting at home with his feet soaking in a basin; he looked angry and was shouting. Although his wife, standing behind him, wore a smile, she was shaking him with both hands on his shoulders. When Secretary Bai came in, Zheng shouted, "Stop!" He kicked the basin angrily, and with one wet foot touching the floor, hopped lightly to the bed for his slippers. With a shout, his wife arched her back to pass the slippers to him. Zheng looked at Secretary Bai, blushed, and said with a smirk, "My mother always said you should give wives a kind heart instead of a kind face."

His wife snapped, "What a male chauvinist!"

Zheng answered back, "Better that than a female chauvinist!"

Surprised at this rancorous scene, Secretary Bai retreated from their house.

But all things considered, Secretary Bai didn't want to lose this man. True, sometimes Zheng Quanzhang scowled at him and spoke sharply against him, which annoyed Secretary Bai—yet still he liked Zheng and wanted him to be his minister of organization. Bai would rather put Ma—such a mean sod—temporarily out of power than penalize Zheng Quanzhang.

Secretary Bai had repeatedly asked the prefecture Party Committee to promote Zheng Quanzhang to minister of the county organization as soon as possible. The last time, the head of the committee office told him that they'd received a letter making many serious allegations against Zheng Quanzhang; the leader had recommended a prompt investigation. He refused to tell Secretary Bai who had written the letter, but he said that Zheng was accused of abusing power for personal gain. Zheng was said to have fraudulently purchased state-controlled commodities, like chemical fertilizer and lumber, and was accused of being conceited and arbitrary, acting high and mighty, and even of having an extramarital affair.

The spurious claims made Secretary Bai bitterly angry. Somebody was counterattacking Zheng Quanzhang. Bai faced a dilemma: on one hand, he could not turn a deaf ear to the malicious attacks or the written communications from the higher authorities, for that would go against the organizational principles; on the other hand, if he sent a working group to investigate the allegations, rumors would spread quickly and ruin Zheng Quanzhang. Unable to resolve the dilemma, Secretary Bai decided to talk to Zheng Quanzhang in person, hoping to keep the accusations under control.

To his surprise, Zheng Quanzhang remained cool and collected, saying only, "I expected this, and I'm ready for whatever happens. Go and investigate!" He didn't show the slightest bit of anger. He calmly requested to address the investigators directly. The county secretary assigned the case and would not address Zheng in person.

Still, although no one knew exactly what happened, news spread overnight all across the county.

"Please send the investigation group," Zheng directed Bai. "Otherwise you will be under suspicion of covering up for me."

At last the investigation group was set up, and Zheng Quanzhang gravely appeared before them. "When I graduated from the Central Cadres School, I bought two bags of urea and two bags of diammonium phosphate for my contracted fields; I purchased them through an old classmate, from his production-service company. I also bought a truckload of urea for my production team, at the state-set price. And with the director's permission, I bought four beams and thirty rafters.

"On my salary of forty-five yuan a month, I couldn't afford the negotiated price of fertilizer and black-market lumber. The kitchen in my parents' house is a thatched shack. The roof leaks whenever it rains—my mother is always complaining about it. I plan to buy more rafters to rebuild it into a tile-roofed kitchen. All the lumber I bought is still in my parents' house.

"As for the woman who often visits me, she was my high school classmate. She likes to discuss social problems with me. All we do is talk together—it's completely innocent."

One investigator asked sarcastically, "Is that all?"

Zheng Quanzhang narrowed his eyes at him and said, "When I was a child, I got a good beating from my mother when I stole some melons from the production team." He paused. "That is all."

The investigators interviewed the production-service corporation, the lumber company, the coworkers of the female classmate, and Zheng Quanzhang's parents.

Secretary Bai's stomach was knotted in pain. He soon learned that the investigation confirmed what Zheng Quanzhang had told them—but nevertheless the county committee held a special meeting and formed an impartial written resolution to be reported to the prefecture committee. Bai knew from experience that other pressures awaited Zheng Quanzhang. He watched the developments with growing concern.

Many visitors tried to squeeze the news out of Secretary Bai, and he noticed people looking inquiringly and suspiciously at Zheng Quanzhang. He began hearing that Zheng had trouble keeping control of those under his command. Villagers from Zheng's hometown started coming to the county to dig for information, and several of Zheng's relatives visited him in quick succession.

Soon Zheng Quanzhang's mother arrived, walking with a cane. It was reported that she'd brought with her a bag of eggs. When she saw her son's angular figure, she cried and said, "Come back home with me! Don't be an official anymore! We returned all the unused lumber, and we'll buy more fertilizer to cover the damage. What is important is you—and you should not worry about the charges. Come home!"

How tough Zheng Quanzhang was! He ignored what was happening to him and went on with his work unfazed, never complaining to anyone. When he met with Secretary Bai to report on his work, he interrupted Bai's attempts to discuss the case with an exhortation to get down to business and leave others alone.

When Zheng turned to leave, he walked away with purposeful, hurried steps, his thin spine sturdy and straight. One could hear the rustling swish of his departing jacket, ragged at the hem. The heels of his cloth-soled shoes were worn and twisted.

But things went from bad to worse. Every day there were new letters from the prefecture Party Committee, implicating Zheng Quanzhang. And then Secretary Bai got some gloomy news: While most of the investigators thought it was nothing serious, there was one voice that held that, although Zheng might not be abusing power for personal gain, he had somehow made purchases that ordinary farmers could not have negotiated. So the final decision was made. Since Zheng Quanzhang had aroused intense public suspicion, he would not be promoted to county minister of organization. Not only would he not be promoted—in the process of streamlining midlevel leadership, Zheng's current position would have to be reconsidered.

Secretary Bai was indignant, but managed to keep a smile on his face and act quiet and genial. He drove to the prefecture committee three nights in a row to battle for justice. But once the committee members had made their decision, they would not yield. Secretary Bai worked to hide his frustration whenever he faced Zheng Quanzhang.

As ordered, Zheng Quanzhang began to transfer his duties to the newly appointed vice-minister of organization.

"I'm going home," he said to Secretary Bai with an apologetic smile. "I've handed over what I should." A humiliating blush crept up his sallow face. "I haven't been home for a long time. I . . . I ask for a few days' leave to go back home." His eyes were sunken so deep that the bones around them seemed to jut out from his face. His eyeballs themselves seemed to be recoiling in fear. But tears welled there when he looked at Secretary Bai. He said, "I'm going back home . . ." He stood up and left, rubbing his eyes. He was still a boy!

Secretary Bai knew that when Zheng Quanzhang walked out of there, out of the county committee courtyard on his way to his hometown, he was beginning a long and difficult journey, an ordeal no smaller than the twenty-five-thousand-li Long March in his personal life, for he'd have to face many people on his way.

As Zheng Quanzhang wheeled his bike out the gate of the county committee courtyard, he came upon Ma Zhankui, who seemed to be waiting for him. Ma was wearing his shades, his face wreathed, his bulging stomach detracting from his height, making him seem even shorter. This time Ma did not hold Zheng Quanzhang's hands tightly; instead, he touched Zheng's hand symbolically.

"Communist Youth League School Zheng!" he said with jeering laughter. "We are alike in being removed from office and power!"

Zheng Quanzhang came to a halt, narrowing his eyes at Ma.

"Yes, we are the same. Dismissed from office."

"Oh, damn it!" cursed Ma Zhankui. "There is no damn truth in this world!"

"No," Zheng Quanzhang replied, "I don't agree with you there."

"Back home?"

"Back home."

"Well, see you later!" Ma said.

"Later."

Zheng Quanzhang wheeled his bike away and Ma Zhankui waddled into the courtyard.

5

Zheng Quanzhang remained at his parents' house.

The virtues of living in the countryside were countless: no one showed any particular concern for the intricacies of the county institutional reform; no one cared about personnel changes; nobody dwelt upon the joys and sorrows of moving up or down in the bureaucracy. Farmers had their own concerns; they minded their own business and attended to the practical things they could see with their own eyes. They were not overjoyed to have a personnel director in the village, nor were they affected by his suddenly losing the position. The villagers would neither try to butter him up nor pour scorn on him. In their eyes, he was only a cadre earning a salary; that was all. His return on leave from work inspired only minimal comment, for his family had never made a big deal of his being head of personnel. Zheng Quanzhang could now enjoy the simplicity, good-heartedness, and warmth of the country folks, as well as the fragrant fields and the joy of labor. Here was a different world, entirely separate from that of the county committee courtyard.

Zheng Quanzhang had sentimental thoughts: he should do more good for these kind people, but now he lacked the power to do so. When he was working at the county committee compound, his work had felt isolated and irrelevant. But now he could see the real significance of that work and the decisions he'd made. He heard the villagers discussing the rising fees for water and electricity; the changing costs of commodities; the complexities of merchandise production, warehousing, civil disputes—and for the first time he saw the dry procedural machinery come to life in the faces of the villagers and in the fields stretching out before him. And his grief weighed more heavily than ever on his heart, especially when he was alone.

His family did their best to care for him. His parents insisted he be offered the best food every day. His wife often urged, "Take a walk outside when you have nothing to do. Don't stay at home all the time; it's not good for you."

And every time his beautiful, healthy wife went out, she'd return with some bit of news to entertain him with. "Sheshe's wife quarreled with her mother-in-law and called her names again! His wife is really a bloody nuisance. Her brother-in-law beat her and her husband, so Sheshe hit him back. I scolded Sheshe that he should keep his shrew wife on a leash and not turn a deaf ear when she shouts abuse to his mother in the courtyard! So Sheshe pushed his wife into the room and took out a handkerchief and swatted his wife on the leg. I asked him if it was enough for him to dust his wife's pants."

Zheng Quanzhang laughed.

When he was overcome with regret, humiliation, and gloom, he went to labor in the fields. If there was no work to do, he would walk in the fields.

One clear day after a rainfall, he stood at noon on the main road outside the village. It was early summer; the sun was shining, and the rain-soaked wheat stretched to the far horizon. The rain-freshened northern mountains stood out crisp and clear. The scene was awash in light blues and deep blues, and the beauty of it brought joy to Zheng's heart, exalted his vision, and took his mind off his problems.

A bay colt appeared on the road. He kicked up his heels and ran off into the distance, then turned back from afar and dashed away again. He seemed determined to revel in the joy of life and youth. Apparently he knew he was being watched, for he played tricks the next time he dashed off. He tilted his body and veered into a stand of poplars beside the road, taking a corner gracefully before dashing out toward the main thoroughfare.

Just then the colt stepped into a roadside puddle, his forehooves skidding so that he fell to his knees. He recovered quickly, standing up and walking onto the main road—sheepishly and slowly now, looking only down at the earth. Soon a truck appeared on the road, heading toward him. He swished his tail, turned around slowly, and stood still on the road, facing away from the oncoming truck. He seemed to be trying to save face with this daring act. His sharp ears were pricked up attentively, the rims turned backward. The truck came nearer, bearing down as the colt slowly began to move. The truck horn was blaring and the earth was shaking. Finally the colt skittered away, his feet barely touching the ground. Careering for a few steps until out of danger, he suddenly remembered his dignity and resumed walking, slowly and princely, marching in step.

Zheng Quanzhang laughed heartily.

That evening, Secretary Bai came to see him. The wise leader, glancing around at Zheng Quanzhang's shack kitchen, said, "I don't want to offer any sympathetic words, for they are useless. What I want to say is, congratulations! For I believe it is a good thing for a young man to fall sometimes; then he has the opportunity to pick himself up and go on and learn lessons from his fall. If an old man falls down, he might break his bones and never get up. But a young man's bones are fresh and strong, and a little stumble does no harm. That's all. You may have a rest. I'm leaving now."

That night, Zheng Quanzhang couldn't sleep. He was remembering his three years in the central school of the Communist Youth League—his aspirations and ambition, the expectations of the central leadership. He remembered his classmates dispersing all over the country and the news they shared in their letters. It seemed that no one was proceeding smoothly or without a hitch. Were there strong hindrances to progress in China? Yes! But so many young men, intellectuals, cadres, party members—people with lofty ideals, or just ordinary people—were trying their best to push the country forward and help bring about progress. The country was progressing; this was the general trend. Retreating led to death.

The most important thing—Zheng had known it back then and he reminded himself now—was to never lose hope, to maintain the spirit of enterprise when faced with misfortune. Refuse neither fine wines nor bitter ones.

"What is the matter with you?" his wife said, lying next to him. "Since Secretary Bai's visit, you've been a circus monkey answering to the gong. You've been nervous all night, turning over, restless . . ."

"I'm not old enough to wet my pants," he replied.

The next day, Zheng Quanzhang went back to work.

Translated by Wen Hui

Jing Fu (1942–2008)

Jing Fu, the pen name of Guo Jingfu, was born in Shangzhou, Shaanxi, and educated in Shangzhou Teachers Training School. Before becoming a professional writer in 1985, he was a teacher. His works include short stories, novellas, novels, and essays. Collections include *The Deep Footprints: The Selected Stories of Jing Fu* and *A Book from Heaven*. Jing Fu's longer works of fiction include *The New Girl*, *The Intellectual Circle*, *The Story of Love and Hatred in Eight-Li Town*, *Hongniang the Go-Between*, and *The Cries of Deer*. He is also the author of *The Seashells*, a collection of essays. His works have received many awards. His short story "The Walking Stick" won the National Excellence Award for Short Stories.

JING FU

The Walking Stick

If my two little grandchildren hadn't used the walking stick as a weapon in their play fight, I would have forgotten about it. When we moved back to Beijing and unloaded the family belongings, it was brought into the small storeroom and laid among the odds and ends. I told myself to remember to move it into my bedroom, but soon I became preoccupied with other things. After returning to the city, I no longer needed it. In Beijing I rely on cars for travel and use elevators for moving up and down inside buildings. No longer do I take walks on dirt roads. So the walking stick has remained in the pile of odds and ends.

Its sudden appearance with my grandchildren made my heart beat faster and reminded me of him. Had he received the gifts I'd sent him? I've worried that perhaps I did the wrong thing in leaving those gifts for him. In my mind's eye I see him stubbornly turning his back on the gifts and walking angrily away, muttering to himself, not looking back a single time. He was always like that.

In the autumn of 1974, for unexplained reasons, I was banished to a remote county in the hill country. The county was thousands of li away from my home in Beijing. It was arranged for me to live in a sanatorium, a rest home for retired cadres.

It was just past midautumn when the rainy weather set in. It rained constantly. Having just arrived, I hadn't adjusted to these new conditions. With no experience to rely on, I hadn't bought and stored enough firewood. My family was on the brink of having no firewood for preparing meals. The institution was quite a distance from town—one li. On rainy days, firewood was scarce in the town market—and to make matters worse, the road leading to town was muddy. Even if wood were available, how could I trek the muddy road to get it ordered? How would the seller get it back to us?

After breakfast the next morning, as I was worrying about our firewood problem, I heard from the courtyard the call of someone selling chopped wood. I rushed out and saw an old man standing in the autumn rain. It seemed as though the falling raindrops were countless threads hanging from the sky.

On the old man's shoulder was a carrying pole with a bundle of wood at each end. On his head slouched a dark-brown straw hat that looked like an enormous mushroom. Rainwater leaked through it, trickling along the deep wrinkles of his face and forming tiny water-falls at his jaw until finally falling to his chest. His ragged black coat was soaked and clung tightly to his body. The legs of his trousers were rolled up above the knees, exposing his mud-spattered legs, and his traditional kudzu-fiber shoes were so plastered with wet earth that they looked like two muddy straw mattresses. His wizened face, with its sunken rainwater-blurred eyes, was aimed at my door.

I walked up to him to help him remove the heavy load of firewood.

"Step aside!" he said. "Watch out for the mud and rainwater!" He headed toward the stairs.

With a brief shake of the pole, he lowered one bundle to the ground, and with a foot on the bundle, he pulled out the pole. Then he turned, straightened up, and put down the other bundle. He placed the carrying pole against the wall; I marveled at his enormous, bony hands. The old man took off his heavy straw hat and wiped the rainwater from his face. He narrowed his eyes to scrutinize me. After looking me up and down, he smiled a toothless smile.

I said to him, "Let's go in the house and get out of the rain!"

"What's with the heavens!" he said. "When rain is needed, it never rains. But when we don't need it, it rains endlessly! The crops are rotting in the field. Aiee!" He sighed. The old man remained standing on the stairway, gazing disapprovingly at the heavy gray sky. A puddle of muddy water formed under his feet.

"Sit down and have a cigarette." I sat on a small stool near his feet and offered him a smoke.

He didn't take the cigarette. He went over to the wall and unfastened a shabby cloth bag from the carrying pole, and then came back to sit on the stool.

"Do you have any hot water?" he asked, untying the strings of the bag.

I poured him a bowl of hot water. "You're such an old man to be out in this weather. Why are you still coming around to sell firewood in the rain?"

He didn't answer me but proceeded to take pieces of coarse-looking greenish-brown cake out of the bag. He broke them into little bits and soaked them in the hot water. Then he asked for a pair of chopsticks and set about eating.

"My teeth are gone, so I have to soften the cake with water." He opened his toothless mouth and poured the soggy pieces of cake down his throat as if he were eating gruel. "The stomachs of hard laborers could handle iron pieces." He absently said whatever was on his mind. "You are running out of firewood, aren't you? This place you live in was hard to track down. I took several detours before I finally got here."

He had come especially to bring me the firewood? But how had this half-deaf, thin old man learned about me?

"Are you used to living here yet?" he asked. "Can the kids stand the climate and the life here? Is the coarse food hard to swallow? Let me tell you, you'd better add a bit more soda to your hominy grits, and cook it a long time. Pickled vegetables would be tasty if you stir-fry some hot peppers to go along with them as seasoning. Meals are of first and foremost importance. You must take good care of your health." He looked steadily at me without blinking an eye, but gave no ear to any of my replies.

"Get me an ax," he said. "Well, this one is OK. Don't stop me! I can chop the firewood in no time, but it's no easy job for you!" Carefully the old man untied the two bundles of firewood and began to cut the long sticks into short pieces and the thick sticks into thin pieces.

"It's a very long way from here to Beijing," he continued. "No matter the distance—we common people know what's going on there in the capital. Good people suffer more hardships. That's been true throughout history, from ancient times to the present. You must eat well! Old people rely more on good eating. I was born on Double Ninth Day, the festival of mountain climbing on the ninth day of the lunar month. We were born in the same year, you and I, but you are not as strong. You've got high blood pressure. You walk with caution. We common people who work with our hands can eat and do labor until we collapse. Once we fall down, that's when our life goes out like a lamp running out of oil. But things are different with you people who work with your minds. Though you are advanced in years and have your share of infirmities, a broken pot outlives a good pot. You should move around often. Don't sit too long. Staying in motion promotes the circulation of blood. It broadens your mind, too. I'm telling the truth."

I thought about all the man's assertions. The Chinese commoners of the older generation have been living a life as simple and humble as dirt and mud. They've grown used to eating coarse food and wearing ragged clothes. They have endured poverty and hardship.

Theirs has been a generation forged by miseries, which also shaped their characters. They have adhered to deep moral values, and they're known for their wisdom. This thin and bent old man was sharing that wisdom and offering a philosophy of life—the philosophy of the ages. Though his words seemed simple and commonplace, they stirred my heart and set me to thinking.

I asked him to stay for dinner, but he declined with a wave of his hand. He said that before going back home, he had to go to the main street to buy medicine for the pigs he raised. He had to get home before dark to feed and pen them up. If no one was around after dark, the pigs might be attacked by wild animals from the woods.

I handed him a five-yuan bill, which he was hesitant to take. I waved my hand to tell him he didn't need to give me any change. He thought for a moment and then took it as he slung his pole on his shoulder and disappeared into the autumn rain.

Quite to my surprise, he soon returned, panting. I thought he'd come back for something he had forgotten, but instead he took out three crumpled slips of paper money from his inside pocket. They were three one-yuan notes. Smoothing out the notes and placing them on my table, he hurried away again.

He must have sensed I was chasing him, for he turned around and said, "My firewood was at the old price!" Gazing at his gradually disappearing figure, I realized that now I too was out in the rain.

Ten days later, just when the firewood was almost used up, the old man returned carrying two more bundles of wood. But this time, a white wooden walking stick was hanging from his shoulder pole. The walking stick looked quite unusual. I assumed he must need it for his return trip. After all, he was sixty-seven years old! But he unfastened it from the pole and said, "I come too late. I'm to blame for your fall. Was it serious?"

Five days ago I'd been told to report to an office. On the way back, I'd stumbled on the edge of a ditch. I wondered how he, who lived thirty li away, had heard about this accident.

He must have sensed my curiosity because he said, "I know everything you've done. Everyone else knows, too. I know you stumbled and fell on some vegetable crops and propped them back up even though you couldn't get yourself to your feet. I also know who put you on his back and carried you home. Nowadays, from the commune all through the district to the county, no official makes a speech without starting with, 'The situation is very good and is getting better and better.' But you never said that. What you say is that the common people haven't got enough to fill their stomachs and they work too hard. You don't think I know about this? Of course I know!"

Solemnly he handed me the walking stick. "From now on," he said, "lean on this walking stick whenever you go out. It was made of milkwood. It may not look good, but it's very solid. I cut and dried it last night. Now try it out to see if the height is right."

I took the walking stick from him. It had the pure smell of new wood. It was made of a whole young milkwood tree, from both the trunk and the root. Tiny plum blossoms were carved on its reddish handle. When I looked closely, I saw that at the tip of the reddish part was a tiny, red, five-pointed star. The star, though irregular, obviously had been carved with great care. Holding the walking stick in my hand, I could imagine the old man, my year mate, holding a small knife and carving solemnly in the dim light of an oil lamp with a flame no bigger than a bean. Cutting one stroke after another, the old man would narrow his eyes into two thin slits and puff out his toothless mouth to blow off the sawdust . . . As I looked at the red star, it seemed that suddenly a sparkle burst forth, triggering my memories of the past, thoughts of the present, and premonitions of the future.

The old man took the walking stick from me and ran his rough hands over it as if rubbing it with sandpaper. He handed it back to me. The walking stick seemed to glow as if it were a holy object. I leaned on it. Its height was just right. It fit perfectly in my hand.

Strangely, I felt a surge of strength rushing through the walking stick directly from the earth, helping me stand firm and steady.

As time passed, the walking stick became my best friend. I never went out without it. When I was feeling weak, it gave me strength and courage. When my spirits were low, it gave me support and consolation. When I was again summoned to make a report, I was stronger because of the support of this very cane, the sight of those tiny plum blossoms on its handle and that red star at its tip. I felt I was a powerhouse, full of strength all over.

The old man came every ten days, rain or shine, frigid cold or sweltering heat. His comings were as precise as the phases of the moon: he arrived with the first quarter moon, the full moon, and the last quarter moon. Every time he would make the same remarks and would cut the firewood he'd brought: thick sticks into thin pieces and long sticks into short pieces. Every time he would ask for a bowl of hot water to soak his pancake pieces in until they were soft enough to eat. Every time he would accept only the "old" price of two yuan, not a single fen more. Every time he would tell about something that had happened in his production team and would follow up the story with his comments and judgments. And every time, he would offer some commonsense advice, like "Persimmon vinegar is tastier when warm" or "Celery boiled in water helps reduce high blood pressure." When these things were all done, he would graciously refuse my offer of a meal, hoist his pole on his shoulder, and set off for home.

It was hard to see a man who was as old as I was traveling such a long distance to deliver a heavy load of firewood. Nor could I endure the idea of him worrying about me. But he always came punctually, never missing a single time. I wanted to give him something—money or old clothes or the like—but he always stubbornly turned and left abruptly. At mealtime, I would often think about the firewood in my kitchen and the old man who had labored so conscientiously to bring it. He seemed like a member of my family, an eccentric elder.

One pleasant winter day in 1976, the wind was gently blowing and the warm sun was shining. The old man came with a heavier load of wood than usual. After putting down his load, he unfastened the old cloth bag from the pole as he'd done every visit. I poured him the customary bowl of hot water. However, this time he didn't set about eating his sopped cake, but instead took five cakes from his bag and handed them to me. The cakes were reddish and disk shaped. With an apologetic smile, he said, "Here are some persimmon cakes. Don't you look down on them! They are for your granddaughter. She may never have eaten anything like them. Rough and coarse though they look, they taste sweet."

I didn't refuse. I took them. I asked him to sit down, but he went to find the ax and set about chopping the firewood. He turned his head from time to time and laughed in my direction. I was quite baffled at all of this. After chopping for a long time, he finally stopped laughing and told me this story:

Pursued by Han Dynasty leader Wang Mang, Liu Xiu had no food to eat, no water to drink. Suffering from hunger and thirst, and without the slightest bit of strength left in him, Liu Xiu lay beside a road like a dead man. Just then a girl named Yin Pearblossom passed by. She was from a common family and was carrying a pot full of wheat gruel to her family doing heavy work in the farm field.

The famished Liu Xiu lifted the lid of the pot and poured the whole meal—enough for two farmers—into his own stomach. He thanked the girl over and over for saving his life.

Later, Liu Xiu ascended to the throne, sitting high on the dragon seat. Every day dozens of cooks prepared food for him. But none of their delicacies from land or sea could satisfy his cravings. He began to suspect that his cooks were not doing their best to serve him, their monarch. After all, he reasoned, their food was not as tasty as the simple gruel he'd eaten from Pearblossom's pot while running for his life. So he decided to execute one cook after each meal.

Seeing their colleagues being killed off, the remaining cooks fell into a great panic. If the executions went on day after day, how many more cooks would be killed and where would it end? After discussing the problem, the cooks sent out a great many people to find that village girl somewhere along the route Liu Xiu had taken years before in his distress.

Fortunately, their efforts were rewarded. The girl was found, and Maid Pearblossom set about cooking her wheat gruel for the emperor.

When the gruel was done, the emperor was served. He looked at the gruel, sniffed it, and flew into a rage. He shouted furiously to have the cook's head cut off. At this, the attendants on the scene knelt down and begged, "No, Your Majesty! Don't do that! Please don't do that!"

The emperor asked angrily, "Why not?"

"The gruel was made by Maid Pearblossom, whom you met when you were in distress," replied the attendants.

Hearing this, the emperor commanded that Pearblossom be brought before him.

The cooks were all seized with fear for Pearblossom. How evil it would be to execute such a lovely young woman!

But Maid Pearblossom went to the palace confidently.

After performing the ritual kowtow before the emperor, Maid Pearblossom rose to her feet and stood, waiting to see how the emperor would deal with her. The emperor approached the maiden, asking questions and eyeing her from head to foot. At length he was convinced that he was not being made a fool, and that the girl before him really was Yin Pearblossom who had once saved his life. Still, he couldn't understand why the same person couldn't make an equally tasty meal!

"Emperor," Maid Pearblossom patiently replied, "the meal you ate that day was made with coarse wheat grits, yet you thought it was delicious. The meal you ate today was made of fine wheat grits that I hand selected, grit by grit. Yet you said it was not delicious. It is not that today's meal was not delicious, but that Your Majesty's stomach, which was empty then, is now already filled with rich food. Let us wait three days. During those three days you shall not eat any food. After three days, your humble servant will cook a meal for you to eat. If you still think my food is not delicious, you can execute me or even have me cut into a thousand pieces. Your humble servant will not utter even a single complaint against you."

The emperor thought for a moment. He realized he had done something terrible in having those innocent cooks executed, and he regretted it deeply. Immediately he ordered that, as a sign of his repentance, a payment of one hundred liang of silver be given to each executed cook's family.

———

Having finished the story, the old man laughed at me once more as his eyes shrunk into two narrow slits. He picked up the walking stick from beside me and examined it from different angles. He ran his hand up and down the handle as if he were sanding a piece of furniture. Then he put the stick back down gently and took his two yuan. Carrying his pole on his shoulder, he walked away.

His story set me to thinking. Why had he told me that story at that particular time?

Ten days passed in the blink of an eye. It was again time for the old man to replenish the supply of firewood. I waited as usual, but he did not come. It was as if the waxing and waning of the moon were no longer governed by the same natural laws. Surely something was terribly wrong.

The next morning, as I was about to set off to town to order a pole load of firewood, a young man entered my courtyard carrying two bundles of wood, one on each end of his pole. He told me that the old man, my year mate, was unable to come because he had hurt his back while cutting firewood on the mountain. The young man had been asked to bring the wood.

I inquired anxiously how badly the old man was hurt, and felt relieved to hear that the injury was not very serious. The young commune member also told me that the old man's hometown had been a stronghold of the Communist Party guerrilla forces during the war. The old man's father, at the age of seventy, had been shot by the Kuomintang, and his head had been hung above the town gate for ten days. The old man himself used to carry messages in those days and had had a reputation as a fleet-footed runner. One time, while he was escorting several leader-comrades across a mountain, his group encountered Kuomintang troops. He drew the enemy soldiers away from his comrades and as a result was captured. When interrogated, he insisted he had been on the mountain to collect medicinal herbs. The enemy troops couldn't find any proof against him, but they still put a bullet through his left leg. Even with the wounded leg, he crawled away to find his lost comrades.

I missed the old man, my year mate, more and more. Frequently I had the urge to pay him a visit, but I never went for fear that my visit might bring him trouble.

I didn't see the old man for several months, which felt like years. During that time, the young woodsman kept me abreast of the old man's condition and sent him my greetings. I earnestly hoped he would recover quickly and looked forward to seeing him again soon.

One day I received a notice telling me to return to Beijing as soon as possible. I spent a few days gathering up and packing my things, hoping for the return of the old woodsman, wishing to see him once more before my departure.

And then there he was, leaning on his staff before me! A lingering illness had made his thin figure even more emaciated. Ignoring my inquiries about his health, as if he had never been injured, he went straight into my kitchen. Surveying my stock of firewood and my walking stick, he sat down. He smiled at me and pulled out of his wicker basket more than a dozen red persimmons.

"I haven't got anything to give you except these persimmons," he said. "What do you think they look like? Do they look like the hearts of oxen? Exactly. They are called ox-heart persimmons. The ox heart . . . have you ever seen an ox heart? An ox heart's tip points straight downward, straighter than the hearts of some humans."

I gazed for a long while at the rows of persimmons. What he said was true—these persimmons did look like ox hearts. Nothing less than ox hearts!

I wanted to give him money and clothes so that he'd be able to take better care of himself, but I feared my offer might insult him. Shortly before my departure for Beijing, I entrusted my neighbor— an official who'd been reinstated by the local government to a leader-ship position—with some gifts to pass along to him. I said to myself, this time he will not turn down my gifts.

It has been two months since I returned to Beijing, where meals are not cooked over smoking firewood. Once I returned here, I no longer thought about how meals were cooked. I was always busy with my work. My memory of the old man gradually began to fade away.

Today I happened to see the walking stick, and it reminded me of the old man and of my gifts to him. Snatching the stick from my grandson's hand, I stroked it gently as if I were stroking a child who had been naughty. I saw the tiny red star and shook the dust off it. It gleamed brightly once more, like a blazing fire. The plum blossoms were distinct on that handle with the smooth reddish surface—still warm from the stroke of the old man's rough hands.

No sooner had I scattered the playing children and lost myself in thought—standing alone in the courtyard in the evening sun with the walking stick in my hand—than my grandson flew back to me like a little bird, with a package in his arms.

"Grandpa, here's something mailed from our hometown!" He happily called the small county where we had spent four years "our hometown." In his arms was a parcel sent from that small county. A warm feeling of nostalgia swept over me.

Without wasting a second, I took the package from my grandson and opened it to find the things I had given to the old man. They were being returned along with a letter from my neighbor, whom I'd asked to deliver the gifts to the woodsman.

The letter said that the old man, my year mate, had adamantly refused to accept my gifts and had reacted with great anger. My former neighbor had no choice but to send the money and other gifts back to me. He tactfully related what the old man had said:

"There are hundreds and thousands of old farmers like me in China. The farmers in our country far outnumber the old folks. Can he give every one of them these things and this much money? Now he's in office in Beijing, shouldering an important responsibility. If he would only keep us farmers in his heart, it would be more precious than any gift of gold or silver."

Having read the letter, I had to ask myself, are you close to the people?

I couldn't say no, but neither could I say yes. The judgment could only be passed by people like the woodsman. His image appeared once more before my eyes: his skinny figure, his tattered clothes, his wrinkled face, his slightly hunched back, his load of firewood carried on the ends of the carrying pole, the way he leaned on his walking stick . . . He didn't know how to make flattering, insincere remarks. A bowlful of sopped cakes in hot water could make him feel content.

Yet all that time, he had placed my family in his heart and cared about every necessity of our lives. He was even concerned about our ailments. He was as simple and unsophisticated as the earth. His heart was as clear and pure as the sky. It is the thousands and millions of people like him and their descendents who make up the majority of our civilized, modern nation. It is they who prop up our country with their bony bodies and rough hands. Throughout times of difficulties and hardships and brutal wars, it was they who dauntlessly and unselfishly protected us, raised and nurtured us, shared our anxieties, and gave us encouragement.

If we were separated from them, it would be as though we holders of high positions, along with our revolution, were cut off from the sunshine and the air. As though our feet were not touching the solid earth beneath.

I find I am pressing the walking stick close to my chest. But I have no idea when I began doing so.

Translated by Du Lixia

Gao Jianqun

Gao Jianqun, a contemporary Chinese novelist and a native of Xi'an, was born in 1953. He entered China's literary scene in 1976 with *On the Frontier*, and later published *A Remote White House*. In 1993 his masterpiece *The Last Xiongnu* was released, which eventually led to the so-called Eastward Expedition of the Shaanxi Writers Group. Now he has published five novels, some twenty novellas, and eight collections of essays. The excerpt here, "A Trip for Love," is taken from *The Last Countryside*, one part of his *Trilogy of the Northwest*. Gao is now also a vice-director of the Shaanxi Writers Association and of the Shaanxi Confederation of Literature Circles.

6

Gao Jianqun

A Trip for Love: The Story of an Unmarried Mother

Good Luck Town—in Chinese we call it "Double Six" to mean good luck—is a remote and secluded place, far away from the outside world. Not because the world turns away from it and its nearby satellite villages, nor because it is slow in responding to the pace of the outside world, but simply because of its isolated location. The Creator, alas, is not quite generous, for He creates some places rich, flourishing with gold and silver, and others simply, with bare and barren land and poor people.

But the seclusion of Good Luck Town is mitigated by the highway, and also the traffic, and especially the bus that carries people to and from this place.

Should a bus happen to stop and stay for a while here in the small town—even if it's a short stay—it may leave a story. Perhaps a long story.

And you see—even now, while we are talking, here comes a bus ready to stop at the south end of the town, near the mediator's office managed by Hillock Zhang. Obviously, after the long, hard journey, the vehicle is exhausted, covered with dust all over and sagging under a mountain of luggage on its roof. It is simply out of breath!

A short while ago, just before the bus came to a stop, a fashionable woman of unknown age was looking excitedly out from the bus window, pointing to each village and naming it as the bus passed: "Jia Terrace . . . Feng Terrace . . ." and so on.

Now the bus rolls to a stop in the town.

The woman gets off first, followed by a large trunk handed down by several men. Look! A beautiful face invites many helping hands.

"Thanks!" she says in a standard Beijing dialect as the bus pulls away.

She moves toward the town, struggling to manage her cumbersome luggage.

Hillock Zhang is sitting on the terrace, reading *Reference News*. Literate Li, his assistant, who has nothing to do, takes an afternoon sunbath.

"Uncle Zhang," says Li, "some woman is approaching, and she's so beautiful!"

Roused from his paper, Hillock Zhang glances at the woman, shaking his head in disapproval.

"Why bother?" scoffs Zhang. "A woman like that looks good from afar, but when she's closer—a pig! From a distance that woman looks good simply because of her dress and manner, but a closer examination will reveal her true nature. She may be unfortunate in her nose or eyes or even in a woeful facial expression. But a pig is different. Close up, it looms quite large, while from afar it seemed merely a small figure, even delicate."

"Ahem." Li the Literate warns his boss by clearing his throat, for the woman is close enough now to be seen clearly. She's wearing a pink dress and high-heeled shoes, walking on long, slim legs. Her face is lightly powdered. A pair of sunglasses balances on her nose.

"How well dressed she is!" whispers Zhang as the woman approaches.

"Are there any hotels available here in town, sir?"

"No."

"Any place to stay the night?"

"There is a guesthouse, you see, over there—those three stories. The ground floor is for dining, and the other two above are for living. Just over there. Lift your foot, and it's yours."

"Thank you, sir!"

And off she goes.

Literate Li steps forward. His face reflects a growing concern for the woman, as her luggage is too large to be balanced by legs so long and slim. But Li is too shy to offer his help, so he merely watches her move away.

With his eyes still on the figure of the woman disappearing, Li asks Zhang, "How old is she? Can you guess, Uncle?"

"Never ask the age of a city woman." More experienced in life, Zhang advises, "Her face may be worth a look in the broad daylight. But night will reveal a face covered with pumpkin and cucumber pulp—watermelon rind and the like, which makes her face that of a ghost's. A woman will be cared for if her face is good; she has no concerns in the world, just good drink and good food her whole life through. Everything is just good for her! But a countrywoman, my goodness, must use her hands to dig up food from the land, and her face is, well, quite secondary. And so when you ask me about this woman's age, you give me a challenge. Twenty? Right. Thirty? Right. And even forty, I dare say, could be right for her."

"Nonsense. That makes no sense at all!" Li answers back, unsatisfied. "Uncle Zhang, you are experienced. Tell me, do you believe this woman is still pure, or not?"

"That, I can answer for you," Zhang says, brimming with pride. "My experience says to look at her hips and legs first, and then her waist and lips. Mr. Zhang is no whistle-blower, but judging from how she walks, I'd bet that city woman is no maiden!"

Literate Li watches the woman move away, entranced.

The woman approaches the guesthouse and checks in. For her name, she fills in "Nan, Duckweed." ("Nan," her surname, literally means "from the South.") She enters "Manager" for her profession, and pauses awhile for her age, finally writing in "adult." For place of residence, she writes "Beijing." She identifies this little town as her final destination. Under "Reason for Traveling," she enters "Personal."

"Hello," the attendant greets her. "What kind of room would you like?"

"The best one you have," the woman replies, and the arrangements are made.

She goes upstairs. "We also serve food here!" a voice shouts from behind her.

Half an hour later, the woman comes back downstairs. She has put on a jacket because of the cool mountain air. She inspects the tables to see which is the best, the cleanest. Once seated, she picks up a pair of chopsticks from a bamboo box and cleans them with a piece of napkin, holding the chopsticks in her right hand.

The wait for her food is long and makes her anxious—but this is the pace of things in a small town. The woman feels tired after her long bus journey and keeps dozing off, one elbow propped on the table and her hand on her forehead.

A child's face suddenly appears from under the table.

Startled at the motion, Duckweed Nan opens her eyes.

The child gazes at her and mumbles, "Legs in flood, lips in blood!"

"What did you say? Hey!" She senses something funny in the child's speech.

"Legs in flood, lips in blood!" the child repeats loudly.

A waitress arrives with a plate of dumplings. Beet-red, she yells at the child: "Naughty, Qiong Qiong! Be careful, or you're going to get it!"

Making faces, the child escapes from under the table and runs into the street, looking for a new way to amuse herself.

The waitress places the plate on the table.

"What did she say?" asks Duckweed.

"She is cursing you, saying that your legs are bare like a fisherman's and your lips so red, like a vampire's."

"Oh, is that so?" Duckweed finds herself offended, instinctively tugging at her skirt and neckline as if to cover herself up.

She secures a dumpling with the chopsticks, takes a bite, and then puts it down. Her eyebrows pucker at the bad taste.

To the waitress nearby, she says, "I saw a tall old fellow standing on the terrace, reading a newspaper. Is that Zhang, the party secretary of the town?"

"Yes, that's right. He is Hillock Zhang. We call him Uncle Zhang. He's not a party secretary anymore, you know. He's just a mediator in the town, playing the part of peacemaker in conflicts. Helping people in trouble get out of trouble."

"Yes, I noticed the sign on the wall when I passed by. And what is your name?"

"Asiatic Plantain," the other answers.

"Then, Plantain, I need your help. Would you go and ask Hillock Zhang to come over to my room in the evening? Just tell him that my name is Duckweed Nan and that I'm an educated young woman from Beijing, settling down in this military outpost."

"All right."

———

Night falls in the small town. Dim streetlights extinguish, one after another, from the insufficient power. The moon hangs brightly in the sky, casting the mountain's large shadow over half the town, the mountain looming faintly in outline. All is silent except for the barking of someone's dog nearby. In the distance, a stream murmurs along the ravine. Closer, dripping water can be heard.

Plantain leads the way, and Hillock Zhang and Literate Li follow.

"Yes," Zhang is saying, "at that time, educated young people came from Beijing to settle down in northern Shaanxi by the tens of thousands—at least twenty-six or twenty-seven thousand. Now, you see, only a few hundred remain. But through hard life experience, these cubs have grown into tigers. Some are in America, some in Japan, others in Australia and other countries. Some have become writers, some journalists, and still others managers of some kind. Rough times can temper a personality! Can you imagine what our society would be like if that generation had grown up differently?"

Literate Li asks, "What about Duckweed Nan? Do you know her?"

"No. She was not in my brigade. But I remember seeing her name on the list of education activists from Dazhai in the people's commune."

"But her visit here is a mystery. She didn't go to the town hall, nor to the village head, but merely to you. Why?"

They come upon the guesthouse, and Zhang steps forward and knocks on the door.

Duckweed appears at the open door.

Hers is the best room in the guesthouse of such a small town. Furnished with a TV, a pair of sofas, a desk, a double bed, and, most importantly, a bathroom, it is just like a room in a city house.

"Ha, ha!" Zhang enters the room and launches into his opening speech. Nan turns off the TV, instantly attentive.

"Cadres from Beijing—excellent!" Zhang declares. "Whether they be soldiers in the army or students at college or workers in a factory, they no longer visit their parents but us folks, in Spring Festivals or the like, saying 'our brigade' this and 'our family' that. Nowadays they have their own families and work even harder, but they keep on writing to us, sending their good wishes to every house and home."

"Party Secretary Zhang, your speech moves me deeply!" Nan says. "Would you like tea or coffee?"

"Tea for me," Zhang says.

"Coffee? I've seen it only in movies. Is it tasty?" Li asks shyly, glancing at the hostess and then ducking his head down again.

"It's pretty good. Why not try it?"

The service begins right away, each enjoying his share, and at last the hostess makes a coffee for herself, with her own cup that she brought with her.

Nan produces a pack of 555 brand cigarettes and places them before Zhang.

"I already have some," says Zhang, pointing to his own pack of cigarettes.

Silence prevails for a moment. Zhang looks at Duckweed, and Duckweed looks at Zhang.

Zhang suspects that the woman has something on her mind, something hidden, and notices how her hands fumble while serving him tea. She's a person of position with no reason to be nervous before them. Perhaps it's only the excitement of a cadre returning to her second home. But to Zhang it seems like something personal.

Literate Li takes a sip of his coffee, and the bitterness leaves him with a sour face. He's about to speak, but the tension in the air overwhelms him.

"I have something to say," Duckweed announces, "but I'm not sure how to put it." Turning serious, she walks to the other end of the room and bolts the door. She lights a cigarette and begins to smoke it.

"You can tell me, your uncle Zhang. I'm not a party secretary anymore; I'm a mediator now. I go around Good Luck Town trying to make things work out or smooth things out. Don't treat me like an outsider; you can come to me for help."

"But how can I say it to you?" Duckweed begins sobbing.

"Just say it. I'm ready to listen to you," the mediator encourages. "I'm experienced, and my ears are attuned. The world is a complex bundle of things, and anything queer or crazy might happen. Whatever happens, though, happens for a reason."

Duckweed stops sobbing and begins to tell her story. "I had a child when I was in the countryside—about twenty years ago."

"I guessed as much, even before you said anything," confides Zhang.

"I'm planning to go to my brigade tomorrow. May I tell you the whole story on the way, if you'd be willing to keep me company?" asks Duckweed.

Uncle Zhang nods. "No problem."

"Uncle, this is a present for you. And your reward is not included." Duckweed fetches a bag from the cupboard, showing Uncle Zhang a bottle of wine, two cartons of cigarettes, and some high-end tonics. She has come prepared.

"No, that wouldn't be right." Zhang waves his hands to reject the offering. "You are looking down upon me. I'm your uncle Zhang!"

"Don't treat me like an outsider—just like you said," Duckweed retorts cleverly. "Please accept these gifts as tokens of my respect for you, or else I'll be horribly upset."

"Well, then, we'll take them." Zhang signals to Literate Li.

Li does what he is told.

Early the next morning, a three-wheeled tractor moves out of the town and enters the road along the valley in the mountains. It zigzags across a stream, making a big noise all the way. The driver is Little Islet, whom everyone knows.

The tractor carries Duckweed Nan, Hillock Zhang, and Literate Li away from the town.

Duckweed holds a video recorder in her hand, its small bag hanging from her shoulder. Against the backdrop of tractor noise, Duckweed is telling her story.

"He was a demobilized soldier, very handsome, a typical native of Suide County. It was during the Spring Festival, and I was on duty while others were off at home. I was alone in the cabin and scared at night. And so I knocked on his door, the door of my landlord, and lay down on the kang, sleeping with the man I loved. Shortly after that, I found out I was pregnant. I was scared. I could do nothing but tighten my waist belt while working in the field. Finally, I told him the secret and asked him for help.

"That night by the river, he said, 'I can marry you.'

"I told him, 'No. I'm going back to work in the city.'

"'You can accuse me of rape, for the sake of your own reputation,' he offered. 'I will go to jail for eight years, and then I'll get out.'"

"That's true," Zhang cuts in. "According to the CPC document issued in the fall of 1970, anyone who raped an educated girl would be sentenced to eight years in jail. Every commune member knew those terms. But how did you respond, dear girl?"

"How could I betray him? I shook my head firmly. I reminded him that I was the one who'd knocked on his door. At that, he turned away and left me without a word. He was upset. Before long, news came that he had died at the construction site on the Zhang River, when the dam caved in."

A vivid image flashes across Zhang's mind: a good man, always with an army cap on his head. He says, "He was found under a frozen block of soil. I was one of the men responsible for the construction, you know."

Duckweed continues her story. "My friends, kind women, treated me so well that they wouldn't allow me to work in the field, instead arranging for me to cook at home. I gave birth in October. The dates hanging in the tree were extremely big and red that year; I still remember them.

"But how to deal with the little creature was a problem. I told my friend, 'Take her from me, and leave her outside the village. If someone kind enough picks her up, she'll enjoy a full, happy life.' The baby burst into a loud cry at the door, and I called them back inside and kissed her one last time. Then I wrapped her little body in the army jacket I loved best and handed her over to my friends."

The tractor booms loudly and shudders hard before it comes to a stop. A narrow path stretches ahead.

"Uncle Zhang, I can't go any farther," says Little Islet. "You can walk from here." Turning off of the main road along the stream, they begin climbing the hillock.

"Wait a moment!" Duckweed shouts. She leads the way down. Before them a date tree stands tall, and Duckweed photographs it for a while. Then she takes a picture of the village between the woods and the hills in the distance. She moves under the date tree and kneels down for a closer look. There is nothing remarkable there except for a kind of spinachlike plant amid the grass.

Hillock Zhang approaches. "Is this where they left her?" he asks.

"Yes, I'm sure it was here." Duckweed removes her sunglasses for a closer look, as if she might suddenly find the child.

"I can't have any more children, you know, Uncle, so this child is very important to me."

Zhang stands there, not knowing what to say.

"Party Secretary," she asks, "is it possible that she's already dead?"

"Silly question! Whatever comes into being in this world is supposed to live, for one reason or another. You know what they say: A piglet is born with food for three days."

"Oh, I do hope she survived somehow," Duckweed says. "What do you call this grass?"

"Plantain. Asiatic plantain."

"Plantain?" repeats Duckweed. She takes a picture of the plant.

Duckweed Nan asks Literate Li to shoot a photo of her with the plant and date tree. Li waves his hands and says, "No, no. This is the first time I've even seen such a machine."

"It's easy. Just frame the picture you want and shoot. This is on, this is off." Li listens attentively and masters it immediately.

Nan starts to head for the village. Li holds the camera before his eyes, following her pace. Zhang follows Li, but slowly.

From above, a local housewife looks down into the courtyard. Duckweed stops and shouts to her. "Are you Pillar's Wife?"

"Who are you?"

"I'm Duckweed. I saw you long ago at your wedding ceremony. We were pulling the handcart at the construction site. Remember?"

"I remember that! Here in the mountains we have fewer things to remember, you know. We think of you whenever we have the chance."

"You were always the most beautiful wife in the village."

"Not anymore. I'm over forty already! Come and sit for a while in my cabin, please!"

"I'd love to, but not now. First I have to go to the cadres' cabin in the back valley, and then I'll come back for visits from door to door."

"OK, I'll be waiting."

Another courtyard echoes with the sound of a huge roller on a millstone. Duckweed climbs up the steep incline to see.

"Aunt, you are still alive?" Duckweed's hands fly up to cover her mouth in surprise.

Her aunt is pushing the roller around. She stops, drying her eyes with the front of her garment, not knowing who is greeting her.

"I beg your pardon. Sorry. Aunt, it's Duckweed. We young people mourned sadly because we were told that you had passed away!"

"Yeah, Nan! You still remember your aunt? I fell seriously ill but did not die. The king of hell licked my nose and found it bare—so he spared me!"

Duckweed helps push the roller as her aunt sweeps the millet toward the center of the millstone.

"Why don't you go in and sit in the cabin, my child?"

"Not now. Dear Aunt, it is so nice to see you well. I promise to come back once I return from the village."

"I will serve you good food when you come back."

"Well, until then, here's a small token of my regard. Do take it." Duckweed gives her dear aunt 200 yuan.

"To see you again is enough for me. Why should I need money? I have no use for it."

"It's not just for you. And besides, I'd have no idea what to buy for you."

"Oh, then I'll accept it, my child."

Auntie puts the money into the front of her garment. The roller starts up again.

"Duckweed Nan is here! Duckweed Nan is here!" People shout to each other across another courtyard.

"I'm coming. I'm coming!" Duckweed answers.

"You're not used to this mountain path. Let us help you up."

"I can manage. I used to be able to carry a bag of beans up here. I think I can do it!"

Nan does have some trouble climbing the steep yard. She takes her steps one by one, with difficulty because of her high-heeled leather shoes. Li stops shooting and offers her a helping hand, but Nan refuses to take it.

"Duckweed Nan! Duckweed Nan!" Local people stand in line, jumping and clapping, shouting their welcomes. A tall boy reaches her first and grasps her hands.

"Who are you?" Nan asks. "You're not a member of this brigade, are you?"

"I'm Doggie. I was only this tall when you were here in the brigade."

"Doggie—you always had a runny nose, didn't you?"

"Um . . ." Doggie grins shyly.

More helping hands reach her, and Li continues to shoot the colorful scene with Nan's video camera.

The village is called Little Clear Creek. Zhang knows it like the back of his hand. He was surprised last night when he heard Nan's story; such a big event happened here twenty years ago, and he didn't know a thing about it.

Back at the date tree, when Nan was wondering if the child might be dead, he was quick to find the words to comfort her—but in truth, he was not so sure the little creature could have survived for very long.

Treat a dead horse as though it's alive. Zhang considers the present situation. Now that Nan has committed her story to his care, he believes he should do his best to help her. Besides, he feels especially responsible for this young woman. For many reasons, the northern Shaanxi folk are closely related with the Beijing cadres. When Zhang was the party secretary of the town, it was he who brought them by donkey cart from the county town into the village, and it was he who saw them off, one by one, when they left to return to city life. Naturally he has a deep, lasting affection for these young people.

The very arrival of Duckweed Nan in Little Clear Creek is a blessing. A festival atmosphere hangs in the village. Shouts echo throughout the valley, and Nan's name is spreading quickly to every family. They treat her as they would their own daughters; every face turns from gloomy to smiling. She is the daughter of the whole village.

Zhang is especially excited—but the excitement mingles with other feelings in his heart. Being somewhat sensitive, he avoids the bustling scene and falls a few steps behind the crowd. For one thing, he fears that he cannot bear the commotion. For another, he has already started working out the matter that Nan entrusted to him. When it comes to one's private affairs, he thinks, a secret inquiry is better than a public one.

Zhang enters the village by himself.

Pillar's Wife is standing high above the courtyard, watching. She sees Zhang and greets him with a question: "Uncle Zhang, have you come because of Duckweed?"

"Oh, well, yes."

"Why has she come here?"

"No special reason. She's now a higher-up at a company in Beijing. She's checking out our village, uh, to possibly build a date-processing factory."

"I don't believe that. Who on earth would throw money into this poor valley? She must have come for something else."

"Not everyone is like you. Believe me or don't; I don't care."

"She came for something else, I'm sure," Pillar's Wife mutters to herself.

Zhang shoots her a dirty look and continues on his way.

———

The heavy roller squeezes along the millstone. Duckweed's old aunt pushes the roller around along an invisible track. But she fumbles for the money her niece gave her—more money than she's ever had in her life. As the locals would say, it's burning a hole in her pocket.

The pushing suddenly ceases.

"Who's there?" Without turning her head, she withdraws one of her hands from her waist. "Who is so kind as to visit me?" Her voice sounds like a warm smile.

"Hillock Zhang, from the Zhang River."

The rolling resumes, lightly, with a helping hand from the man.

"Hillock Zhang, have you come with Duckweed?"

"I have little business to do in town. I've come for two reasons. First, to accompany Duckweed, since she's a newcomer. Second, to see if you are still alive, my old friend. In the fifties—the last century!—just after the Liberation, you were the model beauty around here!"

"Age and a beard haven't made you mature at all. Where will I hide my old face if the young people hear your nonsense?"

"Well, then, let's get down to business. I must ask you for a definite answer, Double Blessing's Mother."

"So serious you seem to be. How can I know anything so serious?"

"Serious or not serious, you treat me as if I were speaking non-sense. How would you prefer me to behave?"

Double Blessing's Mother smiles broadly. Anyone who remembers her younger days can see that she is pleased through and through. "OK," she relents. "What is the matter? Just tell me."

"Aha. We are both aging, and half our lives are gone. We could grow used to anything and not be alarmed. Don't you agree?"

"Would you please get to the point instead of beating about the bush?"

"It's a long story," Zhang says. "About twenty years ago, exactly the third year when the Beijing cadres settled down in our brigade, right at the season when the dates turned red, someone may have found something by the road just outside the village. Did you ever hear of anyone who might have seen or heard of anything like that?"

"Like what?"

"A baby."

"A baby?" Duckweed's aunt gasps. "How sinful! Who would ever leave a baby out there?"

"You see, I even warned you, and you're still alarmed. Don't worry about who did it. Our focus is the baby itself. Do you know if anyone picked it up, even among our neighboring villages?"

"Oh, I can see what you're getting at. You want to implicate Duckweed in this, don't you? You'll never do that. Duckweed is innocent —pure through and through. I couldn't care less about what you say unless you first take that back."

"That would be out of the question, Double Blessing's Mother. To tell you the truth, it is Duckweed who has come by air and bus to our village to search every corner for the baby. Her conscience won't let her bury this forever in her heart. Besides, she can no longer bear a child, you know."

Double Blessing's Mother thinks for a minute and says gravely, "I really don't know. I would tell you if I knew. How pitiful this is; Duckweed, my poor child!"

"Think again. Try to remember."

"There's no need for that. Do you think someone who found a child in the village could keep it a secret for so long and from so many people? No way!"

"This time spent with you has been useless. Such idle talk, and all for nothing!" Zhang feels discouraged. "I'm going."

———

Duckweed Nan arrives at a clearing where three cabins sit facing a soil cliff.

The cabins were built originally for the cadres to settle down in the country. After the cadres returned to the city, one cabin was used as the village hall, and the other two became classrooms of the village school.

Now all the villagers, old and young, are gathered here in front of the cabins. The village head—a middle-aged man, about the same age as Duckweed—has decreed that every household bring their best food here to make an impromptu potluck reception for Duckweed. In the center of the courtyard is a large stone table, heaped with red dates, peanuts, boiled corn, squash soup, and more. The village head himself has carried a huge watermelon and cut it open for everybody to share.

As the school hour draws to a close, pupils begin to crowd like herds of sheep, laughing and playing, adding to the festival atmosphere.

Soon everyone takes a seat. One of the wives suggests that Duckweed should sing a song for everyone, and the others all agree. The local people remember what a good singer Nan always was.

Duckweed feels a little nervous. She's excited but also hesitant, as if she were a stranger here.

The village head interrupts to say, "Our Duckweed is out of breath after a long journey. Let's give her some time to prepare. I will sing for you first!" At the top of his lungs he begins to shout the song "A Widower Cried for His Deceased Wife."

When he finishes, Duckweed stands up and smooths her dress. She says, "I will sing 'Wandering Chants' for you. This is my favorite song. I first learned it in Little Clear Creek, and I later returned to it in the army. I often sang it in the office. These days I sing it at karaoke with friends. It always reminds me of northern Shaanxi. It reminds me of all of you."

Duckweed clears her throat and begins to sing. Her earnest face and voice spark a memory for the locals—that of an educated girl with two braids in a Red Guard uniform.

Wild geese southward flying,
Fly faster, faster, if you can.
Carry my message to Beijing, saying
That we miss our leader Mao Zedong.

Just then Hillock Zhang arrives and immerses himself in the excitement of the scene. The melody and the sincere way Duckweed sings seem like an invitation. The singer winks at him, and he motions for her to continue. Zhang retreats to the edge of the crowd, bending down to wipe his moist eyes with a sleeve.

The village head approaches and entreats Zhang to rest in the large cabin. Zhang waves a hand to dismiss the invitation. Determined to help Uncle Zhang feel more comfortable, the village head pulls a stool from beneath one of the other guests, and Zhang finally agrees to be seated.

The singing continues.

Zhang catches the village head by his arm and motions for him to squat down next to the stool. "Sir, do you know anyone who had a child in this village, more or less around this time of year, in the fall of 1971?"

"Fall . . . '71 . . . no, definitely no one. The winter of 1970 was the field reconstruction campaign, and each person worked in his or her own area. How could someone have a child? Even if they wanted to, there's no way!"

"Don't answer so quickly. Think carefully. Try to remember! Let's go through every household, one by one."

"Oh, including those with married women?"

"Sure."

"Well, in that case, Pillar's family, of course. Asiatic Plantain was born that year in the fall. There was a bumper harvest of dates that year, you'll recall."

"Plantain! Ha ha, Plantain!" That's it! An image flashes through Zhang's mind—a memory of Duckweed taking pictures of the plantain grass under the date tree. He knew someone would know something about the child. It couldn't have happened without someone being aware of a trace, some clue. Zhang realizes that Plantain, now married, is none other than the short waitress in the guesthouse of the town. To think—Duckweed's daughter was there right in front of Duckweed's own eyes!

Patting his forehead, satisfied with this breakthrough, Zhang rises and gives the village head a grateful smile before taking his leave. He decides to go talk to Pillar's Wife.

The village head remains hovering next to the stool, puzzled by the whole matter.

Nan continues singing, one song leading into another. She is completely absorbed in the performance, showcasing her passion for and devotion to the place and people before her. She feels herself giving in to the atmosphere of celebration.

Kneeling, standing, always adjusting to capture the best possible angle, Literate Li snaps away with his camera.

———

"Pillar's Wife, please come inside with me; I have something important to say to you."

Pillar's Wife watches the outside world before her cabin. She has remained at home in the yard, not joining the crowd to watch the performance. Something is stirring in her mind, though she's not sure what it is. Startled by the sudden interruption, she turns to find Mr. Zhang, an elder, which puts her at ease.

"Whatever you have to say to me, just say it here, outside. That way I can enjoy the view while you speak."

"As you wish."

Mr. Zhang crouches down into a low talking position.

Pillar's Wife, who should squat for the sake of politeness, remains standing, apparently unconcerned with social graces. What's more, she slowly turns her body away from Mr. Zhang, so that her side is toward the elder. She ignores the suggestion of haughtiness that this posture implies.

Zhang snorts. "I don't mind haughtiness. I'm a straightforward, uncomplicated man. Regardless of how you behave, I'm going to tell you the truth."

"It would be better if you didn't speak. I'm not willing to listen."

"Whether you listen or not, dear Pillar's Wife, I must speak. Is your daughter, the one who's married and living in town, named Asiatic Plantain? It's an easy question."

"Yes, why? What's the matter? Is it wrong to name her that?"

"Hold on, I mean no criticism. But I must know: is Asiatic Plantain your own flesh and blood, or are you not her biological parent?"

"What does that really mean, 'flesh and blood'? Who is to say?"

"I knew it." Zhang is energized by the answer. He moves to stand up.

Before Zhang can fully rise, Pillar's Wife turns to face him directly, one hand on her hip and the other pointing in Zhang's face. She scolds: "Hillock Zhang, I'll spare your old wrinkled face, but only because you're a few days older than me; otherwise you'd be about to lose face quickly in Little Clear Creek. I myself would tear to pieces anyone who dared to imply what you're implying. I tell you, this daughter of mine is my own flesh and blood."

She pauses to remember.

"I, too, was pregnant for ten months and had a painful delivery."

The stream of abuse that follows arouses no hatred in Zhang. He returns the old woman's curses not with a curse but with a smile, saying, "Pillar's Wife, you are a woman, a mother. You must know how much a woman suffers in losing a child. It's torture for a mother to miss her child for so long, never knowing what has become of her."

"That's not my business. If she could tear herself away in the past, she should be strong enough to stay away from the child now."

"Pillar's Wife, your claim betrays the truth even if you don't want it to. The baby who was delivered twenty years ago by Duckweed is your Plantain, whom you must have adopted as your own at that very same time."

"Uncle Zhang, stop abusing me with these vile accusations, this evil scheming! Go ahead and try to prove it. I've done and said nothing to suggest that I am not the biological mother of Plantain."

Before Zhang can respond, Pillar arrives home from the hilltop with a hoe slanted across his shoulder. He shouts his greeting across the courtyard as he approaches. "Uncle Zhang, what a blessing! What wind blows you to this narrow and remote place?"

"Pillar, my friend. The road is available to all who seek it. I come on behalf of Duckweed."

"Yes, I was out working the fields when I heard that Nan has come, and I ran home at once to see her."

"Pillar, I've been talking to your wife about something quite serious. Now that you're here, I'll tell you."

"Don't bother, Uncle Zhang. I know all about it—about Duckweed."

"You know?" Zhang is caught off guard.

Pillar's Wife tries to restrain her husband lest he disclose every-thing, but her husband waves a signal to stop her, saying, "Sleeping cannot bother the eyelid. My darling, it's time to tell the truth."

The wife grows angry and slumps on the ground in protest.

Pillar slowly begins to tell the whole story.

"Some twenty years ago, my wife became pregnant, but we lost the baby to a miscarriage. I wrapped the baby's body carefully with straw and went out in the dark to the hillside to bury it. On my way back to the village, I noticed a young woman on the outskirts, placing something under a tree. She heard my footsteps and hurried away. I was curious about what she was doing out there by herself and went to look. As I got closer, I saw that she'd left a newborn baby, wrapped tenderly in an army uniform. I picked it up, and it cried out in need."

"And so you named the baby Plantain because she was found on a cluster of plantain grass, is that right?"

"Right, though it was my wife who named her. She was still reel-ing from our own loss when I came home with the baby. Immediately she took the infant to her breast and began feeding her. As soon as the baby was settled in her arms, she stopped crying. It was uncanny! Later my wife named the child Asiatic Plantain, for the reasons you already know. Uncle Zhang, my wife loves the girl as only a mother can, and I love her, too. We never really believed we were not her bio-logical parents. Yet somehow, a part of me suspected that someday her birth mother would come to find her."

"Duckweed never said she wanted to take your daughter away. Rather, she said she'd like to come to see you."

"I've been thinking it through," Pillar says, "and I've come to a conclusion. A married daughter is like water poured out, as they say. And Plantain could easily have another mother in addition to the one she has always known. Isn't that something good? To be honest, our conditions are so poor in the country that the child grew up as a shepherd, without even a day of schooling. I'm afraid Duckweed will be disappointed with how we've cared for Plantain."

Pillar's Wife breaks in angrily. "Ridiculous! Bringing a child up is not an easy job; dreary nursing and endless cleaning make for hard work and a toilsome life. Don't try to shift the blame to me, damn you!"

Zhang, however, refuses to take her bait. He turns to Pillar to ask, "Did you ever tell Plantain? Does she know?"

"No, I never did," Pillar replies softly. "Simpleminded Plantain is not at all aware of it. We never uttered a word, for fear that an improper past would hurt her chances for a happy life."

Feeling neglected, Pillar's Wife hastens to cut in. "Uncle Zhang, suppose Nan does convince us that she's the birth mother. She's not likely to convince our daughter so easily. Plantain will most likely hate Nan and bitterly reject her. Don't you see that?"

"My wife is right, Uncle Zhang. Plantain is hard to convince—of anything. There's no guarantee that she'll be willing to accept Nan. Before you tell Duckweed the truth, perhaps you should go first to Plantain and try to sound her out on the matter. If Plantain is willing to meet Nan, then it's OK with us. Otherwise, you'd be wise to tell Duckweed to go home without revealing any more secrets."

"Pillar, you are right to say so," Zhang agrees. Exhausted, he manages to stand up, with more than a little effort.

Pillar turns gently to his wife. "Why don't you go out to the celebration and enjoy yourself?"

"I'm not feeling well. You go," his wife whispers.

The celebration in front of the school is nearing its end. Lunchtime approaches, and a great feast is laid out. People are eating and drinking around the stone table. Dates, potatoes and sweet potatoes, corn, squash porridge—everything is served with joy. Kids are running in twos and threes with corncobs in their hands, making a noisy scene.

A bell rings, and the pupils return to their classroom. The grounds are suddenly half-empty and far quieter. Men smoke in groups or drink tea, while the women chat about their own affairs.

Duckweed sets a carton of cigarettes on the table, inviting people to help themselves. Then she picks up the camera and resumes filming the villagers. Afterward, she enters the school and continues shooting portraits of each and every child.

The children are hard at work in their classroom. The day's text is entitled *Little Hero Yulai*. The teacher reads it first, followed by a group reading out loud:

I am a good child;

I love the Chinese Communist Party.

The children's voices merge in a sweet, clear sound, full of life and vigor.

"These are the cabins built for the educated young people from Beijing," Nan declares before her video camera, "funded by the Beijing government. Now they have become the classrooms of the Little Clear Creek school. When I arrived, the lovely students were already in class."

Retreating sadly, Nan climbs the hillside, gaining a bird's-eye view of the village. While she speaks, Literate Li takes up the video camera to film her commentary.

"This is Little Clear Creek, an ordinary village in northern Shaanxi Plateau. I lived in this place for three years as a younger woman, and it is here that I left my . . . my . . . past."

Nan chokes on her words, unable to speak. She takes the camera from Li, turns it off, and then hands it back to him. Leaning against a big tree, she begins sobbing, tears streaming down her cheeks.

After a while, she hears someone calling her from behind. "Duckweed, Duckweed! Do you recognize my voice?"

Wiping away her tears, she turns to see a surprisingly young-looking man.

"Pillar! You look just the same as before. You haven't changed!"

"I was working on the hillside when I heard people shouting your name, and I ran like a hurricane to come see you."

Behind him trails Hillock Zhang, who has taken notice of Nan's distress, saying, "Let's go back, it's too high and cool here."

On their way down, Duckweed hangs back and confides to Uncle Zhang, "I feel depressed. I need a good cry."

"Go ahead, my child. Nobody will laugh at you. It will be a release for you."

"Are there any clues yet?" she asks tentatively.

"Hard to say." Zhang scratches his head, glancing at Pillar a few steps ahead.

Evening approaches and the sun begins to set. Duckweed knows she has to tear herself away from the village, so she travels from door to door saying her good-byes.

Women—young and old, married and unmarried—tug at her sleeve, saying good-bye with sorrowful voices. Duckweed is bathed in tears. No one is willing to let her go, so they walk hand in hand for a long stretch.

Duckweed confides to the women that with her three years of experience in the village, she believes she will be more satisfied, more content, in the long run. She learned a lot, she says, and owes so much to those three years. Tempered by hard country life, she is now able to deal with any difficulty—whether in the army, in an office, or working as a business manager, as she has in recent years, on leave with pay suspension. She is her own boss.

She tells them with great seriousness that she has a good plan to supply some money to the village, so that they can build a date-processing factory. Two problems should be considered, she advises: one, the market, and two, technique. She will be responsible, she says, for creating a market. The technique problem can be addressed by inviting an expert to visit the village and write up a feasibility report.

She adds that she would like to bring the video recording she's made to her colleagues, but that she will send a copy back to Little Clear Creek.

The villagers have nothing comparable to offer their dear daughter in return, other than their best dates, squash, and buckwheat flour. They fill a large bag for Duckweed, but she struggles under the weight of their generosity. Since she's not strong enough to carry the gift, Zhang steps in to offer a solution. "I have an assistant," he shouts. "Li the Literate—he can carry your gifts for Duckweed."

All the offerings create a heavy burden on the shoulders of Li, who protests that he serves simply as a beast of burden!

Hillock Zhang looks back as the tractor starts to sputter. He catches sight of Pillar's Wife standing in front of her cabin, drying her tears. She, too, is seeing them off.

The three-wheeled tractor booms away down the path, leaving the village behind in the distance. Silence settles there in the dark, the only sound the retreating hum of the tractor. No one utters a word, but excitement still lingers in their hearts.

———

The next morning, Duckweed gets up later than usual. Her habit of rising early, carefully cultivated in the army, has been forsaken this morning.

She seats herself at a table in the dining hall, her droopy eyes betraying a sleepless night. It's as if she's in a trance. Overexcited and still exhausted, she is not quite back to herself, even after a night in bed.

"A remote, small, mountainous village . . ." She can't help humming this familiar song. The tune begins to energize her, and she considers how right she was to come and visit the village, even aside from her personal reasons. Twenty years have already passed, and she has returned to this place of growth only once. She silently chides herself for not having come sooner.

The waitress brings a bowl of buckwheat noodles in mutton soup. It's Duckweed's favorite food. In their twenties, she and her friends would enjoy this soup whenever they came to town, if for no other reason than for the nutrition, which was severely lacking in those days.

But today the mutton soup doesn't taste as good as her memories. Duckweed isn't sure whether the difference is in the soup or in herself. Probably the latter, she decides charitably, for the pace of any such change in mountain life is quite sluggish.

The waitress offers her more soup, and adds some with a spoon at Duckweed's gesture. The waitress is named Plantain, Duckweed recalls.

Here Plantain stands before her, short and buxom, just shy of five feet tall. Her official uniform indicates that at least one of her family members is serving in the army. Her hair is thick and black, plaited into two braids down her back. Her chest swells from inside her jacket, suggesting a womanly figure despite the shapeless army garb. Duckweed imagines how strong Plantain's child must be, considering the mother's form. The name of Plantain's daughter suddenly comes to her: Qiong Qiong.

Plantain seems nervous. Seeing Duckweed watching her so closely, she turns away self-consciously and rushes off.

Pushing the empty bowl aside, Duckweed considers her plan to visit Hillock Zhang, who probably has something to tell her after yesterday. Of course, as her elder, Zhang must also be visited out of courtesy, out of respect.

She heads outside. Qiong Qiong is playing on the doorstep; she casts the child a hearty smile. She is so lovely, Duckweed thinks.

"Legs in flood; lips in blood," the little girl chants when she sees Duckweed. She's poised to run the moment someone approaches to scold or strike her.

Duckweed is in an especially fine mood and is not at all annoyed at the child's taunting. She smiles at her lovingly.

"Qiong Qiong, would you come walk with me for a while? I have candy to share with you." To add credence to her claim, Duckweed produces several candies from her handbag.

The effect on the girl is obvious; she instantly warms up to Duckweed in the face of this temptation. Duckweed removes a candy wrapper and puts a sweet morsel into the girl's little mouth.

Within minutes, Qiong Qiong is as tame as a puppy.

"Auntie!" she calls to Duckweed in her sweetest voice. Duckweed takes her by the hand, walking toward the mediator's office.

The newly appointed auntie and niece walk along and take in the view. They stop in several shops along the way. When they finally arrive at the mediator's office, Duckweed learns that Uncle Zhang has gone to the guesthouse to see her. He must have a reason for going there instead of waiting for me, she thinks. So she and the girl turn around and head back to where they came from.

Perhaps overly spoiled by her mother, Qiong Qiong quickly grows tired from their long walk, and she begins pestering her auntie to carry her almost the entire way. Duckweed, who has had no child to carry ever since she gave her baby up to the woods, is not inclined to give in to the girl. And besides, this little child looks like she needs the exercise. So Duckweed just ignores the girl's pleas.

Halfway home, Qiong Qiong absolutely refuses to take another step. She begins yelling at her newfound auntie and rolling around on the ground in a childish tantrum. Duckweed has little choice but to bend down and, dusting the child off, pick her up and carry her the rest of the way to the guesthouse. She quietly regrets taking this naughty child with her.

Duckweed struggles to keep her balance along the path as she maneuvers Qiong Qiong in her arms. Then suddenly her eye is drawn to a pendant around the child's neck.

It is something like a locket, a kind typically worn by a child from the time he or she is one month old until the age of thirteen. But the one before her eyes is not typical; it is a Chairman Mao badge, once very popular during the Cultural Revolution but now rarely seen. Here its function has been transformed into a traditional one, serving as a good-luck charm in true country fashion. Duckweed recalls the taxis in Beijing that have Mao badges hanging inside to serve as talismans for luck and safety.

With highlighted cheeks and swept-back gray hair, Mao's image on the badge is so familiar to Duckweed that she recognizes instantly that she was once the owner of this badge.

How could that be? But certainly it is true. It was her second winter in northern Shaanxi; Duckweed received the pendant during the provincial meeting for agricultural-education activists from Dazhai. In a flash, her memories flood back to her. The badge had been pinned on the Red Guard uniform she'd used to cloak her poor child—her own flesh and blood, whom Duckweed wrapped tenderly before giving to her friends to abandon in the woods.

In the thrill of discovery, Duckweed grabs for the badge and turns it over. Oh! She finds a line of words: Shaanxi provincial meeting for agricultural-education activists from Dazhai, 1970.

"Don't touch that! Mom said it's Grandpa's!" Qiong Qiong resents her aunt for this intrusion.

"Let's go and find your mother, my child." Her voice trembles with delight. Pressing Qiong Qiong closer to her breast, she quickens her pace.

With Qiong Qiong's help, Duckweed finds Plantain's home and stops just outside her small room. She can hear two voices conversing, a woman's and a man's.

First, Plantain's voice pleads with Uncle Zhang: "Uncle Zhang, this must be some sort of cruel joke! A strange woman appears and declares she is my mother from who knows where, for no reason— someone I've never seen or heard of. I say, you tell her to keep her hands off me and out of my life. I'll never accept her as my mother."

Zhang is annoyed. "Nan comes all the way by air and bus to see you because she's trying to make things right. Don't you see she did this out of love? She made a mistake in the past and did not treat you well, and now she's trying to atone for what she did. Can't you see that?"

"No. I really don't see that. Can you find a drugstore where a remedy for horrible mistakes is sold? If my father had not picked me up from outside the village, I would have become a square meal for a wolf in the wilderness. Is that something she can atone for?"

"How can you say these things? How can you insult your own mother? It's a blessing to have her as a mother. Don't you see?"

"I don't care. I would happily do without that kind of blessing, if you insist on calling it that. Uncle Zhang, perhaps you want a mother like that. Tell that woman that I have only one mother, and she is in Little Clear Creek. I'd rather go begging with her my whole life, until even she pushes me away!"

"What a wild child!" wails Zhang, feeling particularly old.

"Mommy, Mommy!" cries Qiong Qiong, her little hand patting at the door.

Plantain opens the door. Nan enters, hesitant. Plantain sees Qiong Qiong in Nan's arms, and she freezes. Then she takes her child from Duckweed, yelling, "Shame on you, Qiong Qiong! How can you let your beautiful dress touch that woman's arms? You dirty-bones!"

"Plantain, please, watch your language!" Zhang tries to calm her.

Duckweed looks at Plantain, tears welling in her eyes. She says to Zhang, "Uncle Zhang, do not blame Plantain. Let her pour out her complaints at me. It will be a relief to me. No matter what insults she hurls at me, I can withstand it!"

At this gesture of calm tolerance from Nan, Plantain stands dumbfounded, speechless. Her lips tremble.

The air feels like it will explode. Zhang plays the part of a mediator, saying, "Plantain got the news just a moment ago, and she's still trying to wrap her mind around all of this. I'm sure she'll grow more comfortable with the facts in a couple of days. Am I right?"

Holding her child tightly in her arms, Plantain remains silent for a while and then releases a sudden loud cry. Duckweed, too, begins crying without restraint. Knowing that he should give these emotional women their privacy, Zhang leaves the room.

———

It's a sunny autumn day, and a golden wind caresses the faces of those outside. Nan is walking happily along a street of Good Luck Town with Qiong Qiong warm in her arms. After some shopping, Qiong Qiong has a new look. She is now a city girl, in leather shoes and smart trousers with suspenders. She clutches a piece of candy in one hand.

"Auntie, are you one of us? Are you from Good Luck Town?" she asks Nan.

"No, I'm just passing through. I leave in a couple days. Work is waiting for me in Beijing."

"Is Beijing far, far away?"

"Yes, far, far away. You'd go by plane." She looks up into the air.

"Auntie, I want to go with you. I would have a new dress and candy every day. I'd fly in the air, on an airplane!"

"Oh, now." Nan is amazed by the intensity of her feelings for this little one. Warmth permeates her body. Is this maternal love? She cannot tell. She sets Qiong Qiong down on her feet, giving the girl a gentle kiss.

Zhang catches sight of the exchange as he approaches from the other end of the street. The older man is deeply touched.

"Qiong Qiong, you are so pretty!" he says. "I almost didn't recognize you."

The child does not hide her joy at being complimented. "Auntie bought this for me. She's going to take me into the air on an airplane!"

"Qiong Qiong, you could call her 'Grandma' instead of 'Auntie.' How would you like that?"

"'Grandma'! Auntie, should I do that?"

Duckweed nods her consent slowly, a bit uneasy at the suggestion.

"Grandma." The child's voice is sweet.

The little one shakes herself free of her grandmother's hand and runs off to play.

"Perhaps I've been too self-conscious even to imagine it," says Duckweed, "but I never dreamed of having someone call me 'Grandma.' I still feel like a young girl myself—I am one in my memory, just a girl in a Red Guard uniform with two braids, jumping and laughing and playing around. It feels like just yesterday!"

"Yes," says Zhang. "But the youngest of the cadres' generation is now around forty, or fifty, or even more. And twenty-five years have passed for those who came here in the winter of 1968 or spring of '69. City people don't show their age, but those who live a country life are already clearly grandparents!"

"Aging occurs everywhere, for everyone. I'm no exception. Time and tide wait for no man!"

Hillock asks how Asiatic Plantain is doing now with the news of her birth.

Duckweed recounts for him how Plantain kept crying the previous night, saying nothing. But, Duckweed says, she recognizes that this is radical news for Plantain. She owes Plantain a great deal, and so she doesn't want to demand too much from her. Now that she has learned her grown daughter's whereabouts and has spent time with her in person, she's satisfied.

Zhang says that the news seems to have put Plantain into a state of shock. "Just give her time to get through it. Patience is your job now."

Duckweed nods her agreement.

Zhang promises that he'll go again to Pillar's in Little Clear Creek. Now that the matter is out in the open, he believes it wise to keep the couple involved—to nudge them a little bit more to his side and to secure their support.

Without wasting another second, Zhang heads off.

Plantain is waiting in front of the guesthouse, her child by her side, when Duckweed arrives.

She's still puzzled. Seeing that city woman walking toward her—who is she?—Plantain is not yet convinced that the woman known to her as "legs in flood, lips in blood" will turn out to be Qiong Qiong's grandmother. It's just too unbelievable!

The drama of city life, so remote until now, has suddenly become part of their everyday lives. Is it a mistake or a misfortune?

"Grandma!" Qiong Qiong shouts and tries to run to Nan.

Oh, let there be mercy on her—this lonely city figure in the village, Plantain thinks. She looks older these days in this small town. Her shining face is no longer shining, and wrinkles have begun to spread around her eyes. Her hair, once styled and flattering, is now covered in dust, turning gray and thinning.

"Grandma!" Qiong Qiong shouts again, and this time she is released to run from one mother to the other.

Nan picks the child up and steps forward to utter a greeting: "Plantain."

Plantain avoids Nan's eye contact. Looking down at her toes, she confesses quietly, "I'm not yet used to calling a stranger 'Mother.' May I call you 'Auntie'? Perhaps that will change sometime in the future. OK?"

"Anything is OK." Duckweed accepts without delay. She adds, "Plantain, I fell ill with a puerperal fever while giving birth to you. Now I'm unable to have any more children. But now that I've found my only daughter, I can never be lonely."

Sincerity begets sincerity. Duckweed's confession has a great effect on Plantain. She tells Duckweed that her father and mother have come, by her request, and that they are waiting in Nan's room, ready to talk with her.

"Where is your husband?" Duckweed asks.

"He's away in the army."

"Tell your father and mother that whatever they need, they should just tell me. And you, too—you should never hesitate to ask me for anything. You've suffered so much already, my dear child—"

"I'm OK," Plantain cuts in. "I have plenty of food and clothes; there's nothing else that I need. And my parents are very proud and self-reliant, so they'd never accept your offer of help, I'm afraid."

"Then will you consider leaving with me?"

"How could I, when I'm a housewife here?"

Duckweed pauses. "Would you consent to let me take Qiong Qiong with me back to Beijing?"

"Let me think it over."

"If I take Qiong Qiong to raise her, I can promise her a bright future. It's time for her to go to kindergarten. An education is so important."

Even for Good Luck Town, which has been the backdrop for many notable events, the story of Duckweed Nan and Asiatic Plantain is especially moving and unique.

Literate Li refers to it as "a trip for love." It is perhaps the most beautiful story we have ever heard.

The next day, after the Midautumn Festival, Duckweed Nan, together with her granddaughter, Qiong Qiong, prepares to leave this small town.

Around noon, the sun is shining in the bright autumn sky. A bus comes from the north, from the grassland. It stops at the town exactly where Nan got off the day she arrived.

Among the people who have come to see Duckweed Nan off are Pillar and his wife and Plantain, their daughter, in whose arms her little Qiong Qiong still rests.

Hillock Zhang, the chief mediator, is also present; under his order, his mediators stand in a ceremonious line along the road.

The bus stops. It is time to go.

Pillar lifts the big trunk and loads it onto the bus.

Wrapping her arms around Plantain's shoulders, Duckweed cannot bear to tear herself away.

The bus sounds the horn, urging the party to conclude.

"Pillar, Pillar's Wife—my brother and sister, I am grateful to you for your efforts in raising Plantain. I promise to come and see all of you often—and especially to see Plantain, my dear child."

With these words, Duckweed takes Qiong Qiong from Plantain's hands and climbs the steps onto the bus.

The bus moves forward. Plantain follows alongside it for as long as she can.

Nan waves from inside, shouting, "Plantain, believe me. I will treat Qiong Qiong as a princess for the whole world to admire. I promise you!"

A gust of wind carries her voice across the distance.

Half an hour later, when Duckweed's voice has trailed away, when the people have returned to their homes and jobs, when here again is an empty place where nothing seems to happen, two figures stand high on the terrace before the mediator's office. They are Hillock Zhang and Literate Li. The former turns to the latter.

"Now, about the age of that city woman over there, can you tell?"

Translated by Wang Hongyin

Li Tianfang

Li Tianfang is one of China's most popular authors. She is the former vice-chair of the Shaanxi Federation of Literary and Art Circles, a member of the Chinese Writers Association, the State Council allowance expert, and a part-time professor at Brown University.

Li's first publication was in *People's Literature* magazine in 1964. She has published ten collections of works that include prose, novels, short stories, essays, and journalism. She is best known for her major novel *Moon's Crater*, the prose collection *Secret*, the short story collections *Love's Unknown Number* and *Accidentally*, and the collections *Li Tianfang's Prose Selections*, *Plant a Land of Sun Flowers*, *Green Wine Glass*, *Mountain after Mountain*, *The Yan'an Essays*, and *Wild Goose Flying South*. She has won more than twenty prizes for her writing. Many of her works have been selected as required texts by primary schools, secondary schools, and universities in China, and they appear in several anthologies.

7

Li Tianfang

Love's Unknown Variable

He drifted away and back, away and back, but still he avoided falling into that bottomless, dark abyss.

He had been in this kind of coma several times before—the kind that seemed just like death—but each time he had managed to come to instead of passing away. Each time, just like now, he had lain in the hospital bed unconscious for several days. Each time he would eventually return to consciousness, would eventually stand up and return to the school, to his blackboard, and explain dual linear equations and factorization.

But this time, he worried that he would not stand up again. An exhausted and weary feeling pressed tightly on every part of his body. His left leg was numb and heavy. His left arm was numb and heavy. It seemed like these things were not his anymore. They were out of sorts, clumsy, refusing to obey their master's orders.

Ever since regaining consciousness, he had somehow known that the life in his body was coming to an end. Doctors' whispers, along with his wife's and son's sad expressions, confirmed his premonition. But even without these clues, he understood well that at his age, with his history of heart trouble and this latest stroke, it was unlikely that he'd have a full recovery. He didn't need a stethoscope to sense that his heartbeats were weak and powerless, his heart an aged, rusty clock whose pendulum was growing loose and slow.

Why didn't it stop swinging altogether? Why hadn't he died that morning, right after class, when he'd fallen in front of his alarmed students? Many stroke patients died that way, without much pain. So why did he, after lying motionless in the hospital bed for several days, stroll back into life? What was he still worried about? What did he have left to do? Was there something he didn't want to leave behind?

Doctors urged him to keep absolutely calm, urged him not to worry, not to get excited, not even to think about anything. But after returning from unconsciousness, it was hard to follow such orders. These days he couldn't help but think of long-past times.

Was he afraid to leave behind his wooden triangle ruler, his compasses, his little chalk box? It would be only natural for someone who'd devoted forty years of life to a single occupation—interesting or monotonous—to have difficulty tearing himself away from it.

Zhao Yiru was nostalgic about everything related to the school. Beginning as a village teacher when he was twenty years old, he had traveled down a long road. Though he could not say that he was proud of every step on the road, overall those steps were solid. Now, throughout the town he enjoyed a great reputation as the founder of a new way of teaching mathematics. His teaching and his scholarly research were respected by his colleagues. The year before last, at a celebration of his fortieth teaching anniversary as well as his sixtieth birthday, the education bureau chief had spoken words of high praise, saying he hoped that young teachers would follow in Zhao Yiru's footsteps, devoting love and dedication to their teaching careers.

He could be proud of some parts of his life and content with others. As an ordinary person, his upright character and diligent work had earned him honest respect and fair judgments. Weren't these good enough to comfort his old heart? Looking back, he found nothing to be ashamed of.

As for his family, he believed he had treated them well. When he was nineteen he had married a woman two years older than himself. It was not until he was forty-five that he brought his wife from their hometown to visit the school where he taught. By then she already looked like an old woman. The students were surprised. Why, they wondered, had their handsome and dignified teacher married an old village woman, one who looked like she could be his older sister?

But soon they changed their attitudes. They saw how much this elderly couple respected and loved each other. From then on, each time the school showed a movie or held a New Year's celebration or other social event, the teacher showed up with his wife; like any young couple, they sat shoulder to shoulder as they watched the movie or performance.

Their son was their true comfort. The boy's facial structure took nothing from his mother but much from his father. He had his father's long, rectangular face, deep-set eyes, and straight nose. Whenever father and son were together, other teachers would exclaim, "Look, a pair of matching figures!" Some people simply called them "Big Algebra" and "Little Algebra." The son was his father's shadow. Zhao Yiru knew that after he left this world, he would live on through his son.

He had raised his son to be an independent man. He was confident that his son would do fine in this world after the father had departed. So why did Zhao Yiru feel so worried and anxious as he lay on the hospital bed?

His eyelids were heavy; he opened his eyes with great difficulty. He gazed kindly at his son, wanting to say something; he moved his lips, but no sound came out.

Sitting by the bed, the son saw that his father was awake. He bent down hastily. "Daddy, want some water?"

Slowly his father shook his chin, which jutted out from the quilt. "Want some medicine?"

The old man shook his head again. Water and medicine did not concern him. The expression on his face showed an inner struggle. Finally he made a decision. He gazed at his son again and said, "Write . . . write a letter for Daddy. Do you . . . do you have some paper?"

His clumsy tongue made his words sound stiff, and his voice was unclear, but his son understood. The youth pulled out a notebook from his pocket and waited for his father's words.

"No. Send . . . send a telegram. A letter . . . too slow." His lips started to tremble. He tried hard to still them, shutting his eyes slightly for a moment, and then continued. "You write. Write, 'Time is up. Eager to see you . . .'"

The pen in his son's hand stopped in midair. He looked at his father, surprised. All the family members were there in the room. Whom was this telegram for?

Zhao Yiru was silent. His face had turned red; he avoided his son's gaze. Instead he looked out the hospital window, staring at a remote place. After a long time, he turned his head and answered his son's unspoken question. "To . . . to your aunt."

The son looked puzzled. As far as he knew, he didn't have an aunt. But Zhao Yiru ignored his son's confusion. He muttered the recipient's name and address, one word after another, with much difficulty. They were in his memory, the name and the address, and he could recite them without thinking, as if he used them every day. The son recorded the father's words with great care. Still, Zhao Yiru was afraid that his son would make a mistake. He asked him to read the telegram aloud, word for word. Then, with relief, he urged his son to send it out quickly.

Afterward, Zhao Yiru felt even weaker. He was tired and uncomfortable. He didn't speak or ask for anything. If someone gave him water, he drank; if someone gave him food, he ate. Other than that, he lay in bed with his eyes closed and his body still, as if he had fallen into a deep sleep. But in fact, he did not sleep at all. He opened his eyes every time there was a sound at the ward door. He stared at whoever entered. Sometimes it was his wife, sometimes his son, or sometimes just visitors to other patients in the ward. When he'd identified the visitor, he closed his eyes at once, leaving deep disappointment on his face.

On the third day after the telegram, when it was almost dark, a cool breeze blew into the ward, bringing with it the fragrance of the big mimosa tree that grew outside. Zhao Yiru, who had spent another day in despair, was extremely exhausted and had just fallen into a sound sleep.

At that moment, an old woman walked into the ward. From her expression and attire, one could see at once that she was a dignified country doctor or a country teacher. She wore clean, simple clothes, and her white hair was bound neatly at the back of her head, leaving her face looking pale and sad. She stepped into the ward without greeting anyone. She stopped just inside the door as her eyes searched the room, moving from one bed to the next until, as they settled on the corner bed, the sleeping Zhao Yiru suddenly, magically awoke. When his eyes met the woman's, he immediately sat up straight, as if he'd been electrified.

This sudden burst of life startled his son and his wife, as well as the other patients in the ward, but the old man didn't notice. Surprised and excited, he stared at the woman walking toward him. Two streams of tears ran down his face. The old woman hastened her steps. When she reached Zhao's bed, her face was also full of tears. In front of all the other patients, the two white-haired people stared at each other, shedding silent tears. They did not move for a long time.

Finally, Zhao Yiru could not hold on any longer. His body shook. He fell stiffly back onto the bed. The old woman seized his hand. She firmly held his head and slowly lowered it onto the pillow like a loving mother gently putting down her sleeping baby. With tears still on his face, Zhao Yiru fell soundly asleep. His face looked serene and satisfied. He never woke again.

The old woman looked at Zhao Yiru's face for the last time and gently covered his body with the quilt. Straightening up, she wiped her tears away, smoothed her hair, and thanked the relatives for sending her Zhao Yiru's telegram.

Then, ignoring the curious looks from Zhao Yiru's family, the old woman silently opened her cloth bundle and took out an embroidered pillow made of white satin. Carefully she put it under the head of the dead man. The snow-white pillow and the scarlet embroidery somehow bespoke a fiery youth, a pure and innocent childhood, and a binding love.

Zhao Yiru's son, both terribly sad and wholly confused, felt that he should stop this woman who was behaving so eccentrically. He looked at his mother with a question in his eyes, silently asking, do you know who this woman is?

His mother shook her head. She didn't know who the old woman was or why she had appeared at her husband's deathbed. Yet she had made a promise to her husband on one of his last nights, when all was quiet and everyone else was asleep. The old man had asked her to sit down beside him and had looked at her steadily for a long time. Then he'd said to her, "For my sake, please excuse whatever unexpected things happen at my death."

She had asked him what he meant, but the old man had offered no explanation. He had never used such an urgent tone of voice with her before, nor had he ever looked at her in such a grave way. Quietly she had promised to do as he wished; she would excuse him for whatever might happen.

The appearance of the old woman, who seemed to be about the wife's own age, shocked her and made her sad. Her heart told her to reject the old woman. Still, she felt sure that in forty years of marriage, her husband had never been unfaithful. Even at this moment she could not find fault with him. She resolved to honor her dead husband's last wish. A kind and generous woman, she accepted and forgave what was happening before her.

The old woman from afar asked that the embroidered white-satin pillow be cremated with the old man. She participated in the entire funeral and watched as Zhao Yiru's lanky figure became ashes and was put into a small, delicate case. Then, without any explanation, she quietly left.

Naturally everyone was curious. The townspeople kept talking about this rare story, speculating about what might have occurred between the two. Gradually they came to a conclusion: there must have been a grand and unusual love between Zhao Yiru and the white-haired woman. It must have begun when they were very young and been interrupted for some unknown reason. But neither time nor distance had truly separated them; an invisible thread had linked them together till the ends of their lives.

Some imagined the story in even greater detail. They hypothesized that when the love affair had ended, the two lovers had made a promise that they would see each other one more time at the very last moment of their lives. They vowed that when the first one died, the other would attend the funeral and reveal their love to family of the deceased.

This seemed far-fetched—but since no facts were forthcoming, the townspeople had only their imaginations to explain the strange events.

Many folks were upset by this rumor; they thought it showed disrespect to the dead. Besides, the story was hard to believe in light of the evidence. Everyone knew well that the math teacher, who'd been reserved and unsociable, had lived an upright life. A strict, straightforward life; even a boring one. His days had centered entirely on home and school, linking the two places as if they were points on a single line, a line that he'd traveled every day of his adult life. How could he possibly have been a participant in such a romantic story?

How could such a great love have been hidden beneath such a non-descript life, only to be revealed at the very end?

Whatever story people imagined, the answer remained out of reach. The townspeople wished they could wake up Zhao Yiru and ask him to reveal the true story. It was such a pity that he could no longer explain what had happened. Praise or censure, blame or commendation, now people would have to reach their own conclusions.

Alas, it turned out that Zhao Yiru had been an obstinate and eccentric old man. He spent his whole lifetime in front of the blackboard, solving complex and difficult mathematical equations, explaining so many X and Y values. And yet, at the end, he left the world a great, unsolved variable!

Translated by Zhang Yujin

Ye Guangqin

Ye Guangqin, born in Beijing, Manchu, studied under the Xi'an Literary Federation and became a full-time author in 1995. She worked as vice-chair of the Federation and acted as deputy secretary of the Zhouzhi County Committee, focusing on the environment and animal protection. She lived for a long time in the Old Town village, Houzhenzi, in the hinterland of the Qinling Mountains.

Ye Guangqin's major works include the novels *Inharmonious Siblings, My Pathetic Eldest Sister, Beijing Herbs, Family Photo, Inside the Gate of Heavenly Purity, Picking Mulberry Seeds, Qingmuchuan Town,* and *Snakehead Highness,* as well as the nonfiction works *Luofu River without Diaries* and *Jade Carving.* Many of her works have been adapted for film, including *Green for Go, Red for Stop; Beijing Herbs;* and *The Marriage Certificate.* Her novella *Down the Drain* won the Lu Xun Literature Prize, and *Luofu River without Diaries* won the National Minority Literature Prize.

8

Ye Guangqin

Rain: The Story of Hiroshima

1

In the apartment next door live two middle-aged sisters. The oldest sister's last name is Yamamoto; the other's is Shibata. Yamamoto is their original family name. The younger sister was married once; she kept her husband's name after they divorced. The elder sister has never married. So their mailbox at the front door is labeled Etako Yamamoto and Yoko Shibata. The characters for "Etako" (柯) and "Yoko" (榕) are not commonly used in Japanese. Once I asked them about their names; they told me they were named by their father, who was a Japanese-language teacher in middle school before World War II.

Sister Yamamoto, born in the year of the tiger (1938), is sixty-seven years of age now; sister Shibata, born in the year of the horse (1942), is sixty-three. Despite their age difference, they look alike. Each has single eyelids and a big, round, baby face. Their skin is smooth and delicate. When they were young, they must have looked like the women of beauty in traditional Japanese portraits.

But when they encounter other people, they don't act alike. Sister Shibata will stand to the side, bowing down slowly, murmuring simple pleasantries for quite some time, making you feel that you have to respond in kind and greet her with endless respect. Sister Yamamoto, on the other hand, is cool and reasonable. She bows down a little when she greets others, but with less courtesy. She speaks faster, louder, more clearly, and is never wordy or long-winded. Although she looks cool and mild tempered, she is warmhearted inside.

Every morning, when Sister Yamamoto cleans her doorsteps, she cleans mine as well. Or if I am not at home when the weather changes and it begins to rain, she brings in my clothes that are hanging in the courtyard to dry. This may be common in my home country of China, but it's rather rare in a modern Japanese city. Around here, if it begins to rain during the day and your clothes are hanging outside to dry, nobody will take them in for you. In fact, neighbors living in the same apartment building often don't know each other at all. As an old Chinese saying goes, you know the voices of the dogs and chickens next door, but you do not know the voices of the people there. So I feel lucky and honored to have neighbors as kind as these two sisters.

Yamamoto, the elder sister, likes to wear old-fashioned dresses. She favors dark-brown skirts, with coffee-colored shoes and an amber necklace. Her clothes appear somber and plain at first glance, but a closer look reveals the high quality and attention that go into her carefully selected outfits. The younger sister, Shibata, tends more toward colorful clothes, especially bright reds and greens. Sometimes she even wears sportswear, although she is over sixty years old.

Sister Yamamoto's hair, almost all white, is well combed and styled. She wears a curling ponytail at the back of her head. Sister

Shibata's hair is white with a little gray, permed short with a streak of light purple at the front. She looks somewhat amusing.

I enjoy watching the sisters when they go out in their traditional Japanese attire. If the elder sister wears a kimono the color of lotus root, embroidered with small cherry flowers, the younger sister will dress in a light-blue kimono with a grassy design. When the elder sister wears primrose yellow, the younger sister chooses light pink. As a pair they're always elegantly dressed, beautiful, and fresh look-ing, clicking through the neighborhood in their Japanese clogs. They greet everyone politely as they go on their way, smiles on their faces. They seem so stately and attractive, like immortal figures drifting down from the sky or old angels from heaven.

A thought always occurs to me when I see them passing by: I should invite the two sisters to China and introduce them to a fash-ion-design school; there they could share with the students their expertise in makeup, clothing, and color coordination. They are clearly experts.

Of course, to dress and coif yourself so well, you need money. I can only assume that the family is well off; their traditional garb and the jewels and pearls they wear must be extremely valuable.

The two sisters are entitled considerable annuities and free state-supplied medical care because they are survivors of the atomic bombs. They seem to be so strong and healthy, without any appar-ent physical maladies, year-round. Unlike me—on any given day you might find me with a cold or some stomach problem, and I do have to go to the hospital to see my doctor now and then.

When the sisters run into me around our apartments, some-times they say, "Ye-san, you need some exercise and discipline. You look great, but you are putting on some weight these days."

Their normal exercise routine is to walk their dog in the park. They have a big, gray Akita Inu dog. Tall, with two white dots at its eyebrows, it closely resembles a wolf. The sisters called it Kamo.

Kamo is a common Japanese man's name, so I assume that Kamo is a male dog.

Dogs are not allowed in this apartment community, but the managers don't do anything about Kamo because the sisters claim that he's already an "old man" and an old man has a right to live a simple and peaceful life. The apartment managers did come once to try to take the dog away. Kamo started to bark at the managers, fiercely baring his great teeth, his fur standing on end. Next door I could hear the loud, low growls from deep in the animal's throat. It sounded like he would have thrown himself upon the managers had he not been tied up with his leash. Since then, Kamo and the managers have been implacable enemies. No one else in the complex is afraid of Kamo except the managers.

One time, a manager pulled me aside to speak about the dog. "If Kamo, the alpha dog of Juniper Hill, causes any problem for you," he said, "or even just a slight inconvenience, you are entitled to my immediate response and the full support of the community office, and the sisters will be sued in court."

Our community is situated atop the beautiful Juniper Hill, with an excellent view of the western end of Hiroshima Beach. Not many Hiroshima residents are natives; most of the people in this city have migrated from elsewhere. Of course, almost all the native inhabitants of downtown Hiroshima were killed in the atomic bombings sixty years ago; very few survived the attack.

The Juniper Hill community comprises several blocks, including the beautiful white building where the sisters and I live. It was built in the late 1990s. Before that, this area was only a long, natural slope covered with juniper trees.

Most of the residents here live on the first floor. Each terrace apartment has a patio and then a small lawn outlined with an iron fence. Of course, only those of us on the first floor have the benefit of these lawns; those on the second and third floors are not so lucky.

The sisters have a nice doghouse for Kamo in the southeast corner of the lawn; he stays there quietly during the day. In the evening he moves to the patio, gazing steadily through the glass door, waiting for the sisters to take him for a walk. The sisters like to walk Kamo in the open area. This has become a routine sight in the neighborhood: the wolflike dog, his gray fur shining in the sunset, his collar attached to two leashes, one held by each sister. The dog looks big, strong, and powerful, while the sisters look slim, dainty, and well mannered. The dog and his two masters form a triangle, walking quietly and peacefully along the dam on the Ōta River plain. Neighbors and visitors often stare as they pass by.

Each sister holds a plastic bag in her hand. Yamamoto's bag contains a small shovel for collecting Kamo's waste. Shibata's bag holds a small dish, which they fill with food or water when the dog needs a rest along the way.

Kamo knows well with whom he is walking; he never runs but keeps a steady, princely pace, like a royal horse galloping in front of the palace, not walking but dancing to a rhythm. Throughout the walk, Kamo communicates his joy via his big tail, swishing and waggling it, pleasing the sisters.

The dog knows where to stop for a break and where to eat or drink—spots where the sisters can enjoy the beautiful views and the evening sunset, and where there are chairs and stone stools as well as vending machines. Kamo likes apple juice and knows which machine sells his favorite treat. There's never any doubt about it: when Kamo stops and glares at the appropriate vending machine, Shibata will draw out a ten-yen coin and put it into the slot, wait for the ding sound, draw out another ten-yen coin and again put it in and wait for the ding. She could easily find a hundred-yen coin in her purse or pocket, but she prefers to draw out the ten-yen coins one by one, sharing with Kamo the anticipation of hearing the dings accumulate. When she has paid all the requisite coins, the can of juice drops from its slot with a loud bang. Kamo then pounces, opening the small door with his mouth and gripping the can, offering it to Shibata's hand. Shibata pours the yellow juice into the small food dish, patting Kamo's head and saying, "Go for it, boy. Just what you've been waiting for."

Sometimes Shibata intentionally stops putting coins into the machine, waiting. Kamo is not stupid; he can count, and he barks once, loudly, to urge her to continue.

After the apple juice break, they continue on their way. Where to walk, where to rest, even which bushes Kamo may approach for shitting and urinating—these are all predictable features of their walk. Nothing changes.

I really admire their lifestyle and their attitude. I can't think of a single detail of their life that seems to be unsatisfactory to them. At this age, many people grow complacent and then bored. But the sisters seem to enjoy every single day. Seeing them reminds me of the TV series *The Happy Life of Bigmouth Zhang Damin*. It was based on a book by Liu Heng; I read it years ago, back in China. What is a "happy life"? Surely it is this—the life these sisters enjoy. When I am old, I can only hope to have as happy and comfortable a life as they're enjoying today. I'd count myself lucky even just to have as wonderful a dog as theirs.

The Yamamoto sisters have few relatives around. Sometimes a middle-aged man comes to visit them. He must be one of the next generation of the Yamamoto or Shibata family. In Japanese, he addresses both sisters as "Dear Mama," in a warm and affectionate way. How can I guess their relationship, when he calls them both "Mama"? Meanwhile, the two sisters address the middle-aged man as "Kamo"—the same name as their dog! "Kamo, Kamo," the sisters will say, and the man responds with a prompt and clear "Hai!" ("yes" in Japanese).

Whenever the man is visiting, Kamo the dog stays outside, lying docilely in a corner of the patio, quiet and unobtrusive.

Every time Kamo comes to visit the sisters, he always brings a large bundle of yellow daisies. Several times I've seen him just as he arrived at their door, stopping for a moment to catch his breath. Sometimes he lays the flowers on the ground while he waits for the door to open. Since it takes some time for the aging sisters to come to the door, he uses those moments to comb his hair, straighten his tie, and pick up the bundle of flowers again, arranging it carefully in his arms. When the sisters finally open the door, they're greeted with the sight of a well-dressed, handsome, and vital young man.

Kamo's visit doesn't usually last long. He may leave after just a brief chat. Sometimes he'll help the two sisters with some household chore—watering the flowers on the terrace, cleaning the yard, moving items in or out, adjusting the satellite receiver at the fence. The sisters seem to enjoy sitting on their sofa and issuing instructions: Left! Right! A little higher! He follows their orders willingly and happily.

Kamo's skin is clean and white; you can even see his blue veins underneath. Sometimes I think that if Kamo were female, he'd be a pretty lady, maybe even a TV star. But it seems that Kamo is only an ordinary worker in a large company, the type who doesn't stand out and will never rise to prominence. From his obedient, eager-to-please demeanor with the sisters, it's easy to see what role he must play at work.

These pleasant visits seem to grow increasingly rare, though. Lately there are many more times when Kamo the dog is at home and Kamo the man is not around. These days, sometimes Kamo doesn't appear for as long as one or two months; the sisters wait patiently, expectantly, for him to come. Normally they save all the difficult manual household tasks for him. But if enough time goes by without a visit, or a task requires immediate assistance, like bringing the flowerpots inside when it gets cold out, then the sisters are forced to turn to me for help. They'll nervously and politely address me as "Ye-san" and timidly ask for help, trying hard to avoid causing me any inconvenience. As for me, I'm happy for them to prevail on me as directly and frankly as they do Kamo; after all, they're as old as my eldest aunts.

I've had the chance to visit their apartment several times. Their rooms are tidy and spotlessly clean. It's the traditional Japanese custom for all tools and utensils, every vestige of daily life, to be neatly hidden away during the day. Every pillow or quilt from the nighttime is stored up on the shelves in the morning, leaving the bare tatami in a now-empty room. To all appearances, these people never sleep. Likewise in the kitchen: there are no vessels, spoons, or pans piled up; no containers of oil, salt, soy sauce, vinegar. It's so clean that you might even wonder if these people ever eat at home—or eat at all.

All these customs the sisters adhere to completely, with one exception: flowers. All over the apartment there are flowers. In the sitting room, the bedrooms, on the dining table, atop the piano, and even around the toilet, you'll find light-yellow daisies. Wherever you look, there are daisies. They even grow outside along the fence—a tiny variety, all in yellow. Linger a moment in any room and you will smell the daisy's light, fresh scent. Perhaps it's just me, but that smell always reminds me of funerals.

Still, the whole place feels cool and light. The spartan environment doesn't exactly match the sisters' elegant style in dress and appearance—but they must like it that way. In comparison, my own apartment is always in a state of chaos. The books I'm reading are scattered everywhere—next to the toilet, across the windowsill, all over the floor. Sofa cushions tossed on the tatami, dirty socks on top of the TV. My disorderly life, with not even a nod to aesthetics or propriety, is a far cry from the traditional Japanese tranquility of my neighbors.

Whenever I help the sisters with any small task, they offer me something in return as a gift. It may be some cookies or a clever toy, always well selected and dignified. Madame Yamamoto always offers me a kind suggestion or well-meaning bit of advice along with the gift. Perhaps she'll tell me that I'd look better with a particular type of makeup powder, or that my hairstyle would be more elegant if I used a pearl hair clip. I always listen attentively and follow their advice, going out to buy the powder and starting to use the hair clip with the pearl decoration. They're always surprised and delighted, enjoying my improvement and feeling satisfied that their suggestions were followed.

My husband often warns me to keep my distance from our Japanese neighbors, not to accept any gifts or advice from them. He tries to stop me from dropping by their apartment. He thinks I'm too susceptible to others and should develop my own ideas and my own judgment. He thinks it would be better for me to stay away. He'll often quote some proverb or saying that he reads in the paper. Distance makes beauty, he'll say.

I object to his suggestions and warnings; I see no harm in helping the sisters now and then. I do have my own ideas, and I am strong-minded. But I enjoy the sisters' little gifts; I find myself eager for their advice and the precious, tiny objects. I can't stop opening my hands for them. My husband is out working every day, leaving early in the morning and returning late at night, like the Japanese salarymen that he works with. I'm left alone all day in our spacious rooms. I only want some interesting and amusing way to pass the time; sitting around the house all day will make a person bored and depressed. It's good for me, I think, to have something useful to do, to help the sisters.

My Japanese visa shows that I'm an "accompanying spouse"— that is to say, a housewife. My husband is the breadwinner. My visa status does not allow me to hold a paid job; I can only stay at home, idle all day, doing nothing, like a monkey in a cage. I move, desultory, from the terrace to the sitting room, from the kitchen to the bedroom. I might eat some slices of orange or apple; have a cup of tea, a few bites of cookie; do some reading for no purpose. I'm smart and capable; I can do lots of things well—and yet I'm not allowed to do anything. You feel empty and lonely when you have nothing to do; it's a kind of sickness.

At times like this, I always think of my friends back home in China. Where are they? What are they doing? I think of my desktop computer, which I'd work at almost every day; sometimes strange words would appear after certain random keystrokes, perhaps the result of some naughty virus.

Back in China, I had my work; no matter what else I did, I was a writer. But here in Japan, unable to work, I'm nothing but a house-wife. How can this be? Even in the apartment next door, the two old sisters are busy—busier than I am, anyway. I hear their clicking clogs—going out, coming back, going out again. Apparently they have a lot to do. I know that Yamamoto is a member of the *paiju* club, and she teaches a kimono class. And Shibata is a member of the senior citizens' glee club, a council member, and on the staff of the *Housewives Salon*. The two sisters are enjoying an enriching life, and their daily appointments are well arranged, scheduled, and man-aged; they have many interests, and they enjoy their activities. How I wish I could join in their circle and team up with them. It is hard, having nothing to do.

One day I'm out on my terrace, hanging some clothes to dry, when I hear Shibata singing and Yamamoto playing the piano. Shibata's voice is clear and loud, while Yamamoto strikes the piano keys with force.

No matter wherever you may be wandering about,
There is always gathering and leaving, happiness and sorrow.
It is really a small, small world.
The small world is like a round, round circle,
So let us stretch out our hands and love each other.
The spacious sky and the far-reaching ocean
Will be resting in our heart.
Our hearts will be hosting the small world;
There is everything and a loving story.

They're singing a well-known children's song, popular in Hiroshima, called "Small, Small World." Almost everyone here seems to know it. In downtown Hiroshima, at the gate of the big SOGO department store, there is a tall clock like Big Ben. At the top of every hour, the clock clicks and rings, and toy figures come out and sing this song in chorus. A crowd often gathers to watch the mechanical performance. I don't know when it became the song of the local people, the song of Hiroshima, but whenever someone in the city feels like singing, this song is sure to be heard. Listening to "Small, Small World" as sung by the sisters, I feel like one of the enthusiastic crowd come to see the performance of the toys. I feel young and innocent, rejuvenated. I feel the tranquility of "seeing the mountain as a mountain."

Shibata sings the song repeatedly while Yamamoto accompanies her on the piano. They show no sign of tiring. I wouldn't say Shibata is a good singer; sometimes she goes off-key, and she can't quite reach the highest notes, even when she tries an awkward falsetto to get there. Also, the piano is very old and out of tune. However, I admire the attitude and spirit of the sisters; they have the courage and ambition to do what they enjoy, with no thought to how others might judge them. If it were me, I would have given up in fear that I wasn't good enough. But Shibata is Shibata: she likes to sing, and the more she does it, the more she feels like herself. She's not doing it for anyone else's sake.

At noon, after lunch, I go down to the mailbox to pick up my mail, unconsciously singing "Small, Small World" under my breath. Just then I see the sisters going out, well dressed as usual. Shibata hears me murmuring the song; she bows to me and apologizes for her loud singing earlier, which must have intruded on my quiet morning at home. I tell her no, it's OK, because I like that song. Shibata tells me that their chorus will be performing "Small, Small World," and she'll be singing in the alto section. She has to practice, as she doesn't want to make any mistakes. Without thinking about it, I ask Shibata if I could join the chorus and sing "Small, Small World" with them too. Shibata laughs. No, she tells me, because it's a senior citizens' chorus; the minimum age is fifty-five.

But Shibata says that if I'm looking for something to do, she could bring me to their kimono class, where I could learn how to wear the kimono. I tell her I'll have to check with my husband first—but I know he'll never agree to let me go to that, and I know there's no need to discuss it with him. Besides, the kimono class costs money—and I don't even have a kimono. Anyway, I tell myself, what use do I have for kimono lessons? I'm not Japanese.

Shibata nods and starts to go, but then turns back and tells me quietly, "Your red sweater doesn't go with the blue trousers you're wearing. There is a Japanese proverb: match red cloth with blue, even the dog will dislike you." I don't know what to say. At home I dress sloppily, for comfort, without giving much thought to my clothing. I've never been good at putting together stylish outfits or finding items that flatter my appearance. What's the point in paying attention to that now, when I hardly ever leave my house? Why would I spend time carefully doing my makeup in the morning, only to stay by myself all day and then wash it off again at night? Just for practice?

But then a voice in my head says, maybe just for fun, or to make yourself happy, or because you never know what will happen.

I don't know where that voice came from. But I'm starting to realize that I need to do something for myself.

2

The sisters next door are capable and indomitable. They don't fear anything—except the rain.

I've known people who were afraid of thunder, storms, strong winds, but until I met the sisters I had never known anyone who was truly afraid of rain. It doesn't matter whether it's a light drizzle or a heavy downpour; both Sister Yamamoto and Sister Shibata will be breathless, anxious, holed up in their apartment and refusing to go anywhere, even out onto their terrace. No chorus practice, no kimono class, no outside activities whatsoever. No appointment is important enough to induce them to go out in the rain. They're always telling me that, as a woman, I must be fully made-up every day, even alone at home, that it's always worthwhile to make my face beautiful. But when it rains, the sisters' faces grow dark, looking tarnished and old; they transform into tired *obasans*.

When the cherry blossoms start fading away, it will be the rainy season in Hiroshima. Then rain will fall constantly, steadily, endlessly. Our whole area, including Juniper Hill and the Seto Inland Sea Beach at the foot of the hill, will be drenched in rain. During the rainy season, it's as if the whole city is underwater. It's wet everywhere—wherever you go, whatever you touch, anything you intend to hold in your hand, it will be wet. If you don't diligently clean the surfaces in and around your home, mold will grow on everything; even the quilt that you sleep under at night will smell like mildew. You can keep your dehumidifier on all day, roaring nonstop, but it's of little use. Your skin will feel clammy and unpleasant. Even when there's a rare and brief respite you dare not open your window, or a humid wind will come blowing into your room. During the rainy season you daily feel ill at ease, upset, smothered, bad tempered for no apparent reason. The rainy season is a season of discomfort.

During this period, the sisters next door are depressed and listless. They don't come out to go shopping; they don't even take out their trash. For a whole week, I neither see nor hear any evidence of them at all. No one sings or plays "Small, Small World."

Peering from the terrace between our two apartments, I can see Kamo, their lovely dog. He's lying in his kennel, his head low and his tail even lower. There's rainwater in his bowl; his food dish is empty. His shiny gray fur has become flaxen and looks disheveled. He is quietly, halfheartedly growling. His ears are pointed back, and his eyes look watery. His small world must be sad and dreary right now.

Kamo notices me looking in his direction from my terrace and slowly, lazily wags his tail once or twice, an automatic hello. Then he puts his head back down on his paws and closes his eyes. He knows that no food is served when it rains. No going out and walking in the yard, no prancing in the open field. No apple juice. He has to endure these miseries—whether it rains for a week or even a month.

I feel sorry for Kamo. Kamo the dog, that is. He's powerless, at the mercy of the humans around him. He needs help and care. I tear off a piece of the pancake that I'm eating and toss it to him; it falls close to his kennel. He opens one eye and sees it land, but doesn't move. I throw another piece his way; this time he slowly stands up, turns around, and lies down again, now with his rear and tail to me. I go back to my kitchen, looking around. In the refrigerator I find the piece of Canton sausage that I brought back with me from China; I've been saving it for quite some time. I throw the sausage to Kamo, and it lands on his back and then rolls to the ground near the fence. This is not working as expected; Kamo is neither excited nor interested. I keep trying, over and over, until most of the food and snacks from my kitchen are strewn across the sisters' lawn. Like his masters, Kamo the dog is not coming out. All my food is arrayed on the grass like sacrificial offerings to the rain god.

I start hoping that Kamo-san, that meek man, will come soon and bring some liveliness to this stagnant scene. He can help stir the still waters here.

But Kamo—the man—doesn't come.

In the late afternoon my husband gets home from work. I tell him about my day. He looks at the yard next door and sees all the chunks of food that I threw, now soaked and swollen and rotting, transformed by the rain. He asks me to quit putting my oar in their boat. He says this is Japan, not China. Here, he says, there is always some hidden request when people communicate with each other. My husband tells me that the principle for living a peaceful life here in Japan and in other Western countries is: do not cause trouble for others. Or: mind your own business. The Chinese proverb when you have trouble, you will have kind support from all directions may be right in China, but it doesn't apply at all here in Japan. If I'm always voluntarily stretching out my hands to help others, he says, getting into other people's business, they'll lose respect for me. I'll be considered uneducated and inferior.

That night, I cannot fall asleep. I lie in bed mulling it over. Who is right? Is it better to stay away from those who may need help, in order to avoid causing trouble for them? Or, on the other hand, am I right to stretch out my hand to offer my assistance to others in a time of need? Are my actions good or bad? I don't know. Is there a way that both concepts could be integrated into one? That is, can you volunteer to help others without causing them trouble?

In the morning, my husband finds me pensive and quiet, not chatting with him as usual. He thinks that I'm unhappy, worried. So he offers me 20,000 yen in pocket money and urges me to go to Tokuyama City, west of Hiroshima, for a walk or a tour. He encourages me to go have some fun—take some pictures if I like. He reminds me that my good friend Deng Youmei used to work in Tokuyama when she was younger; I could go take some pictures for her sake.

So the next day, I go to Tokuyama as suggested. It is still raining. I agreed to go for fun and a change of pace, not to take pictures. God knows where in Tokuyama Deng Youmei used to work.

Tokuyama is just as wet as Hiroshima. I walk around, stopping to buy a beautiful dog collar from a shop near the train station. I feel pity for Kamo. He is innocent and vulnerable, left uncared for in the rain for days. Sure, he can be a handful, but he still deserves to be cared for. He deserves to be cared for by me.

Back at home, I don't want my husband to see or know about the dog collar. I carefully wrap it in paper and hide it in the bottom of a drawer. When the weather is fine again, I'll visit the sisters and give them the collar in front of Kamo. I want to let Kamo know that I have a gift for him. He is also my friend. Next time it rains, I'll send him food again; maybe this time he'll accept my offering.

At the beginning of each season, the apartment management office distributes paper bags for each household's trash. The management office posts a notice on the bulletin board, asking each family to go and get theirs at an appointed time. The bags will not be available after the scheduled distribution. There's a common house for community public gatherings, unlocked and open for scheduled activities and locked at all other times. The managers work only part-time; I assume they have other jobs as well. So at the designated time, I go to the common house to fetch the two bundles of bags for my family. The manager checks his list and crosses off my husband's name. Then he says, "Good, you're in 104—can you get the bags to 103 as well? You know, the home of the alpha dog? These bags will be mildewed if they're left in storage too long."

Four bundles of paper bags are not hard to carry. Why not? I'm about to nod and say yes, when I remember my husband's warnings: Do not cause trouble. Mind your own business. I feel confused, and I hesitate. The manager notices my delay but looks down and makes a mark on his list, murmuring, "OK, 103. It's raining, so the two obasans won't come out anyway." He puts four bundles of paper bags in my hands.

It's too late to argue or negotiate. They are in my hands, and I have to do this favor for the sisters.

Holding my umbrella, I run quickly back to our apartment unit with the four bundles of bags, trying to keep them dry. I stop at my neighbors' door and ring the bell. I'm hoping that the sisters will invite me in so I can see what they've been doing all this time while cooped up in their rooms.

After several minutes, Sister Yamamoto sees me through the video monitor and answers in a weak voice. "Is that Ye-san?"

"Yes," I answer. "The manager asked me to bring you your trash bags."

"Sorry to cause you so much trouble," Sister Yamamoto says. "Please leave them at the door. Thanks a lot."

Sister Yamamoto does not open the door. I leave the paper bags on the doorstep.

Those two bundles of paper bags are there for a whole week. I go out in the morning, and the bags are there. I go out at noon to do some shopping, and the bags are still there, untouched. The sisters have not opened their door even once. How strange!

I start to worry. Back home in China, from time to time we'd hear on the news about some old man in a foreign country who was found dead in his room after several months. The political public relations offices held them up as examples of the selfishness and lack of humanity in the capitalist countries. I don't want to see that happen in my neighborhood. I tell my husband about my worry and concern. He glares at me and angrily says that I am seriously sick. He tells me I'm watching too much negative TV.

But I care about others, I protest.

He says to me, "Do not make trouble for yourself while you're idle."

My husband has worked abroad for many years; he is cool-minded. He cares about his work and his home; he does not care about other people's business. As he always says himself: it's good to live in another culture and encounter other people, but don't get too involved. It seems that when he was working back at home in China, his coworkers put too much pressure on him to combine his work and home lives.

I say to him, "What is the meaning of life, then, if not to live together with your fellow man? You need to have relationships with other people. Care for others, and let others care for you. You can't be alone in the world, with your single window to the outside, dealing only with your wife at home and your own shoes when you walk. You have to be part of the world, and the world is other people."

He replies, "I don't want to argue with you. I don't want to play with words. You idle about at home all day; you want to argue and talk to other people just to make sure your lips still work."

Sometimes, two people get in the habit of arguing over something or even nothing as a way of amusing themselves.

The next morning, my husband gets up early and heads out to work. But he suddenly comes back in, shouting. I'm still lying lazily in bed. "Get up," he shouts from the doorway. "I see a *gang* in the morning sky!"

I know what he means. "Gang" is a slang word for "rainbow." Only those kids of the old Beijing residents, Beijing natives of our generation, call a rainbow "gang." If you say "gang" in today's Beijing, nine out of ten people won't understand you. My husband still uses all those old words and sayings; he doesn't change with the times. I don't know how he teaches his modern students at the university; sometimes I wonder if he's doing a good job.

Still in my pajamas, I rush to the terrace. From there I see, rising above the ocean, a beautiful blue sky. After endless days of rain, it is bright and clear. In the east, the morning sun emerges above a white cloud, beams of light pouring into the awakening sea. In the west, on the horizon, a vivid rainbow bridges the northern and southern sky like a colorful gate, uniting the mountain on this side and the sea on the other. The rainbow drifts with the cloud, coming closer and closer. In almost no time, the rainbow bridge is just over my head and I am under the bridge—ha! I want to shout along with my husband, for the rainbow and for the clear day.

Kamo, the dog next door, is bravely barking and barking at the rainbow. It's a rare sight, and he is overexcited. I see that our neighbors' lawn has been cleaned off; the bits of pancake and meat and other food are all gone. In Kamo's food dish there is fresh dog food.

The rainbow has faded, disappearing as quickly as it appeared. No more bridge; who knows where it goes. The big, bright sun pushes its way out of the clouds, bathing the field in splendid yellow. A light fog rises from the foot of the hill, spreading slowly and quietly along the hillside. Some kind of sesame-colored bird squeaks sharply, frightened, as if being pursued. A bushy-tailed squirrel slips down from the tree and escapes into the hedges. The cool wind blows in from the sea, bringing the salty smell of fish and brine, kissing my face and whispering in my ear like a lover. I stretch, feeling comfortable and cozy.

This will be a clear day.

I have to carry my heavy, wet quilt out and hang it to dry in the yard.

When I go out my front door to take out the trash, I meet Sister Yamamoto, cleaning her doorway. She greets me with a clear and healthy "Good morning!" Her made-up face looks fresh, and her eyes look happy. She's wearing an apricot-yellow shirt, looking like the rising morning sun. In comparison, my blue nightgown seems poor and ugly. I can't reconcile the sight of this confident, elegantly dressed lady with the image of the cowardly, disheveled, depressed obasan who stayed in her dark room for days on end. Maybe my husband is right; maybe everybody does have a private life that they never show to another living soul.

The rains are gone and it's another clear day. The sisters again return to their normal vivacious lives. They go out to walk their dog, Kamo. They go out to join their chorus and sing. They go out and participate in all their pleasant routine activities. Their small world is filled with sunshine and joy. It's as if those unhappy, tedious, tough, and disgusting rainy days never even happened.

3

Now that the long rainy season is over, hot and humid weather is on its way. Soon it will be August. Kamo, the dog next door, seems to be ill; he's not eating well. I see the sisters repeatedly squatting down at Kamo's kennel, trying to convince the dog to take his medicine, as you'd do with a small child. Over the fence, I suggest to the sisters that an injection of the medicine would be easier and save them a lot of trouble.

Sister Yamamoto, busy dealing with Kamo, doesn't reply. Sister Shibata comes over to me and says, "It's not medicine; it's only some nutritional fluid for dogs. Kamo is not sick, he's just getting old; today he lost another tooth. You know, in human years he's more than eighty years old."

Oh. Kamo is becoming a dog with no teeth.

Shibata turns back and looks at the dog, who seems tired and listless. She says that even though Kamo isn't eating anymore, he is happy.

"Yes," I say, "Kamo must be happy."

August 6 is the memorial of the atomic bombings in Hiroshima. Five-color paper-crane decorations hang over all the doorways, in memory of the event. I'm too shy to ask the sisters about the relatives and close friends they must have lost that day. It's an intensely private issue; I don't want to bring them pain. I would never ask unless they were openly willing and wanted to talk about it. But from their active, engaged attitude toward life, it's obvious that they weren't much affected.

Some families hang a national flag on their door. In the Guotai Temple Cemetery near our community, fresh flowers are placed on the ground. Countless people come to pay their respects and mourn their beloved. The tolling of a melodious bell can be heard all around the temple area. Bundles of flowers appear along the roadside, atop the river dam, and in the corners of the walls.

All these memories of the dead. Memories of the day sixty years ago when more than 140,000 people died from the atomic bombing and nuclear fallout. The torch built after the war, to keep the flame of peace alive, still burns behind the monument. It is said that the flame shall be kept burning until there are no more nuclear weapons in the world.

On TV there are continuous reports and interviews as well as live coverage of the memorial ceremony at the Peace Square. They broadcast the story of Sadako, a young girl who died several years after the bombings because of leukemia from the radiation. During her treatment in the hospital, her friend told her that if you make a thousand paper cranes, your wish comes true. Sadako used all the medicine-packing paper she could find to make hundreds of tiny paper cranes, praying for peace and health. She made 664 cranes before she died. Those little paper cranes were perfect and elegant, each only half the size of a fingernail. The story celebrates the power and determination of that little girl.

Early in the morning, the two sisters, both wearing their beautiful black kimonos embroidered with waterbirds, start walking toward the square to take part in the gatherings. Each carries a large folder and writing pad; they plan to invite everyone they pass to sign a petition in protest of nuclear weapons. Because I'm the first person they see as they head out, I am lucky enough to be the first one invited to sign. Looking into their sincere and confident faces, I have no reason not to sign my name. I'm certain that everyone they approach will gladly sign as well.

Again my husband scolds me, arguing that I should never sign such a document. My status here in Japan is that of an accompanying spouse, he reminds me, a foreigner who must not involve herself in national politics—and that includes signing a petition.

"But what if I already signed?" I ask. "Should I report myself to someone?"

"If you already signed, then you've violated the law of the National Immigration Bureau," he tells me. "You could one day be expelled from the country."

Expel me. Expel me from this country. Do it now. Surely someone else is eagerly awaiting a visa to come here; myself, I'd just as soon leave.

He replies, "Why don't you think of it in another way? If there had been no atomic bombing, if those one hundred forty thousand people had not been sacrificed, how would World War II ever have ended? If those thousands of deaths hadn't happened, how many times more Chinese, and people from other war-torn countries, would have had to be killed before the war ended?" He shakes his head. "They say you are stupid and silly, that you can't think for yourself. I'm starting to believe it. How is it that you're a senior council member of the Writers Confederation? How can you even be a so-called writer, with so little achievement or understanding?"

I tell him that the Writers Confederation aims to stop the use of atomic bombs in the world. "We cannot allow atomic bombs," I argue with him, "at any time, anywhere in the world."

My husband is angry now. He starts to shout at me: "Go away, you silly old lady. You can't change the meaning of things! You're talking nonsense. You're no different from the crazy sisters next door! You are ugly."

That night, still angry, I refuse to cook dinner for him. In the end, we both go out to a nearby restaurant. Eyeing a large, well-cooked prawn, fried to a golden yellow, my husband suddenly says, "Today is the Hiroshima memorial, when the locals remember the sad sufferings of their loved ones. How can you eat these nice, well-cooked prawns and have such a good appetite? How can that be?"

I stare at him for a minute and then pick up the large prawn and put it in my mouth, eating it whole.

———

Midnight, August 6, it starts to rain—heavily, a cloudburst.

A strong windstorm rises up; rain pours into the yard and the house. The windows shudder and even the window frames begin to tremble. The curtains inside seem to inhale and exhale. Large white birds struggle hard against the window. Cold raindrops begin to pour inside the house. It's pitch dark outside. I can hear nothing but the roaring sound of the storm: the falling rain, the raging winds, the ocean waves crashing against the rocks on the shore. The chorus crescendos, and the sound grows strange and monstrous. Huaaa, the rain falls, hitting the tree leaves. Huuuu, the wind rolls, roaring and crawling along the cliff of the mountain. Shuaaa, the waves crash and roar from the dark sea, attacking the shore. Everything that can move is moving. Kooong, looong, a series of thunderclaps come after the lightning. I imagine thousands of horses and warriors in the ancient battlefield of the dark valley, pale and ghastly lightning revealing the roaring woods. I see the yielding trees struggling in the blowing rainfall, the billowing curtains of seawater and the mysterious mist fleetingly visible in the lightning. Hoolaa . . . hoolaa . . . hoolaaaaa . . . It seems like the whole world will be swallowed up in an enormous vortex, like the Bermuda Triangle, with no way to escape.

I believe that right now everybody in Hiroshima is awake and awaiting the end of the storm and the coming of the morning sun. Nobody but a fool would be asleep. Nobody is laughing or talking. We are all praying and worrying for the outcome. Here on Jupiter Hill, we all fear that the hill might crack and crash in suddenly, and the stone and mud will all be washed away to the deep ocean gulf.

All of a sudden the storm stops. There's a quiet moment—almost stagnant. Absolute emptiness; no one even breathes. And then here it comes again: hoolaa . . . hoolaa . . . even stronger than before.

I can hear, between the gusts of wind and crashes of waves, the sound of my husband sleeping, his deep breathing and snoring. He is sound asleep. You could carry him to the shore and throw him into the rolling sea, against the waves; still he would sleep.

When I look at the curtains, I suddenly think of the window: Did I leave it open? I'd better go check! Then I remember my washed clothes hanging in the yard. Nobody has been out to gather them in. I try to awaken my husband. Wearily he murmurs, "What the hell are you doing now?"

I say, "The sky is falling down on us."

"That's OK," he mutters. "Don't worry. If the sky is falling down on us, the third floor will catch it. You don't have to worry about it." He tells me he's been awake the whole time, through the lightning and the stormy night. He's been thinking hard about his students' essays and their homework, he says. He's not asleep at all.

I ask him to go out and help bring in the clothes hanging in the yard.

He says, "Leave it wet, since it's wet already. Why should we bother to bring them in? Leave them in the rain."

Soon after this conversation, I hear his snoring again. He must be thinking very deeply about those essays. I walk to the gate of the terrace and find that the clothes I hung out in the meadow yesterday are all gone. Who knows where they are now, blown away by the windstorm.

A moving spot of light catches my eye; it's from a flashlight next door. Turning in that direction, I see the two sisters busily working in their yard—in the midst of this terrible stormy night! Are they out there digging for treasure?

I sense a new writing project welling up in me; there's a story to be written here. It reminds me of the murder scenes from various TV shows: the old woman, nervous and afraid of the rain, hurriedly laboring in the dark night, fighting against the thunderstorm . . .

The next morning, I get up early. I learn from the sisters that Kamo passed away in the night. At night we experience great difficulties.

The door of the sisters' apartment is left wide open so that Kamo's soul and spirit may go freely to where it belongs. The sisters dress in traditional funeral attire: black skirts and tops, long necklaces of black pearls. Their clothes are clean and light; they mourn their dog just as fully as you'd mourn a human relative.

Kamo was my friend, too. So I go out and buy a bouquet of flowers for the sisters, to pay my condolences for their sad loss. A beloved animal and a longtime companion has passed away; they must be very sad and in low spirits.

Since the door is open, I enter their apartment with the bundle of flowers. I see the body of Kamo, dressed officially, lying in the center of the sitting room. His fur has been recently washed and cleaned, dried with the hair dryer. His body is covered with a small blanket. Sister Yamamoto and Sister Shibata are sitting on each side of Kamo, quiet and solemn. But they look calm, not distressed and mournful as I had imagined.

Sister Yamamoto accepts my flowers and places them near Kamo's head. Sister Shibata tells me that the people from the funeral home will be there soon; the body of Kamo shall be given to them for proper treatment. That is more appropriate, she says.

I dare not ask them what kind of funeral home it is—a funeral home for humans or for animals? Pets are very popular in Japan; when a pet dies, there are special organizations to handle the remains. You can't simply throw the dead body in the trash can.

Since I've come to pay my condolences to Kamo, that lovely dog, I should say something—to him and to the sisters. I offer some kind words about him, his beauty and talents. The two sisters smile at me silently while I murmur my praise for Kamo. Then I say that perhaps they will someday find another Akita Inu dog to love. I say that Akitas like Kamo are clever, smart, and faithful. The sisters sit still, not saying a word.

The vehicle comes at noon. Kamo's body is put into a small wooden box and carried out to the vehicle; the kennel and the plastic food dish go with him as well. Now Kamo is gone, as if he disappeared into thin air. He enjoyed his long, lovely life, and then one morning it vanished, simply and without leaving a trace, quietly, as if it never existed. But I do feel and taste something palpable from his passing, something light and ineffable; the loss is there, but you can't touch it. It's hard to describe.

My heart feels empty. It's strange to stand there on the terrace, looking at the neighboring yard, green and also empty. Kamo is not there. The lawn is still there, but now the southeast corner is vacant. Only the green grass, swaying in the breeze, quivers slightly with life. The sky overhead is blue and clean; white clouds float along, going somewhere. The sea, reaching far from the hillside, rolls its waves in mist. The bright white sun comes to shine over the land, dazzling. I smell the tempting, appetizing scent of fried garlic coming from someone's kitchen.

I think, this is life, and life goes on with time.

Time flies.

4

After the heavy storm that day and night and the death of Kamo the dog, the flowers and bushes next door become withered. It is high time for Kamo the pale-faced young man to come see the sisters. But still he does not come. I wait for the sisters to call me for help moving their flowerpots, as the days are getting short and cold. But they do not call, either.

The year's end has arrived. Both Sister Yamamoto and Sister Shibata are getting busier by the day. They study in an Esperanto class two half days a week. The class is held in a study center at Hiroshima Station; they go there by bus. I don't really understand what Esperanto is, nor what it's used for. It is said to be an artificial language (but aren't all languages man-made and artificial?) invented by a doctor in Poland, intended to be scientific, systematic, easy to learn and understand. Apparently there are Esperanto associations throughout the world, bringing people together to communicate in a single language. It's a new and largely unknown language. I have no personal interest in learning it or helping it take hold. However, the sisters next door are learning it; they have the courage and patience to do so. They have the ambition and curiosity for it—and for many new things. Sometimes I feel that they're living a most precious life. They are extraordinary.

When you live with the extraordinary as your next-door neighbors, seeing them almost every day, you may start to feel a little scared.

One day, out of curiosity, I approach the sisters and ask them if Esperanto is easy to learn. Sister Yamamoto says yes, it is simple and easy. Sister Shibata says it is interesting. I ask them how to say "atomic bomb" in Esperanto. Yamamoto says, "*Pahung.*" Shibata also says, "Pahung."

Uncertain, I say, "It is pahung?"

They both say, "Yes, it is pahung."

The younger sister adds, "Pa means flash of lightning and hung means explosion."

At the time, I think that they're kidding, making fun of me. Two years later, I will have the chance to visit the United States of America and meet a professor who teaches Esperanto in a university. I will ask him for the pronunciation of "atomic bomb" in Esperanto, and he will tell me clearly that it is pronounced "pahung." I will know then that the sisters were serious.

But today, they try to convince me to come to the Esperanto class with them. I say that I can't even manage to learn Japanese well while living in Japan. Esperanto will have to wait; I can't use Esperanto to buy cabbage at the Juniper Hill market.

Increasingly I start hearing the sisters working hard to memorize the Esperanto vocabulary. Auto, *naiwude, shisise* . . . It sounds strange and funny to my ears. The two sisters even write letters to each other in Esperanto, and then seriously go to the post office and mail them! They collect the letters they receive from each other, mailed from and dispatched to the very same address. Each sister dutifully replies to the letters she receives, all in order to practice this made-up language. I start to worry that I'll receive a letter in Esperanto as well.

The Japanese are always busy during the year-end period. One of the major projects that keeps them busy is writing celebratory greeting cards to friends and relatives. They bring their piles of New Year's cards to the post office, and the post office distributes the cards on New Year's Day, beginning in the early morning. Nearly every household receives bundles of New Year's cards. The more cards you receive, the more popular you appear to others and the better your reputation among the neighborhood.

The other project at this time of year is preparing New Year's presents. These presents, known as "New Year celebration gifts," are usually given to close relatives or friends. No matter how far away, the shop owners are responsible for delivering the gifts to the recipients. Most shop owners hire temporary staff at this time of year to help handle the deliveries. They drive to the recipient's home and call his or her name out loud, ostentatiously, thereby boosting the recipient's status.

The sisters usually send New Year's cards to each other via the post office. They send New Year's gifts to each other, too. Yamamoto will call a shop to deliver one box of golden fish cake, addressed to Shibata. A few days later, Shibata will call for a package of mountain mushroom to be delivered to Yamamoto. I call the shop to deliver a beautiful handkerchief to each of the sisters, but shipped as two separate gifts, at different times. In return for my gifts, I receive their reward, a beautiful skirt made of wool.

My husband says that we're living right next door—we don't need to play games like children, just for amusement. I say, what's wrong with amusement? It's our life; we ought to make it more vivid and exciting.

My husband says this is not a project for busy people; it's for idlers who have no real work to do.

And I say, who will care for others, if not idlers?

There's another traditional Japanese custom that people follow at this time of year. Families who experienced bereavement at any time during the year are not supposed to receive any New Year's greetings. They notify all their friends and relatives so that they don't receive any cards.

Two days before Christmas, the sisters order a beautiful Christmas tree; they ask the flower shop to deliver it to their door. They plant the Christmas tree in the middle of the lawn, covering nearly a third of the outdoor space. They'd originally planned to plant the tree in a pot in their sitting room, but because the room is so small and the space under the ceiling so low, they decided to plant it outdoors. Now the sisters have a lot of work to do, going in and out of the house, decorating the tree and buying fancy and unique toys. They are so excited and happy. They spend most of their daytime hours arranging the small objects perfectly on the Christmas tree. In most families, this is the work of the children. The sisters seem to enjoy it, the ongoing reminder of the importance of the holiday, the fun of the decorating.

I ask them over the fence whether they're planning to host a big Christmas party at home. Sister Shibata answers yes. She says that they hope I can join them for the party, and she asks if I might help them make Chinese jiaozi, dumplings, for their guests as the main dish. Sister Yamamoto quickly brings a pen and writing pad and asks me to write the shopping list for them so that they can prepare the necessary wheat flour, meat, vegetables, and seasonings. I say that I will prepare and bring jiaozi as my donation and gift to the guests. The sisters are so happy and excited, clapping their hands like children.

———

It's Christmas Day. In the morning, I go out to buy two heads of cabbage and a kilo of minced meat. On the way back, walking up the slope, I meet with the postman, heading toward our building. We know each other; he's learning Chinese in a language class downtown and is always eager to practice his Chinese with me. He says, in Chinese, that there is a letter for me and also a postcard for my next-door neighbors. While he talks, he hands me the letter. I take it from him and see the clean white postcard for my neighbors. The message, printed in size-three bold black characters, reads clearly:

Due to the sad and sorrowful bereavement over the loss of our loved one this year, we regret that we will not send New Year's greeting cards to you. Please accept our apologies.

And beneath that, in smaller characters:

Our elder son, Kamo (aged 43), passed away in May this year. We appreciate and give our hearty thanks to all for the kindness and generous help offered to him while he was with us. We remain in prayer. Please accept our best wishes and may God bless you.

Heisei, Year 14, December

The card is signed:

Shibata

Kamo. Kamo. Is that the man Kamo, who used to come often to help the sisters?

The postman points at the postcard and says in Chinese: "Letter for master. Death of the sun."

I tell him, it is not the master—this letter is from her husband. And it's not "sun," but "son"; it says that her son, Kamo, died.

The postman nods and says, "Yes, her son, Kamo."

He tries to pronounce the Chinese "er" (兒) for son, but he always pronounces it "e." I have no time to care about that. I just want to ask him for sure: whose son?

He says, "Obasan."

"Please speak in Chinese," I say. "Which obasan do you mean?"

He shows me the postcard and points at the two Chinese characters there: Shibata (柴田). He clears his throat, stammers several times; he still cannot speak out the family name of Shibata in Chinese. Finally, he switches to Japanese. He says, "It is Sister Shibata's son, Kamo. He died of leukemia."

Suddenly my head feels numb. No wonder Kamo hasn't come around for the last six months or so. He died last May of leukemia. I can't help but think of the sisters—how brave and strong they are! Although they endured such enormous misfortune and unbearable sorrow, they remained so steady, calm, and quiet. They're like a silent stream drifting downhill; undercurrents and eddies, ups and downs, flow beneath the happy surface. From above, no spray arises; all appears calm and even. What strong characters they must have to act like this; how tough and stoic they must be. These happy sisters, enduring such a heavy burden on their shoulders, and yet they stand straight as the juniper tree, not bending a bit. Even now they are preparing for their Christmas party, inviting relatives and friends to come over and enjoy.

For the whole morning, I'm overcome with emotion; for the whole afternoon, I cannot calm down, my heart beating fast and sorrow in my throat. I think of Kamo, the pale young man. He was the son of Sister Shibata and he died before his mother. At her age, she lost her son. His grieving mother who is busy preparing for the Christmas party. Busy and walking about in the yard, smiling contentedly . . .

I begin to think about myself. Several years ago, back home in China, I had work-related conflicts and thought I was misunderstood; I even cried about it in front of several officemates. Upset and angry because I hadn't been treated well, I seriously considered suicide. How impetuous I was.

The Christmas party at Sister Shibata's house is good. Almost all the participants are elderly natives of Hiroshima. They are recognized at the national level as treasures in this city. These old men and women have come from all over the city to attend this party. It could not have been easy for them to come. Sister Shibata tells me that they organize a party like this every year, and each year, the number of participants grows smaller. These people are the stars in the sky, but they are falling down one by one. And today all these shining stars are gathering at Juniper Hill.

From all the way at the bottom of the hill you can see the twinkling lights of the Christmas tree. But here in the sisters' apartment, more stars shine. These are the stars that survived the atomic bombing sixty years ago. They are still alive.

The guests prove to be very talkative, happy and at ease. As the old proverb says, dew is water that survives the ocean. This group of people endured the miseries of Hell, fighting against the devils, escaping and surviving so many disasters. And yet, deep in their hearts, they are happy. They deserve the enjoyment of a happy life every day.

I'm working busily in my kitchen, preparing the minced meat and vegetables for the Chinese jiaozi. Sister Yamamoto has sent one old woman named Uchida to help me. Yamamoto tells me that Uchida has visited China before, so she must know how to cook Chinese jiaozi. But Uchida, this old woman who had jiaozi years ago once, has no idea how jiaozi are made, how to put the filling into the dumplings. She can keep me company, but she can't help, because she doesn't know what to do.

So Uchida stands by my side, talking to me. She says she was Yamamoto's schoolmate when they were in senior high school. On the very day of the bombing, she and Yamamoto were together. The two were best friends; they shared the misfortunes and disaster, and together they survived the atomic bombing. She married four times in her life, Uchida tells me, so she has five family names. "Uchida" is the name of her last husband's family. Her marriage is complicated and miserable, she says. Uchida tells me that women who survived the A-bombing could never have a good marriage.

I try to change the subject and ask about my neighbors, the sisters. She says that the sisters have experienced similar misfortune, if maybe a bit less than her own.

5

It was the evening of August 5, 1945. The dreadful alarm horn went on the whole evening. After a quick supper, all the people fled to the air-raid shelters.

It was August in Hiroshima, so it was stuffy and humid. The air inside the bunkers was no good at all—stuffy, hot, humid, moldy. People had to crowd on the wet floor in the cavelike shelters, hoping for the alarm to cease. Everyone wanted to go home and take a shower and rest. The morning of August 6 arrived, and the air-raid alarm finally ended. People started to head home, sweaty and tired. Years of continuous war had brought the whole country of Japan into profound poverty and exhaustion; the feeling of war weariness was their constant companion. It was hard, not knowing when the war would end or what the outcome would be.

Hiroshima was home to the most important military base in Japan during the war period. Etajima Island in the Seto Inland Sea was the command center of the Japanese Royal Navy. The military factories and shipbuilding factories in Hiroshima were the backbone of military logistics and weapons supplies. Ujina Port served as the launching site of the Japanese forces; from there Japan could invade the Chinese mainland. Thousands of Japanese soldiers boarded military boats, fully armed, and traveled across the Japanese sea to fight for the emperor and for their so-called East Asia Prosperity Plan.

Meanwhile, thousands of bodies of soldiers who'd died in the war, their bone ashes packed in white cloth, were shipped back via Ujina Port to their final destinations, their family homes. The local residents were used to the quiet parade of grieving relatives walking to the cemetery, the familiar white packages in their arms, containing the remains of their husbands or sons.

August 6 was a bright, clear day—blue sky with few clouds overhead. The Japanese call this a very fine day, or great fine day—just like the term in Chinese for a bright, clear day after snow. But that early morning, the weather was already hot. You'd be sweating after just a few steps in the open air.

The Yamamoto family left the shelter, heading for home. Father Yamamoto looked at the blue sky above and said, "No rain. Even a little rain would cool us off." He turned back and looked at his wife and at his daughter Etako. Etako smiled at her father, saying nothing. Father Yamamoto waved at them, paused for a moment, and then started making his way toward the station. He was going downtown, where he was a teacher in a middle school. Etako's mother, watching him leave, said her usual good-bye: "We'll be waiting for you to come home soon."

Etako was in senior high school. She would graduate soon. Today she looked forward to seeing her friend, getting together after school to do their homework and get some exercise. In her small handbag, there was a lunch box with some food that her mother had made for her the night before. The rice was a little bit rotten and had a bad smell. Etako dared not complain to her mother about it; she knew their rationed food was limited.

Her mother had packed the rice and green beans for Etako because the girl had physical labor to do today. Etako and her classmates had been busy working for some months already, disassembling and clearing away damaged houses. It was very hard and dirty work. They were asked to dismantle the easily flammable buildings and remove the furniture in order to avoid large-scale fires during the air raids. All this work was organized by the urban Hiroshima schools and carried out by the students. It was all done for no pay—no compensation whatsoever. Everybody was working while half-starving. The students talked about little else but food.

After saying good-bye to Etako for the day, Mother Yamamoto held her younger daughter, Yoko, in her arms and began to make her way home. Yoko had been sick with fever the night before and had cried throughout the night. Mother had to go find some medicine for her.

The family had stayed in the air-raid shelter for only a short time, but in Etako's memory, it had been a terribly long time since they'd had any fun together. As an adult, when Etako thought of her family, her father, she remembered the vision of the air-raid shelter where they had stayed that morning. But for young Etako, the schoolgirl, it was a large family gathering that was recorded in her memory—a gathering in a place with a beautiful view and the feeling that nothing would ever change.

Etako and her classmate Uchida were assigned to go to the western region of Hiroshima and clean the dismantled houses there. She remembers it vividly even now. It was just after eight o'clock. She and her classmates arrived at the work site. Nearby there was a trolley-bus station where they could go to get some drinking water. The big clock in the station lounge was just striking eight. A trolley bus rushed into the station, full of commuters crowded onto the bus, impatient to get to work. The captain, standing at the back of the platform, blew his copper whistle loudly, warning the passengers to stand back.

Etako and her classmates finished their water and were about to leave the station when they heard an approaching fighter plane overhead. It was a B-29 bomber. Etako could tell it easily from its roaring sound. Because air raids were common at any time of day, the residents of Hiroshima had become experts in recognizing the planes flying overhead. They didn't need to look up, only to listen; their ears could tell the type and model of every plane. Uchida stood at the station platform, pointing to the sky and shouting to her classmates: "Look, it's the B-29 transformer flight. It's coming again."

Everybody stopped what they were doing and looked up into the blue sky. There were two big bomber planes flying over the city of Hiroshima from east to west. The silver planes were dazzling, almost too bright to look at in the morning sunlight. Everything was in mist. The students launched into discussions of where the planes had come from and where they might be going.

Bang! Suddenly a loud, heavy sound and a flash, a white flash of lightning. And there, rising in the sky, another sun, much bigger and more powerful, shining far too brightly over all the construction and the buildings, and then fading away from view. The students automatically covered their eyes with their hands. The flash was so bright and strong that it left them shaking, cold, on that August morning. It was a cold that penetrated their skin, sunk into their bones. That froze them.

Then they heard a shocking sound coming from the sky: a colossal explosion followed by a gigantic, black cloud. A wave of solid heat shot at them, a burning wave overwhelming their bodies, their senses. Blisters rose instantly on their arms, faces, bodies—and then the skin started peeling. Hardened and burned. You could see clothes on fire in the flaming smoke.

They were all in shock. They wanted to shout in pain, in terror, but the scene was silent. Their throats and their lungs were filled up with burning heat. The cloud exploded, grew exponentially, a giant mushroom. The fire-wind blew strong and hard, bearing down with unimaginable power, knocking down every building, every tree, everything that had been standing just minutes ago. They were all on fire, the city was on fire, everything . . .

Etako and her classmate Uchida were thrown down into a small drainage ditch under the side steps, and then the walls of the ditch collapsed on top of them. Deadly pieces of the station wall began raining down over them. They held each other tight, listening to the crashing sounds around them. They felt the trembling of the ground underneath them. They didn't know if they were still alive or dead or in a nightmare, dreaming. Solid items were flying about over their heads. Shards of broken glass flew through the air like arrows, piercing everything in their path.

The two girls lay still in the ditch, their eyes closed, holding their breath. They felt like they were falling into a deep abyss, an underworld where menacing devils and beasts howled and growled, huge boulders rolling and slamming each other. They knew for sure that whatever was happening was unlike anything that had ever happened before in this life.

About forty minutes passed. They were awake. Alive. They struggled to crawl up from the ditch, seriously burned, wounded, blood on their arms and legs. They came up from that underworld to find that the world had entirely changed. Everything was different. All their classmates—everyone who'd remained above ground in the open square where they themselves had stood—those people were all burned to death, unrecognizable in their appearance and shape. Some had been killed by the flying glass-shard arrows, some hit by pieces of the building turned into jagged missiles. A few still writhed on the ground, struggling for their last breaths.

Burnt earth was exposed to them as far as their eyes could reach. No buildings remained standing. The trolley bus that had pulled into the station just before the bombing was now only an iron frame. None of its passengers had survived. The copper whistle that the captain had used to command attention was now a sharp copper slice, embedded in a piece of tile on the crumbled station roof.

The skin of Etako's arm came apart, the bleeding flesh sliced, exposed. It felt so alien that it wasn't painful at all. She wanted to go and look for her teacher; she wanted to ask the teacher for permission to go home at once to see her mother and her little sister. She couldn't find her teacher anywhere, only his wire eyeglasses frames, twisted into a curving shape, lying on the ground.

Etako's home was in Yokogawa, just a few blocks away. She tried to run toward her home. On her way she saw many, many dead bodies floating in the Yokogawa River. Many heavily wounded people were running about, not knowing where to go for safety. Their eyes looked straight ahead, not thinking, only running, struggling.

And then, from a distance, Etako saw her home. It was no longer a home, only a pile of broken bricks and gravel. She ran toward it, the heap of smoking rubble. She fell upon it and tried to dig hard into the bricks with her bleeding hands, looking for anything recognizable.

At the spot where the kitchen might have been, she found the body of her mother. She'd been killed by a large, black pole that had fallen on the house; her cooking scoop was still in her hand. Her head had been hit directly by the heavy pole, breaking her skull to pieces. Her face was not there, not in any identifiable form. Her body was still slightly warm and soft. Etako gently shook her mother's body, trying to awaken her from her deep sleep. Numb, in shock, Etako told her mother that she must wake up to care for little Yoko. If mother died, who would take care of her sister? And who would take care of her father? Her mother's body was perched in a crawling position, arms splayed unnaturally. Etako tugged hard on her mother's arms and legs, trying to help her into a more comfortable position. But she was unable to do so amid the rubble, and so her mother remained as she'd fallen.

Etako found Yoko, her little sister, at the hinge of their gate; she was alive. When the shock wave had struck the house, their Akita Inu dog, named Kamo, had stood over Yoko to block her from the shrapnel and debris. As he stood protecting the little girl, Kamo's body was punched through with shards of broken glass. He didn't look like a dog; he looked like a large wound. Later, when they cleared the site and removed Kamo's body, they found that one large shard of glass had pierced his heart.

Etako held her younger sister, Yoko, tightly in her arms, sitting by their mother's side. She wanted to cry, but no sound came from her throat.

That afternoon, it started to rain—heavy, black rain. Down with the raindrops came all the dirt and dust that had been forced up into the air during the shock. Everywhere the air smelled burnt. It was as if a huge, black pan lid covered the whole city of Hiroshima.

The black rain washed Etako and her younger sister until they were completely drenched. They had nowhere to go, nowhere to hide from the black rain. They did not even try to evade it, allowing the rainwater to flow down their limbs and bodies, down their faces. Yoko was too nervous and frightened to cry; she held tightly to her elder sister's neck, wanting to never let go.

Dark, black clouds hung above the scorched ground washed by black rain. Every house was reduced to piles of brick and rubble. There were a few people digging into the piles, looking for their relatives or their belongings, for anything they might be able to find. The rain continued to fall, pouring down from the sky. The heat of the rain hitting ash created smoke where it fell. Ugly water blisters mushroomed here and there on the ground. Black rain ran down along the damaged buildings, leaving black slashes across the once-white walls. Etako looked at the black smears, feeling sad and hopeless.

Her whole world had suddenly changed. What had happened? What would happen now? No one could say for sure. She felt the weight on her back and shoulders: her younger sister, Yoko, was lying quietly now on Etako's back, black rainwater dripping from her face onto Etako's neck, cold and itchy. After quite some time, Yoko put out her little finger and pointed to the black marks down the wall. In a childish murmur she said, "Rain, rain, black rain, Yoko is afraid of the rain . . ."

Etako and Yoko rested at the remains of their damaged house, sitting there listlessly and waiting for their father to come home. The black rain, after falling heavily and fast, stopped suddenly without warning. After the rain, the sun came out again. It was another sunny morning in Hiroshima. But Hiroshima was no longer there.

Yamamoto Etako was no longer there, either—at least, not as she had been before that morning. Long after the event, Etako learned that the black rainfall, although it hadn't lasted very long, had caused the survivors lifelong injury; deadly injury. This rain would cause them endless pain thereafter.

Etako and Yoko have been afraid of rain ever since.

Their father never did return home; he was gone forever. He had been teaching in his school downtown. The bomb exploded in the air 577 meters above his head. The temperature at the center of the explosion was over 6,000 degrees; at that temperature everything evaporates, leaving only a trace of ash and dust behind.

And so Etako assumed the responsibility of taking care of her sister. They lived in the temporary tent encampment built for the survivors. At the remains of their house, she found the tiny yellow daisy flowers that were the first plants to grow after the bombing of Hiroshima. The daisies struggled their way from the broken bricks and ash, weak and sickly flower buds reaching for the breeze. Days later, the flowers blossomed in the field, viable, fresh, and beautiful. Soon after, in the shade of their wall another daisy flower blossomed. Then another near the wall with the black rainwater marks.

She had wanted to get married, with her younger sister accompanying her. But Etako's blood was found to have been affected by the radiation from the bomb. There were obvious changes in it, and her health would always be in question. Yoko, however, seemed to remain healthy; no abnormalities were found after several medical checks. The sisters appreciated this blessing of God over their family. It was a miracle of life: not everyone who survived the disaster would turn out to be sick.

In honor of Kamo, their brave dog who'd saved Yoko during the bombing, they started to raise a second Kamo—and then after him, a third. They raised one Kamo after another; the dogs had become a constant part of their life together.

Yoko grew up and got married. The man's family was wary of his deciding to marry a Hiroshima girl, a survivor of the bombing. Yoko had had to provide them with all the documents and medical reports, had endured all the strict examinations and evaluations. In Etako's eyes the scrutiny had been an insult to her family's dignity. But for the sake of Yoko's happiness and her future, they allowed it.

Yoko got married joyfully. She left the family and moved to her new home in Nagoya with her new husband. She was married to an honest and dependable man. Shibata Shoji was a bus driver, a man of duty. He and Yoko came frequently to Hiroshima to visit Etako. Shibata was kindhearted and easygoing. Two years later, their son was born; they named him Kamo. The infant was found to have some blood abnormalities and was eventually diagnosed with leukemia. Throughout his childhood he was often sickly and was frequently in the hospital. The medical reports said that Kamo was sick because of his mother's radiation exposure. This would be an extremely frequent finding in the generation of babies born to survivors of the bombing.

Shibata Shoji did not say anything about Kamo's leukemia to his family. But Yoko decided the she must leave the Shibata family. She didn't want to bring into the world another child who'd been poisoned from the bombs. After Yoko left the family Shibata, Kamo had a new mother—his stepmother Shizuko—who gave birth to two healthy sons, Kikuo and Kiyoo.

Yoko kept the family name of "Shibata," because it was also her son's family name. She wanted always to have the same name as her son.

6

The new semester started and my husband's work transferred him from Hiroshima to Tokyo. When we were preparing to move, as I was cleaning and packing our things, I found in the bottom of a drawer the dog collar I'd once bought for Kamo. I couldn't find an appropriate time to bring it to my next-door neighbors, but I couldn't bear to throw it away. So I decided to bring it with me to my new house in Tokyo; maybe one day I would have a dog myself.

When we settled down in Tokyo, I was eager to meet our new neighbors in the apartment next door. They were a newly married couple. They both sported hair dyed yellow; they both wore stylish curvy jeans. Both the man and the woman liked to wear big earrings. When I'd run into them at the elevator or our doorstep, they never took the initiative to greet me unless I opened my mouth and said hello first. The couple seldom even spoke to each other—each was always looking intently at his or her mobile phone, clicking on the keypad, busily sending messages or e-mails to someone else.

I told my husband that I still thought frequently of the Yamamoto sisters in Hiroshima and wanted to write something about them and for them.

My husband said, "What could you possibly write? They're just two elderly sisters and an old dog, and the dog is dead. The sun sets also, and the two sisters are still living happily and enjoying their life. Isn't that all?"

I said, "It is that simple, indeed, a simple story. But hearing it from your mouth, in your words, it does sound like nonsense."

Written in Hiroshima in 2002
Translated by Qin Quan'an

Xiao Lei

Xiao Lei was born in Heyang County, Shaanxi Province. Xiao Lei has published collections of lyric poetry including *Adolescence, The Land Reluctant to Part, The Graceful God of Fragrance and Happiness,* and a collection of narrative poetry *The Porter's Love.* His collections of journalism include *Wild Gild Geese Flying South, In the Distant Place, The Olympics of Literature,* and *Personal Experience in Hollywood.* He has published a collection of novellas, *Persistent Unrequited Love: A Trilogy,* and a novel, *Lunar Craters,* as well as the nonfiction release *Jin Jie.* His recent publications include the lyric poems "Singing of Energy Resource" and "Mandate of Heaven," and journalism pieces "Prince of the Desert" and "The Remote Apricot River." He has won a dozen awards for literature and his writings are featured in several anthologies.

His calligraphy has been displayed in a number of exhibitions; published in newspapers, magazines, and albums; included in various collections; and widely collected throughout the world.

9

Xiao Lei

Who Would Go to the Scaffold

Folks who lived in this area preferred to sing the words in a play rather than speak them. Therefore it was said that they were "singing in a play" rather than "acting in a play."

Now and then Liang Xiangqian wondered why this was so. Was it because Shaanxi opera, which had been popular from generation to generation for thousands of years, so touched people's hearts with its charming tunes? Or was it because not everyone could act in Shaanxi opera, and therefore it was a comfort to those who could sing a few lines but couldn't act? His conclusion was that both of these explanations applied.

Indeed, what made this particular Lantern Festival so special was that it included a performance of Shaanxi opera.

In the late afternoon on the fourteenth day of the first lunar month, when the sun was about to set, the master actors came by appointment, one after another, from nearby villages and assembled behind the stage of Liangjia Village. In this area, when any village planned to put on a Shaanxi opera performance, it was unnecessary to invite the county or provincial theatrical troupes, because every village had its own master actors. When a performance was arranged, master actors from nearby villages and communes would assemble at the village, and actors would be available for every type of traditional opera role—including *dan* (female), *sheng* (male), *jing* (painted face), *mo* (middle-aged man), and the clown. Since the plays were all traditional ones following fixed conventions, there was no need for rehearsal. As soon as the various roles were allocated by the director, the performance of a complete series could start immediately with the beating of drums and striking of gongs.

The director of the performance that night was Hei Lao from Liangjia Village. At over thirty years of age, he was an expert farmer and master actor, especially known far and near for playing the female role. He had learned every line of about a hundred plays.

The performance for tonight, he decided, would be *Eight Garments*. He chose this play to go first because it was splendid. It included every type of role—sheng, dan, jing, mo, and clown—and there was lots of action, like when the evildoer was executed by being cut in two at the waist, and when the heroine cut her own throat, and when Bao Wenzheng cut off the criminal's head with his dragon-head hay cutter, and the judgment at Yama's palace. In short, every unique skill and stunt in traditional Shaanxi opera was included in *Eight Garments*, and Hei Lao knew that this play would enjoy high popularity far and wide. If they performed this play first, everything would get off to a good start. Afterward, when other villages wanted to give a performance, they would certainly invite Hei Lao's troupe.

Now, behind the stage, Hei Lao was assigning roles to the appropriate actors. He assigned the aged male role of Yang Lian, the young male role of Zhang Chengyu, the painted-face role of Bai Shigang, the aged clown (the constable), and the young clown (the mayor).

Naturally, the young female role of Du Xiuying belonged exclusively to Hei Lao. When all these roles were assigned, Hei Lao realized to his surprise that the master actor who'd play the aged squire Ma Hong hadn't shown up. It turned out that he'd contracted a serious illness and was confined to the kang for days. Who would play Ma Hong?

Hei Lao was worried. Everybody was busy preparing. The man in charge of the costume trunks was distributing costumes among the actors, and those who had their roles were beginning to get ready. Some were putting on their costumes, and some were applying face paints. The role of the aged squire was not a major one, but still the show couldn't go on without it. What would Hei Lao do?

Worse still, starting in the late afternoon, a great tidal wave of theatergoers had rolled in from far and near. By dusk, the theater was throbbing with people, forming a clamorous atmosphere like crashing waves. Two large oil lamps had been hung high above the stage, and people gazed at the stage with expectant eyes as if waiting eagerly for the sun to rise. He couldn't disappoint them!

In fact, the villagers had been discussing the performance among themselves for months. There had been a drought the previous summer, and men and women wearing wicker helmets, in bare feet and with their trouser legs rolled up, had knelt in front of the Black Dragon Cave to pray for rain. The old Dragon King had manifested his power, and the rain had spilled down. Thanks to the saturating rain, which lasted for a whole day and whole night, the dying cotton plants were brought back to life, and the seedlings of corn, broomcorn millet, millet, black soybean, and green gram sprang up like mushrooms from the parched fields of wheat stubble. There was a great sense of relief among the desperate farmers, as if they had been rescued from a sea of fire. They had vowed to give serialized theatrical performances to thank the gods.

Since the tenth day of the first lunar month, the whole village had been busy preparing for the grand performance. Opposite the stage, a cloth awning was put up and banners were hung depicting heavenly officials riding on auspicious clouds to give blessings. Offerings were laid out on the square table; the smoke of incense curled up above them. Inside the awning was the shrine of the Dragon King. The villagers had placed him in the center, believing that this god of clouds and rain loved seeing a play as much as the villagers did. The performances at this Lantern Festival were to be held especially in the Dragon King's honor.

The expectations, from both man and god, put Hei Lao under tremendous pressure. Everything else was ready; all that was needed was the actor. Where could he be found? Even if he could be kneaded with clay, it would take time!

Hei Lao was at his wits' end, as desperate as an ant on a hot pan. At the back of the stage, two boys—Liang Xiangqian, the younger, and Wang Shiyun, the elder—watched the developing dilemma. The boys were both learning drama from Hei Lao during the winter holiday and were now assigned to act walk-on parts. They saw their master's desperate position and felt as anxious and helpless as he did.

All of a sudden, Wang Shiyun, taking a deep breath and blinking a pair of big, round eyes, made a request to Hei Lao. Timid as a rabbit, he said, "Master Hei, if there is no way out, let me take over."

"Go away! Get out of here!" scolded Hei Lao. Unable to solve his problem and seeing the reckless boy overreaching himself, he burst with rage. "You can't even remember the simple line 'It's a real pity.' How could I count on you to act in a new play?" To cover up his own helplessness and anxiety, Hei Lao didn't hesitate to poke the poor boy's sore spot. Liang Xiangqian couldn't help feeling embarrassed for his friend.

Indeed, although he had big eyes, bushy eyebrows, and a strong constitution, Wang Shiyun was not good at his studies or writing Chinese characters, nor was he fit as an actor. He would often forget the text he'd been taught. Even if you started him out with a hint—like "Man's nature at birth is good," which is the first line of

Three-Character Classic—he wouldn't remember the next line ("Man is born good"). Even if "Zhao, Qian, Sun, Li," the first line of *The Hundred Surnames*, was prompted, he would forget the next—"Zhou, Wu, Zheng, Wang"—even though Wang was his own surname.

As for learning to write Chinese characters, he could not even hold a writing brush firmly and properly. To determine whether he had learned this skill, his teacher used to sneak up on him and pull up his brush all of a sudden, staining the boy's palm black. Whenever this happened, Wang Shiyun would get a runny nose, and he would wipe his nose with the back of his ink-stained hand, turning his face as black as the flowery-faced role in Beijing opera.

In their drama class with Hei Lao, Wang Shiyun, with his thick and powerful back and shoulders, his big ears and head, was asked to play the aged male role in *A Reluctant Farewell*. But once on the stage, he could remember only the first few words—"It's a real pity"—and forgot all the rest of the lines. Motionless and speechless in the center of the stage, he had blinked his black, beanlike eyes and stood looking like a big sack of grain.

At first, Hei Lao had taught him word by word and sung in demonstration: "It's a real pity that my daughter has a hard lot, married a bad man named Xu Sheng." But even after Wang Shiyun had been taught dozens of times, he could still remember only the first few words, forgetting all the rest. Hei Lao had flown into a fury and given the poor boy a resounding slap on the face, hitting him so hard that the boy's black skullcap flew off and tumbled about on the ground. Liang Xiangqian, who was standing by and learning to play the young male role of Xu Sheng, had found the scene rather amusing—but he dared not laugh out loud. Instead he quickly took to his feet and pretended to go to the lavatory.

Since Wang Shiyun couldn't manage the major roles, he was given minor ones. One time, the boy had played the role of an old domestic servant. He had tottered onto the stage and introduced himself by saying, "I'm eighty-two years of age . . ." As he spoke he tried to stroke his long, white beard, only to find he had forgotten to wear it—and so he ran backstage to fetch it. It was at that point that Hei Lao lost all hope of turning the boy into a good actor, and the mentor reassigned the boy to a silent role.

After that, Wang Shiyun played the dog in *Killing a Dog as a Warning to His Wife*, and the tiger in *Wu Song Kills a Tiger*. He went wrong again in playing the tiger when he forgot the right time to die. His head covered with a yellow robe as the tiger, he fought a fierce duel with Wu Song, a hero of great valor. They fought hand-to-hand from stage left to stage right, from upstage to downstage, repeatedly without end, until Wu Song got so tired that he threw himself upon the stage floor. But even then Wang Shiyun didn't give up, instead lifting the robe a bit to peep at what was happening. Out of anger, the drumbeater at the side of the stage kicked him on his bottom so hard that the tiger went head over heels and rolled into the wings. Such had been Wang Shiyun's ignominious experiences in the theater.

Now, seeing his master filled with worry over the vacant actor, Wang Shiyun only wanted to help. But Hei Lao dared not entrust Wang Shiyun with such an important task—this poor pupil who could not even remember the line "It's a real pity." Neither could he forget that die-hard tiger. He knew that this boy with the big, black eyes was full of courage and generosity, but he could not accept Wang Shiyun's offer.

Seeing Wang Shiyun thus rejected, Liang Xiangqian thought to himself, this guy has plenty of guts! He remembered that once Wang Shiyun had caught a dead fish from a cistern and secretly put it between the pages of a classmate's textbook. When the little girl had opened the book with delight, she'd screamed in surprise and then fainted. By the time she came to, she found her crotch wet all over. Her parents wouldn't let Wang Shiyun off easily, and his own father gave him a sound beating with the club.

Liang Xiangqian was immersed in his memories as he painted his face and put on his costume. So lost in thought was he that he didn't notice his master scrutinizing his face. Like a drowning man who suddenly found a straw to clutch at, Hei Lao cried with delight, "You act the part!"

"Me?" Young Xiangqian was astonished and excited.

"Yes, you play Ma Hong," ordered Hei Lao, looking at the innocent little boy.

"But I haven't learned to play Ma Hong," replied Xiangqian hesitantly.

"I'll teach you right away."

"Will that do?" asked Xiangqian, agreeably surprised.

"Sure," Hei Lao replied decisively. "There's little time left. Quick, put on your makeup and costume. Sing the lines after me." He began applying greasepaint to Xiangqian's face to make the base, then picked up a brush to paint his eyebrows, added a bit of white powder on the ridge of his nose, and then created a white beard of three linked sections with a part down the middle. Finally the master put a yellow robe on the boy. Thus Liang Xiangqian was quickly transformed into a queer old squire.

With that accomplished, Hei Lao sat down at the dressing table, took out his costume and supplies, and made himself up as the beautiful country girl Du Xiuying.

Meanwhile, Wang Shiyun, who had tried to relieve his master of worries, had been ridiculed and humiliated right to his face. He sat on the costume trunk feeling sad, sniffling and fixing his round eyes in envy on Liang Xiangqian, who was being prepared for the role. Wang Shiyun was filled with remorse and self-reproach: he was worthless, unable to lend a hand at a critical moment.

In contrast, Liang Xiangqian now felt rather pleased with himself, for the master not only thought highly of him and entrusted him with an important task, but, more importantly, he would take part in a complete series. Step by step he would play an increasingly important role and get to observe up close how master actors performed.

.Proud of himself, he laughed up his sleeve at Wang Shiyun, who was several years his elder.

Liang Xiangqian knew that his smirk was covered up by his white face paint and the white beard of three linked sections. Instead, Wang Shiyun might think he was showing sincere pity and consolation. As expected, Wang Shiyun rose to his feet from the trunk, came over to his friend, and said encouragingly, "Don't feel sorry for me. You'll do a great kindness to our master if you can play the role well."

The drum sounded three times, and the noisy audience below the stage grew quiet; it was as if the wind had stopped blowing and the rain had ceased to fall. And then the complete series of *Eight Garments* formally began. Liang Xiangqian, hiding behind the back curtain, watched the performance intently, although he didn't fully understand what was going on. Not until many years later would Liang Xiangqian, then an adult, really grasp the plot of the play.

Eight Garments tells the story of Zhang Chengyu, a young scholar. Zhang wants to go to the capital to sit for an imperial examination, but he is penniless and has no traveling expenses, so he goes to his uncle, his mother's brother, to borrow some money. His uncle, who's also hard up for money at the moment, tells his daughter Du Xiuying to pack up a parcel of garments for his nephew to pawn. As Du Xiuying feels love for her older cousin, she does him an additional favor: she puts ten silver coins from her private savings between the eight garments. Then, for fear that her cousin might not understand her secret gesture, she adds one embroidered shoe as a token of love.

Zhang Chengyu is so absorbed with his books that he doesn't bother to look into the valuable parcel of eight garments. He goes straight to the pawnshop and willingly exchanges the parcel for only five silver coins.

Just then Bai Shigang, a burglar, sneaks into the house of Ma Hong, a rich and powerful person, and kills Ma Cheng, a servant, and steals some clothing. The family retainer yells to the squire for help.

Liang Xiangqian was still watching, entranced with the performance, when Hei Lao nudged him to be ready for his appearance. As if by magic, Master Hei Lao had transformed himself into Du Xiuying and looked as pretty as a fairy, with hairpin rings swaying on his head, large eyes, upwardly slanting eyebrows, and cherry lips. He was dressed in a blue satin coat with tassels and a red silk skirt with ribbons floating on both sides. Liang Xiangqian marveled at the transformation.

But although Hei Lao was dressed as a beautiful maiden, he remained himself, a stern teacher. He pulled up his long skirt and gave Liang Xiangqian earnest instructions, directing him in how to speak and act on the stage, seeing to it that the boy had learned all of his lines by heart. Satisfied, Hei Lao raised the back curtain and pushed the fully equipped Liang Xiangqian onto the stage. Liang Xiangqian, with his long robe and long beard, instantly became the character Ma Hong.

Appearing on the stage, Ma Hong gave his opening speech. "I wear a fur-lined jacket and boots; they all call me a fat turtle," he said. He then demanded, "Why did you people call for me?"

"A burglar killed your servant Ma Cheng," his retainer answered.

"Where was he killed?" Liang Xiangqian as Ma Hong inquired. When the squire arrived at the scene, he poured out endless grievances. "People, stay at home; disaster comes like a bolt from the blue," said Ma Hong. Then he wrote an urgent report and asked the retainer to present it immediately to the county magistrate, Yang Lian.

While Liang Xiangqian was acting onstage, Hei Lao had his heart in his mouth. Having been an actor for twenty years, Hei Lao had experienced endless dangers, but he had never run a risk like letting a child act a completely new role on the spur of the moment. What if the novice failed? If he forgot a line, took a wrong step, or missed a cue, the performance would be ruined.

But as luck would have it, the pupil did not let his master down. He was so smart that he instantly learned by heart everything his master taught, and he acted perfectly on the stage. Hei Lao was thrilled; as the boy withdrew from the stage, the master hugged him closely in his arms.

Liang Xiangqian was then only seven years old and had just started school. The Taoist robe was far too large for him, and he was nothing like a bearded old squire—but he could remember everything as it was taught to him, and he acted perfectly. Even the master actors were amazed at his remarkable performance. They kept saying to Hei Lao, "That kid is really talented and quick-witted. He has the makings of a good actor. And you are a brilliant master. It is just as the saying goes: a great master brings up brilliant disciples." Hearing their affirmations, Hei Lao was so wild with joy that he burst out laughing boisterously, forgetting that he was dressed as Du Xiuying, a delicate and pretty girl with a hapless fate.

Liang Xiangqian was as pleased with himself as his master was. Not because the other actors spoke highly of his intelligence; he was well aware of his own brightness and cleverness and had heard as much many times from the adult villagers and his schoolmates.

What's more, Hei Lao, his master, had already affirmed the boy's emerging talents. When Hei Lao played the young female, he often needed a supporting actor, so he had taught the boy to take on these minor roles. When he played Hu Fenglian in *Hiding in the Boat*, he taught the boy to act as Tian Yuchuan. In one scene of that play, Hu Fenglian has to awaken Tian Yuchuan, who's sound asleep, but she's embarrassed to pull him because, according to the rules of etiquette at that time, a man and a woman should not touch each other when giving or receiving something. So the woman makes the boat toss a little by rocking it gently in order to awaken him. Later, in class, when Liang Xiangqian's desk mate was dozing off and he was afraid that the teacher would catch her napping, he rocked the desk a little to wake her up.

When Hei Lao played Bai Yunxian in *The Broken Bridge*, he taught the boy to act the part of Xu Xian. To incite the audience's emotions, Hei Lao would add "my dear husband" to the end of every line he sang, dragging out the three words dramatically. Hei Lao asked Liang Xiangqian to do the same, adding "my dear wife" to every line and extending the three words as he sang in the character of Xu Xian.

Every time *The Broken Bridge* was performed, Hei Lao sang the line, "Since you went to the Golden Mountain Temple to burn incense, my dear husband . . ."

Then young Xiangqian would sing the next line: "Not a single night have I failed to wait for you till the moon rose over the western tower, my dear wife."

Such antiphonal singing, the characters responding to each other, was filled with emotion and sounded sweet to the ear; the performance was always a great success.

Hei Lao often spoke highly of the boy and firmly believed that he would have a bright future. Whenever a play was put on in a nearby village, he would take the boy with him to act a small role in it.

So the praise from his master and the other actors now was not what thrilled the boy. What made him most happy about playing Ma Hong was that he could stay on the stage throughout the performance, watching the whole play at close range. He seemed to be a born theater fan. For as long as he could remember, whenever a play was put on in a neighboring village, he would eagerly go to watch, no matter how far away it was. And he never once missed a performance in his own village.

If a village was too poor to put on a full-length drama, a playlet was performed. The playlet of his hometown was a unique marionette show, locally known as *The Monkey on Thread Show*. He could even be entranced with this simple kind of show, taking the puppets for humans.

Once, watching *The Return of Zhou Ren to His Master's Mansion*, he was completely absorbed in the plot although only puppet shadows appeared on the screen. The boy took it all in: Zhou Ren's anguish and regret; the tragic sight of his wife's suicide after her failure to kill the evil prime minister; Zhou Ren being grievously wronged, beaten brutally; and then the character kneeling before his wife's grave, crying piteously and digging at the earth in order to join his dear wife in the same grave. It all so moved the young boy that he cried bitter tears, and his eyes remained red and swollen till the next day.

Later, a Pu opera troupe of Shaanxi Province came to Liang Xiangqian's hometown, but he had no money to buy a ticket. He got glazed printing paper, cut it to the size of a ticket, drew lines on it, and copied the words from a real ticket. Then, every day while the audiences were busy entering the theater, he joined the crowd, held the fake ticket in his palm, and waved it in front of the ticket collector before sneaking into the theater.

When Liang Xiangqian watched the play about a cowherd and a girl weaver, he was so moved by the wonderful story that his eyes secretly welled up. And when he saw the play *Song Jiang's Third Attack on the Zhu Family Manor*, he leapt for joy when the father and sons of the Zhu family were badly defeated by the greenwood heroes.

One day, however, Liang Xiangqian was late for the theater, arriving after the theatergoers had all entered. He repeated his usual trick of waving a fake ticket—but this time he was caught on the spot and driven away by the ticket collector. Since he couldn't enter the theater to watch the play *Cutting through the Hill to Save His Mother*, the boy sat under a tree to listen to the aria and the melody from the musical instruments, picturing the plays he had seen over the past two days.

Where had the girl weaver come from when she took a bath by the Dragonhead Spring? And where did the clamorous springwater come from? The five warriors of the Zhu family had been either pierced through with a sword or hacked to death in the face with a chopper; how did the blade enter into the chest, and then how did the blade emerge from the back? And again, how did the chopper stick to the face and not fall down? He remained perplexed about these intriguing questions.

But now Liang Xiangqian was playing the squire, and he was overjoyed that he could stay on the stage to see through all the secrets and know how the make-believe suicide was committed.

The evolution of the play's story continued. It turns out that Bai Shigang, the burglar and murderer, is an office attendant from the county headquarters who likes to indulge in excessive drinking and gambling in his spare time. When he grows short of money, he commits the heinous crime. Then he takes advantage of the fact that Zhang Chengyu, the young scholar, has pawned his valuable parcel for less money than it was worth. Bai Shigang brings a false charge against the scholar and incites Ma Hong to take the stand. Then Du Xiuying, the scholar's cousin, together with her father and aunt, come to the county headquarters, beating the drum in an appeal to redress the wrong. Yang Lian, the county magistrate, has to pass judgment on the case again.

Backstage, Liang Xiangqian was busily reviewing the spoken parts and librettos Hei Lao had just taught him. This time there was much more to memorize. Some lines were to be spoken, and others sung. For fear of forgetting any and thus spoiling the whole thing, the boy sat on the costume trunk repeatedly reciting the words to himself. Suddenly, the supervisor called for the appearance of Ma Hong onstage. Hearing the call, Liang Xiangqian jumped off the trunk, donned the squire's cap and the long white beard, picked up the yellow robe, and ran to the stage in fear and trepidation.

Transformed into Ma Hong, the boy sang to the county magistrate, "I come up to make a deep bow. I'm summoned to Your Honor's presence, but why?"

There appeared here a long section of responsive singing as each character present in the courtroom was interrogated by the county magistrate. Each character gave his or her account of the case, raised questions, explained, and bore witness. They sang one after another in a quick tempo, closely linked together. Liang Xiangqian, as Ma Hong, was among the antiphonal singers. Finally, Hei Lao, playing Du Xiuying, interrogated in anger.

"Who sewed the eight garments? And who made the embroidered shoe?"

Liang Xiangqian responded at once by singing, "The eight garments my daughter sewed, and the embroidered shoe my daughter made."

Yang Lian, the county magistrate, continued to inquire. "Tell me your daughter's name."

"My daughter is Ma Qunying," Liang Xiangqian responded in song.

An urgent order was issued by the magistrate to bring Ma Qunying there at once. Acting on the instructions of her father to give false evidence, Ma Qunying said, "The eight garments were sewn by me, and so was the embroidered shoe."

Du Xiuying, who had in fact made the garments and the shoe, was finding it hard to defend herself. Faced with the uproarious mocking laughter of the official runners and the despotic power of the county magistrate, she looked up to heaven resignedly and sighed heavily, singing, "Peals of laughter from the runners make my face turn red with embarrassment. With a kitchen knife in my hand, I'll kill myself to relieve my misery." Then, overcome with shame and grief, Du Xiuying cut her own throat.

Liang Xiangqian was fascinated by the tricks of performance. Hei Lao, as Du Xiuying, flapped the ground with the shining kitchen knife in his right hand; at the same time, with his left hand, he suddenly removed his white shawl and tossed it into the air. The audience thought it was the knife, not the shawl, that was tossed into the air, so the audience's attention was diverted to the movement in the air. Hei Lao seized the chance to put the knife in his right hand on his neck, and at that very moment, Wang Shiyun, who played a county runner, spurted a mouthful of red water onto Hei Lao's neck.

Thus blood sprayed out, the charming young maiden was covered in blood, and all the audience cried out in alarm at once.

Liang Xiangqian saw with his own eyes, close-up, the ins and outs of all the tricks; he was impressed and dismayed at the same time. As an insider, he admired the perfect performance of the tricks and the cleverness of turning sleight of hand into reality. And as a spectator, he was dismayed at the result of the tricks and the sudden ruin of an innocent girl by a falsehood. Thinking of himself as the squire who'd told lies and caused the maiden's death, he was guilt stricken and not quite himself, both in his heart and in his body.

Seeing Wang Shiyun standing by in a black mandarin jacket, playing a county runner, Liang Xiangqian envied that role. The runner's act of spurting a mouthful of red water on Du Xiuying seemed to show his sympathy for the poor girl. Moreover, Liang Xiangqian felt empathy for his friend's frustration at being denied the speaking part; the older boy had suffered an unjust grievance, just like Du Xiuying.

Liang Xiangqian began to feel jealous of Wang Shiyun. How lucky he was to play a county runner, just standing by as Du Xiuying cut her own throat, even spurting a mouthful of red water on her neck, and still getting to see the ins and outs of the theater tricks. How enjoyable! Wang Shiyun had gained the upper hand after all. Liang Xiangqian felt a strong sense of loss.

The story of the play continued. Because of Ma Hong's false testimony, the scholar was beaten to death by Bai Shigang, and the girl committed suicide, which startled the judge in the Palace of Hell. Determined to review and redress all unjust, false, and mishandled cases for the ghosts of wronged persons, the wise judge in the netherworld requested that the King of Hell conduct a new trial. The master actor who played the King of Hell was said to be at his best when displaying his tusks; this stunt was protected by patent, to be performed only on the stage but never revealed elsewhere.

The master actor was now sitting backstage applying his makeup. His face was painted dark green and then dusted with golden powder; his lips were then painted crimson and again dusted with gold. Afterward, when he put on the queer large, red robe, he at once had a ghastly look. If he bared his tusks, Liang Xiangqian imagined, surely he would more resemble the green-faced and long-toothed King of Hell with a bloody mouth. It was a pity that he would not show his long teeth now, and no one knew where he hid them.

After an eerie sound from beating drums and striking gongs, the King of Hell, led by four ghosts and the judge, appeared on the stage. The King of Hell struck his pose and then let forth a roar that could shake heaven and earth. "A tall Taoist cap I wear on my head, the saw-toothed tusks lining both sides of my mouth, the drum made of human skin beaten on the side—I'll preside at the trial and administer justice."

Sitting in his ghostly palace, having interrogated a bunch of criminals and the ghosts of those who'd been wronged, the King of Hell roared, "The grievances heard make me boil with rage; I grind my teeth in fury."

His two tusks, which had stood upward like two sharp swords, now bent and twined around his neck like two snakes and then drew back to his mouth, making a clicking noise all the while. Meanwhile Liang Xiangqian, as Ma Hong, knelt in the Hall of Darkness during the trial by the King of Hell. Now and then he raised his head, admiring the superb stunt. But it was hard for him to discover the secret of the trick from his kneeling position at a distance from the King of Hell, who was sitting high on the platform.

Wang Shiyun, however, was much luckier. Playing a ghost, with pitch-black face paint and a red beard, he followed the King of Hell wherever he went as the cases were tried. He supported the king's right arm and left leg with his hands and then rested his head against the king's back. Now and then the king would turn around toward the ghost to drop a hint, and the two tusks seemed to be entwining and swaying just in front of Wang Shiyun's eyes. Liang Xiangqian was so envious of Wang Shiyun that he, with his eye sockets painted white, could only stare, dumbstruck.

All of a sudden the King of Hell shouted, "Bai Shigang is to be hung up in the eastern porch, and Ma Hong is to be detained in the western porch!" Before Liang Xiangqian knew what had happened, he was taken away by two devils to the backstage.

The detention of the criminals was no trivial matter. Word of the trial by the King of Hell came to Bao Wenzheng, a just and upright magistrate. Bao Wenzheng held a court session in the chief minister's official residence to uphold justice.

Backstage, Hei Lao was telling Liang Xiangqian the story and instructing him on how to act. "The King of Hell has the scholar Zhang Chengyu, who was beaten to death, brought back to life. And the soul of Du Xiuying, who was wronged and driven to death, finds reincarnation in Ma Qunying's corpse," he said. "Thus, Ma Qunying becomes Du Xiuying and marries her cousin Zhang Chengyu in the magistrate's court. Afterward, Bao Wenzheng punishes the evildoers: Bai Shigang, the looter and murderer, is to be cut in two at the waist, and Ma Hong, the perjurer, is to be put under the bronze hay cutter and beheaded."

On hearing this, little Xiangqian burst out crying with fear, begging tearfully to his master, "I quit. I won't act anymore!" It wasn't the cutting a living person in half at the waist, taking out a person's intestines and stomach, or cutting a person's head off with a bronze hay cutter—these were all interesting theatrical scenes that the boy desired to watch with his own eyes. But he had never imagined that the person to be beheaded was none other than Ma Hong, whose role he was playing!

Backstage lay an iron hay cutter borrowed from a villager. Village productions used no stage props, so usually real items were borrowed from local villagers instead. The iron hay cutter could slice a bale of millet straw or cornstalk to short pieces with a stroke;

impetuous and careless young men often lost their fingers or even an arm while chopping hay. And now a living person's head would be put under the shining blade of the cutter. Who wouldn't be frightened out of his wits!

Not only was the blade of the cutter gleaming with death, but to heighten the dramatic effect, Master Hei Lao had requested a pad of yellow paper with each sheet folded diagonally; he'd ordered these leaves pasted on both the blade and block of the cutter. Perhaps this was intended as an offering to the gods for protecting the actors from accidental injury. But the more devoutly they prayed to the gods for blessings, the more dangerous this trick appeared to be. Since the cutter was pasted with sheets of yellow paper all over, when the handle of the cutter was raised, all the sheets swayed together in the breeze, making a continuous rustling noise that added to the dramatic atmosphere of dread. It was no wonder that young Liang Xiangqian begged tearfully not to play Ma Hong anymore!

After three beats of the drum, the bronze cutter is laid.
I'll be rock firm in executing the law.
Whoever breaks the law must be beheaded,
No matter whether they're sons of princes and nobles.

After the dark-complexioned Lord Bao, with a half-moon painted on his forehead, sung out the order in a hoarse voice, the red-faced Wang Chao and black-faced Ma Han obeyed the order to bring up the criminals before the court. Just at that critical moment, however, Liang Xiangqian was behind the curtain refusing to appear onstage, although Master Hei Lao, now worried to death, tried everything he could think of to persuade him. Instead, Xiangqian began weeping more violently, shedding streams of tears and phlegm. The boy was so frightened that he threw himself to the ground, paralyzed, just like the play's condemned criminal who was to be executed.

At this point, filled with both worry and irritation, Master Hei Lao gave Liang Xiangqian—still in white beard and face paint—a violent slap in the face. As if his anger hadn't fully vented itself in the slap, Hei Lao cursed roundly, "I thought you were a piece of real gold, master-actor material; never did I imagine you were less than a piece of worn sackcloth, a sheer good-for-nothing. Just tell me, how am I supposed to deal with such an embarrassing situation?" Hei Lao lifted his hand to deliver another violent slap to Liang Xiangqian, who was choking with sobs.

Suddenly, someone grabbed his arm. Hei Lao turned and saw Wang Shiyun. Shiyun had just played a silent county runner, and then a silent ghost. Having finished his walk-on roles, he had nothing more to do for the moment; he'd been waiting quietly for the scene where the criminals would be executed. When he saw his master Hei Lao being worried to death and burning with wrath, he approached Hei Lao on tiptoe, gingerly, as if he had a rabbit tucked into his bosom. Nervously and timidly he said, "Master, if there is no other way out, let me act instead. Xiangqian is scared, but I'm not."

Hei Lao was taken aback at first and was about to lose his temper, but not for an instant did his arm stop in the air. As if meeting with a savior, Hei Lao embraced Wang Shiyun's shoulder with his arm and cried out excitedly in the shrill voice of the young girl he was playing: "Aha, it's settled! The role suits you best now—there are no lines for you in the next part! Quick, change your makeup and costume. The role now suits you!"

With that, Hei Lao grabbed a white brush and painted the ridge of Shiyun's nose and his eye sockets white, and then he tore the white beard off Liang Xiangqian's mouth and put it on Shiyun's. "The retainer's red trousers are OK for the condemned prisoner. Bring a red felt cap—a red felt cap, please!" shouted Hei Lao as he took hold of a red felt cap from the old property man's hand and put it on Shiyun's head. "Go on!" he said excitedly.

The two actors playing Wang Chao and Ma Han gave a roar from behind the back curtain and carried the new Ma Hong around the stage. Afterward, they put the condemned prisoner's head under the shining blade of the hay cutter on which the sheets of yellow paper were rustling in the wind.

Because of the beating and scolding by Hei Lao, as well as his own shame and fear, Liang Xiangqian sat on the costume trunk, sobbing and wiping his tears. More than that, he was inwardly disturbed: because his cowardice had led him to quit at a critical moment, Wang Shiyun had to be taken away to the court to be beheaded. It was improper to turn a dangerous and terrifying job that one was unwilling to do over to one's senior. Moreover, the hay cutter was a real one that could truly chop a person in half. Would he have an easy conscience if Wang Shiyun's head were accidentally cut off like a watermelon?

Liang Xiangqian forgot his own shame and began to worry about his friend. He jumped down from the trunk, tiptoed to the back curtain, and peeked underneath to see what would happen.

Bai Shigang, the murderer, was about to be executed. Bai Shigang was stripped to the waist and bound to a pillar. The red-bearded executioner stabbed a broadsword into Bai Shigang's belly, and the criminal spurted a mouthful of red water, spattering both of them. When the broadsword was drawn out, the executioner pulled a length of intestine from Bai Shigang's waistband, gnawed on it, and then went on to pull out the intestine, hand over hand, twining the bloody and swollen entrails around his own neck until they accumulated thickly.

Women and girls in the audience screamed with fright, and some children were so scared that they hid themselves in their mothers' arms. However, Liang Xiangqian knew it was all fiction. What the executioner pulled out was not human intestines, but a pig's small intestines left over from a slaughter the previous day. The pig's intestines had been washed clean, left out to dry, and then hidden in Bai Shigang's waistband. They were stretched and inflated as they were pulled out of the actor's costume. Knowing all the secrets, Liang Xiangqian didn't feel a bit surprised; he even laughed secretly at those in the audience who were so foolish as to be frightened, screaming and yelling. Little wonder people often said, "Actors are madmen while audiences are fools."

The boy was pondering the serious question of "madmen" and "fools" when he heard Bao Wenzheng roar, "Cut!" Liang Xiangqian was startled by Lord Bao's roar. His attention snapped to the gleaming white blade cutting into the neck of Wang Shiyun, who was costumed in the red felt cap and white beard. In an instant, with an earsplitting crash, the blade descended, and now blood was spurting in all directions—and Wang Shiyun's head separated from his neck! Wang Shiyun's head was rolling like a watermelon on the other side of the cutter; simultaneously, with a crash and a shudder, the red felt cap became a blood-red pot, and the long white beard became a cloud of smoke. When Liang Xiangqian saw with his own eyes his friend's head cut off with the hay cutter, just like those careless young men who lost fingers and arms to the blade, he could not help crying out "Aaah!" He threw himself onto the blue brick floor behind the curtain and fainted.

The performance came to an end and the curtain fell, but the unexpected accident backstage threw the actors into utter confusion. Still in his makeup and costume, Wang Shiyun dashed over to Xiangqian, holding the junior student in his arms and calling repeatedly, "Xiangqian, what's wrong? Xiangqian, what's wrong?" After a long while, it seemed that Xiangqian's soul returned faintly and slowly, and gradually a trace of breath appeared from his nose.

But as soon as his eyes half-opened and he saw the head with the red felt cap and white beard, the boy cried out hysterically, "Ghost, ghost, bring a piece of red cloth to cover my eyes!" He struggled to run away, but Shiyun only held him more tightly. To the small face as pale as death and two eyes staring vacantly, the older boy said, "Xiangqian, it's me. It's me!"

Liang Xiangqian fixed his eyes on the red felt cap, intending to raise his hand, but instead he blurted out, "Ah, blood! Bring a piece of red cloth to cover my face!" Suddenly Xiangqian's pants grew wet and hot. Wang Shiyun looked down and saw that the junior student had been so terribly frightened that he had pissed in his pants without realizing. The older student couldn't help feeling sorry for Xiangqian; slowly he explained, "It was playacting. It was fake, not real!"

"It was playacting, not real?" Xiangqian asked, staring blankly.

"If you don't believe me, have a feel of my head." Wang Shiyun held Xiangqian's hand and pulled it up to the red felt cap he was wearing. Liang Xiangqian felt the red cap with a trembling hand. After a long while, he said with a quivering voice, "But I saw your head rolling on the other side of the cutter . . ."

"No, it was our master Hei Lao's head," Wang Shiyun explained. "When the blade came down, Wang Chao and Ma Han dragged my body aside and my head, together with my body, fell to this side of the cutter, while on the other side, a head popped up from under the table. That head was also wearing a red cap and a white beard, with eye sockets painted white, shaking like a rattle-drum—just like a human head being cut off! When the head stopped rolling, I saw that it was Master Hei Lao, acting under the table."

"Was it really fake?" Liang Xiangqian was still not quite convinced. Having acted the whole night, he was utterly confused about truth and fiction. A good person had turned villain, a living person had been put to death, and a dead person had come back to life. The fake had become real, and the real had changed into the fake. A fool had become a wise man, and then a wise man turned into a fool. A nobleman had become a humble one, and the most valued one had suddenly turned worthless. Once it had been ideal to play this role; later it was better to play that one. What was playacting, and what was reality?

The cloud of dense fog and the terrifying vision of beheading still swayed before the eyes of Liang Xiangqian, who had pissed in his pants. Later, when his pants had been dry for many years, he was still lost in that cloud of fog, often unable to tell whether what was happening around him was mere play on the stage or the true essence of the human world.

Translated by Yang Narang

Zhao Xi

Zhao Xi, born in 1940, studied biology at Shaanxi Normal University. He worked in the biology department there and then went on to work for the Shaanxi Provincial Planning Committee; the writing team and political work team of Shaanxi Revolutionary Committee; Shaanxi Provincial Committee, Communist Youth League; Shaanxi Literary Federation; and Shaanxi Provincial Writers Association.

Zhao Xi served as deputy director of Shaanxi Provincial Committee Office of Communist Youth League; deputy editor in chief of *Shaanxi Youth*; a party member of Shaanxi Literary Federation; editor in chief of *Oriental* magazine; and party secretary and vice-chairman of the Shaanxi Provincial Writers Association.

His main works include the collections of novellas and short stories *Soul of the Great Wall*, *White Grape Legend*, and *Moon on the Eighteenth Day of a Lunar Month*. He has published five novels: *Love and Dream*, *My Daughter River*, *Green Blood*, *Wolf Dam*, and *Playing the Mast*. *My Daughter River* won the Shaanxi Double-Five Award for Literature. In 1992, a reading of the novel was held in Beijing and broadcast on China National Radio. The book details the life struggles of a group of young people living in the mountains during the reform era.

10

ZHAO XI

The Soul of the Great Wall

1

July is the springtime of the frontier north of the Great Wall. Hoping to draw a picture of the Great Wall that could reflect the spirit of China, I came to the border town at this time each year.

The desert, grassland, sand hills, and red *lao'an* flowers under the glow of a splendid sunset had the beauty of a soft, golden garment. I sat on the ruins of a beacon tower, drinking in the miracle of the scenery of the frontier. In this area, the ancient Great Wall was half-buried. Only a curved line of ridge remained, winding far into the distance. Still, this weather-beaten relic maintained an imposing grandeur as it stretched across the vast wilderness and off to the horizon.

There was a profound stillness. Not a sound could be heard. A soft wind carried the scent of sage from the grass pools. A small wheat-colored bird shook its wings and chirped now and again. Like the ancient Great Wall, everything in the desert, from the grove of snow-white oleaster to the verdant grass and wildflowers, appeared solemn and serene.

I was touched as I looked at this magnificent scroll of scenery. I thought of the history of some two thousand years ago: a history of the scourge of violent times, the cruel labor of building the Great Wall, and the story of Meng Jiangnü, the legendary figure of the Qin Dynasty—when her husband died while building the Great Wall, her tears moved heaven and earth and caused the Wall to collapse. I thought of the folk song:

The sky is gray, gray,
And the steppe wide, wide.
Over the grass that the wind has battered low
Sheep and oxen roam.

The history was past, but this backbone of the nation remained there, traversing the land. I couldn't go on painting. I sank into contemplation. Half the face of the russet setting sun lingered at the vanishing point of the desert, and flaming clouds drifted above the horizon.

What was it that suddenly broke the twilight serenity? An ethereal sound came from the foot of the Wall. Jingle, jingle, jingle . . . It was silvery and delightful. And then it was no more. It disappeared like the song of a brook or a bamboo flute played by a frontier guard centuries ago.

Following the direction of the sound, I saw a herd of donkeys grazing leisurely on the green fringe of grass at the foot of the Wall. They looked like a swarm of black ants trooping through the field. And then: jingle, jingle. The sound of the small bells rang clearer and louder.

I was stirred and my heart leapt. It was as though the Great Wall had come alive and moved and smiled. Was it whispering?

The frisky, rambling donkeys on the verge of the Wall drew my interest. I longed to draw a picture. It could be called *Grazing at Dusk under the Great Wall.* And so I took out my palette and began to paint.

2

Engrossed in my painting, I suddenly heard a heavy cough from below the beacon tower. I stopped and looked down. At first I saw the back of a figure in a faded black shirt, emerging from the grass. His form appeared beside the collapsed part of the Wall and then headed in my direction. Finally, he turned onto the Great Wall and I saw that he was an old, bent man.

A straw rope hung from his waist, and though it was July and a warm day, he wore a coarse cotton undercoat. In his hand he carried a small stick to round up the donkeys. Although his mustache was white, his face and the patch of bare chest that showed from his open collar were red with health. He smiled in a kindly way and his eyes glittered from his rugged, weather-beaten face.

Naturally the sight of the old herdsman of the northern frontier inspired me and became part of my canvas. I greeted him while returning to my painting. "Hello! What are you doing?"

"I'm a donkey herder." He smiled as he removed a plastic tarp from his pack and then sat down on the ground. The plastic served him as a rain jacket and ground cloth. His posture was fantastic against the splendid backdrop of the sunset, the rolling profile of the Wall, and the vast expanse of desert.

He was cheerful. Years of herding donkeys along the Great Wall had given him few chances to meet strangers. On meeting me, he poured out his warmth as if I were an old friend. He asked me with interest, "Where are you from?"

"Guanzhong."

"Ah, yes; your accent tells me you're from Huazhou." He chuckled. "Why, I've been to Huazhou once. Years ago there was an uprising there and it was a tough fight. In those days I was with the revolutionary Liu Zhidan. Your land is level and flat and the noodles you eat are long and wide. Huazhou has lots of white flour and red-bean gruel, isn't that so?"

Incredible! I was awestruck by this old donkey herder. Had he been part of the Weihua uprising? I asked, "Were you in the Red Army?"

"Oh my, that was forty years ago—when I was your age. I was fearless and daring. Traveled north and south as if nothing could harm me. The uprising failed. I rode around attacking the Japanese devils and chasing the Dazui bandits around Mount Tian in Xinjiang. I got wounded in the leg and then I retired."

I learned that he was sixty-eight and that his wife was dead. She'd left behind a daughter of nineteen.

"Aren't Red Army veterans supported with food, clothing, fuel, and education?" I asked. "I thought the Five Guarantee Policy ordered local governments to take care of that."

He shook his head. "I can still move around and don't need that relief. Years ago, I was given a subsidy of twenty-five yuan a month. But during the Cultural Revolution, they said I was a fraud. They couldn't find the papers to prove my Party membership or that I belonged to the Red Army. So they took my name off the relief roll and took away the payments." He heaved a sigh. "In those days, we rushed about here and there fighting in battles all the time. How could a 'file' be kept?"

"Oh, it's too bad that that happened."

He smiled cheerfully. "I can still move around. Even if I can't do heavy work, I can look after the donkeys. But I do have difficulty walking now. My daughter pitied me and dropped out of school; now she tends the donkeys with me. She runs fast, so I don't have to worry about the donkeys chewing on trees or eating the crops."

I was overcome with emotion. "You shed blood for the country and have nothing left. Don't you want some help?"

"No, no." The old man shook his head. "The leader of the commune is very kind, and he wrote an affidavit for me. The county government asked me to find a witness, but all the witnesses are dead. No one can provide proof. I'm just a little drop of dew. I'm a nobody."

I suddenly heard a rustling behind me. As nimble as a little lamb, a young girl jumped out in front of us. She was not very tall and yet she was smartly turned out, wearing a blue blouse and a pair of green trousers that were patched at the knee. Her bare brown ankles were visible above a pair of grass-green rubber shoes. On her back she carried a load of hay that was dotted with red, purple, blue, and white wildflowers. Concealed among the flowers, her pretty oval face had the flush of dawn. A beam of light danced from a pair of charming eyes. At the corner of her small and exquisite mouth she held a sprig of red lao'an flower. She impressed me as a lively and mischievous girl.

She didn't say a word—just inclined her head, watching me paint. She couldn't conceal her delight at seeing me sketching her father, the old Red Army man. Eventually she jumped behind her father and shook his shoulder: "It's getting cold. Let's go home, Dad." She spoke with a sweet, girlish voice.

At that moment I heard the jingling of the bells and felt something warm by my side. I was surprised to see that the black donkeys had climbed onto the battlement with the girl and seemed to be giving my picture a stolid look.

"My daughter's name is Liuhua—she's named for the lao'an flower. She tends the donkeys with me every day."

I said, "She's still young; she should go to school."

The old man replied, "In recent years, it was a mess here in the dust bowl region. No food could be found, and so most men migrated to other places—and that left no one to herd the donkeys. We can't just let the commune break down, can we? So Liuhua quit school."

Liuhua lowered her head and kicked a clod of earth.

As they prepared to leave, I colored in the sketch of the old Red Army man and presented it to him. He shook my hand joyfully. "Comrade, please come to our village and drop in sometime when you're free. There'll be food in the fall, and Liuhua will make sweet glutinous millet cake and stewed mutton for you."

Liuhua was silent. She took her father's arm and led him down from the beacon tower. I gazed at the back of the old Red Army man and his daughter as they faded into the wilderness, barely visible through the evening mist. Suddenly, loneliness filled my heart as if I had lost something.

After a long while I could still hear the jingle of the bells. Their sound rang out merrily, like hundreds of birds singing in unison or a brook rippling through a forest. The sound echoed over the expanse of the Great Wall, and all at once I saw Liuhua jump onto the back of a donkey and wave at me with a bunch of wildflowers in her hand. The jingle of the donkey bells rushed into my soul like a song from the bottom of a maiden's heart.

3

Two years later, I returned to the border town.

The lao'an trees were in bloom. The thickets of lao'an blossoms were like the red glow of dawn that set off the ancient Great Wall, extending far into the distance. Beyond the Great Wall lay an expanse of grass and myriads of flowers. As before, it was the springtime of July in the region.

I lodged in the primary school of a village along the Wall. To my surprise, classes were already suspended. The head of the commune who escorted me there told me that the schoolteacher, Wang Junhai, had recently been promoted to clerk for the local Chinese Youth League at a nearby commune named Gaojia. No one had yet been found to take his place, and so the school was closed.

Wang Junhai was apparently a versatile young man. When he was in the village, he painted, sang, and played musical instruments all by himself. In the clay cottage where I stayed, I saw remnants of a musical score on the wall and a pile of discarded music books at the end of the kang.

As usual, I walked along the Great Wall. It had just rained and the air was particularly fresh and clean. Around spots that had been sand heaps a few years back, some groves of elms and acacia had been planted. A sand road bearing tractor-tire marks wound into the heart of the woods. A small canal of silicate bricks passed among the trees. The ancient Great Wall was tinged pale green; it looked almost alive as it stretched into the desert and off again to the horizon. There was a profound serenity here.

Having feasted my eyes on the beautiful scenery of the border-land, I returned to the primary school. I heard something stirring in the kitchen; the smell of tasty food filled the air. Then a figure in a red shirt flashed past the doorway.

"It's time for lunch, Comrade!"

It was a girl's voice outside the door—and when I looked up I was speechless. Liuhua! It was indeed the girl I'd encountered on the Great Wall two years before. She was taller now and more slender. She wore a red shirt of homespun plaid, and her braid was hidden under a blue cotton school cap. Her eyes seemed bigger and darker, and they glistened unfathomably.

"Liuhua!"

"You are . . . ?"

"I drew a picture for your father at the Great Wall near the border town, one summer."

Her dark eyes twinkled and a faint smile emerged at the corners of her mouth. She didn't say anything, but she lowered her head.

Little had I imagined that she lived in this village and was called upon to cook for me! I chatted with her and learned that she was still

255

herding the donkeys with her father. But the old man was sick these days and couldn't stir when the weather changed.

A bowl of white rice and a porcelain dish of mutton were served. I was amazed that they had such fine rice in this poor, remote area of the northern frontier.

"We grew some rice in the river bend," she said, sitting opposite me without eating. She spoke softly; it was obvious that she was now grown-up and shy.

I took a swallow of the rice and asked, "How much rice do you reap in a year? And how much can be rationed to the commune members?"

She gave a strained smile. "There are only some dozens of acres of farmland. Rice is for the visiting cadres. Sometimes it's ordered when a commune meeting is held. We get a small amount rationed to us during the Spring Festival."

She said nothing further. Yet there was something in her eyes that looked too much like a deep, tranquil lake.

One evening after supper, I said, "Let's go to your home. I want to see your father."

Liuhua was agitated and shook her head, saying, "No, no!" She looked distressed. At last she said, "Dad is sick and the room is dirty."

She lowered her head and was choked with sobs.

We walked along the winding sand road. In the summer night the sky was all the more blue above the frontier fort. The light of the moon touched the Great Wall and formed a silver line.

When we passed through a lao'an grove, I saw lamplight coming from the donkey shed and heard the jingle of the donkey bells. How familiar and genial were those little bells. Yet it looked dreary in the silence of the night.

Neither of us uttered a sound. The small yard of the donkey shed was fenced with a mud wall. The lamplight came from a side room of the hut. I entered; this was her home. In the light of a small oil lamp, the old Red Army man was lying on his side on the mud-brick kang.

He coughed repeatedly; his bare, brown back was bent. When he saw me he continued to cough, but his eyes lit up with joy.

He rose and spoke happily into my ear: "It has been two years. You still remember me."

I held his hot hands and said loudly, "I came here to draw a picture of the Great Wall and see you, too."

"Ho!" He smiled merrily. "The Great Wall! You must do it well. When you finish it would you give me one?"

Liuhua quietly left the room while we chatted about the old days. I asked him about the relief payment.

"The allowance was finally granted. But Director Wang of our commune said that once the county government implements the policy for me, then Liuhua might be given a job in the county seat." He seemed upset. His white mustache fluttered. "We don't like that idea. If everyone leaves the village, then who will grow the crops? We shouldn't give trouble to the Party as some people did. Once they got promoted to high positions, they began using their power for their own benefit, planning the future for their own children. I've hated that all my life."

He fumbled for some tobacco leaves in a shallow basket and packed them into a sheep-bone pipe. He drew on the pipe and then passed it to me. He seemed to pout a bit beneath his mustache and said with a heavy heart, "In recent years I haven't been feeling well, but I'm not giving up easily. There is one thing that troubles me, though, and that is Liuhua's marriage. I just can't let go!"

He sighed and then continued. "A few years ago, Junhai, the local schoolteacher, fell in love with Liuhua. The lad is clever and honey-mouthed, and he kept writing her love letters. He even wrote her poems that I couldn't understand. Liuhua is unsophisticated. Soon they were engaged. Who would have known? Then Junhai left the village and got established as the Youth League secretary of the commune and never came back. Liuhua's engagement was put aside. My daughter was heartbroken; I was seized with regret and fell ill. What ·can I do?"

The old man lay down on his stomach on the rim of the kang and coughed incessantly. I patted his back and tried to comfort him, but I was too indignant to speak.

It was late at night when I left the mud hut. A curve of crescent light hung at the zenith of the sapphire sky. Sitting on a tree trunk in the middle of the yard, Liuhua was bathed in the soft moonlight as though coated with frost. Silent and motionless, she sat there like a jade statue.

I lay wide-awake that night in the room of the primary school. That July evening in the north by the Great Wall was fresh and cool. Now and then a dog barked and the wind murmured. The night wind blew on the paper windowpane. The jingling of donkey bells echoed in my ear. The sound, mellow and clear, reverberated in the cool night air.

4

I made a special trip to the commune seat for the sake of Liuhua. It turned out that it was Director Wang of the commune who had escorted me to the village when I'd first arrived.

Wang heaved a sigh and said, "Alas, there's little that can be done to save Liuhua's engagement. I went to talk to Junhai, but he said his mother wouldn't consent. Junhai has been promoted and now has a permanent urban residency, while Liuhua is just a peasant. I'm am afraid it wouldn't work."

Nevertheless, Wang did offer some hope. He told me that he'd reported Liuhua's situation to the county government, and the replacement policy suggested that it might be possible to find Liuhua another job. Wang smiled and added, "If she has a job, then there will be hope for a marriage."

It was almost lunchtime when I returned to the village. The sun shone high over the vast expanse of grassland. The line of the Great Wall faded into the endless sea of sand. The desert was still except for an occasional bird's cry; it was almost soundless.

As soon as I climbed up onto the Great Wall battlement, I heard the familiar jingle of donkey bells resounding from beyond the grass pool. Soon I saw those black, antlike donkeys faintly in the grass.

I looked far into the distance; the bells rang merrily. Ah, Liuhua—it must be she tending the donkeys. I ran toward the other side of the grass pool, shouting, "Liuhua, Liuhua . . ."

But there was no answer. Not until I reached the donkeys did I discern, immersed in the waist-deep grass, the back of a twisting and turning figure wearing a patched, dark-blue shirt. Now I could see clearly that it was the Red Army man, stooped in the grass, using a scythe to cut fodder. His back shook with the labor.

He was clearly very ill—but what sustained him was grazing the donkeys. I tried to call to him, but the words caught in my throat.

The old man turned and, wiping the sweat off his forehead, shouted at me, "Hurry back for lunch. It has already passed dinnertime. You must be starving."

Suddenly he collapsed onto the grass, still smiling at me. His gaunt, sallow face and naked chest streamed with sweat.

"You're sick," I said in a pained voice. "You need to rest. It is such a hot day, you—"

He interrupted: "Work is a cure for all kinds of illnesses. I work, I sweat, and the illness is gone. Besides, Liu'er, my little Liuhua, does all the cooking, so I just need to 'cook' for the donkeys." He laughed good-naturedly. When he untied his haying band, a few potatoes were revealed.

I said, "You go back to eat something warm. I'll look after the donkeys for you."

The old Red Army man said, "These potatoes are cooked and they're tasty." He blew the dust off the potatoes and began eating.

"Let me have one."

"No, not for you." He pulled a long face. "You're an artist and your stomach is delicate. We have white rice for you. These are not good enough to feed the donkeys."

He would not give me a potato, but stuffed one big lump into the mouth of a small, grayish donkey crouched at his feet, coaxing, "Come on, you greedy little girl, here's something tasty for you."

He soon ate up the potatoes and wiped his mouth. Then he stood with a bent back and walked slowly to a small stream. He shouted, "Are you thirsty? Here's sweet springwater."

"What? Sweet water? In this desolate desert?"

"Ho, ho, you've never had it before? The springwater in the desert is sweeter than sugar."

The old Red Army man bowed down over the edge of the pond and gulped down several mouthfuls of fresh water. He wiped the beads of water off his mustache and slurped, "Great! Fantastic! How sweet!"

He pulled out a hollow grass stem and handed it to me. "You suck it with the stem. It's cool and nice."

I thrust the stem into the water and began to drink. He was right. "How sweet and cool. I've never had such delicious springwater before."

Seeing me so content, the old man said to me with a smile, "Young man, you should know that the reason the people here on the northern frontier are so healthy and robust is the sweet springwater!" He laughed heartily again, which induced the donkeys to cluster around and jingle their bells with a merry sound.

At noon the next day, Liuhua rushed into my room. Eyes wide, she asked me, "Comrade, do you have the commune's official seal?"

"What is it?" I asked. I noticed that she carried a sack of food on her back.

"It's my dad. He had a fever when he came home late last night, and he also has diarrhea. Actually, he's been sick for some time, but I did not think that today . . ."

I hurried to the commune clinic. The old Red Army man was lying on the bed; a woman doctor was giving him an injection. His face was sallow. The sight of me brought a glimmering light to his eyes; his mouth twitched a bit and he whispered to me, "It doesn't matter, doesn't matter. Live to work and die without regret. We are just little dewdrops and nothing more. Go to your work. Don't delay!"

Luihua went to the grain shop to exchange food stamps. The doctor told me that because the old man had suffered from diarrhea for some time, he was seriously dehydrated. Because he was elderly, she was afraid that . . . She trailed off.

A cold shudder passed through me.

Liuhua came back from the grain shop. She flopped down, dejected. The grain shop would not buy back her food stamps. They only exchanged food stamps for corn and millet.

I resolved to visit the stubborn unit and go through the procedures. As I was preparing to leave, the doctor glanced at Liuhua and made a signal with her lips. "I'm afraid the old man won't pull through."

I was shaken. Dear God! Could it be that the old veteran was passing as if being blown away by a gust of wind?

5

The Red Army man was buried at the foot of the Great Wall, beneath the grassland where the wildflowers blossomed, under his beloved land where he'd left his footprints and to which he had dedicated his life.

No pursuit, no ambition.

Even on his deathbed, he'd held the hands of Director Wang and mumbled, "Don't spend the country's money on me. I'm just a little drop of dew. I haven't done anything. Don't trouble the Party. Please find Liuhua an honest peasant for a husband."

After the Red Army man was buried, his identification problem was resolved—but it was too late. Director Wang held the piece of paper in his hand and bent his head in bitter mourning.

Soon afterward, it was arranged that Liuhua would work as an assistant in the shop of the supply-and-marketing cooperative in the neighboring village. Commune Director Wang came to meet Liuhua in person on a small tractor.

The atmosphere was joyful in the little yard of the donkey shed. Liuhua came out of the small room and approached the tractor through a throng of villagers.

Yet she did not get on to the tractor at once. Instead, she looked around at the donkey shed. Look! The long-eared donkeys were craning their necks to gape at Liuhua.

At that instant, the donkey bells rang out clearer and louder than ever, and a naughty gray foal leapt to Liuhua's side and nuzzled her with its white nose.

Liuhua stood there as if rooted to the spot, stroking the pointed ears of the foal. The little donkey shook its head, and the bell jingled merrily.

Liuhua looked up and asked the leader of the production brigade, "Who will take care of the donkeys after I leave?"

The leader replied, "Don't worry, there's someone to take over."

Liuhua didn't move. She frowned and murmured, "But it's already time for someone to graze the donkeys."

Director Wang was anxious. "Hurry, Liuhua. Leave them. You've got a job—that's the important thing. Maybe when you're settled in Liang Village you and Junhai can be together. Let's go."

Liuhua was stunned at these words. She quickly turned her head and stared at Wang. Her black eyes shot out a sharp, cutting light. In an instant, she turned and went back into her father's small room. She threw down her small bundle and picked up the herding stick.

Coming back out with it, she said coldly, "I'm not going to Liang. I'll stay here and graze the donkeys."

6

It was dusk. Liuhua wasn't back yet. I sat on the battlement of the Great Wall, gazing into the vast desert and grassland. Around me grew the same green grass and wildflowers. But now the scene included a small mound of yellow soil at the foot of the Wall: the grave of the Red Army man. The sunset cast a russet-golden light upon the grassland and shone on the long, curving form of the Wall extending eastward to the sea.

There was the same stillness. The sky seemed higher above; the clouds were paler. The earth looked expansive and immense. This was the real Great Wall, I thought to myself. It wasn't as grand here as at Badaling, which attracts so many tourists. It was modest and true. This part of the Wall had been scoured by time and the turmoil of war for over two thousand years, and only a weathered mass remained. Nonetheless, it was solid and high. The flesh and blood of countless anonymous heroes like the Red Army man had brought it into existence. Their effort created this unadorned backbone of iron traversing the land from Shanhaiguan—the eastern "pass between the sea and mountains"—to the desert. Untouched by the world's cares, it traveled from the Qin Dynasty into the world's future.

I sat on the battlement of the ancient Great Wall and watched the sunset glow in the western sky over the grasslands and yellow sand. I was still conceiving my painting in my heart. But somehow, I could not help but be concerned about Liuhua, and I longed to see the donkeys she cared for. Yet stretching before me were only the vast sea of sand and the verdant plain. Nothing more could be seen. Where was she?

Suddenly the evening breeze carried the familiar jingle of donkey bells. They seemed far off and the sound was dim, but their music reached me clearly. It was always peaceful along the Great Wall, and yet that tranquil line carried an intrinsic power that overwhelmed me. At that moment I felt that the Great Wall was alive and that it smiled. Oh, you sleepless soul! What message do you whisper to our motherland and the posterity of China?

Translated by Liu Danling

Feng Jiqi

Born in Qishan County, Shaanxi Province, Feng Jiqi is a CPC member who studied writing in the Department of Chinese Language and Literature at Northwest University, graduating in 1990. He has worked as a correspondent and station-master at the radio station of Beiguo Town, Qishan County; editor and director of the editing office in the *Chinese and Foreign Documentary Literature Magazine* Company; and director of the editing office in the *Yanhe River Magazine* Company. He made his literary debut in 1983 and joined the Chinese Writers Association in 1994. Now he writes full time, working for the Shaanxi Provincial Writers Association.

His works include the prose collections *Tell Your Life to Yourself*, *People's Testimony*, and *Nothing Retained*; short story collections *Thirty Short Stories* and *My Farmer Parents*; and the novels *Season of Silence*, *Under the Big Tree*, *Knocking at the Door*, *Knife*, and *Village*. His works have won first prize for the Galaxy Documentary Literature of Shaanxi Province, the Shaanxi Double-Five Literature Prize for a Collection of Stories, the Shaanxi Double-Five Literature Prize for a Collection of Essays, and the Nine-Headed Bird novel award.

Feng Jiqi

The Butcher's Knife

The old butcher Ma Changyi was using a grindstone to sharpen his knife in his courtyard. The grindstone was set on a stair under the eaves of his house, which saved him from bending down when he sat on a stool by the stairs. The knife could be made sharp only on a grindstone like this one, deep pea-green in color and fine in quality. The knife, used to kill pigs, was shaped like a willow leaf; it was one foot three inches long and three inches wide, with a smooth, oil-covered handle. Ma Changyi was sharpening all three of his knives in turn: two willow-leaf knives and a chopper.

With his right hand tightly gripping the handle, and three fingers of his left hand pressing, like a Chinese doctor taking a patient's pulse, against the body of the knife, Ma Changyi waved his arms to and fro. He appeared to be careless and absentminded, but in fact he gave great attention to the amount of pressure he used so that the blade would not become blunted. The knife was double bladed; after he finished one blade, he switched the handle to his left hand and continued with the other.

Above the grindstone on another stair there was a china bowl of clear water, from which he took out a tuft of cloth to sprinkle water on the knife. The water scattered across the edge and then ran down the blade.

The springtime sun was pleasant. Rays of sunshine, as intimate and cordial as the knife itself, seemed to be sliced by the leaf-shaped knife. The walls, the doors, and the windows of his house all glowed with happiness when the courtyard was turned white by the gleam of the knife. On the grindstone the sunlight, as thin as muslin, sparkled with every movement of the blade. The light seemed liquid, flowing in all directions.

Ma's perfectly focused attention followed each long and short stroke of the knife on the grindstone. His ears were sensitively attuned to the sound made between knife and grindstone. The sound, as soft as a waving wheat stalk, was reserved and restrained, not the least bit wild or insolent.

The old butcher Ma Changyi had always sharpened his knives this way. The courtyard had a soft, warm atmosphere, with a slight sweet smell from the heated metal. Ma Changyi was as calm as the knife he was sharpening, but there was a trace of subtle joy in his stern face.

As he worked, Ma's hands left the knife. The knife, however, continued moving back and forth, controlled by invisible hands. Ma Changyi moved his stool a little distance away from the step and fixed his eyes on the knife. Like a mechanical gear in a lathe, the knife was moving with the same rhythm it had followed in Ma's hands a moment before. Ma Changyi showed no surprise; this was just what he expected to see. Like a painter, he was appreciating his newly completed work.

Ma Jianhua, the butcher's son, came in and out through the gate several times. He said nothing when he saw his father sharpening the knife; it had become the older man's daily routine. Five years had passed since his father had stopped working as a butcher, but he'd never stopped playing with his knives.

As a young man, Ma Changyi, the butcher, had been well known in Songling Village and throughout Nanbao County. He could skillfully kill a pig and, step by step, make it clean and white.

When the pig was lifted onto his table, he'd remove his coat or jacket and work wearing only a vest, open at the top so that his hairy chest showed through. He'd take up the rope that was used to bind up the pig, wrapping it around his own waist, and begin his work.

With the knife held tightly between his teeth, he'd use his right leg to press heavily upon the pig's belly, his left foot placed solidly on the ground. His right hand grasped the pig's front hip while his left hand held the pig's snout. Once the butcher was in position, his left hand jerked the pig's head back with a sudden force; the pig was unable to utter a sound. Taking up the knife in his right hand, he stabbed it at a slant into the pig's neck. The whole action was finished in the blink of an eye. It was like a match being struck.

The butcher seemed to stab with great force, but in fact he used precisely enough pressure to pierce the pig's heart, and not a bit more. When he pulled out the knife, he caught hold of the belly and squeezed. The pig's blood ran into a basin through the cut in the neck. Thanks to the butcher's agility, once the pig was dead its blood was almost immediately drained from its body. Then the skin became very white and bright.

The next step was to remove the pig's hair in boiling water. The key was to mix cold water into boiling water so that the water was just the right temperature. If the water was too hot, it would damage the skin; if the water was too cold, the hair couldn't be removed. To check the temperature of the boiling water, Ma Changyi would plunge three fingers into the water and immediately pull them out again. To cool it down he would add a bucket of cold water and then another three ladles of cold water. Now he knew the water's temperature without touching it.

Once the pig was submerged in the mixed water, Ma Changyi would roll up his sleeves and plung his arms into the water. In a short time, the pig's hair had been removed. Then the pig was put back on the table, and Ma Changyi would begin to demonstrate his knife skills.

First he would use his willow-leaf-shaped knife to scrape the pig's body, twice. Before finishing, he would cut a hole near one back leg. With a skewer he'd stab into the pig's body along the inner side of the skin. After inhaling a long and deep breath, as if drawing magical powers from somewhere between heaven and earth, Ma Changyi blew on the knife, his mouth nearly touching the blade. At this moment his emotions were aroused and his desire burned deep inside; his four limbs became as stiff and vigorous as the skewer. With his mouth seemingly welded to the pig, he would blow on the blade with a short breath; his cheeks bulged and his eyes opened wide. He'd alternate a long and deep breath with a short and light breath.

This blowing ritual was so rhythmic, enjoyable, and wonderful that he could blow thirty-two times on one inhale. His eyes lit up; he was fully enjoying his work, reveling in it. Women watching would hold their own breath, their eyes wide; some shed warm tears. Ma Changyi would lift his eyes from the pig and sweep them over the women's peach-blossom faces. A nearly indiscernible smile made his brow crease lightly.

Ma's mouth soon left the knife. His hands tightly holding the pig's leg, he'd exhale a long breath. His expression would be self-contented. Sweat would run down his face.

After he'd bound up the opening with flaxen twine, he'd begin again to scrape the pig's whole body with great force, all the way from neck to tail.

The knife took away all the dirty, filthy matter with a rustling sound. He used just enough strength to remove the remaining hair, but not so much as to damage the pig's skin. His feet beside the table seemed to be dancing rhythmically to the knife's every movement. The knife was singing and speaking, too.

At this point Ma Changyi was like a drunkard, intoxicated with his work: shaking his head, waving his arms, and moving his feet in small, fast steps. His face held an intense expression, almost bitter looking, scrunched up as if in great pain, but his eyes glowed with happiness.

In Ma Changyi's hands, the knife bloomed like a flower, proud as the sun, bursting into laughter like a madman. After the butcher scraped the whole pig from left to right, he'd again scrape from top to bottom. The second time, Ma Changyi would hold the handle in his right hand and the knife in his left hand, but after several strokes he'd gradually loosen his grip. The knife moved obediently over the pig's body with exactly the proper strength. It worked more freely now, scraping away all the remaining hair tucked into the wrinkled crevices of the pig's head. The scraping sound was as clear and melodious as a person tapping his fingers on a drum. Squatting down beside the pig, Ma Changyi watched the movement of the knife with a smile on his face.

The crowd of onlookers was startled to see the knife perform for Ma Changyi without his controlling it.

When the pigskin was scraped clean, Ma Changyi moved to cut open the pig's belly. He placed the knife's tip gently, just on the line formed between the pig's belly and its anus. He pressed the blade lightly and a line appeared, like a masterful brushstroke on a piece of white paper. Abruptly, he stilled the knife. His right hand held the handle lightly, while his left hand suddenly hit a spot on the handle not covered by his right. The belly, like two doors, opened with a clang, and the tripe and intestines poured out.

Laying down the knife, the butcher grasped a two-foot-long, smooth, oiled stick to prop the belly open, allowing a stream of hot air to burst out. At this moment, he'd shout in a low voice, "Get away!" As the crowd shrank back, he would quickly grab a handful of cottonlike steaming grease from inside the belly and put it into his mouth. He'd tilt his head back and promptly dispatch the grease to his stomach. Often, women would spontaneously utter an amazed "ah!" Ma Changyi didn't look at them at all; he took up the knife again and continued his work.

The willow-leaf-shaped knife was an amazement to the villagers. They couldn't help sighing and gasping in surprise. Some young women, in particular, exclaimed, "The knife, the knife!" They gazed at Ma Changyi in admiration.

Ma Changyi appeared untouched by their gaze, though he certainly knew what their eyes meant. Sometimes a flirtatious woman would pat him on the shoulder, saying, "Brother Ma, tell me what magic you have performed."

Turning around for a glimpse at the woman, he'd reply casually, "It's not magic, but skill from my years of practice."

Some thought the knife a monster; when Changyi put it down, a curious man would take it up and test its sharpness by cutting his own hair. The man would loosen his grasp to see if the knife would move on its own, but the knife always refused and would fall to the ground, nearly slicing off the man's foot. The villagers sensed the strangeness of the knife, but they couldn't figure out why the same knife would move automatically like a machine in Ma's hands.

——

Now, on his stairs under the eaves, Ma Changyi turned to see a woman standing before him. She was a beggar and had made a living in Songling for a long time; all the villagers knew her. She was in her forties or a bit younger, known to be a native of Wudu County in Gansu Province.

Without a word, the woman fixed her eyes on the knife moving automatically on the grindstone, free of Ma's touch. Her mouth half-open, she blinked at the back-and-forth movement of the knife. The knife had captured her gaze as well as her heart. She seemed nervous; one hand was clenched in a fist and the other grasped a corner of her clothing.

Ma Changyi took the knife from the grindstone. The beggar relaxed and nodded as if to show her admiration. The butcher took out ten yuan from his pocket and gave the money to the beggar.

The woman said, "The knife, your knife?"

Angrily Ma Changyi bent down and picked up his knife. It gleamed. The beggar suddenly trembled, and her face turned pale. Ma Changyi said impatiently, "You are not to come here anymore!"

The beggar turned and quickly disappeared. Ma Changyi glanced at the woman's back, finding it upright and her hips plump, not sullen and loose.

Ma Changyi, now retired these past five years, continued to sharpen his knives. Then, as he always did, he took the knives and walked toward the gate.

At the passage between the new building and his own house, he encountered two girls who worked at his son's restaurant. Thanks to a custom granted by Fengshan County, dozens of households ran catering businesses. But Ma Jianhua's building was located just beside the highway, giving his business an advantage. In his building, the first and second floors were occupied by the restaurant, and the third floor was a dance hall. On Sundays, many city dwellers from Xishui City and the provincial capital would tour Zhougong Temple; from there they would come to the village to rest and dine.

Thanks to his brisk business, Ma Jianhua employed more waitresses than any other restaurant in the village. The two girls at Ma

Changyi's gate had been working at the restaurant only a short time. Seeing the knife in Ma's fist, they were so scared that they instantly covered their breasts with their hands. They lowered their heads, letting him pass without saying a word.

Ma Jianhua would replace the old waitresses with new, younger, and prettier ones every three months. Ma Changyi never concerned himself with his son's business. To him, each of the girls was a stranger. Although he often went to his son's restaurant to dine, none of the girls' faces remained in his memory.

One early spring night, when he had just fallen asleep, Ma Changyi was awakened by the sounds of cries. First he heard his daughter-in-law crying and then another girl's cries. Unable to go back to sleep, he sat up but didn't go out right away. He went to his wooden cabinet and took up the knife he had sharpened that day. His rough hand moved lightly over it, producing a sound as slight as waving wheat. The knife felt cool and smooth in his hand. After stroking the knife twice, he licked the blade with the tip of his tongue. It tasted like iron, a mixture of sweet and salty. When he put down the knife, the courtyard had fallen silent again.

Ma Changyi left his room. Walking lightly, he crossed the yard, which was bathed in fluid moonlight, and went up to the second floor. He knew his son and daughter-in-law didn't share a room, that his son had a room of his own on the second floor, where he spent most of his free time. Upstairs he stopped at his son's door. He could hear the sounds of his son in bed with a girl. He wanted to leave, but his feet refused to move.

The girl was twittering and sobbing, and then there was silence. Was that the slim girl who often served him a meal? Or was it the fat girl with fair skin? Or was it the girl from Sichuan Province with the big, round eyes? Ma Changyi could hear nothing but the sound of the moon burning on the roof of the building. He went back downstairs softly.

———

Ma Jianhua had one hobby: collecting girls' hair. Whenever he went to bed with a girl, he would collect several strands of her hair and stick them in his diary, labeled with a number. His wife had long suspected that her husband was unfaithful, but she couldn't find a way to confront him until she discovered his revolting habit. When she found the diary, she also saw that the numbers went up to sixteen. She was startled and went to confront him; he only cursed her and sent her out of his room.

Ma Changyi was aware of the differences between him and his son; they had different ways of living. Ma Changyi had tried to change his son, but in vain.

When he was a student in middle school, Ma Jianhua didn't behave well. One time, he and two classmates had left the school and put up a stall to sell vegetables, without saying anything to their teacher. When Ma Changyi found out, he threatened his son with the knife, saying, "Set your mind to study, or I'll cut off your hands."

The son had stretched out his arm and said, "Go ahead, cut here!"

The butcher's face had turned sallow in anger. He threw down the knife and left.

Later, when his son failed the college entrance examination, Ma Changyi tried to persuade him to repeat his studies for a second year, but Ma Jianhua refused to listen to him; instead he went to the county seat and found a job managing a snooker hall. Ma Changyi went there and broke all the billiard sticks. Nevertheless, his son still went his own way.

Ma Changyi, who had been a butcher for half his life, longed to see his son's success. He wished only that his son not follow in his footsteps as a peasant butcher.

When Ma Jianhua had been a child, studying in primary school, his father used to make him kneel down as a punishment, but most of the time the boy was obedient. When Ma Changyi's son was born, the butcher was much older than most of the other village fathers of his generation; therefore he devoted more love to his son than to his daughter. He still remembered one night when his son had a severe stomachache; he'd carried the boy on his back to the county hospital, in spite of the heavy rain and cold wind, his wife holding an umbrella over them.

When their son entered high school, the couple bought no new clothing the entire year in order to save enough money to allow their son to dine in the teachers' canteen, which served better food. They did everything they could to benefit their son's studies and his future—but he refused to follow the road laid out for him.

When Ma Jianhua got married, Ma Changyi no longer worried about his son's future. Still, he tried to teach the lad how to conduct himself in society by setting a good example, hoping Jianhua would become an honest, kind person who dealt fairly in business. Whenever he pointed out these lessons, his son made no reply but simply smiled. The father couldn't fathom what lay in his son's mind.

It was apparent to Ma Changyi that his son and daughter-in-law were not on good terms, and he knew that his son had affairs with the girls from his restaurant. But how could he talk with his son about such things? The old to the young? Sometimes he felt he could forgive his son, for whenever he turned on the TV, what he saw was men and women wrapped in each other's arms, or a man going to bed with a woman, or a woman being the third party in a couple's marriage. No wonder young men had been so influenced. At other times he couldn't forgive his son at all, for it was immoral for a married man to go to bed with another woman. He couldn't let his son live such a life.

It was only when he was sharpening the knife that he could forget all these thoughts.

Knife in hand, Ma Changyi left the courtyard, crossed the main road, and came around to Muck Street behind his yard, where there was a stack of dried wheat straw and a stack of firewood. He waved his knife and stabbed it into the straw as if into his enemy. He stabbed with a quick motion, producing a sound like that of cutting hair. Pulling out, stabbing in, pulling out, stabbing in—Ma moved around the stack, repeating the maneuver. He unfastened his buttons and rolled up his sleeves. He appeared to be greatly excited. After stabbing dozens of times, he scraped his knife on a pile of hard firewood; it sounded like knife scraping bone. The knife became blunted and its blade turned flat.

Looking at the knife, he smiled grimly. Then he returned to his courtyard and immediately set to sharpening it again. After he made it sharp, he would blunt it, and then sharpen, and then blunt. It was his daily routine.

———

Ma Jianhua had wanted to pull down all five rooms of the old one-story house when he was putting up the new building in the courtyard, but Ma Changyi wouldn't allow it. The older man preferred to live in the house he had built himself. Therefore, three old rooms were pulled down and the other two remained, dull in tone and ill-matched to the impressive new building. A stranger passing by would think that Ma Jianhua was practicing "one country, two systems" at home, leaving his father in a shack while the son enjoyed relative comfort. In fact, the younger man had had no choice but to yield to his father's stubbornness. He often tried to persuade his father to have the old house pulled down, but his father always remained silent. If Ma Jianhua continued to press the matter, Ma Changyi would take up the knife and scrape his own leg. Seeing this, Ma Jianhua would drop the argument.

When Ma Changyi had originally built his five-room house, many Songling villagers cast envious eyes on him, saying Ma Changyi was a successful, capable man. The house was a highlight of his life and career. The year after the house was built, he had gotten married and then lived with his wife in the house for decades. But to his bitter sorrow, his wife, who was ten years younger than he, died five years ago. She was only forty-nine years old when she died. On her deathbed she asked him to sit beside her so she could smell her husband's body. It was the smell of knives and butchered pig's meat, a smell that had kept her company for thirty years.

The first night of their marriage, when he wanted to go to bed with her, she shed painful tears and said, "You are harder than your knife!"

He replied, "The harder a man is, the more he's loved by a woman. Don't believe it? Just have a try!"

At first his wife couldn't bear the smell of the meat and the frightening blade between his legs, but after some time, the woman grew greedy for the smell. The strong, hot, sticky scent on its own would arouse her intense desire. When they were in bed together, she'd say lustily, "You're so hard—do whatever you like."

When Ma Changyi came home after killing pigs, his wife would hold the knife bag and slide out the knife. It was her way of hinting, and he readily took the hint. Then the smells of meat and iron filled every corner of the house.

When she was alive, she used to assist Ma in his work—helping him sharpen his knives, or holding the pig's leg for him, or pulling out the pig's intestines in order to remove the waste.

Ma Changyi and his wife had hard times, too. Like most peasants, they labored for three periods of the day—early morning, late morning, and afternoon. Sometimes they'd have to labor in the evening as well. They had only one pair of work trousers between them. Ma Changyi gallantly insisted that his wife wear the trousers, while the woman refused so that her husband could wear them. Often neither one would give in, both of them choosing to endure the cold instead. When they were both working at the reservoir construction site, alternating shifts, whichever of the couple was currently on the job would wear the pants.

In winter, they went to cut firewood near Beishan Mountain. Ma Changyi cut firewood at the bottom of the valley while his wife carried the firewood out of the valley. Standing at the foot of the mountain, Ma Changyi looked up at the woman's bent and curved back, and his eyes suddenly brimmed with tears. What a good woman! When she returned for the next load, as he bound up the firewood and loaded it on her back, he gazed at her sweat-moistened, flushed face and could no longer control himself. He rushed to lift her and made her lie down on her back without even releasing the bundle strapped to her, so that she lay on top of the firewood. Before the woman could pull her arms from the rope, he had already removed her trousers. His blood was boiling with urgency. Bending over her body, he said, "You just lie down. I won't let you carry firewood—you just carry the butcher Ma Changyi."

With her arms around his waist, she said emotionally, "I will carry you, and carry you for my whole life."

In Ma's eyes, there was no better woman. No one could take his wife's place. He had a rough appearance but a considerate heart. More than once he had said to himself, "I have to provide her with better clothing and better food. I'll make more money with my knife so that she can live a better life."

In the winter of 1985, Ma Changyi was called to kill pigs for the peasants in Beiyang Village. He spent five days in a row killing pigs before he returned to Songling.

That night when he entered his home, smelling strongly of blood, his wife noticed that he looked gloomy. Something was wrong, but she didn't know what. Without a word, Ma Changyi threw himself down on the kang and stared at the ceiling. The woman removed his cotton-padded shoes and socks. She covered his legs with the quilt. When she went to untie the buttons of his cotton jacket, he pushed her hand away and took the jacket off himself. The bloody scent grew stronger; it was coming from his body. When she lay down beside him, she found a white cloth wrapped around his hairy chest. She asked him what had happened; he remained silent.

She untied the white cloth and found a bloody cut across the left side of his chest. Startled, she asked, "Did this happen while you were slaughtering pigs?" Ma Changyi nodded his head. "But for years you've never had an accident when you killed a pig." She shook her head incredulously.

Ma Changyi didn't reply, but this strong, stoic man began to shed tears, so his wife asked no more questions. After applying some medicine to the wound, she dressed it with a strip of clean, white gauze.

That night, Ma Changyi tossed and turned on the kang. His wife asked him, "Is it painful?"

He told her it was not a physical pain, but a mental one. His wife hugged him from behind. Ma Changyi said, "Hold me tightly, tightly." Holding each other, the couple slept that way until daybreak.

Ma's birthday fell a week later, on January 2. That night the couple had a busy and beautiful time in bed, just as they had when they were young, making the earth and the ocean shake. When they finished, Ma Changyi, not wanting to keep a secret from his wife, told her how he had gotten the wound on his chest.

On the night of December 27, after the day's slaughters were finished, his host had entertained him with fat meat and wine. Later, his host went out to bring meat to his mother-in-law. Ma Changyi was sleeping in a spare room for the night when the host's wife pushed the door open and came in. She quickly stripped off her clothes and crawled under Ma's quilt. Before Ma Changyi realized what was happening, the woman had already put out the light, and while one hand reached under the quilt for his manhood, the other stroked his hairy chest.

His heart beating fast, Ma turned around and caught sight of his knife bag on the cabinet. The knife was as bright as a lamp; in that light he could see his wife, her face an image of health, kindness, intimacy, and affection. He heard the knife saying, "Ma Changyi, you said you would love me for your whole life, and that you would never give your heart to another woman. Is that true?" Hearing the knife crying in the bag, Ma quickly pushed the naked woman away, turned on the light, and jumped off the bed. He reached into the bag for the knife. Turning pale with fright, the hostess heard Ma Changyi asking her to leave immediately. Before she'd crossed the threshold, Ma Changyi had already made a cut in his chest with his knife. He spent the rest of the night in the host's cowshed.

When Ma finished recounting the story, his trembling wife held him in her arms. He wanted to continue speaking, but she stopped him. She suggested letting his manly blade speak instead, and Ma Changyi had another busy and beautiful time with his wife in bed.

Afterward, his wife asked him tenderly, "Changyi, this knife is yours, and also mine, right?"

Ma Changyi replied, "Yes, and yes."

His wife laughed.

When his wife left this world, Ma Changyi was sick with grief. Wherever he went, he felt empty: in the house, in the courtyard, in the whole world. His nights were sleepless.

The knife always brought his wife's figure to mind, so Ma took the knife with him wherever he went. His unusual behavior frightened the villagers, including his son. Eventually some village cadres were able to convince Ma Changyi not to bring the knife into the field, to his relatives' homes, or to the market. But he often got out of bed at midnight to sharpen the knife in the courtyard. He felt restless if he didn't sharpen his knife even for one day.

After his wife died, he found ten pairs of shoes in the cabinet, all handmade by her. Ma Changyi took them all out, looked at them for a while, and set them on top of the cabinet. Every few days he would take the shoes out and dry them in the sun, and then store them again atop the cabinet. Five years passed; he had never put any of the shoes on his feet. At night, after gazing at all the shoes for a long time, he would smell them, inhaling the smell of cloth, the needle, the thread, the color, and a smell he couldn't quite identify. He would put his hands into the shoes, absorbing their warmth, softness, smoothness.

The butcher's daughter-in-law always wondered why her father-in-law had the shoes displayed on the cabinet. She thought he wanted to show the villagers how devoted her mother-in-law had been. One day she put the ten pairs of shoes back inside the cabinet. Ma Changyi grew sullen and told her to take them out.

She said, "They'll get dirty. Besides, why don't you ever wear them?"

"None of your business," Ma Changyi said. "Just take them out and put them on top of the cabinet."

The daughter-in-law had to take all the shoes back out and display them on the cabinet as before.

———

The night the dance hall opened, Ma Jianhua was worried that the music from the speakers would disturb his father's sleep, so he tried to keep the volume at a reasonable level. At eleven o'clock that night, he came down to the courtyard to see if his father had fallen asleep. Upon entering the courtyard, he saw his father sharpening a knife. A bright moon was drifting in the sky above the silvery white yard. The moonlight, like the tongue of a cow, was licking Ma's silvery-white body, which looked transparent, like an artifact of the moonlight. Ma Changyi was deeply absorbed in sharpening his knife. The knife glittered crisply under the bright moon.

Standing at a distance, Ma Jianhua could see his father swaying slightly, his feet beating rhythmically to the movement of his body, which was also the rhythm of the dance music upstairs. It looked like his father was not so much sharpening a knife as dancing with a knife. The butcher waved the leaflike knife, admiring it in varying positions. The knife was burning like the moonlight. Ma Jianhua couldn't see his father's expression; he could only see the knife dancing happily in the courtyard, under the bright, fine moonlight. Ma Jianhua could see nothing but the knife. The whole yard was filled with its overwhelming smell.

He didn't have the patience to see more. He went back upstairs quietly.

The following day, when the father and the son met, they had only to look into each other's eyes; after an embarrassed moment, they passed each other without a word.

One night, Ma Changyi came up to the third floor and stood quietly outside the dance hall, still as a wooden stake. Ma Jianhua pulled the door open; seeing his father there, he invited the older man in to have a look. Ma Changyi said, "I am only sharpening my knife." Only then did Ma Jianhua notice that his father was holding the knife.

Ma Jianhua said, "Just put your knife back and then come in, have a look. You've never seen how the young people dance."

His father replied, "I want to bring the knife with me. There's nothing to be afraid of."

"Bring it if you want," Ma Jianhua said.

The father followed his son into the dance hall. Intoxicated by the music, the young people inside didn't notice Ma with his knife. The butcher took a seat on a bench, holding the knife in his lap. When the colored lights swept over the hall, the knife, ablaze in color and waves of light, seemed like a natural part of the scene.

A girl with large breasts and a wide bottom came over to Ma Changyi. She was going to ask him to dance; she hadn't noticed the knife. Unaware that the girl had had an affair with his son, Ma Changyi raised the knife from his lap. He only meant to explain that he wasn't there to dance, just to have a look. But the girl, seeing the knife reflect a dazzling gleam, screamed and rushed toward the crowd as if chased by a murderer.

Back in the courtyard, Ma Changyi sat beside the step under the house eaves and began sharpening the knife again. After a while, he put his thumb on the blade to feel its sharpness. Then he took the knife to a poplar next to an outhouse in the backyard. He chopped off all the branches of the poplar with the force and speed of a much younger man. He was torturing the knife, as the knife was torturing him.

"You are useless!" he shouted. "What can I do with you?"

Returning to the dance hall, Ma Changyi knew that he'd scared the girl, but his eyes couldn't help searching for her. He saw her dancing in a man's arms. The girl was turning round and round, swaying along with the music. He blinked and saw that her clothes had been cast away. Ma's eyes were filled with the vision of plump nipples and fleshy hips.

He gripped the knife handle tightly, hearing a dull sound in his ears. The girl's fleshy white body was swaying before his eyes, making him feel dizzy. The sound of the music was at some times like corn stalks crushed under a tractor, and at other times like a pig's fatty meat being cut away from bone. Colored lights poured down like rain. It felt like what skimmed overhead was not colored light, but countless knives. They were as soft as noodles but still retained their sharpness.

Ma Changyi had played with knives his whole life and had never feared them. Tonight, however, the sensation of all the knives above his head scared him out of his wits. Vaguely he saw one bloody cut after another on his body; he felt pain all over as if needles were piercing his chest. The knife fell to the floor with a loud bang, overwhelming the noise of the music.

Suddenly the music stopped—the dancing was over for the night. Ma Changyi's thoughts were interrupted by girls' shouts, laughter, and the footsteps of the crowd heading downstairs. With difficulty he bent down to pick up the knife. Leaning on it with its tip pointed toward the ground, he struggled back into his own old, shabby house.

———

One day between late summer and early autumn, the villagers found the dead body of the woman beggar. She had been stabbed to death on the edge of a swamp. Curious, Ma Jianhua joined the onlookers.

The woman beggar, her limbs stretched out, lay prone at the foot of the slope leading to the swamp. Her hair hung loosely over her face. There was a large stab wound in her back. She had been wearing her shoes with the back part squashed flat, so that her heels stuck out of them. She was neatly dressed; it looked like she was only sleeping, facedown.

Standing beside the body, the villagers whispered, "Who would stab this woman to death?" Several of them let out a sympathetic sigh. "She looks so nice. What a pity!"

Ma Jianhua squeezed into the crowd to have a glimpse. After seeing the hole in her back, he left, feeling sick.

When he entered the yard, Ma Jianhua could no longer keep from throwing up. Ma Changyi, who sat sharpening his knife, asked his son, "What's the matter?"

Ma Jianhua answered, "A killing. I have seen a killing."

"Who was killed?" his father asked.

Ma Jianhua answered, "Someone killed the woman beggar."

Ma Changyi replied, "Do you think that is worthy of your attention? Haven't you seen a dead person before?" He sprayed some clean water on the knife and was again lost in his work.

In the afternoon, the body was taken away by the local police. Afterward, two policemen came to the village and went door-to-door in search of clues.

When the policemen came to his door, Ma Jianhua didn't conceal anything about what he knew.

"Did you know the woman beggar?" asked one officer.

"Yes, I did," answered Ma Jianhua.

"When did you see her last?"

"About a month ago."

"Who in the village is most likely to have any hatred toward the woman?"

"I don't know."

"Why do you think someone would want to kill a beggar?"

"It couldn't have been a murder for money. How much money could a beggar have?"

"Do you think she was raped and then killed?" asked the police, scrutinizing his face.

"I suppose someone is so thirsty as to eat snow." Ma Jianhua smiled.

"Then you don't think she was raped?"

"Only a guess," said Ma Jianhua. "Without any evidence I dare not draw a conclusion."

The policemen spent three days looking into the case in Songling but uncovered no clues about the killer. Since the victim was no more than a beggar, they had little motivation to pursue the investigation. After all, it is difficult to solve a case without any clues.

Just when the police were preparing to put the case aside for the time being, something happened in the village. To the villagers' surprise and shock, Ma Changyi committed suicide.

For a couple of days prior, Ma Changyi hadn't sharpened his knife.

At lunchtime that day, Ma Changyi didn't show up in his son's restaurant as he usually did. Thinking his father wasn't feeling well, the son left him alone so he could rest. After lunch, when there were fewer customers, he went into his father's old house. Ten pairs of shoes were still neatly displayed on top of the cabinet. His father lay on the bed, covered with the quilt from head to toe.

Thinking he was asleep, the son called, "Father!" But his father made no reply. He called again, and still his father remained motionless.

His heart suddenly seized with fear; Ma Jianhua could smell blood and iron. Drawing closer to the bed, he lifted the quilt and saw a pool of blood. Three knives lay beside his father. The butcher had sliced the vein in his arm. His body had already stiffened.

Translated by Zhang Yihong

Li Kangmei

Born in Weinan City, Shaanxi Province, Li Kangmei graduated from the Department of Chinese Language and Literature, Northwest University, in 1989. Before that, in 1970, he had joined the army and worked as a soldier of 5307 Unit, as a temp at Weinan Fuel Company, and as a professional writer at the Art Institute. He is the fourth standing director of the Shaanxi Provincial Writers Association and chairman of the Weinan Writers Association. He made his literary debut in 1981 and joined the Chinese Writers Association in 1994.

Li Kangmei's works include the novels *Fissura Marginalis*, *Forever*, and *Roses Are Still Red*; the novellas *Chilly Winds and Cold Rains*, *Family Problems*, *Thick Soil*, *Snowfield*, *Revenge*, *Battle of Official Career*, *Go to the Post*, and *Female County Magistrate*; and the TV series *Old Circumvallation*. His *Li Kangmei Corpus* is a three-volume opus. His work has won the Shaanxi Double-Five Literature Prize, the China Central Television Best Script Prize, and the Torrent Excellent Works of Henan Province Award.

12

LI KANGMEI

The Portrait of the Ancestor

A true June sun looks down. In its bright light, her extended shadow moves energetically. Solemnly she brandishes the broom as the splashed water soaks into the earth. Her loose, white gown is a lonely cloud floating in the drifting dusty fog, but from the sky it looks like a mass of rags. The ground is as clean as if it has been freshly wiped by a cloth. A pungent scent rises from the earth.

A bar tightly latches the gate. In the yard, a stripe of white hemp is tied between two pegs, projecting a pitch-black shadow arc against the dark-yellow land.

She trembles with excitement, holding the ancestral portrait with both hands. It seems like the austere ancestor on the long, mounted scroll might blow away with the wind as she wipes, but she doesn't slacken in her ritual cleansing. This annual ritual causes the ancestor on the ancient rice paper to become haggard and frail. She must be careful not to let his portrait be exposed to the sun nor left in the damp to grow moldy.

First she unfolds the scroll on the kang. The stiff and yellowish underlay sends out a cracking sound like raindrops falling on withered leaves. Carefully intent, she feels her sparse hair damp with sweat and her skin shiny as wet glass. More than once she experiences a leaping-up disturbance of some kind, a sudden tightening in her body. It makes her wonder about this portrait of sitting men whose heroic handsomeness is compelling enough to attract any woman. Though the once-vivid color has faded with time, the central figure's lifelike gentle, merciful face once again penetrates deep into her imagination. He wears an ancient outfit. His long, thick hair, bound by a stripe of gold, stands tall; a golden belt circles the waist of his mauve robe.

This ancestor, in fact, belongs to all those villagers who respect him as "the grandfather." A distant conflict among the kindred long ago caused a regretful separation between him and his wife. Those dissatisfied with the local harsh living conditions chose to emigrate stealthily. But surprisingly, during their midnight leaving, they did not take the scroll with the male ancestor's portrait. Whether they acted out of sympathy or anxiety is not clear. In any case, the scroll is now incomplete—the female portrait is missing, a sad vacancy. Fortunately the portrait of the male ancestor still has the power to hold the pieces of the village together.

In the past, on lunar New Year's Day, the portrait was unfolded on the wide wall of the ancestral temple before every inhabitant; the forefather in the scroll would sit solemnly upright, receiving the people who made deep bows before him. Even after the temple was rebuilt as a school, the scroll remained at the hall for a couple of New Year's Days. Only the chief of the village was entitled to keep this precious scroll.

But now, the scroll has been left in the care of an outsider, a middle-aged woman who has never been the chief of the settlements. Her dead father-in-law once was the chief, and her ex-husband succeeded him. But the latter quit the position and now is a contractor in town. He rarely comes back to this home, for he has remarried. They are no longer husband and wife.

The portrait has almost been forgotten by the local villagers.

Her ex-husband did not think to hand the portrait over when quitting as chief. The current chief is a young lad; he called the portrait "the thing" when she offered it from both hands with respect. He allowed his aunt—that's what he called her— to keep it safe and sound.

She carried the thing under her arm when she went home, with a wild mix of emotions. Thus suddenly honored, she had a sense of irrevocable responsibility. The young chief instructed her to keep the scroll "safe and sound," smiling trustingly. She knew nothing of the rituals that had been involved prior to her marriage, only the single fact that the keeper would be responsible for accepting all tributes dedicated to the ancestral portrait. Later, the tributes eventually ceased. But she felt that the guardian of the portrait must continue to represent its supreme stature and value in the village.

She remembers how her father-in-law, in the small hours of the first day of the lunar New Year, would ask his wife to take out the portrait from some secret place in the closet. Then, escorted by firecrackers all the way to the school hall, and after the villagers crowded in, he would be the first to worship with three kowtows. He would stand beside the portrait, witnessing as the villagers one by one made their three deep bows of respect. Her family shared the honor of escorting the portrait and kowtowing early because of her father-in-law.

She had memorized all the rules of the ritual before her mother-in-law had left the scene. The portrait was presented twice a year— once on the first day of the lunar New Year, and again on the sixth of June. Her ex-husband had performed the sacred ritual for a few years after her father-in-law's death. Although the lunar ceremony gradually lost its grandeur, the portrait continued to be faithfully presented twice a year. Then her ex-husband decided with deep regret: no more public display, but we can still hang it at home. Her family continued to be very faithful worshippers.

Now the portrait is left in her care. Her name, Huang Xishou, means "fine hands," but it can also mean a woman from a different family.

The sunlight passes through the window onto the kang, where the portrait is in half-light and half-dark. After she finishes washing her hands and face in the kitchen, she notes the sunlight shining on half the portrait and turns pale with fright. While she and her husband were still married, he admonished her that the rules must not be broken and the portrait must always be protected from direct sunlight.

She eventually began to put a sheet over the rope holding the portrait. Then another sheet covered the portrait itself. Her ex-husband approved. Today she continues this practice skillfully, pulling the portrait into the shadows gently and then quickly draping a single bedsheet over it.

Unexpectedly, she feels her eyes grow moist. Her hands, busy spreading the sheets, turn rigid. The brand-new sheet is decorated with brilliantly colored pine and a crane: the pine boughs are lush and the white crane, symbolizing health and longevity, dramatically extends its wings. This is a gift from her daughter and has been kept in the bottom of the box. At the end of last year, when her son and daughter paid a visit, her son brought her a variety of foodstuffs, and her daughter, the sheet. She remembers how deeply satisfied she was when she first took it into her hands. Impulsively, as she put the sheet into the box, she thought of asking them to kowtow to the portrait on the first day of the New Year. The memory of that moment excites and thrills her, but her daughter had to go to her husband's family to celebrate the arrival of the New Year. And her son could not stay either. Already the straw boss of his father, he has to split his filial piety—half to his mother, half to his father while guarding the construction site.

A knock stops the tears in her eyes.

Persuaded by her children, she has changed her living habits in recent years: eating well to lead a happy life, remembering things worth remembering, and forgetting things not worth the bother.

"Who is it?" She walks into the yard.

"Me," answers a man.

"What is it?" she asks.

"Open the door to talk." The man remains outside.

"Not today, I'm not going to . . ." She has kept today's ritual as the main secret of her heart for years, but her secret almost slips out on hearing his voice. She swallows and smiles at herself silently.

A couple of years ago, she was anxious about no one taking over the portrait, but later, she started hoping that the memory of the portrait would disappear gradually among the villagers. When her ex-husband dumped her and started a new family, she was pleased to be left with his ancestor. She long ago decided that the moment before she passed away, she would ask all the villagers to gather around her and would offer them the portrait as a dedicated treasure, leaving all the villagers gaping and in tears.

What kind of honor will that be?

He chuckles outside, then gets close to the door and keeps his voice low: "I'm not going to . . . with you . . . I am going to . . ."

She raises her voice: "Not today, no matter what happens!" Today's portrait drying is a heavy responsibility. The day has become holy to her, and she must keep herself clean for the sake of her sacred ancestor, resisting the insistent man outside. "You, you . . . you make me anxious!"

"You may be anxious, not me."

She doesn't answer.

"OK, OK, I will come tonight." The footsteps recede.

She stands in the yard for a while, feeling a little guilty. Truthfully, her days would be boring and hard without him. He is an educated man, dealing with everything about her thoughtfully and delicately. For instance, he asked a craftsman to install water pipes for her in the yard, but to others he said: "Huang's ex-husband is still a good-hearted man—see, he takes care of her life in one way or another, even though they're not a couple anymore." And when harvest season approached, he secretly borrowed farming machines to give her a hand in the fields, then told others: "See, though this husband and wife were together for only one night, love lingers on for a hundred."

Sometimes, she is also grateful to her ex-husband, who gave her the freedom to taste this sweet, destroying her stereotyped notion that every man is the same.

Her ex-husband never valued much about her, such as her fine hands. But her new friend kneads and squeezes her hands from every fingertip, licking and sucking them with his lips and tongue. After every inch of the palms and backs of her hands are caressed, she giggles like a young sweetheart.

The sight of the white hemp rope rescues her from indulgent self-absorption. Drawing her lips together, straightening the edge of her gown and running her fingers through her half-wet hair, she grows calm and again feels a sense of awe, standing before the portrait lying on the kang. She pulls back the sheet, wondering whether the ancestor will glare at her in anger. But his bushy eyebrows and big eyes are as benign as usual, only a little blurred and languid with age.

Then she smells the scent of the mothballs coming from the brand-new sheet.

While taking out the sheet her nose became numb. She is too nervous to breathe, but her conversation with the man in the yard clears her mind as well as her nose. It was her ex-husband who required her to jam in a few protective mothballs, though now she has turned to her mother-in-law's practice and stuffs in tobacco leaves.

The scroll becomes reshaped by the new sheet, the gift of her daughter. Her daughter bought the sheet to demonstrate her filial piety. She wasn't thinking of the portrait. She only hoped to add some color to her mother's room. If using such a sheet to wrap the portrait is in any way a mistake, the mother must take the blame.

In previous years she used the denim sheet from the kang as the bottom layer and covered the portrait with a hand-dyed door curtain. Since the curtain has many holes, she is glad to replace it with the new sheet.

The mothballs smell stronger and fresher than the tobacco leaves. She repeatedly sniffs the scent. It reminds her of the smell of the man outside when he stayed with her.

"Lay the portrait in the sun in a hurry!" she orders herself. But the man's interruption agitates her. The benign face of the ancestor, however, restores her calm.

Pulling the denim sheet from the kang and throwing it on the rope in the yard, she stretches it flat from one end to the other. Then she's suddenly filled with shame and pulls the sheet down rapidly. The sheet was rinsed just a few days ago. It is tracelessly clean. The light shines through it. Nevertheless, the thought of the man causes her to pull it down.

Her ex-husband slept with her on this sheet for years, but she never felt shame when she dried the portrait in the sun. She probably wouldn't have felt this way today, either, if her new friend hadn't come knocking at such an untimely moment. Thinking of what they did on the sheet, she throws it on the bench under the eaves and considers what to replace it with.

After a while, her eyes light up. She takes out the sheet she has saved in the closet for her son. Though her son barely visits her, it is the ideal choice. He is the rightful descendant, and so he's qualified to line up with the portrait. He will also be the new chief if he doesn't leave the village.

So she completes the drying procedure with the portrait in the middle, her daughter's sheet under it, and her son's on top.

After the drying process is finished, simply and securely, she covers the gate with the denim sheet to resist peeking outside. Having completed her task, she sits on a stool in the shadows, enjoying the sunshine with the ancestor.

She drowses under the dry heat of the sun, but then quickly awakens, worrying that the wind will blow the portrait off the rope. Besides, the time in the sun must be carefully calculated, for the scroll is fragile.

Footsteps hasten to the outside door. This time she simply does not answer. There is a gentle knock. Then the man moves back and begins to think aloud:

"Xishou, what happened today? I want to talk to you about a good thing . . ." After a quiet moment, he murmurs softly, temptingly, "Your hands, your fine hands . . ."

She is half-seduced; her hands under her knees begin to tremble out of control. But she calms herself by sucking her fingers in her own mouth. If it were not for the secret hanging on the rope, she would open the door.

She again hears his steps. Suddenly frightened, he yells at her, "What's on your mind? Don't be nervous, you don't—"

She interrupts, "I'm OK! Everything is fine! Why don't you come later tonight?"

"As long as you're OK . . ." He leaves in relief.

After he leaves, her mind relaxes and stretches out. The covered portrait with the two layered sheets flies in the wind. But she sees them separately. The top sheet is her son's—he soars lightly and joyfully like a free flag. The portrait is heavy—he breathes deeply and wheezes. The bottom sheet . . . but her mind is cut off from involving her daughter—it's improper. Stop it! She tells herself to close her eyes at once and calm her restless heart. She will always relate someone to the portrait on the antique paper. It was her father-in-law years ago, then her ex-husband. In the past the portrait symbolized power. Then the portrait and power became less closely connected. Sometimes it's only a portrait, but sometimes, it is the spirit of the entire village.

The man outside also has a different family now. He used to be a teacher in the village school and then became accepted as a son-in-law living in his wife's home. From that he became a member of the village. She is willing to associate him with the portrait, but he has already become confusedly entangled in her mind. It was wise to put her son's sheet on top so that she would think first of her son. All things change in the world; you don't know what will happen tomorrow. Another day the villagers may be keen to worship their forefathers again, looking eagerly for the face of the ancestor. Then the keeper of the portrait will be the one who boards the altar first and gives orders to everyone in glory.

Thinking of such a scene, she opens her eyes in pleasure and almost jumps into the room, ladling out a basin of cold water. The cool wash delivers the appropriate sobriety. Cleansed from fatigue, her face glows as fresh as a new bride.

Her father-in-law had been the keeper of the portrait for three years when she became a bride. So her wedding was much grander than that of any other woman in the village. She clearly remembers her father-in-law perched solemnly in the sitting room, receiving gifts and congratulations respectfully, holding a long-stemmed Chinese pipe.

The old man died with the same satisfied smile, because he was sure his offspring was still the keeper of the portrait. It's too bad that her ex-husband left home and forgot it. She has now charged her son with being the keeper. She has faith he'll be mature enough to undertake the responsibility when she's no longer able. After a few years she'll need to advise him about the portrait. Hopefully the important obligation will help him grow up quickly. Regrettably, her daughter-in-law can neither know the glory of her ex-husband's keeping it nor learn how her mother-in-law has fulfilled the trust of protecting it all her life.

A few slight cracks appear in the portrait in the June sun, and the shadow moves to the east. The duration of the ritual drying grows shorter, and thus must be done more carefully, year by year. She had meant to roll the scroll on the rope, but the appearance of a crack makes her give up that dangerous idea. With the help of the stick, she carries the portrait with the sheets, and then slowly puts all three of them on the kang to cool off.

The sun burns away the mothball smell. The sharp odor of tobacco leaves remains. The tobacco leaves better protect against bugs, but there are no longer raw tobacco leaves at home. Her ex-husband would be the proper one to ask for some from the neighbors; for her, a woman alone, to ask would cause too many rumors. With no fresh leaves available, she rolls the old leaves into the scroll to prevent the bugs and then puts a few mothballs in the sheet her daughter sent. Then she wraps both the sheets and the portrait in the red-silk cloth.

The ritual is complete when she finally encloses the portrait. After taking the denim sheet off the gate and laying it on the mattress, she wearily lies down on the kang. As usual, she thinks about whether the portrait is an image made up by the painter or a true picture of the ancestor. After displaying or drying the portrait, pondering that question always invites her to fall into a long, sweet, satisfying sleep.

That night, the man comes as promised.

She has already forgotten her daytime ritual reservations when she opens the door to him. She feels only eager expectation. The man takes her hands the moment he enters. She quickly becomes as soft as mud, almost losing her ability to walk. He lifts her from her knees straight to the kang. His hands grope for the lamp cord to turn the light on, but she begs him: "Don't turn on the light."

He agrees and sits in the dark. Her hands clutch his shoulders as soon as he turns his face to her. He falls to the kang and she immediately throws herself on his chest. But the man remains as calm as the face of the ancestor in the portrait. She can't understand why he is so restrained.

"Are you trying to make me lose my mind?" she babbles.

"Ha!" He grins at her and then touches her bosom. "You closed the door tightly today."

"It was broad daylight." She tears open her clothes and her body is quivering.

The more she quivers, the calmer the man remains. It is as if, facing a deliciously cooked dish on the table, he ponders whether it might taste bad when it's either too cold or too hot. He waits for just the right moment, caressing her to make her almost come. Then he takes his hand away and says:

"Let's talk!"

"What? Can't you wait until after . . . ?" She is gasping.

"Now is the best time!" He's made up his mind.

"Do this first and then . . ."

"Talk first!"

In a few words he tells her that one of his old coworkers bought out of his job and went into the antique business. As a result, he's now so rich his wallet is as thick as a brick, and he even owns a car.

"I came to your home today, but your door was closed so tightly."

"I won't stop you if you leave with him." Sobbing, she feels aggrieved and insulted. Then she sobers up. "You should save your words for your wife and kids."

"I'm not talking about leaving."

"I won't take one penny, even if he gives you a hundred, as long as you stay with me." She takes his hands again in love.

"Don't rush. I still have other things . . ."

She brushes his hands off and sits up in annoyance, buttoning her gown.

He senses he is pushing her too hard. He again caresses her fine hands, licking every fingertip skillfully. And she again fills with sexual desire and moves into his arms. But he goes blank, wondering whether to talk with her frankly before or after the sex. Feeling his hesitation, she tells him he can speak directly. There is nothing they can't talk about with each other.

Neither feels good about the way things are.

He goes straight to the point. "Do you keep an old portrait?"

"Yes . . . no, oh . . ." She's reluctant to leave her state of happy desire, painfully unwilling to acknowledge his all-too-plain question.

"It costs a fortune!"

"What fortune? I don't need a fortune."

"It's a piece of wastepaper in your hand!"

Her quivering ceases. The delicious high coming from her fingertips falls off quickly and vanishes. He continues to lick her fingertips and tenderly throws himself on her on the kang. She remains motionless as a corpse. Dropping her fingers, he tries to find her lips with his. But it is useless. She turns her face, avoiding his kiss and making noises as if she were going to vomit. Then she pushes him away with all her strength. As before, he chins into the middle of her bosom, but it doesn't help. He thought the prospect of a large fortune would excite her, but her mind is elsewhere.

"You keep the portrait!" he asserts.

"Nonsense!"

"You keep it!"

"Fuck you!" she responds angrily.

"There is a portrait of a male ancestor; the female one is lost." He ignores her anger.

Finally she sits up. Bang! She turns the light on and moves to the edge of the kang. She sits like the ancestor in the portrait with her hands on her knees and her feet on the ground. But her face is grim and twisted.

"What are you doing? Let's sleep together and talk lazily."

"Get out! Your blind wife is waiting!"

"OK, no damn portrait, let's have sex, OK?"

She stands up solemnly and tidies her disheveled gown.

He sighs deeply in regret, striving for a last chance with his soft tone. "That's their ancestors, not yours, nor mine. It is literally a portrait worth nothing."

She is hurt and shocked. Such words would disturb her if she did not remember the reverence in her father-in-law's face and that his son's sheet once wrapped the portrait. Without knowing why, she lies, "He took the portrait when we divorced. It's the only thing he asked for."

"You are stupid! That thing is probably worth more than all your other possessions!"

"It's his ancestor, after all, no matter how valuable it might be."

He sits up, disappointed. But to keep his relationship with her, he begs her to come back to bed.

She leans on the door frame, holding her elbows. Her defiance glows in her eyes.

He smiles bitterly. "My goddess, you are my ancestor. You cannot leave me like the portrait did."

She bursts into laughter and points outside. "I'm no longer in the mood tonight." She is satisfied with his last words—he called her his ancestor.

They walk to the gate, one behind the other.

His wife with cataracts is groping along the village paths. She scolds in a small voice as she walks along, "You are a shame to my ancestor, you are a shame!"

He slips away from his wife hurriedly. Hearing his retreating steps, his wife erects her ears and chases after him with twittering steps. "I am the one who is ashamed of my ancestor!"

Huang Xishou stands beside the doorway for a long while. She is annoyed by the half-blind woman's open insult to the ancestor. Then she thinks, but she is the one who truly belongs to the village.

She makes up her mind. She will break with the man whose family name is not from the village. She will find a local man who respects the ancestor.

Translated by Li Meng

Hong Ke

Hong Ke was born Yang Hongke in 1962 in Qi Shan County, Shaanxi Province. He graduated from the Chinese department of Shaanxi Baoji Normal College. Hong Ke is a member of the Shaanxi Writers Association and now teaches in the School of Liberal Arts of Shaanxi Normal University. He went to Xinjiang Autonomous Region in 1986 and lived in Kui Tun for ten years.

Hong Ke started publishing his work in 1983. He has written about five million words, encompassing six novels including *The Rider to the West* and *Big River*, and eight collections of novellas and short stories, including *The Pretty Enslaved Sheep*, *Riding Over Tian Shan Mountain*, and *The Sun Sprouts*. He has received many literary prizes, including the Lu Xun Literary Award, the Feng Mu Literary Award, the Zhuang Zhong Literary Award, the Novel Award of China Novel Society, and awards from several magazines.

13

HONG KE

One Family in the Desert

Before dawn, the old man went out the gate of his house with a shovel on his shoulder, heading onto the road toward his farm field. His grandson followed, holding an orange juice bottle. The bottle, as long as the Child's arm, almost touched the ground as if he were dragging a sheep or a dog. Two years before, the Child's father had brought the bottle of orange juice from the town over a hundred miles away. Grandfather, with hands as strong as bear paws, quickly broke the nylon string around the bottle neck and replaced it with cowhide. All the local cows and dogs had begun to wear such cowhide strings around their necks. The cowhide string became the symbol of village property, and wearing their cowhide strings, the animals would come back to the village by themselves.

Grandfather knew his grandson. A cowhide string was fastened around his bottle. His drinking water now also came from bottles instead of directly from the well. The Child preferred to drink from the bottle, and adults let him do what he liked. Cows and dogs also drank their water from the bottle: the Child poured water from the bottle into the feed trough. The bottle bounced in his arms, causing the water to slosh inside. The eyes of the cows shone like diamonds in the manger. The bottle was heavy, filled with water, and the Child shifted it from hand to hand. The heavy bottle made his arms grow in length. Grandfather said, "Longer arms mean you're growing up. Don't worry, work harder!"

The Child was happy and content while working. But Mom complained to Dad, "He should go to school; he should use his head." Dad told Grandfather that going to school was good. Grandfather laughed so gleefully his mustache trembled and his eyes disappeared into his wrinkled face. The house, too, was laughing. Its windows quivered like the flapping wings of birds. The white poplars in the yard clapped their leaves against the sky.

Mom was drawn from the front of the house into the backyard. Grandfather and the Child lived in back, while Mom and Dad lived in front. There was a big yard in between. Every family in the desert had a big yard surrounded by either bricks or fencing. A few years ago, Dad and Mom had gone to the distant town to do some business. They seldom came back home, so the front house stayed quiet. Dad came home occasionally, while Mom almost never did.

Dad told Grandfather that the town was hectic and life there was busy, and Grandfather believed it to be so. "Life in town should be busier than in the village," Grandfather responded. "Busier life is better!" Then he added, "But don't work your wife too hard!" He glanced at Dad, implying that a man should be busier.

The Child came to understand this many years later, but Dad didn't understand it. Nevertheless, he nodded his head and said yes. He did this habitually, whether he understood what people were saying or not. No wonder Mom thought he was stupid. Dad could manage with village things, but in town Mom was better.

Hearing Grandfather's happy laughter, Mom joined them. "Tomorrow we will take the Child with us to town." Mom never missed such a good opportunity.

Grandfather said coldly, "You will send him to school next year, won't you?"

Mom was shocked by Grandfather's sudden change. Her struggles in the business world had not prepared her for the old man's sudden turn. She stood in silence for a few seconds. "He should go to primary school next year. This year he's supposed to go to kindergarten. He is six, but in town, two- or three-year-old kids go to kindergarten."

"My grandson can get his kindergarten education from me."

Mom kept silent, but with a smirk on her face. Dad started talking. The Child remembered that Dad always said something in a stubborn way, and Mom always gave him such opportunities. Local people called Dad's way of talking *piao liangqiang*—"stubborn talking." It was always the same. He burst into a rage, then turned his head sideways and asked Grandfather: "How can you give him a kindergarten education? Kindergarten education must be provided in school."

Staring at his stubborn son, Grandfather rolled a cannonlike cigarette, held it in his mouth, and puffed. He coughed several times. If Dad would remain silent, the embarrassing situation would not last long. But Dad got angrier and repeated his comment about education in a school. That drove Grandfather to stiffen deeper into silence. This was what Mom hoped and expected. Only after many years did the Child come to understand that hostile dynamic.

In the moment, he just played with the yellow dog. Even chickens and dogs preferred to stay away from a child his age. The dog suffered from being nearby. If the Child stayed with Grandfather, the dog shied away. When the Child played with other kids, the dog followed Grandfather closely. The dog barked from under the child's bottom. It sounded like the child was farting.

Dad did not give up, pressing Grandfather for an answer. Grandfather said unhappily, "The potatoes are not harvested, and my boy is a good helping hand." Grandfather knew what Dad would answer. He put his hand on the Child's head with his eyes closed, totally ignoring Dad and Mom. Like the Mountain God, his face emotionless, he heard nothing Dad said.

Dad, inspired by Mom, spoke his mind. "What can a broom-size kid do? I will stay another day and harvest all the potatoes in the morning."

Grandfather kept silent, his hand still resting on the Child's head. But the head became warm and active under Grandfather's hand and started talking. "I grew the potatoes with Grandfather, but you're going to harvest them? That's not fair!" Grandfather's eyes opened, and he happily hugged the Child together with the dog in his arms. Grandfather was the mightiest hero on earth, glaring at Dad and Mom.

"Mind your own business," Dad said. "Do not speak without thinking."

Early the next morning, Grandfather took the young boy and walked out of the village. The dog followed for a short distance and then went back to guarding the home.

Corn, cotton, and sunflowers had all been harvested. Some of the land was plowed, so the field seemed wide open with a few stems of corn and sunflowers shivering in the wind. The stubble looked yellowish-black, worn out after the harvest had been taken away. The ground itself appeared worn, with sand dunes in the front. The Sun rose slowly, dull and sleepy.

A year earlier, Grandfather had explained to the Child that the Sun seemed lazy only because it was so far away. The Child, however, was suspicious. He didn't think the Sun was so far away. Several times the Child murmured, "It's a window." The Sun rising over the dunes was like a window slowly opening, as if pushed by two men who left the village and ran across the field to the horizon while the village and the Earth slept soundly. Their wheat, corn, and sunflower fields were near the village, but the one with the potatoes was far away.

A day or so later, when Grandfather woke the Child, the dog was still sleepy. The Child spilled several drops of warm water into the dog's ears from a bottle. The dog first howled in its dream and then dropped its head as though hit by a bullet and could not wake up again.

"That's the Sun licking your bottom."

"Why not licking your bottom?"

"There is no shit scar on Grandfather's bottom; that is why the Sun does not like licking it."

"There is no scar on mine either."

"You dirty boy, thick pancake-like shit scars cover your bottom."

"No shit scar on me!" the Child shouted in anger.

When he was two or three years old, Mom had taught him to use paper to wipe his bottom, while other village kids used stones or leaves. Mom asked him to wash his bottom before he went to Grandfather's to sleep. Mom also told him to say "bottom" instead of the vulgar local word, *gou zi*. Mom picked up many good things in the small town when she was there on business. But when the Child stayed with Grandfather, he always said *gou zi*.

The angry Child pulled down his trousers and pushed his buttocks high for Grandfather to check the scars. "Any scars? Any scars?"

Smiling, Grandfather patted the small buttocks. "Scars can't be wiped or washed off. If you followed Grandfather to the field in the early morning, all the scars would fall off after a few steps."

The Child was still angry, but Grandfather soothed him, saying, "More scars are a good thing. They mean you are closer to the Sun."

The Child mumbled, "I don't like anybody pushing forward and backward behind my bottom."

"Then run after the bottom of the Sun."

When the Child was again awakened by his Grandfather in the early morning, he was very excited to find that the Sun did not have a bottom.

Many years later, the Child still remembered that scene—Grandfather and the Child running toward the Sun at dawn. On this special morning, a pair of supernatural eyes jumped from the bottom of his heart into the sky, looking down at the hurrying Grandfather and Child. The Child cried out in surprise. Suddenly he recognized that he was looking at himself through his own eyes.

This realization was crucial, and this self-examination was repeated day after day until gradually it became a habit. After many years the Child understood it was a good habit. The Sun was like an open window only in the morning, as it rose slowly over the sand dune.

Grandfather said, "The Sun is still far away from us."

It had turned bright by the time they arrived at their field. Grandfather dug a pit in the ground and made a fire with a few clumps of *suosuo* grass. The grass burned robustly and the fire drove away the cold. The grass was smokeless when it burned, like magma fresh from underground. When the Child saw pictures of volcano eruptions at school, he always thought of Grandfather's campfire.

The child sat close to the fire, and Grandfather dug. Plump potatoes rolled out of the sandy soil with little effort. The Child long remembered that cool, earthy, wet fragrance from the first potato. The smell reminded him of a cow teat.

Grandfather was very skillful. No potatoes were bruised or damaged. The Child sensed the fresh, rich juice of the potatoes. He became hot from the fire, and beads of sweat appeared on his nose. He grasped a rolling potato with his hands. Two hands were needed. The potato felt wild, fresh out of the sandy soil. It tried to escape from his hands. Although he did everything he could to hang on, it jumped out of his hand and escaped.

The Child grabbed at three of them, one after another, but they all escaped. Worse, the struggle with the potatoes sapped his strength. The Child grew tired. He stood beside Grandfather, eyes wide open, watching the old man drag all those potatoes from the ground. The cool, wet, and earthy fragrance from the piles of potatoes rushed through the air. The Child sneezed several times, and Grandfather told him to warm himself by the fire. So he did.

It was said that the wolf, snake, tiger, and leopard were all afraid of fire. Potatoes acted like animals. Strangely, however, the Child could not smell the potato fragrance near the fire. He moved a bit away and again enjoyed the good smell.

The Child had no choice but to remain by the fire, watching Grandfather's skillful digging. The sun brightened gradually. Sunbeams like arrows from far away struck his back. Soon Grandfather was covered in arrows. He flung up his arms like a folk hero with thousands of arrows in his heart. He bent forward and showed no signs of giving up.

The golden arrows from the Sun became so dense they could not plunge into Grandfather. He never stopped digging. One potato after another rolled from the soil, and finally the ground was emptied. He loosened his hands and stuck the shovel into the earth. The suosuo grass burned out and the tongues of fire disappeared. The red grass stems cracked and turned into soft ashes. Grandfather buried five potatoes in the fire. The potatoes seared and struggled. Potatoes were strong. Red embers became dark ash. Another fragrant smell emerged. The Child cried out and ran toward the sand dune. The baked potato smell was much stronger than the smell of the fresh earth. He stopped running because the eyes ran faster. Far away toward the horizon, the potato fragrance soared, and it screamed to him like a flock of birds. Grandfather told him all people on earth could smell it.

"Would they come?"

"They are most distinguished guests. Of course they will come."

Grandfather sat with his legs crossed, like a Buddha praying piously. He believed the greatest kindness was in inviting someone to eat. The potatoes in the fire seemed to pray and wait quietly while giving off their powerful scent. To attract guests from far away, the smell became increasingly strong. The Sun stopped at its zenith in the sky. Grandfather scattered the ashes and took one potato. The Child might eat it first; he always ate baked potatoes at home. Grandfather peeled the potato skillfully and wolfed it down as if it were a delicacy.

Eventually a stranger was attracted by the smell. According to Grandfather, the one who smelled the fragrance first was the most respected guest. This most respected guest was like a big stone, emotionless and dull. His hands and feet were stiff; the only active part of his body was his nose. Without saying a word, Grandfather offered water, which was to say the orange juice bottle. The guest rinsed his mouth and washed his hands. He sipped once. As if sipping wine, he swallowed slowly and with difficulty. After a long pause, he sipped again; five times altogether.

Grandfather presented two well-baked potatoes and asked the stranger to choose. He knew which one he would prefer and kept that one in hand. Grandfather peeled the potato. A mist burst out like the potato was an exploding grenade. The smell became stronger. Grandfather handed the hot, tasty potato to the stranger, who started to eat. The potato was too hot. He squatted on the ground, eating with difficulty, as if fighting a ferocious animal. His shoulder and head trembled like the *campo* wrestlers who fought their finals. When the final wrestling began, everyone at the Mongolian Na Da Mu Festival would hold their breath. Silent wrestling was amazing. Sometimes it lasted for an hour. Even the earth trembled.

In time, Grandfather handed over the second potato. The Child saw that the second one had not been peeled. He realized the stranger wanted to enjoy the peeling himself. When he got yet a third, the stranger raised the potato and looked at it under the Sun. He quickly peeled off the skin and exposed the flesh inside like a piece of tender meat dug from the depths of the earth. He ate it with the Sun hanging over his head like a lamp. He ate the potato in a vigorous yet solemn fashion, as if he were enjoying a great feast. He forgot himself while enjoying the banquet. When he finished, he wiped his mouth with his hand and walked away with his head held high, without saying good-bye or even looking at Grandfather.

"He did not even say 'thank you,' Grandfather."

"He thanked the sky and the earth."

The last potato in the fire belonged to Grandfather. He peeled the yellowish-black potato but did not rush to eat it. Instead he left enough time for the fragrant smell to pour out until the whole area was overwhelmed by it. Grandfather took one bite. "Grandfather could eat eight in one breath when he was young," Grandfather murmured, and then he began to sing. But he sang about mutton, not potatoes.

Brother's meat,
You did not have when I came,
With fat mutton in your hand!

Grandfather repeatedly sang about the fat mutton. Many years later when he had grown up, the Child realized that Grandfather was singing about an enchanting love story from his youth. When Grandfather was carried away by his song, he regarded the Child as his close friend and spoke out his private words: "Meat is good, but the meat eater—man—is better." To Grandfather his grandson was a buddy. "Be grateful to meat eaters."

They made another fire, buried another five potatoes in the hot ash, and then left for home. The Child turned frequently to look back. The potato smell had spread several miles ahead of them. The Sun was setting. As Grandfather often said, "The Sun is kowtowing to the potatoes."

The Child had read some cartoon books brought by Mom from the town. She told him stories explaining the pictures in the book. Accordingly, he knew that everything on earth depended on the Sun for growth. He told this to Grandfather. However, Grandfather's theories were all centered on the earth. He insisted that the Sun was kowtowing to the potatoes.

"Look with your own eyes. What is the Sun doing?"

Like a desert whirlwind, the smell from the fire overwhelmed the Sun; thus it faltered. Grandfather and the Child stretched their necks to watch the brilliant Sun set in the desert. As Grandfather predicted, the Sun knelt down on the dusty dune suddenly. Now he had more to say.

"Corn, wheat, sunflower, and cotton give life to the Sun. Potatoes are even greater. They make the Sun get into the ground."

Immediately the Child thought of similar plants like sugar beets and carrots. Grandfather stroked the Child's big head with satisfaction. The Child also thought of peanuts. Though peanuts were not cultivated in central Asia, everyone knew that peanuts grew underground like potatoes, carrots, and sugar beets. It was as though his intelligence increased with his Grandfather stroking his head. The hand, dry and hard like suosuo grass, was covered with cracks all over. It was this hand that empowered his head. Like a flash of lightning, the suosuo grass on the sand dune appeared in his head. The dry suosuo grass resembled Grandfather's hand. With his own eyes he saw it burning, smokeless. The vigorous, pure fire looked like the tongue of flame fired from a gun, like a cartoon depiction of magma erupting from a volcano. The big fire from the grass melted the earth. It was this pair of magic hands that were stroking his head.

Owl was soaring across the autumn sky, the vastest and highest sky where he could demonstrate his flying skills. The Child thought of birds and beasts on the earth. He felt his heart beating rapidly, but then it calmed. The big, hovering hand over his head stopped, and the flying owl came to a standstill in the sky as well. Everyone in the desert knew that the bird had masterful control. Owl timed his flight perfectly. The Sun had knelt on the sand dune to kowtow to the last crop on the earth—the potatoes. The Sun should be grateful to the owl, a product of the sky. Owl had picked up the sweeping, fragrant potato smell soaring like a whirlwind into the sky. He knew what was going on.

Grandfather quietly took his hand back, but the Child still associated the hand with the owl. The Child's face was as red as the fire; his powerful imagination was also visible. Since the Child thought he grew the potatoes by himself, it was unnecessary to describe their fragrant smell when they were ripening.

Three days later, Grandfather transported all the potatoes in his carriage. The Child and dog went with him. Dog liked to bark and jump around the village. When they arrived at the field near the entrance, the dog's barks became so subdued they sounded like sobs. His voice almost suffocated. The vast desert humbled the dog. Taking a cue from the potatoes, the dog buried his mouth into the earth. No more barks were heard.

The Child helped his Grandfather silently. He checked the ashes of the fire and found that all the baked potatoes had been taken away. They had been eaten and gone far away. He hoped people from the farthest places on earth would come here. This bold idea stirred his mind, and he could not refrain from launching a stone like a rocket. He remained in that throwing position long after the stone was released. He felt like a mighty launching pad that sent the most sophisticated aircraft into outer space from the depth of Zhun Ge'er Basin. The Child cried out from the excitement in his heart.

"I will thank you all; I will thank you all!"

He cried out again and again. Gradually he realized that even his loudest shouts were voiceless, merely in his mind. He knelt down unconsciously. He did not know that kneeling indicated appreciation or gratitude. It was just a simple action that needed no explanation. It would never occur to him that the Sun too, like him, knelt down. He simply did one thing after another.

He dug a small pit and lit a fire with the firewood he'd picked up. He did not use Grandfather's suosuo grass, but dry cow dung instead. Everybody knew that dry cow dung was the best firewood in the desert. In winter it was the major fuel. In autumn, women and children collected dry cow dung and stockpiled it in the yard like gold to help them survive the severest winter. He was used to picking up dry cow dung.

He lit a pile of dung. The smoke from cow dung was not straight. Signal smoke usually soared directly into the sky like a long spear, but smoke from cow dung dispersed into the sky like rivers into the sea and became invisible or blended. He buried potatoes in the ashes of the dung. He knew that this launch would travel farther than a rocket. He did this confidently like an adult. Once finished, he dusted his hands.

Grandfather watched the Child closely from beginning to end. He coughed when he felt satisfied. Behind the carriage, he lit a hand-made cigarette to smoke his excitement away.

The Child seemed to be the only one on earth. He became intoxicated in this self-absorbed state for a very long time. The boundless quiet was wonderful. Many years later, the Child was not the Child anymore, but the quiet remained in his mind, together with this vast field and this special moment, forever. There were two stories about Grandfather's potato planting. One was that the sandy soil far away from the village could produce good-quality potatoes, even though everyone else wanted to grow crops near the village. The other was that the sandy soil had been chosen by Grandfather for his tomb. This soil was surrounded by typical Zhun Ge'er sand dunes, covered by red willows and suosuo grass. Apart from Grandfather's potato farming, this soil served as a perfect place for those who had passed away.

But Grandfather outlived his own expectations. Even after it was predicted that he would soon be gone, he still lived a very healthy life. His coffin was prepared in advance. His wife had passed over ten years earlier, and he buried her in the potato field where the oasis and desert met. Grandmother was said to be ill all the time, and the medicine she took equaled the amount of food she consumed. She suffered more than enough and asked Grandfather by all means to bury her remains in a quiet place. "You should not feel obliged to accompany me. You should find a good tomb. I've spoiled your whole life and I feel embarrassed and guilty."

"What's gotten into you, old lady?" He did what should be done, ignoring her words. When he strolled around the tomb, he refused to remain idle, clearing the weeds away from it. Once finished, he pushed the shovel into the ground, not feeling tired at all. The crust of the sandy soil, covered by thin grass, easily turned over. In a short time, he turned a big stretch of land. When the morning passed and the Sun reached its peak, a vast field had been turned over.

It was springtime. Grass sprouted, trees budded, and everything came to life. A newly turned field was next to her tomb, and the place didn't feel so desolate. Before his work, though sandy date trees and red willows grew on her tomb, it had still seemed desolate. It was the turned earth that made a difference. The earth gave off a unique smell from its depths. The breathing of the earth touched his face in a tender and sensuous way. The old woman was not dead: her tomb was alive.

He was very excited. He planted potatoes there. Potatoes from this sandy soil were fresh and big. He had directed the Sun to the tomb field and potatoes were the children of the Sun. He'd come to understand this when he was very young.

The next fall, around the end of August, the Child left Grandfather for school in town. Dog was very excited. Dog had restrained himself for as long as half a year and now he could not control himself. Dog licked the Child's hand and wagged his tail freely. Everyone could sense his great joy. Dog alone would now enjoy the happiness of staying with Grandfather.

Grandfather—

When the village disappeared from view, the Child was in tears. He was a child, anyway, and could not control himself anymore.

In school the Child behaved like a real man. Nobody despised him, including teachers. Not just the ordinary teachers, but even the one from Beijing. The trend was to come to the West voluntarily to support education there. Her lecture was great. Some discs, brought by university students, were played on TV for after-class activities. Students from the farthest reaches of the desert saw the Old Palace, the Winter Palace, and the Great Wall. Teachers would ask questions about those things in class. Maybe it was predestined that the Child was the first to be asked a question by the Beijing teacher. He didn't answer in a loud voice, but he spoke very clearly. "Beijing is very good, but it is rather remote."

At first the teacher could not believe her ears. She asked again. The other students' eyes opened wide, thinking the answer wrong. But the Child again spoke clearly: "Beijing is very good, but it is rather remote."

The classroom became quiet. This teacher with her glasses was very young, maybe in her twenties. She took off her glasses, wiped them, and put them back on. She approached the Child, asked his name, and touched his head.

"I have a brother the same age as you."

She returned to the front of the class and told the students about her hometown. Her hometown was in an impoverished, mountainous area far inland. She'd studied hard and successfully before attending a university in Beijing.

"Only when I was in my second year as a university student did I understand what the Child said just now. He said it so well."

Translated by Ren Huilian and Hu Zongfeng

Mo Shen

Mo Shen is the pen name of Sun Shugan. Born in Wuxi City, Jiangsu Province, he graduated from the Training Institute of Chinese Literature. He worked in the countryside of Qinling Mountains in 1968, and from 1972 he worked in succession as a freight yard porter of Baoji Station, a reporter of Xi'an Railway, deputy chairman of the Literary Federation of Xi'an Railway Bureau, a screenwriter and director of the Literature Division of Xi'an Film Studio, and a major author.

Mo Shen is director, standing director, presidium member, and vice-chairman of the Shaanxi Provincial Writers Association. He made his literary debut in 1977 and joined the Chinese Writers Association in 1979. His works include the novels *Carnal Thoughts* and *Time*; the novella collection *Life Is Gathering Together*; the collections of short stories *Yun Chunhua*, *Dream Has Gone*, and *Treasure*; the nonfiction titles *Travel to Eastern Europe* and *Great Beijing-Kowloon Railway*, *Making a Fortune in Russia*, *Love Is Born in Death*, and *Sprint*; and the TV series *Wind from the Boundary* (four episodes) and *Eastern Tide* (twenty-two episodes), as well as film adaptations of a number of his books.

14

MO SHEN

Mountain Forest Lasting Forever

Rustles from around the woods alert Old Jia Qiu and he looks around. Yes, it's the little black bear! Only a furry face shows, the little black eyes wide open, looking at the outside world from between the trees.

Jia crouches down carefully, trying to be quiet. At the same time he aims his gun at the bear. Jia is ready to press the trigger. With a bang, those little black eyes will close forever.

Old Jia is known far and wide as a hunter. Years before, a crack shot challenged his marksmanship and invited him to a contest. The crack shot started the contest by killing a little sparrow. Jia showed no hint of hurry and asked, "Do you see the butterfly on that branch?" His gun fired. A close look revealed a hole in the branch and a pair of wings falling down to the ground. The bullet hit right between the two wings.

The little bear makes no movement, waiting silently. It holds its breath, and even its eyeballs stop moving; it blends itself into the rock and the woods. Five minutes, then ten minutes pass. Jia can't wait anymore—but he puts down his gun. This little cub can never change its fate; down in the hollow its mother is groaning with severe suffering.

Jia turns back, waits for a moment, and steps behind a huge rock. He leans against the rock, fills up his pipe, lights it, and smokes.

In the hollow, the wounded black bear gets worn out and stops groaning. A silence covers the woods; even the birds are silent. All is silent. No trace of a breeze, no gurgling of the stream; everything is frozen. Only a cloud floats high in the sky.

Jia has never seen the sea. People who have been in the mountains for generations never see a truck or a bus, let alone the sea. He learned about the blue sea from those intellectuals who came during that time when cadres were sent to live and work in the countryside. According to them, the sea is as beautiful as the blue sky. But their description made him all the more puzzled. He always wondered why the vast blue sea hadn't devoured the huge Qinling Range like the blue sky had.

Old Jia has become one with the huge mountains. He loves sitting on the sunny slope and enjoying the caress of the sun; he loves to close his eyes and listen to the rustling of trees in a pleasant breeze. For him every little stream is filled with life, and he can understand the tears and laughter of each branch of every tree. For him the blue sky is like a strict father, and the mountain a tender and kind mother. Once in a while storms and lightning howl, seeming to devastate the whole mountain range, but the mountain is tolerant and can bear everything. She melts all the ice and snow into clear streams like milk, nurturing everything that grows in the mountains. The sky and the mountain rely on each other day and night, through summer and winter.

Years ago, a group of prospectors told Jia that the earth would be gone someday and so with it the mountains. But he'd never believe it, for he has a determined feeling that the blue sky will always stay with the blue mountains as long as the years last.

The tobacco in his pipe has burnt out, and Jia feels a trace of coldness in his back, which urges him to straighten himself up. This is the way of the remote mountains. No matter how hot it is outside, the heat will vanish as soon as you enter the forest. It seems that those speechless rocks, the sky-blocking trees, the rotten leaves over the slopes, and the streams meandering along the mountain foot all have a certain magic power. Dwelling here for thousands of years, they keep the air clean and pleasant and bestow a special chill to every inch of ground here. If you lie here for only a few minutes, you'll be pierced with a cold that will sink into your core. Old Jia once had such an experience. When he was young he thought himself strong enough and lay down on the rotten leaves for a rest, but when he opened his eyes he found his arms and legs unable to move, although his mind was still clear. Luckily some others found him and carried him home.

His throat feels a little uneasy, but he forces himself to hold the coughing. He used to cough whenever he smoked, but he's never succeeded in giving up smoking. It is said that people in town have to take night shifts, to rack their brains to write, to ponder over problems, and to socialize with other people—and therefore cigarettes become their wonder drug to keep them refreshed, the tool to aid their thoughts, the media for socializing. But why did Jia start smoking? The intellectuals once asked Old Jia, but he gave no answer. Thinking it over later, he found his answer: he is lonely.

The mountains in front of him extend all the way to the far distance. They have not only held Jia's steps and vision but have also blocked his thoughts and even his life prospects. However, a person needs contact with the outside world. He needs to get close to nature; he needs to feel the leaking water drops and the rustling leaves; he needs to live with living animals—a cat, a dog, even the buzzing flies and bees.

Jia can shake off everything when he is completely engaged in his work, but when he stands on top of the mountains for a rest he feels vacuous and totally at a loss, feels like he's been frozen into something as still as the lifeless rocks. At those times, various unanswerable questions enter his mind. What is the universe? Which is larger, the earth or the sky? Why should human beings live in between the earth and the sky?

It is true that there were no human beings in the past and the world was nothing but chaos. He learned from those prospectors that there used to be a vast sea here, with only sediment and lava. Gradually the ground grew out of the sea and reduced again under the sea, until one billion years ago a mass shifting of the plates of the earth forced the sea to recede, and thus the ground rose up to form the mountains that are now known as the Qinling Range. Jia has no concept as to how long one billion years is, but he knows it is a long period. He understands that he is actually living in a place with neither origin nor end. All these profound questions stay with him, perplexing him. What an afflicting thing, when a person is alive but knows nothing about himself or the world around him!

——

The heart-stricken howls are heard once again. It's the wounded mother bear.

Jia draws calmly on the smoking pipe and blows out with the same calmness, not even turning his head. This suggests that he is a weather-beaten, experienced hunter. His tact shows not only in his calmness but also in his complexion. He is thin and has a face etched with wrinkles. When he squints in his usual manner, his expressionless and gloomy eyes can stay motionless for several minutes, which makes him look like a statue. Because he was born in this special environment, all the joints in his fingers bulge out like gnarls and the hands feel like hard, cold boards or stones, with no body heat.

Only after you have held them tightly for a long time can you feel the liquid flowing deep inside those boards or stones . . .

Having hunted a muntjac and a couple of golden pheasants in the morning, Jia then continued his hunting up the other side of the mountains. Around here various tendrils blocked the sky, and rocks in grotesque formation rose up into the air, which provided a perfect habitat for boars.

With only two bullets left, Jia expected to meet a boar. He made his way forward to a Chinese catalpa, where he detected a mass of boar footprints. Following those tracks, which disappeared in just a few steps, Jia stopped to observe the trees around him. Boars like to rub their skin against tree trunks and thus should have left certain hints. Soon he found some hairs on a tree trunk. Moving forward, Jia heard a strange noise and something in front of him took him aback: a boa constrictor just slithering its way out from behind a rock, its bucket-thick body cutting a path through the bush. The snake wriggled its huge girth toward a two-meter-wide crevice as if nobody was around.

Jia stayed still behind a tree, daring not to heave a breath—for it would have been impossible for Jia to kill the snake with only two bullets, and a wise hunter should be brave and decisive and know when to retreat and escape. He carefully stepped backward for about ten meters and then turned and picked up his heels at once. He ran fast and didn't stop for a breath until he was sure that the snake could never catch him. He sat there for ten minutes and was just ready to rise up, but he again heard something. Looking toward the sound, he saw the mother bear behind a rock and, amazingly, the baby bear walking behind.

Jia crouched on one knee and gazed at them, slightly nervous. He held his gun in his hands, already loaded with bullets, but he knew that he could never fire at the bear in such a spot and with such a short distance. Once, a hunter named San Wa had shot at a bear moving toward him, and the bullet hit the bear's underbelly.

Inflamed and with great suffering, the bear howled and sprang at San Wa. With only one claw, the bear exposed the white bones in San Wa's shoulder. A good hunter should never fire at a bear or a boar moving toward him.

The bear sniffed around as if looking for food or having detected something suspicious. Jia remained motionless, hiding himself behind a tree, for he knew that the bear was less agile than the leopard and also less tricky. As long as you make no noise, a bear will detect nothing—Jia was pretty sure the bear didn't realize the danger around it and was looking for food and offering it to the cub. Later the black bear led the little cub to move to the left.

As the bears went left, Jia dashed down the slope. Years of hunting in the mountains had turned him into a sturdy man. He reached the bottom of the slope and climbed up the opposite slope using the bush to hide. Attaining a satisfactory position, he halted and groped his way back to a place where he could see the bears clearly.

This was a perfect position: lying fifty meters between the two slopes, he was in an absolutely secure harbor. Whether he hit his target or not, the bear could never turn back and throw itself in his direction.

He held his gun in his hands. The bears continued searching for food—calm, little realizing that danger was near. Just as Jia was about to pull the trigger, the bear suddenly threw up its head, straightening itself with caution, and looked over its shoulders to glance around. It would have been a perfect opportunity, but the body of the bear was mostly blocked by a tree. Jia had to wait for the next chance. Then, as soon as the bear lifted its head and revealed itself from behind the trunk, Jia pulled the trigger without even taking aim. Suddenly the whole hollow resounded with a crisp crack, startling a flock of birds to flutter about. Shocked and astounded, the bear looked backward and then rolled down the slope with a terrible howl.

Without even a momentary hesitation, Jia aimed skillfully at the little bear. The bear was frightened and was running away desperately, its chubby body wriggling amid the rocks. Confidently Jia aimed his gun at a rock on top of the slope. It stood in a small clearing with no trees or bushes around, providing a natural shooting range. The little bear, however, was running. But just as Jia was ready to pull the trigger, the little bear suddenly tumbled over, which saved its life. When it climbed up again it changed direction and ran into the long grasses behind the rocks.

Now, back in the moment, Jia is a little dampened and withdraws his gun. The mother bear is howling in pain. From the sound of the howl, Jia is pretty sure that the bear is not fatally hurt. He looks down the hollow and sees the bear lying on the grassland covered with blood. Jia aims his gun again at the bear, ready to finish the game, but it is still early and the sun is high above his head. From experience, he judges that the little bear will not be protected from the horror and will come out to pry about. Jia puts his gun on the ground and begins to bide his time and take a rest.

He thinks of a bear he shot last year. When he had cut through its bosom, the bear showed lean meat a couple of inches thick. He cut the paws off and sold them in the market in town. With that money he bought his foster son a suit of cotton-padded clothes, a tufted cap with ear shades, and a bundle of pencils. Back home he hid the rest of the money in the cracks in the wall. He had to save for a new cabin. His foster son was only six years old, but time flies and a dozen years would pass in merely a blink. He needed money to get his son a wife. In the faraway mountains, a wife is not an easy thing to find.

Crackles of branches are heard again in the woods. Jia holds up his gun with great care and pokes through the tendrils to search the opposite slope. It is surely the little bear, its eyes wide open and full of dread. The cub is still crouching behind a tree. Dull as the little bear seemed, it is still a living thing and certainly has its survival instinct.

Jia sits down again for a rest. He has enough time and experience to wait out the little bear.

In front of him the mountain range is still standing there, stretching to the distance, persuading people into believing it resembles the entire world. It is not easy to live in this world. A hunter, for instance, has to make a living by hunting. The more he hunts, the better his life will be. This seems easy to understand, but quite a few stories handed down from the ancestors are about sharpshooters turning beggar in the end. In one story, a hunter hunted everything he saw; even the pregnant rabbits and staggering cubs could not escape his gun. At last all the wild animals were scared of him and ran away to faraway places. In the end he could get nothing and had to chase the animals to the depths of remote mountains seldom frequented by hunters. There he lost his way and died from hunger, with his shining gun in his hands. The story is not heartwarming, but it is quite old, for it is handed down from generation to generation. It's like an enlightening lesson delivered in the most basic manner for those hunters, but nobody can say for sure what it's supposed to mean. The hunter was totally engaged with hunting all the time. When people are focused on pursuing a better life, perhaps everything worth having becomes dull and tasteless.

With a move of his Adam's apple, Jia narrows his eyes and returns his focus to his surroundings.

Beside the rock is a leafless tree. Even with some effort, Jia cannot identify it. Suddenly he feels that this tree reminds him of something in his inner heart, but he can't say what it is. He stares at the tree for a while, and then it comes to him: the tree is like him in that it is also alone here. Jia has been a bachelor all his life; his only son was brought to him from outside the mountains. He never wanted to be alone but he is doomed to be, for just like the tree left here on the rock, he was born in the remote mountains . . .

Jia grumbles to himself—several words but nothing meaningful. Mountain people have the habit of talking to themselves. The words don't matter so much as the act of talking to somebody, your voice reaching two ears. Just as, if you were hit on the head with a stick, you would certainly utter something—it's our instinct.

He draws out his steel, ready to strike it on the flint. Considering for a moment, he puts it back and takes out something else. It's a delicate lighter that he asked someone to buy for him from outside the mountains. It's so much more convenient than the flint. In fact, the flint is outdated and should have been discarded, but he is loath to part with his flint.

One time, years ago, he shot a bear but refused to sell the gallbladder to a merchant who offered one hundred yuan. When another man asked to buy the gallbladder for five yuan, Jia gave it to him for nothing; he knew that the guy needed the gallbladder to cure his old mother of her eye disease. How strange a person he is! And yet, many things in the world are just as strange as Old Jia!

He lights up a cigarette, inhales heavily, and blows out the smoke until he can feel it throughout his body. As he exhales he looks at another leafless tree. Without a second glance, Jia recognizes it as sumac. Sumac is a strange tree: it excretes a poisonous sap that makes people itchy and swollen all over their body. There's an old saying that goes, sumac is mad; it kisses you nowhere but the balls. That year, prospectors touched a sumac and later had swollen eyes and were found scratching all day long with their hands in their trousers.

His foster son was once kissed by the sumac. Jia smeared egg white and leek juice to cure his son. His foster son had been brought to him from outside the mountains. That winter, a group of displaced people begged all the way here from Gansu Province and sold the boy to him for three leopard skins. Outsiders teased him about exchanging such a skinny kid for three precious hides, saying that was paying for doing the favor of bringing the kid back and raising him. Jia didn't think of it that way. He had insisted on offering the kid's father three skins. He himself had never been a father, but he felt that this trade gave him a better understanding of what being a father meant. Of what value are these skins, these fortunes? All these things count for nothing compared to a child; a child is the most precious thing in the world. A child is the core of one's life, the very basis for a harmonious family.

After being hurt by the bear, San Wa was paralyzed. So when those prospectors came here, Old Jia tried his best to persuade a prospector to sleep with San Wa's wife. Before long, San Wa's wife was pregnant. The prospector was handsome and open-minded; his seed shouldn't be too bad! After the child was born, San Wa was pleased and gave his best offerings to his guest. The prospector, however, was bitterly punished by his team leader. The punishment was so severe that the prospector shed tears of humiliation. Jia could not stand by and watch; he came out to give the leader a good scolding. How on earth could this man understand? He had never lived in the remote mountains and didn't know what it was like. Didn't he understand the difficulty of just surviving here, generation to generation? It was perfectly justified for a woman to sleep with a man. If not this man, then it would be some other; there was nothing curious about that. It is true that, in sleeping with a local woman, the prospector had violated the rules of his team, but shouldn't the leader take into account that, as a result, a lively little life had come to earth?

Jia straightens himself. He feels a surge of confidence and pride rising inside him whenever he thinks of that baby. He'd never had such a feeling before: he feels that the profound and huge mountains are everlasting and that many sturdy things in the mountains are also everlasting. These things show great tenacity and indomitable perseverance, almost more beautiful and powerful than the mountain itself.

Jia hears a rustling sound once again, this time with greater force. He looks up and sees that the red sun has disappeared. Up the slopes, darkness is gathering its forces. Back in the shady area a dense mist is already collecting. Dusk will fall in a while; the little bear will surely show itself soon.

Jia takes his gun and begins to probe his way through the long grasses.

Sure enough, the little cub is looking around on the opposite slope, seeming to realize that it's in danger. Its round eyes glance about, showing a trace of childishness as well as worry and fear. The little bear hesitates for a while and then can't help but extend one paw and scurry over a rock. A moment later, it peers out from the grasses and hurtles downward into the depth of the hollow. Its rump twists clumsily from side to side all the way down the slope.

Seeing its awkward way of moving, Jia can't hold his laughter. He is aiming at the cub the whole time; his finger has never left the trigger for even a second. He could pull the trigger at any time and set a crack echoing through the hollow, but instead he waits with great patience, for a good hunter should wait for the best chance to shoot.

Finally the little bear stumbles to the floor of the hollow. Jia can hear its gasps and groans. Why is it groaning? It's obviously saying something! The cub is pouring out its feelings to its mother in a language Jia cannot understand. At that critical moment, Jia is only waiting for the cub to stand still.

Finally the little bear stands still. Jia aims his gun at the bear's heart and is ready to pull the trigger. Suddenly the little bear throws itself toward its mother. It is so excited that it's actually running to the mother bear. Seeing her child, the mother bear throws up her thick paws with the same excitement and utters a strange sound at the same time. It is not a howl, nor is it a painful groan. It must have a special meaning. Is it a warning for the little bear to escape at once? Or a comfort for having found its way back to her? Nobody can say. Old Jia, however, suddenly feels a throb rising up inside himself.

Finally, the little bear throws himself to his mother, desperately pushing with his head against the mother bear. Later, he begins to lick the bloodstains on his mother's bosom, his mouth uttering a special growl; it sounds like sobbing or wailing. The mother seems to have forgotten her own severe pains and grows tender and soft, making no noise, gently nuzzling the little bear. They seem to have forgotten the danger around them and embrace each other tightly.

Crack!

The gun fires and the whole mountain range shudders. The dense smoke of gunpowder momentarily blocks Jia's view and then fades. But what has happened? At the pivotal moment, Jia's hand trembled so violently that his gun shook and the bullet missed its mark!

Jia looks at his gun with surprise, his gun leaning against the rock listlessly with the muzzle pointing downward. Now something wet and soft seems to rise from the bottom of his heart. It shrouds him and leaves him a little at a loss. He doesn't know what he should do. Eventually he raises his head, realizing dusk is already climbing up around him.

A silence prevails in the woods.

It's a silence that will last forever.

Translated by Ji Wenkai

Wang Peng

Born in Xi'an City, Shaanxi Province, Wang Peng graduated from the Department of Chinese Language and Literature, Peking University, in 1988. He was a staff member of Hanzhong Mass Art Hall, chairman of the Hanzhong Literary Federation, and chairman of the Writers Association. Wang Peng is vice-chairman of the Shaanxi Provincial Writers Association and a standing committee member of the third Shaanxi Literary Federation.

Wang Peng made his literary debut in 1973 and joined the Chinese Writers Association in 1984. His works include the novels *Sacrifice of the Mountain* and *Water Burial*; the collections of short stories *Night of Rape in Blossom*, *Secret*, and *Black Peony and Her Husband*; the prose collections *Continuous Homesickness*, *Beijing Records*, and *Hanzhong Woman*; and the biographies *Vagrants' Footprints* and *Mountains and Rivers*.

15

WANG PENG

Sister Yinxiu

This story has to begin ten years ago.

She was thirty years old then, and people called her Sister Yinxiu. Her husband had just died, leaving her with a seven- or eight-year-old son. Her mother-in-law had headed the village cadre of the women's federation for many years. The older woman was capable and kind, treating Sister Yinxiu like her own daughter. Thanks to her comfort and help, Sister Yinxiu did not plunge into extreme sorrow and loneliness.

By chance, the piggery of the village was in disarray then and the pig keeper was about to be replaced, so Father Qingshun, head of the village, arranged for an offer to be made to Sister Yinxiu for her to be in charge of the piggery.

Accepting the offer, she said to herself, it's good—I know how to handle a piggery since I raised pigs when I was young. Besides, once I engage myself in doing something, I may forget unhappy things. Guifang, Sister Yinxiu's mother-in-law, agreed with her decision; the older woman shared the management of the village and was also concerned about the piggery. Besides, Guifang understood her daughter-in-law very well. For the sake of convenience, Sister Yinxiu brought her son and made their home at the piggery.

Sister Yinxiu was a hardworking and stoic woman who would rather suffer than be a burden on others. There was a saying: food makes a pig fatten. However, at that time, the human beings did not have enough to eat, let alone the pigs! Therefore, though Sister Yinxiu worked very hard, the pigs remained thin. She was so worried that she became preoccupied. She went to Father Qingshun and her mother-in-law several times every day to ask for solutions. Finally, they had an idea. There was a row of newly built factories at the foot of a nearby mountain. Because the factories were on village land, their managers had agreed that villagers could help themselves to the refuse from the workers' dining hall. Discarded vegetables, rinds of melon and fruit, leftover food and wastewater from washing rice and utensils—all this could make a feast for pigs.

That was how Sister Yinxiu met Old Mo, a cook working in the factory dining hall. He was a jocular Sichuanese with a broad forehead and kind eyes. In the entire dining hall, he had the best cooking skills and also the loudest voice. His loud Sichuan accent could be heard over any din. In addition, he was warmhearted and always ready to help.

When she came there the first time, Sister Yinxiu was impressed by the grandeur and spaciousness of the dining hall. The entire kitchen, from floor to ceiling, was covered with ceramic tiles. Very different from the dirty kitchens of the peasants' households, it was dazzlingly white; it stunned this simple provincial woman. Afraid to taint the clean floor, Sister Yinxiu was at a loss about where to put down the buckets for pig food that she'd carried on a pole across her shoulders. Fortunately, Old Mo noticed her uneasiness and greeted her in his loud voice, showing her the collecting place and helping her pick up the discarded vegetables and fruit rinds, thus preventing her from making a fool of herself.

Needless to say, the food carried back from the dining hall became delicacies for the pigs, which ate with gusto until they were content. As long as they eat, they will grow and become pregnant and give birth to piglets, Sister Yinxiu thought with satisfaction, as if she could already see big-bellied sows staggering in the pigsty, followed by groups of piglets. This vision made her grateful for the factory dining hall. It also conjured visions of Old Mo with his broad forehead and kind eyes. How I wish I could meet him again . . .

The next time she came to the kitchen, the discarded vegetables and leftover food had already been collected in two metal buckets. She assumed that Old Mo had done it, in a moment of extraordinary kindness. However, he went on to do that every day, collecting the scraps ahead of time for her. No matter whether she arrived early or late, he was perfectly consistent.

Sister Yinxiu could not help feeling grateful to Old Mo.

Maybe his home is in the countryside, Sister Yinxiu speculated. Otherwise, how could he know the hardships of the country folks and the problems of pig raising? But then, feeling somewhat ashamed, she wondered, but does his wife also raise pigs? Does she also carry food for pigs?

Soon Sister Yinxiu learned that Old Mo did not have a wife. He was still single, although he was nearly forty years old. Impossible! How is it that no woman loves such a good man? Why doesn't he have a family? She didn't believe it at first. When it proved to be true, she felt pity and sorrow for him. Still later, she realized that she secretly felt somewhat happy that Mo was single. Why? Even she herself could not tell. A light of hope emerged dimly in her heart. But this good mood soon gave way to dejection, melancholy, and disappointment, the familiar and pervasive feelings of a widowed woman.

The workers at the dining hall gradually learned that Sister Yinxiu was also single, and their eyes began to dart between her and Old Mo, as if by just watching the pair, the kitchen help could connect the two of them. Often, as soon as Sister Yinxiu stepped into the dining hall, all the clamor suddenly stopped; the young lads making steamed buns and the young maidens cutting vegetables would wink and make faces behind her back. She was aware of their joking. How embarrassing! How can I show my face in here again? She felt irritated and shy at first, but when she considered the meaning of the jokes, a faint smile appeared on her face, dispelling the lonely expression so common to widows.

However, the more she thought about it, the more complicated her sentiments became, as if two forces were struggling against each other in her heart. On her way to the dining hall, she'd be thinking of Old Mo's broad forehead, kind eyes, and tender care; it cast a happy spell on her, making her excited, delighted, and hopeful. But on her way home, seeing the village far ahead wrapped in the smoke of peasants' cooking fires, the fog, and evening mist, she'd feel herself constrained by rules, customs, moral codes, and some unspeakable forces hidden in them, which, though invisible, could control people's fates. Then she would deeply regret her indulgence and decide that on her next trip to the dining hall, she would look at nobody. She resolved to ignore the broad forehead and all such things.

But on her next trip, seeing from a long distance the two tall chimneys of the gleaming kitchen puffing smoke into the sky, her heart could not help throbbing. Besides, when she'd enter the dining hall, Old Mo's kind eyes would be looking toward the door as if welcoming her. Of course, once her eyes met his, he'd look away in a flurry as if he had seen her only by chance. Sister Yinxiu was amused; she clearly detected anxiety and anticipation followed by relief and contentment in his eyes.

How about her? Forgetting her worries, she indulged herself temporarily in a happiness that no one else could know, which filled her heart with hope.

One day in April, as Sister Yinxiu prepared to go to the dining hall, she thought about what to wear. It was late spring, and the change in seasons called for a change in garments. Shall I change my trousers? she asked herself, taking out a pair of blue trousers, her only pants without a patch. She put on her homemade cloth shoes. On top, she wore a thin coat she had not worn for a long time. It had a pastel flower pattern. Before leaving, she looked at herself in her broken half mirror, took loose hair from around her temples and tucked it behind her ears, and fastened a new hairpin. It had been years since she'd been in the mood to dress herself up. She felt a bit coy as she stepped out.

Sister Yinxiu picked up the two buckets for pig food and started her journey. Luckily the village lane was empty, since it was spring and everybody was busy working in the fields. She was in a lighthearted mood, as if she were going to a downtown fair instead of to work. She felt delighted, joyful, expectant. She dimly recalled having felt this kind of feeling before. When? Oh, she remembered: it was when she'd come here for the first time, leaving the small village where she'd spent her childhood. But later . . . how about later? She was reluctant to think further, enjoying the broad view of the open country where the air was clean and comfortable to breathe. The dark cloud in her heart, like the dark cloud in the sky, was suddenly dispelled and a colorful world emerged there, one as beautiful as the spring landscape before her eyes.

Stepping into the bright kitchen, Sister Yinxiu tried to control the pounding of her heart. She intended to welcome passionately for the first time that pair of gentle, caring eyes. But they were not there. She turned toward the cooking range, where several pots of food were in various stages of preparation, but she was disappointed. The familiar and welcoming figure of Old Mo was nowhere to be seen.

He must be off doing some other work now. Perhaps he'll be back here in a moment. She prolonged her stay in the kitchen, drawing out her task as long as she could, but when the other cooks noticed her fresh clothes and started smiling in a knowing way, she decided to leave.

As soon as she left, bitter disappointment seized her, as if something valuable that she'd long anticipated and was confident of winning had suddenly disappeared, leaving her dejected.

As she approached the factory gate, feeling disheartened and oblivious to the movement of the carrying pole on her shoulders, she heard someone call out to her: "Hello? You're going already?"

Looking up, her eyes brightened: it was Old Mo! His voice was the same—as loud and warm as ever. But the look was different. No longer was he dressed in his grease-spattered chef's clothing. He had a fresh haircut and wore brand-new khaki pants, which made his forehead seem even more broad and bright. His eyes seemed more gentle and passionate. At first glance, he looked like a young man in his thirties.

"Whom are you going to date, since you've dressed yourself up?" Sister Yinxiu couldn't help joking with him, forgetting that she, too, had on fresh clothes.

Old Mo blushed and waved his hand repeatedly: "It's my turn to have a holiday today. I just came out to take a walk."

"No wonder I didn't see you in the dining hall." Sister Yinxiu spoke boldly, blushing as soon as she did.

"Even if I were there, you wouldn't have noticed me in that crowded kitchen," Old Mo said.

"Your forehead and voice would make you conspicuous in any crowd," Sister Yinxiu murmured in a gentle, low voice.

"So you paid attention to me?"

"Who would do that?"

As they bantered, a large group of people entered the factory grounds through the gate, and Sister Yinxiu turned to leave.

"Let me help you carry that load," said Old Mo, reaching for the carrying pole.

"It will make your clothes dirty."

"Why can't you wash them for me?"

"Our village is far away and it will waste your time."

"I'm going to the village to buy some vegetables for our dining hall."

Sister Yinxiu was amused; she knew that large dining halls got their vegetables from supply companies, not from the village markets. And even if they did, the cooks themselves would not have done the buying.

Sister Yinxiu realized that Old Mo had been here waiting for her today. She did not let on, but she felt pleased and happy. She didn't protest when Old Mo took over the carrying pole, and she did not consider the appropriateness of his doing so.

How broad was the view in the open country in late spring; the bright sunshine lit up the light-blue sky. A few puffs of white clouds drifted by, looking as soft and light as goose down. In the fields, crops were beginning to show promise. Every shade of green was visible, punctuated by highlights of pink, along with lavender sweet-potato blossoms, favorites among the buzzing bees. With the songs of larks and warm breezes, the scene was no less than intoxicating.

Sister Yinxiu and Old Mo walked shoulder to shoulder on the track in the fields, with Old Mo turning from time to time to chat with her. The picturesque landscape, the pleasant spring breeze, and that subtle feeling sprouting in their two hearts made Sister Yinxiu feel a kind of fresh, sweet happiness that she had never felt before.

Generally speaking, when a thirty-year-old woman who has been married and has a son meets a man, calm reason should triumph over emotional impulse. What caused in Sister Yinxiu this first-love-like emotion, the giddiness of a young maiden, had something to do with her family background and her past.

Ah, beyond this green field, in the valley of the dark-blue mountain, was the place where she had lived in her maidenhood. She had pulled pigweed, brought up her siblings, and washed clothes—and then picked tea, planted rice shoots, raised vegetables, and plowed the fields, taking the place of her mother, who had many children and many illnesses. As if the beauty of her homeland had been incarnated in her, she grew up to be a capable and pretty maiden, attracting the gazes of passersby and young lads. Later, go-betweens came to her home. That was the era of the Great Leap Forward, when peasants traded in the cooking utensils of private households and instead ate in public mess halls, believing this to be the lifestyle of paradise.

"Oh, haven't you heard of Wu Guifang," a go-between said, "head of our commune, a woman well known in the entire province, a model figure? She has an equal footing with the secretary of the Party committee of our county! The son of such a woman is certainly good! It's difficult to find such a family, eh?"

Good! After hearing the go-between's introduction, how could a common peasant family demand more?

Having met only twice, in the atmosphere of that era when even killing flies and mosquitoes had to be done in a Great Leap Forward way, Sister Yinxiu and the son of the well-known woman got married at a Great Leap Forward speed, as if getting married was as casual as buying an ordinary garment or having a simple meal. Even for quite a while after the wedding, Sister Yinxiu and her husband had few words with each other. Only at night did he display his frenzied passion, which was hard either to accept or reject, as he never seemed to care whether she was ill or felt well, much less how she felt about his advances.

Her husband's stubbornness and foolhardiness was as famous as her mother-in-law's prestige and influence in the village. Having attended little school and being the son of a cadre leader in a family used to taking the lead in everything, Sister Yinxiu's husband knew nothing but hard work, swinging a pick from morning to evening. In his eyes, even using a cart instead of a carrying pole to fetch manure from the fields was deceitful. He required Sister Yinxiu to work hard every day for the village. She was expected to carry water, clean the pigsty, feed the pigs, and do the cooking at home. She grew as exhausted as a pack animal, with pains in her loins and back. She could find no one to tell her grievances to; she simply endured.

That kind of life lasted for nearly ten years, until one December day. After weeks of carrying large stones for a river dam, her husband became ill and lay in bed at home. The diagnosis was liver disease caused by exhaustion. Even though she had been a party to her husband's nocturnal passions, and even though she had borne him a son, she became a widow without knowing the sweetness of conjugal life—only the pain and the sorrow.

No wonder Sister Yinxiu felt somewhat intoxicated now as Old Mo was carrying the burden for her. Was she afraid of carrying a burden? Ha! Sister Yinxiu could carry even more. But only she herself knew how this scene compensated for many longings in her dreams.

It was getting dark and, ahead of them, Sister Yinxiu and Old Mo could see village women returning home with loads of pigweed and spring bamboo shoots on their backs. As usual, after returning from work, their husbands were going to meet them. Sister Yinxiu's husband had never done this; he did not have the habit of caring for women. As one woman stretched her aching neck, her husband could be heard playfully saying, "Do you want to carry back the entire mountain?"

Understanding her husband's special way of showing love, the woman explained happily: "Once I went there, I wanted to bring back more . . ."

The delightful scene aroused envy, hope, and longing in Sister Yinxiu's heart. She had never experienced such a moment. She had had only sorrow and tears, which had made her eyesight dim.

But now, Old Mo was indeed carrying the burden for her.

It's good to be seen by others, Sister Yinxiu thought before she suddenly returned from her daydream and blushed, stumbling over some creeping wildflowers. To hide her true feelings, she quickened her steps to walk at Old Mo's side, saying, "Let me carry the scraps . . ." She was about to say, ". . . for fear people might see this"—but she changed the words to, "I have been used to carrying them. You should have a rest."

But Old Mo quickened his own steps, as if he were afraid Sister Yinxiu would snatch the carrying pole from him. Waving his hands, he said: "Let me carry; let me carry. We are the same."

It was clear that Old Mo also felt very excited now.

Odd things often happen in our lives: Sometimes an excellent man readily passes up many outstanding women. Eventually he will be charmed by an ordinary woman who is new to him, enjoying being caught up in a love affair that others cannot understand. Such was the case with Old Mo. An orphan from a village in Sichuan, he had joined the army as a teenager. After serving as an army cook for seven or eight years, he was transferred to the factory to do the same work.

At the beginning, many warmhearted people acted as go-betweens for this simple, honest, passionate, and capable young man, introducing him to many prospective marriage partners—a shop-girl, a restaurant accountant, the driver of a store trailer who was a bit older than him. All of these young ladies were good, but Old Mo either had little to say to them or he was late for their dates. Ultimately he remained single when he was nearly forty years old. However, at the first sight of Sister Yinxiu, middle-aged Old Mo was struck deeply by her slender figure, her gentle temperament, and the timid and lonely expression on her face. He felt excited, exhilarated, restless. It seemed surprising, but communication between two souls has always been a mystery that is so complex and subtle it cannot be understood by an outsider.

Old Mo was carrying the two buckets of pig food with the pole on his shoulders, walking neither too slowly nor too fast at the side of Sister Yinxiu. At first he felt nervous—due perhaps to spending all his time cooped up in the smoky, greasy kitchen, or to the broadness and freshness of the open country, or to his being alone with the object of his affection for the first time. Gradually, though, he calmed. They passed seedlings under the warm sunlight, stirred by the spring breeze; a gurgling stream running over tiny pebbles; fences and tile-roofed cottages half-hidden in the shade of trees and bamboo forests—all sights that reminded Old Mo of his hometown on the flatland of western Sichuan Province. The landscape there was exactly like that of southern Shaanxi Province, now spread out before him.

Suddenly he recalled a scene from his past, one hidden in the far corners of his memory. On a similar track through similarly green fields, similarly carrying two baskets of pig food on his shoulders with a pole, Old Mo had gone to a sweet-potato field as a smokelike mist began to rise. He'd gone there to help a maiden who raised pigs. He would carry back two baskets of pigweed for her. He thought now of how Sister Yinxiu resembled that girl, who had herself been sold like a pig when her parents had financial troubles! In what other ways did Sister Yinxiu resemble the maiden from his past? Was it their similarly slender figures, or their similarly kind and gentle temperaments, or their similarly timid and lonely facial expressions? Old Mo couldn't tell. His love, which had been buried for a long time, stored away like good wine left to age, now made him drunk. He began to stagger . . .

"We're home," said Sister Yinxiu. "Put down your burden, and wipe off your sweat." She handed Old Mo a handkerchief, awakening him from his reverie. Wiping the sweat from his broad forehead, he surveyed the scene: a thriving patch of alfalfa; a few twisted willow trees; two rows of low, tile-roofed houses; a nearby ditch; and endless fields not far away. How similar this piggery was to the one in his memory! He could not help saying, "It must be comfortable to settle down here."

Sister Yinxiu felt flirtatious, but she responded forthrightly. "Don't make fun of us country folks. How can you like the simple cottages here when you live in a grand, tall building!"

"Everyone has his own taste."

"I don't believe it," she replied. "What could you like about this place?"

"You don't understand?"

"You . . ."

"What?"

Then both of them stopped and looked at each other with shy smiles. Each saw instantly in the other's eyes what they had been seeking for a long time.

After that, they met alone together again and again, using as a pretext Sister Yinxiu's favorite black-and-white she-piglet, which could not stand up and needed bone powder to strengthen its weak legs. Old Mo collected all the bones in the dining hall, and together he and Sister Yinxiu smashed and ground the bones into powder and fed the concoction carefully to the lovely black-and-white piglet, treating it like their own child. The piglet entered into the act, raising its head to snort for food and licking Sister Yinxiu's and Old Mo's ankles. The intimate, familial atmosphere was seductive. It was as if warm springs had trickled out of Sister Yinxiu's and Old Mo's hearts and rushed forward, washing away the withered branches and dead leaves that had accumulated along the way. Gradually, the piglet was able to stand up.

A wilting fruit tree that suddenly begins sprouting new leaves and producing good fruit can hardly go unnoticed. And so it was with Sister Yinxiu. She underwent obvious changes, exuding vigor and arousing surprised glances from her neighbors.

When she fed the pigs, she wore a white apron around her waist. How slender and graceful her figure was! With a handkerchief covering her head, she swept and tidied the pigsty. How handsome and warm her face was! As she cut alfalfa with a sickle, anyone seeing her from behind would have mistaken her for a young maiden.

And Old Mo? Now his face was always clean-shaven and he had his hair cut twice a month. He began dressing more tidily and spoke even louder, as if giving voice to his newfound hope and joy.

At this stage, it was time for them to consider their next steps; after all, they were no longer young. Of course, Old Mo had nothing to lose, since he had no family. However, Sister Yinxiu had to consider many things.

Though she had the right to remarry, as a widow, she still had to consider the opinions of her child, her mother-in-law, the elders of her clan, her own parents, and especially her brother, who had just been transferred to the commune to work as a pig-purchasing agent. She would have to consult with all of them.

Besides, what would the villagers think about this? In the past, a similar case in the village had aroused terrible gossip. Remembering it, Sister Yinxiu now imagined she'd seen glances of contempt from eyes behind many doors and windows, pointing fingers of blame behind her back, and mean spitting from people walking past her. She could not help trembling, realizing that the situation was more complex than she'd believed. Her enthusiasm began to fade. She knew she had to think it over.

Indeed, the circumstances were even more insidious than she had imagined. Since the first time Old Mo and Sister Yinxiu had come to the piggery together, gossip had begun to spread like the black wings of a bat, which always fly in dark places. Thanks to her mother-in-law's prestige as a leader in the community and to Sister Yinxiu's own youth and beauty, the widow had attracted quite a few unmarried elderly men in the village. Father Xiayao, for example, always loafed about the piggery, pretending to pick up manure. He'd look Sister Yinxiu up and down from different angles, as if he were examining the teeth and legs of a specimen of livestock. Because of Guifang's prestige, no one dared to act as a go-between for Father Xiayao. But that prestige didn't stop anyone from talking about Sister Yinxiu and Old Mo. They were the objects of extraordinary attention. Busybodies with varying intentions were constantly speculating, voicing their observations. In fact, the village was so filled with gossip it seemed that even the rice in the fields was aware that something was going on between Sister Yinxiu and Old Mo.

With so much gossip, how can I live on in the village? At first she was furious, her eyes brimming with tears. But when she calmed down, she began to ponder: wasn't there always something happening in the village to spark gossip? As time passed, surely people would forget her and Old Mo. The stories about them would be replaced by newer incidents sooner or later. So, without regret, she looked to a practical solution: for this issue, what is important is to get the consent of my mother-in-law.

However, in thinking about how to approach the issue with her mother-in-law, Sister Yinxiu became worried and afraid. Her mother-in-law cared about her, she knew, treating Sister Yinxiu the way any older person treated her own children. "You come before me since I am old," Guifang would say to her. "I don't matter anymore." The words often made Sister Yinxiu feel warm in her heart.

Her mother-in-law had also become widowed at an early age, but somehow she'd remained single, which contributed to her prestige, along with the fact of being a clan elder and for many years the director of the women's federation. Whenever a request was made in the village, as long as someone said, "Grandma Guifang said so," everyone would obey as if induced by an invisible power.

Yinxiu's mother-in-law was very proud of this. "Without a man, I can still support the family and serve the public well!"

Thinking about it, a dark shadow appeared in Sister Yinxiu's heart.

Sister Yinxiu still had a heavy heart as she and Guifang sat together in the yard one night in the middle of autumn. The two women were meditating and watching the moon beyond the fence entwined with creeping vines. The lonely feminine atmosphere finally made Sister Yinxiu pluck up her courage and speak her thoughts, confessing her new love. Afterward she lowered her head uneasily, her heart beating fast as if she were on trial.

"Is he the man who helped you carry pig food?"

The question made Sister Yinxiu uneasy, as if all of her "crimes" had been exposed.

Her mother-in-law's tone was as calm as when she dealt with daily disputes among the women in the village—but the calm tone of voice masked the older woman's anger. She had remained a widow from the day when she had been called Sister Guifang to the day when she was called Grandma Guifang. She believed that only women like her could be considered righteous and moral. She wished that all people in the world, especially widowed women, would follow her example.

And now Sister Yinxiu wanted to remarry! Guifang's own daughter-in-law! It was like stabbing Guifang in the heart. Her prestige would be damaged. How would she give lessons to other women after this? The recent gossip in the village had annoyed her, but she had not expected that it was true. She was angry, and she wanted to give her daughter-in-law a good scolding. But as director of the women's federation she had dealt with people of many personalities, and she knew that scolding would not help the situation.

"Alas, if only Lude were still alive . . ." Grandma Guifang began to speak of her son, weeping in genuine grief. Sister Yinxiu's eyes turned red, too, and she tried to comfort her mother-in-law, knowing that it was not suitable to mention her personal issue again. Thus, the issue was laid aside.

In the first month of the next year, when Sister Yinxiu saw men and women visiting relatives in pairs, her heart stirred. Plucking up her courage, she mentioned her secret hope again to her mother-in-law, but Grandma Guifang had made up her mind: she would allow her daughter-in-law anything but a marriage to Old Mo! She asked Sister Yinxiu in retort: "Does your mother-in-law mistreat you?"

After a long interval, with the encouragement of Old Mo and the rising call from her own heart, Sister Yinxiu could not endure it anymore. Once again she resolutely put forward the issue.

This time, Grandma Guifang called for her grandson, who was growing taller each day, and spoke to Sister Yinxiu about the hardships of bringing up children in old China. The older woman said that things were much easier now than they had been in the past, and she chastised her daughter-in-law for not being grateful for her blessings. Seeing her son looking at her imploringly, Sister Yinxiu could not insist any more. All she could do was bury her face in her quilt and weep for a long time, heartbroken.

Sister Yinxiu had the guts to fight against the gossip in the village, but she dared not oppose Grandma Guifang, because that meant opposing all the elderly in the clan, all the village leaders, and the invisible, intangible force that controlled the destinies of all the people of the village. Didn't she want to work in the pigsty and live in the village anymore?

Old Mo suggested that she consult her brother, the commune's pig-purchasing agent, about their dilemma. If he could speak for her as her brother and a leader of the commune, things might be much easier.

Her brother, who had recently applied to join the Party, received Sister Yinxiu warmly. He had been brought up by this elder sister. The precocious young man wore a contemporary hairstyle and a sports coat with fancy buttons. He offered his sister a glass of water and began cooking dinner for the two of them.

"What? You want to remarry!" Her brother was surprised. He believed that his sister was lucky to be the daughter-in-law of Grandma Guifang, a member of the commune's Party committee. However, seeing his sister's obvious unhappiness, he softened his tone. "But Grandma Guifang is a longtime community leader; even the secretary of the commune's Party committee has to discuss matters with her. So you have to get her consent. As she doesn't agree . . ."

Was there anything more to be said? Sister Yinxiu walked out of the gate of the commune, her face pale, her body trembling. She felt as if a sudden storm had frozen her, turning her yellow and withered, without a sign of life.

Thus, year in and year out, the issue was laid aside.

And as for Old Mo? This simple, kind, and honest cook had always been considerate of his beloved Sister Yinxiu, unwilling to bring her any inconvenience. Now when they met, they were careful not to mention the issue at all. But he, who had been cheerful and talkative, became an eccentric lone soul, addicted to smoking and drinking by himself.

Sister Yinxiu—people now called her Aunt Yinxiu according to the custom, since she was nearly forty years old—still raised pigs. Passersby could see her at work in the piggery. As she fed the pigs, she still wore a white apron around her waist, but it could not be distinguished from the black belt that held it up. She still continued to carry the pig food on a pole across her shoulders, but now her back was stooped and her walk staggered. With a black scarf covering her head, she swept and tidied the pigsty. How thin and pale her face had become. As she cut alfalfa with a sickle, anyone seeing her from behind would have mistaken her for an old woman.

It is true, as Guifang said, that life in the countryside has gotten better and easier in recent years. With the advent of wheat mills and soybean mills, it is no longer necessary to carry pig slop from the dining halls of factories, for wheat and soybean residue can serve as pig food. Although Aunt Yinxiu does not see Old Mo anymore, she still feels contented; she believes that she has a man to love who also loves her, and she can recall the precious time they spent together. This kind of love may be peculiar and odd, but who would dare say it is not valuable, pure, and beautiful?

Near midnight during the tenth Spring Festival since he met Sister Yinxiu, after cooking and cleaning up from the factory's annual dinner party, Old Mo heads back to the factory residences. He indulges his gaze, fixing his eyes on the soft light passing through light-green, apricot-yellow, and lavender curtains in nearby buildings. He hears children's laughter and sweet music, and he sees the silhouettes of lovers in various windows.

Old Mo flicks his cigarette butt to the ground and enters the building for single staff. Usually it is well lighted, but now with young boys and young girls away visiting their families, the light in the empty building is dim. Pushing the door open and staggering to his room, Old Mo clutches a bottle of liquor. He drinks until he is drunk—so drunk that he never wakes up again.

Aunt Yinxiu doesn't get the news until many days later. At first she spends the morning searching for the rod for stirring pig food, though all the while she is holding it in her hand. In the afternoon she can't endure stoically any longer and falls ill, lying in bed for two days. She finally wakes up a little past midnight. Through the window she can see the dim light of the moon and the stars. Somehow, she thinks of that black-and-white she-piglet, her favorite, whose illness she and Old Mo cured. That piglet must have already given birth to many litters of piglets.

Translated by Xiaohui Xue

Zhang Hong

Born in Hong'an County, Hubei Province, Zhang Hong graduated from the Department of Chinese Language and Literature, Hanzhong Normal College, in 1978, and then with the class of writers, from the Department of Chinese Language and Literature, Northwest University, in 1990.

She worked in succession as a teacher's assistant, associate research fellow, editor in chief of *Ankang Literature* magazine, chairman of the Ankang Writers Association, director of the Shaanxi Provincial Writers Association, and vice-chairperson of the Shaanxi Provincial Writers Association.

Zhang Hong made her literary debut in 1980 and joined the Chinese Writers Association in 1994. Her works include the prose collections *Return to the Grass*, *Ephemeral World*, and *Singing Fish*; the novels *Black Box* and *Qingyang Ridge*; and the poetry collection *Red Is My Color*. She won the Literature Prize of Special Zones and the first Jiyuan Literature Prize. Her short stories and poetry are broadly represented in anthologies.

16

ZHANG HONG

Lei Ping'er

The art gallery has employed two kinds of people since the national reform: those who are too incompetent to survive the socialist market, and those who are too artistic to satisfy it. Lei Ping'er is an employee there but is neither of these kinds. She works in the gallery's Reference Room. She is twenty-eight, unmarried, and in an awkward stage of womanhood.

Chinese men in this city have bizarre ideas about women. They call the women who think intelligently and act intelligently "stunners." Stunners are perfect. Other women think intelligently but act with a slight stupidity. These women are adorable.

Other women are like Lei Ping'er—they act stupid and even think stupidly. This is just too much for anyone. Polite people call her "naive." Direct people—namely, her colleagues in the gallery—nickname her "dippy girl."

Lei Ping'er herself knows nothing about this. She is happy with her celibacy and lives a very routine life. Each morning, she practices singing and then dancing in the courtyard of the gallery. She eats breakfast. We could describe this breakfast as "classic." Unlike those who carelessly buy a *shaobing*—a clay-oven roll—in the street to cover the whole morning, Lei Ping'er enjoys freshly cooked congee, along with homemade salted egg and some *mahua*, the twisted crullers fried carefully in sesame oil.

She goes to work, though there is no work to do. Under a tight budget, the gallery can only stock a few magazines and newspapers. Almost no one visits Lei Ping'er in the little Reference Room. But she always finds ways to occupy herself. Once she planted a patch of evening primrose in the yard, and now her first "work" each morning is to water them. The flowers blossom only at night and close again by morning. Lei Ping'er picks a bunch before they bashfully finish their bloom, and then she stands at the gallery's gate and greets her colleagues with a smile. As she hands off each flower with great joy, she urges her colleagues again and again: "Use fresh water!" she says. "The primrose is very fragile!"

The gallery is filled with professional artists—painters, musicians, writers, and calligraphers. They despise Lei Ping'er but hide their contempt with words. For them, life is boring. Why not have some fun and make her talk? The bachelors, especially the young ones, call Lei Ping'er "sister" to lure her into doing things for them. Among them, Lei Ping'er has a favorite: Liu Cong, a college graduate assigned to the gallery.

Liu Cong is smart and good-looking. He chats with Lei Ping'er, teasing her with a brand of kindly respect. It pleases her. He gives her a sincere thanks after eating her homemade pancake, and even lets his gratitude show in his eyes. Lei Ping'er wants to use all her skills to cook for him.

Xi Xia, Liu Cong's girlfriend and a college graduate as well, is even smarter than her boyfriend. She is a writer, and Liu Cong is a painter. Both enjoy some fame in their professions. But they both have a flaw: laziness. They neither sweep an inch of floor nor wipe down their tables. The dust accumulating on those tables gets thick enough to make a drawing in. When they met, Xi Xia seized upon

Lei Ping'er's warmheartedness. She spoke with honey lips and called Lei Ping'er her "little sister," and soon that girl was joyfully at her service.

But in truth Lei Ping'er thinks only about Liu Cong, even as she does favors for Xi Xia.

Besides gardening and helping others, Lei Ping'er has a greater hobby: singing. She once dreamed of learning singing at a national academy of music; she was so determined to attend that she never found herself a partner. It's true! People in the gallery know that she once promised herself never to date a man until college. Then, last year, an experienced admissions officer told her frankly that her chances of admission were "absolutely zero." Since then, she has quit singing.

To be honest, her singing is pretty OK. What is not OK is the way she puts on these exaggerated facial expressions in her performances. Her looks are bad. She is short and chubby and out of shape, which is a bit challenging to the audience's aesthetic standards. Her red cheeks gleam against her swarthy face, and her eyes have contracted pupils that make her look sort of bad or even evil. Thus, Lei Ping'er's good heart is totally betrayed by her looks.

When Lei Ping'er was feeling heartbroken, Liu Cong encouraged her. "Not all good singers were admitted by the Academy of Music," he said. "It's just like those great poets in China's history, like Li Bai and Du Fu. They never, ever won a title in the imperial examination, but they still wrote great poems. There is actually something precise in your singing—it's passion. And great passion can make even the gods weep. Keep practicing. Your effort will definitely be rewarded someday."

With Liu Cong's advice, she instantly goes crazy. She sings in the morning and sings at night. She even sings in the midday sometimes. Soon the whole gallery feels its flesh creep.

People complain to the gallery director. "She is doing this ghost-wailing and wolf-howling all the time," someone says. "When does she plan to give our ears some peace?" Director Xu cannot turn a deaf ear to public opinion. He speaks with Lei Ping'er.

"Lei Ping'er, stop singing! Do you know that your singing is worthless?"

"What do you mean?" she says. "Has my singing ever kept you from finding a lover, or from improving your sex life? You don't have time to teach your artists how to make more money, but you have time to stop my professional development?"

Director Xu is choked by her bluntness. Now, if anyone else complains to him about Lei Ping'er, he loses his temper immediately. "If you're so tough, why don't you talk to that freak yourself?"

One Hu Yong, Liu Cong's buddy, says, "Someone ought to be good at this. You know that old saying that the only one who can untie a bell is the person who tied it? Director Xu, go and ask Liu Cong to stop her. That has to work."

Director Xu comes to Liu Cong's studio. "Dear Liu, can you do a favor for our gallery?" He sits cross-legged with his beard hanging down, and Liu Cong has the urge to boast to his buddies. He doesn't respond to the director's awkward plea.

The director continues. "Everyone is complaining about Lei Ping'er's singing practice now. I asked her to stop, but that f—" He swallows the word "freak" in front of Liu Cong. "But she mistakes me for an evil man. Liu Cong, can you go and ask her to stop? It's driving everyone crazy."

Liu Cong gives an indifferent smile. "I will try, then." In fact, Liu Cong feels quite proud of himself, since he can manipulate a woman the director cannot control.

In the evening, Lei Ping'er takes her homemade *guotie*—fried dumplings—to Liu Cong's studio, complaining to him as well. Liu Cong listens patiently as he eats. Afterward he mentions nonchalantly that it might be better to sing along the river, as the air is fresher there. And especially in the morning—singers can take in some essence of heaven and earth, which is exceptionally great for the voice. He also suggests that Lei Ping'er sing in his studio whenever she needs an audience. "Besides," he says, "a good singer always needs a good listener."

Liu Cong then tells her a story about Bo Ya, a legendary musician in ancient China. Bo Ya had a bosom friend, Zhong Ziqi, who was also a devoted fan of his music. After Zhong's death, the musician stopped playing, as he'd lost the one who best understood his music.

Lei Ping'er is soon moved to tears by the beautiful and philosophical story. "From now on," she says, "I will sing only for you. Those vulgar people in our gallery will never hear my songs again."

For Lei Ping'er, what is said must be done and what is done must be carried to fruition. After that night, she stops her public practice and sings only for Liu Cong in his studio. Although Liu Cong never despised Lei Ping'er, like others in the gallery, he never particularly liked her, either. His kind attitude was merely a reward for Lei Ping'er's kindness. Now that he's with her constantly, he can no longer control his antipathy. Especially when Lei Ping'er sings him those love songs with great passion—for Liu Cong it is totally unbearable, like being hugged and kissed by a gorilla.

He complains to his buddies in private. Xi Xia pats Liu Cong's shoulder and mocks him. "Those who play with fire will perish by fire. What are you complaining for? Poor kid. Be careful—that Lei Ping'er might be in love with you! A bosom friend and a lover are like a pot and a kettle: same color!" Everyone bursts into laughter and makes fun. Liu Cong is deeply regretful. After that, he keeps a distance from Lei Ping'er.

Of course, Lei Ping'er senses nothing. As we have already said, her great strength and her great weakness is stupidity. She never notices those subtle changes in people.

She is now at the peak of pride for having Liu Cong as a bosom friend. One day, she gets an idea to organize a group of old people to teach and practice qigong for free. Soon, at half past five every afternoon, when the sun is slowly setting and the whole world is going out to take a look, people find Lei Ping'er and her group practicing in patches of flowers, breathing the essence of the universe together.

Lei Ping'er has a nice voice and is good at talking. What's more, she speaks with great conviction. Unsurprisingly, a group of retired seniors are easily persuaded and become her followers. Her teaching gives her a sense of pride and dignity. If Liu Cong happens to pass by when she's teaching, she becomes far more serious, making the whole gallery feel both awkward and amused. But as time passes, people get accustomed to the sight. They no longer laugh at her. Instead, they grow a kind of respect for this woman. Some female gallery staff even join her team. In the gallery's courtyard, Lei Ping'er and her qigong group become a special sight.

One day, people are chatting over their tea break. Suddenly Xi Xia says, "Something is wrong with our gallery. A demon or a monster will appear here."

"How come?" says Director Xu.

"Each time I see Lei Ping'er and her group practicing like mad, I feel like doomsday is coming."

Director Xu nods. "True! We have to find a way to stop this freak. It's too much. Her qigong is like an epileptic having a fit. It practically destroys heaven and earth. I don't know who started such a pseudoscience. It's killing me. I will bring this up in our meeting tomorrow. My only worry is that Lei Ping'er won't listen and will keep bugging me."

Hu Yong, casting a sidelong glance at Liu Cong, says, "No worries! We have a master here."

Liu Cong is leisurely enjoying his tea and cigarettes. "In my opinion, that's not enough reason for a meeting. Lei Ping'er is doing nothing wrong, and she only practices when she's off duty. What right do we have to stop her? At work she's the most diligent of anyone, sweeping and mopping the floor every day. She even wipes the windows. Her Reference Room is our favorite place. It's not OK to hurt a person for no good reason. To be honest, I really appreciate her fearless spirit. If you were to tell her that Earth will explode tomorrow, she would still carefully do her regular activities today. That's pretty interesting."

Xi Xia is annoyed. "Wow!" she says. "Please don't tell us you're already bewitched by her." Of course, Xi Xia knows that Liu Cong will never be possessed by Lei Ping'er—that is a true "mission impossible." After four years of dating Liu Cong, she knows him pretty well. Artsy people, she knows, are usually weird. They relate tombs to pregnant women's bellies, hell to the sun, and ugliness to beauty. In her mind, Liu Cong's praise comes from nothing but his sense of ugliness.

Now she ruthlessly mocks Lei Ping'er, imitating her cajoling voice and her coy walk. The skillful mockery makes Director Xu and Hu Yong roar with laughter. Xi Xia is good at art and was born pretty. She not only writes beautiful articles, but is also an expert in singing and dancing. And now she is an excellent actress, as her "Lei Ping'er" is more authentic than Lei Ping'er herself.

Xi Xia is pleased with her performance, but Liu Cong bangs the table and stands up abruptly. "Stop it! I think Lei Ping'er is much prettier than you are!"

Xi Xia is struck, motionless as wood. Liu Cong steps out the door, and she realizes what has happened. Quickly she catches up with him and shouts, "She is prettier? Then why don't you just go out with her? Why are you still with me?"

Liu Cong stands calmly, looking askew at Xi Xia. "Do you think that's impossible?" he says. He walks away, leaving Xi Xia to weep and sob bitterly.

Xi Xia has been with Liu Cong for exactly four years. Although they haven't talked about marriage yet, she firmly believes that Liu Cong loves her, and that she has an indisputable priority in his heart. No one else could bear his absentmindedness and sloppiness. She remembers the comment that her sister once made about their relationship: it's like sticking a flower in a dunghill, so true and so real.

Now it is this dunghill who compares her to the ugliest woman alive, in front of all their friends, and then judges that Xi Xia is worse off! She nearly explodes with anger. Liu Cong is the one who touches the tenderest place in her heart. If this cruelty can be endured, what can't be?

That night, Xi Xia doesn't come to Liu Cong's room as usual. She feels that she was too stupid before. At this station in her fortune and fame, girls like her have all gone to the South for better opportunities. But she stayed and has devoted her love to that penniless artist. Now, to her surprise, he looks down on her. So she decides that she will no longer continue to sacrifice unless Liu Cong surrenders first and apologizes in public.

But Liu Cong has no plan for apology. For a long time now he has felt disgusted with Xi Xia's impulsiveness and flightiness. He feels uneasy each time Xi Xia orders Lei Ping'er to serve her. Xi Xia is unruly and never listens to him. He thinks this moment could be a chance for her to change. If she gets hurt, she will surely learn something from it. So when Hu Yong suggests that he apologize first, he determinedly refuses.

But when the night comes, he feels a bit regretful. Especially when he senses Xi Xia's familiar smell in his bed and recalls her exceedingly fascinating and charming body. He cannot help looking around and feeling a great loss.

———

In February, the gallery organizes a spring outing. The staff wants to climb Wudang Mountain. The city adjoins Wudang Mountain and the trip takes two or three days. Hoping for a chance to make up with Xi Xia, Liu Cong signs up for the tour, though he dislikes traveling in groups. He goes to ask Xi Xia whether she's planning to go or not. She treats him like a total stranger, slamming the door in his face without a word. Liu Cong mopes back to his studio, gloomy.

On the way back, he bumps into the jubilant Lei Ping'er. With a bag of leeks, onions, and ribs in her hands, she laughs like a jovial Buddha. "Oh, gosh. Finally, we can go out for fun. You'll see. I'll make some meatballs and pancakes and spiced eggs and beef. There's enough for you, Xi Xia, and Hu Yong. Tell them just to bring their appetites!" Liu Cong feels a bit irritated at Lei Ping'er. But seeing her happiness and hearing her warmhearted words, he is somehow moved.

He says, "Ping'er, Xi Xia may not go. She's at odds with me right now."

Lei Ping'er is as astonished as if she'd been told that the sun rises from the west. "Oh no," she says. "How can she miss such a good opportunity and such a nice spring? I'll persuade her."

By the time Liu Cong tries to stop her, she has already walked for miles. He shakes his head and tells himself, how good it is to be simple! Xi Xia is just too smart, with too much ego.

When she finds her, Lei Ping'er is struck dumb by the scolding Xi Xia delivers. She stands for a moment, wondering why Xi Xia keeps naming her along with Liu Cong and why she insinuates that the two of them should feel quite content.

But Lei Ping'er is not that stupid. She realizes that their bickering must have something to do with her. The realization delights her. She has a place in Liu Cong's heart.

For the excursion, the gallery invites everybody to bring along his or her family members. The gallery even spends the money to book an entire train carriage, to entertain everyone to their hearts' content. The gallery men are more or less artsy people, generally carefree and unrestrained. But today, during the trip, they are awkwardly reserved and quiet.

Director Xu suddenly remembers Lei Ping'er. "Lei Ping'er, you practice singing every day. Why don't you give us a show?"

"Eh, too shy to sing here!" says Lei Ping'er modestly. To apologize, she takes out her food and invites others to share.

Director Xu eats a mouthful of Lei Ping'er's meatballs. "You are so unreasonable. Normally we don't want you to sing, and you roar day and night. Now we ask you to sing, and you refuse."

"Ping'er," interrupts Liu Cong, "can I have more meatballs?"

Happily she runs to him and gives him her whole bag. "Hey, glutton! It's all yours."

"You should sing," Liu Cong whispers. "Why don't you sing for us?" Lei Ping'er doesn't know which song to choose. Liu Cong winks. "That song, 'Valentine's Day without a Lover,' and 'Never Be Apart'— those are two of your favorites, right?"

She blushes with shyness and bites her fingers. "OK," she announces, "I will sing a song for everyone."

She stands there for a while, giggling and stroking her hair coquettishly, before she begins.

Everyone gets gooseflesh, watching her performance. Thank god! Her voice is good enough to cover up the awkwardness. After this, no one dares to talk to her again, just in case she gets excited and sings without an end.

As the gallery has had a tight budget for years, people seldom partake in activities like these and they normally aren't close with one another. But to everyone's surprise, today different cliques begin to form. Only Lei Ping'er is left alone on the way to the mountain peak. But she doesn't feel lonely at all. She comments on the picturesque scenery and appreciates its beauty. She is full of good cheer.

The aim of the trip is to mount the summit of Wudang Mountain— the Golden Peak. After reaching it, everyone is exhausted and sits to rest. Someone says that the place doesn't live up to its fame. Someone else says that the peak's temple has lost its original mystery and is very disappointing. Liu Cong, noticing the kissing couples around the Buddha and burning joss sticks at the temple, is also terribly bored.

He walks away and sits alone. Instantly, Lei Ping'er appears and sits beside him, speaking to him intimately. "Did you make a wish?"

she asks. Liu Cong shakes his head. "But I did," she continues. She looks at Liu Cong with her childlike innocence. "Guess what! What do you think I wished for?"

Liu Cong smiles. "To find a good husband?"

Lei Ping'er smiles back. "They all say you are very smart, but not this time. When I stood at the temple, my only wish was that you and Xi Xia would make up soon." She lowers her head. "You two make such a nice match," she murmurs. "How lucky she is to be with you! I wish she could cherish her luck. Alas, I am too ugly. Otherwise . . ."

Liu Cong feels suddenly tender and protective. He cannot help kissing her on the forehead. "Ping'er, you are very lovely!" Liu Cong would never be able to imagine how great an impact this kiss has on Lei Ping'er.

Lei Ping'er is a pure and simpleminded girl. It is the first time that someone has kissed her, the first time someone has said those exceptionally beautiful words to her. Above all, that "someone" is the very one she admires and the one who seems unattainable to her.

The kiss makes her fly to the heavens, and those unattainable things suddenly seem attainable. Lei Ping'er loses her head over Liu Cong. She walks to a quiet place, tasting and retasting her happiness. She feels that even the ants on the ground are all coming to congratulate her.

On returning home, Lei Ping'er is truly launched to the heavens by what Xi Xia has done while they were all out of town. Xi Xia went to bed with a government official. On Liu Cong's return, he catches the very scene when he opens Xi Xia's door. Immediately he steps out.

For two days Liu Cong eats nothing, drinks nothing, only smokes. Xi Xia is seized with deep regret. Crying bitterly, she begs on her knees for Liu Cong's forgiveness and explains that she did what she did because Liu Cong doesn't cherish her. She kneels for a whole day.

At dawn, Liu Cong stubs out a cigarette and declares that he has decided to marry Lei Ping'er. Xi Xia will be their maid of honor. He hoists his drawing board on his back and leaves the city.

Xi Xia goes to Lei Ping'er. "Little Sister, you are greatly merciful and compassionate. You are most kind. Please don't take him away. You know I cannot live without him!"

"If you love him that much," says Lei Ping'er, "why did you, in just three days, do that thing with another?"

"You are too simple to understand," Xi Xia cries. "You don't know women!"

"Yes, I am simple. But I know love is to be cherished, and for a lifetime." Lei Ping'er stares at the ceiling, reciting repeatedly, "Cherish for a lifetime, cherish for a lifetime . . ."

———

Two months pass. Liu Cong returns. Both women wear out their eyes looking for him. After three quiet days, Liu Cong steps into Xi Xia's room. Lei Ping'er finds out and keeps to herself for a week, crying in her room. On the eighth evening she comes to Liu Cong's studio, asking when he and Xi Xia are going to get married. He tells her the date is the first of May.

"Oh," says Lei Ping'er. "It is very soon." She stares wordlessly at him, until finally she can speak. "Can you be mine tonight? Please give me one night before you get married. I only need one night in my life!"

Somehow Liu Cong is enchanted enough to hold her in his arms. He takes her head in his hands. "Ping'er, your purity makes me ashamed. Men are evil animals and cannot overcome their weaknesses. My sense of beauty is deceptive."

In his arms, Lei Ping'er feels weak all over. At the moment of being embraced, she quickly unbuttons her dress. Now, removing her underwear, she presents herself to Liu Cong like a lamb yearning for sacrifice. Liu Cong kneels on the floor before her body. His fair-skinned hands move down her swarthy body and finally stop at her sacred place. "I can't. I can't overcome my weakness. I accept all your goodness, but I still can't take all of you. I am an ugly person. You should despise me."

Lei Ping'er sits quietly. No matter how Liu Cong begs her, she just sits and won't put on her clothes.

At daybreak, Lei Ping'er finally gets dressed, feeling as if she is waking from a dream. She kisses Liu Cong on his forehead. "Thank you for the night," she says. "I have offered myself to you this time. You don't want me, but I am still happy."

In the following days, Lei Ping'er is the busiest person in the gallery. She decorates the house, books the wedding reception, buys furniture and electric appliances. She takes on nearly every element of Liu Cong's wedding. She even buys wedding invitation cards and neatly writes in every one. It's like she is preparing a wedding for her beloved son.

Lei Ping'er is made a new woman. There is no more "dippiness" in her, only gentleness and tenderness, making her very adorable. On the morning of the wedding, Lei Ping'er picks armfuls of evening primrose and decorates the bridal chamber. She is an angel. Liu Cong can hardly face her without shedding tears.

———

After the wedding, Lei Ping'er becomes the couple's unofficial house-keeper. Liu Cong has always been a man of arts, and it's quite usual for him to spend day and night in his studio. Now, with Lei Ping'er's meticulous care, he is a true workaholic and spends day after day drawing. Lei Ping'er sends soybean milk, chicken soup, and fresh tea to his studio. Xi Xia is lazy and impatient with house chores. She is more than happy to take advantage of Lei Ping'er's diligence.

Gossip starts to spread that Liu Cong is evil and is captivating Lei Ping'er with his charm. People say he's manipulative and is stealing her youth. Liu Cong is uneasy.

So one day, in private, he implores Lei Ping'er to find a husband. He even tells her that he is a useless person and that it's worthless to long for him.

Lei Ping'er is confused. "Do my words mean nothing to you?" she says. "Do you think a woman can love just anyone?" Liu Cong doesn't dare to continue.

In March of the next year, Xi Xia gives birth to a daughter. The baby plunges the couple's life into chaos. Liu Cong becomes short-tempered, blowing up angrily over tiny things. One day, while changing the baby's diaper, he says, "We should give her away. It is beyond us to raise her." He's sure that Xi Xia will stir a hysterical quarrel with him.

But she doesn't. She comes to agree with him, believing it is better for them to give the baby away. And she even comes up with the perfect candidate: Lei Ping'er. "How weird it is!" she says. "All those parents who have great ambitions for their children. I only want my daughter to be like Lei Ping'er."

"That means you're a real grown-up," Liu Cong replies. "A baby matures a woman."

"So, you agree with me?" she says.

"I've been thinking about this for a long time. But I didn't dare tell you. And I'm also afraid that Lei Ping'er will refuse."

"How come?" says Xi Xia. "Why would she refuse? She might be happy at the idea. Think about it! She even stays single for you. What wouldn't she do?"

The couple takes their baby to visit Lei Ping'er. It is a weekend. Lei Ping'er is washing her clothes and singing loudly. "How bright the sunshine is! How pretty the spring is! I come to the beautiful prairie . . ."

Her home is neat and tidy and smells of the delicate fragrance of her cleaning. There's a pale-green sofa in the living room. Above it, a large painting hangs on the white wall. It is Liu Cong's work. It is called *Spring Wind*. In the painting there are vines of honeysuckle climbing through a window, and a pair of scissors on a desk. It was a gift from Liu Cong when he was first assigned to the gallery. Lei Ping'er had gone to visit him and had gasped with admiration at the painting. "What a bold painter!" she'd said. "How can the spring be cut at your will?" Because of her words, Liu Cong gave her the piece.

Lei Ping'er sees the couple coming and is exceedingly happy. She arranges some snacks—peanuts and sunflower seeds—and makes them tea. She holds the baby in her arms and speaks to her. "Look at you! You are so cute! Your eyes are just like your mother's, and your smile is like your father's. How lovely you are!" She puts the baby in her bed and circles her with pillows and a stuffed puppy. She looks at her from afar and up close, as if appreciating a piece of art.

In the hallway, Liu Cong winks at Xi Xia. She gets the hint and follows Lei Ping'er into the bedroom.

She stands close to Lei Ping'er. "Now look," she says. "You really love this baby. How about we give her to you?"

Lei Ping'er is shocked. She stands. "What? Xi Xia! What did you say?"

"We've talked, Liu Cong and I. Both of us are busy with careers, and we have no energy for this baby. So we want to give her to you. Will you take her?"

Lei Ping'er's face changes. She goes back to the living room. She sits on the sofa and is silent. Xi Xia runs after her. "Will you take her?" she says.

Lei Ping'er looks at her, and then at Liu Cong. Suddenly she strides to the door and throws it open. "Please," she says, "get out, and never come to my place again!"

Liu Cong and Xi Xia are too embarrassed to make any sound. They take their baby and run.

———

Lei Ping'er no longer looks sweetly at the couple. Sometimes, she passes by them as if seeing nothing. It embarrasses the couple. Xi Xia calls Lei Ping'er a freak, and Liu Cong complains that he has lost a good friend.

Lei Ping'er resumes her enthusiasm for work. She asks Director Xu to buy a computer and open a shop for the gallery. She has learned computer skills, and soon she'll master typesetting composition. She plans to earn money for the gallery and is confident she'll make it happen. Director Xu is pleased. "That's great," he says. "You're pioneering new ways for us. Look at us now! Those who were capable and young are all gone. Those who have stayed are thinking of going somewhere else. The rest of the incapable bunch makes no money at all, even if they want to stay. And we need money!"

On the day Lei Ping'er's new photocopy shop opens, Liu Cong comes to her with a gift. It is another painting, one of his own. It's called *A Little Street*. In the painting there are two rows of pillbox buildings and a lonely person in a long and narrow street. Lei Ping'er refuses the gift. She says it is too dark.

Instead she buys a poster of Evander Holyfield, the muscular boxer. She hangs it on the wall. Liu Cong senses her indifference and is disappointed. And it's in this dejection and despondency that he finally goes away.

Translated by Chen Yi

Wu Kejing

Born in 1954 in Fufeng County, Shaanxi Province, Wu Kejing graduated with a master's degree from Northwest University. He once served as deputy editor in chief of *Xi'an Daily* and *Xi'an Evening News*. He was vice-chairman of the Xi'an Literary Federation, is a member of the Shaanxi Provincial Writers Association, and was elected chairman of the Xi'an Writers Association.

His awards include the Chuang Chong-wen Literature Prize, the Bing Xin Prose Prize, and the Liu Qing Literature Prize. He has written many novels, prose pieces, and essays and has been published in a number of literary journals and newspapers. His novella *Blue Flower on the Handcuffs* was awarded the Lu Xun Literature Prize.

His novels include *Wuweishizi Road, False Group, Mr. Sister, Shy Flames, Champion Sheep, The Walls, Martyr Granny, Rope of Desire, Itch, Embroidered Pillow, Qinghai Lake,* and *Beauty and Woman*; prose releases include *Monument, Secular Story, Later Death Monument, Blood-Red Flowers,* and *Secular Prose*; short story collections include *Daily Wisdom, Open the Window, Difficulty of Telling the Truth, Five Women from Weihe River, Plum Blossom Cup,* and *Monument*. His works *Bronze Powder, Shy Flames, Blood-Red Sun,* and *Sad for Brothers* were released as part of the Writers Library Series.

17

Wu Kejing

The Bloodstained Dress

There is blood in man's head. There is water in man's heart.
—a folk saying from Xifu

Naturally Mrs. Spots was wearing a qipao dress the day she came to my hometown.

The villagers had no idea that the dress Mrs. Spots was wearing was called qipao. They all stood alongside the street and watched a graceful Mrs. Spots pass through, too dazed by her appearance to offer her a word of greeting. Even the roosters, who would crow till your ears buzzed every day, kept silent. Even the dogs, who would bark till heaven shook, made no noise. A sudden quiet fell on the small village, chokingly quiet.

Mrs. Spots had been riding in a carriage. She could have stayed in the carriage until she reached the gate of Uncle Spots's grand residence; she could have stepped out, marched in, and sat down in the mistress's grand chair to receive welcome greetings from relatives, maids, servants, and manual laborers. Uncle Spots had many laborers and servants.

He hadn't always been this grand, though. A long time before, he'd organized a gang of bandits and become rich overnight. Then he bought a thousand acres of farmland, built a big house with three layers of deep courtyards and wings, and hired workers and servants, plus a gang of armed guards. Their shadows roamed around the village day and night.

People in Little Castle might hate Uncle Spots from the bottom of their hearts, but they all showered him with flattery as if they owed their very lives to him. Why? Because most of the young people in the thirteen bands of the village had joined Uncle Spots's bandits, all carrying with them the dream that one day they would end up just as rich. Others were tenants on his farmland.

Mrs. Spots, for her part, had long heard of the wealth and power of her husband's family, but, as a graduate from Ginling College, she had been exposed to ideas of democracy and equality and such, and would not—no, never!—want to make a show in front of the village folks. So, still a full li from town, she asked the carriage to stop, lifted the curtain herself, and landed on the ground, light as a swallow.

It was April in Xifu when she arrived. The rapeseed flowers were in full blossom everywhere, and the green wheat farmlands stretched to the horizon. Mrs. Spots drank in the scene. Around her, the bees were buzzing, and colorful butterflies were fluttering here and there. What a charming pastoral scene! Mrs. Spots fell in love with the countryside on this, her first journey to her husband's hometown. She knew that walking into town was not what Mr. Spots would do, but she had her own principles: she must be humble and respectful before the common people.

Uncle Spots was stubborn and ambitious, rarely following other people's advice. But, strangely, he acted upon whatever Mrs. Spots said. Uncle Spots admired nobody but Mrs. Spots. So, on that day, he also got down from his horse and walked into the village with Mrs. Spots, arm in arm, with an air of deep affection.

The dress Mrs. Spots was wearing that day was a qipao made of black-silk brocade. It wrapped her tightly and made her body perfectly curved. Starting from her fair neck, a red arc of qipao glided over her chest like a shooting star. Running along the red arc were evenly spaced, chrysanthemum-shaped, traditional Chinese fabric buttons, glittering like stars in the sky. The small red flowers scattered and bloomed on the black background of qipao. As Mrs. Spots walked along with elegance and nobility, the village folk were struck by their own inferiority and unworthy lives and felt pain in their hearts.

Mrs. Spots smiled kindly at the folks huddling on the side of the street. She greeted them with nods, but none of these people responded to her. Instead, they greeted Uncle Spots shyly. What a pity Mrs. Spots failed to understand that the villagers actually admired her most that day; it was confirmed in the folk stories passed down for years to come.

Later, all the people did remember that Mrs. Spots's qipao was made of black-silk brocade. However, about other details, they differed. The dress's opening front, the edge piping, the fabric buttons, and the flowers on the black silk became the subjects of much controversy. Each villager had his own views. As for the shape of the buttons, for example, some said they were dragonfly-shaped, while others claimed they were frog-shaped, bee-shaped, butterfly-shaped, and swallow-shaped. Some said they were lute-shaped, harp-shaped, bud-shaped. Some said they were chrysanthemum-shaped, orchid-shaped, peach-blossom-shaped, and kapok-shaped. However, the villagers were of one voice about one thing, without any dispute—namely, their judgment about Mrs. Spots.

What everyone said was: "Mrs. Spots was somewhat unusual. She was different from us. Not just a little bit different, but too different!" In their various reports I heard undertones of admiration, but also of jealousy and even hatred.

Uncle Spots had no spots on his face. His face was blackish, chiseled, and typical of a Xifu man in its firmness and courage. The surname of Uncle Spots was not really "Spots." Actually, no one was named "Spots" in the thirteen bands of his village. Where did this name come from? Whether from respect or mockery, he was called Uncle Spots. But the name came entirely from his wife.

———

A short time before Mrs. Spots's arrival in the village, an important event happened. The Japanese army invaded Shanghai. The whistles of flying cannonballs pierced the air, and the roar of planes shook the earth. Both were ripping the nerves of Nanjing City—the capital of the Kuomintang—and of Generalissimo Chiang Kai-shek. The leader was at a loss about what to do next. He gathered his high-ranking military counselors and generals and made a test to know their recommended countermeasures. The question was: "The Japanese army has come; what should we do next?" All weighed their words and wrote ideas carefully. Uncle Spots, as a division commander, responded to the question without hesitation. He took up his writing brush and wrote on the paper with large strokes: FIGHT.

The instant he left the meeting hall, Uncle Spots felt his left eye twitching for no reason. As the saying went, a twitching left eye foretold good luck, while the right eye, bad luck. But what good luck would befall him? His eye had been twitching for a few days without explanation. Then, the officers from the government announced that he was promoted to major general.

A lady came with the officers. She was wearing a qipao. She had long legs and a slender waist. It was a pleasant surprise to hear her say that she had been appointed by the government to be his confidential secretary. This is how Mrs. Spots entered the story.

Uncle Spots was grateful to the government from the bottom of his heart.

Uncle Spots said, "Good."

Uncle Spots was a man of humble birth and few words. Whenever possible, he responded with a single word: "Fight." "Good." On that day he said "Good" chiefly because the secretary's qipao caught his eyes. That qipao, made of bright-pink charmeuse silk, was as smooth as water. It opened in the front on the right side with lute-shaped Chinese fabric buttons. Its design was fashionable, tastefully simple. An embroidered plum blossom was sewn on the most protruding part of her chest and gave a three-dimensional impression. This qipao, flavored with elegance and modesty, brightness and nobility, framed the perfect figure of the secretary. Particularly on the lower part of the dress, where two long slit openings would float up slightly when she walked before him; this became a tantalizing scene for Uncle Spots.

In the days to follow, when Uncle Spots saw the secretary walking past him in her high-heeled shoes and qipao with those side-slash openings, he would lose his head and say automatically, "Good."

It was really good. A few days passed. One night the secretary made the bed for Uncle Spots, and then she unbuttoned her bright-pink charmeuse silk qipao and joined him in bed, amorously.

In the morning they had to get up. The secretary washed the makeup from her face—but she missed a few spots. Uncle Spots collected her in his arms and licked every spot tenderly. Her body was quivering with passion in Uncle Spots's caress. She admired him and said, "The generalissimo said that your word 'Fight' was written carelessly, but that your answer was good. It was right. To the Japanese army, we have only one thing to say: 'Fight.'"

Details from the daily life of Uncle Spots and his secretary spread through Xifu. My folks envied the pair. And yet, Uncle Spots looked humble, illiterate, and reckless; he had organized the bandits and killed many people. He had a terrible reputation in my hometown.

———

He brought his secretary back to his own village. In his hometown, she was not the secretary, but the wife of Uncle Spots.

Mrs. Spots never left my hometown after she came to Xifu. But after traveling there with her, Uncle Spots did not warm the adobe kang at all. He immediately got on his horse and left for the war against Japan. Saying good-bye to Uncle Spots at the entrance of the village, Mrs. Spots lifted her hands and touched his face gently, saying, "There is blood in man's head." Mrs. Spots then took her hand away from his face and pressed it upon her chest, saying, "There is water in man's heart."

The folks heard about her words and failed to understand them but felt they were pleasant to the ears. A few repeated the words: there is blood in man's head; there is water in man's heart.

Mrs. Spots, in the eyes of the village folk, did not understand country life. At the east of the village was her three-hundred-mu private wheatland. The wheat was lush, as thick as the sea. When the wind arose, it would stir up tides of grain. If the wheat had grown for a longer time, it would have been a good harvest. However, Mrs. Spots asked some townspeople to level the wheat. They carried bricks, tiles, lime, and sand. They brought a red flag and set off firecrackers before starting to build. The time frame laid out for them was quite short and urgent. Even the brick kilns far away were baking bricks and tiles day and night, but could not meet the requirements of Mrs. Spots's plan.

After that, Mrs. Spots ordered her guards to lead all the manual laborers on the building site to demolish the temples and theaters of the thirteen bands throughout the village, to satisfy the urgent needs of the new construction. The demolition of the temples and theaters outraged some people. They came together and fought, with their tools and hoes as their weapons. They were courageous but helpless without guns.

Bang! Bang! Mrs. Spots's people were shooting guns into the sky. So the protesters withdrew, knowing they could not win.

Mrs. Spots would go to the building site to inspect, always wearing her qipao. She had so many qipaos—she wore a different one each day. When she was wandering and inspecting the building site in her qipao, the workmen had more drive to work. With sweating faces and working hands, they seized each opportunity to stare at Mrs. Spots.

She was knowledgeable about construction. She'd give advice here and make signs there. The whole plan was completed quickly. Eventually, everyone knew that Mrs. Spots was setting up a new school. The sign on the school gate adopted words by Yu Youren, the doyen of the Republic of China: "Free School of the New China."

Mrs. Spots moved to the school to live. She worked, rested, and ate in a charming house built on a high platform, in the traditional style of a watery town in South China. The folks could see Mrs. Spots in qipao, pacing gracefully on the platform in the glow of sunrise and sunset.

On the platform she set a round, hollowed-out, carved red-mahogany urn. A woman attended to her and gave Mrs. Spots a celadon teacup with a lid. Then she passed Mrs. Spots a vertical flute with two red tassels. Mrs. Spots brought it to her lower lip and played tunes the people of Xifu had never heard. Naturally, the music was quite pleasant. In contrast with *Qinqiang*, a popular opera in Xifu, her melodies sounded more gentle and lovely. Her tunes were favored by the local people. The music made the sky bluer and set birds of all kinds—magpies, swallows, turtledoves—to fluttering in the clouds.

The first group of students came to the school from our provincial capital, Xi'an. Some teachers in Chinese-style robes arrived as well. On the school's opening day, Uncle Spots rushed back. He was the honorary headmaster; Mrs. Spots was the acting headmaster. All the students lined up on the playground for the opening ceremony. Uncle Spots asked Mrs. Spots to make a speech. Rather than yielding to him, she stepped forward from Uncle Spots's side and started to speak with elegance and ease. She had spoken only a few words when suddenly Uncle Spots shouted loudly at the students, "Open your legs!"

Mrs. Spots understood Uncle Spots's vernacular. She looked back at Uncle Spots and smiled; then she turned to the assembled group, bowed in apology, and said, "At ease, please."

"Open your legs" became a joke about Uncle Spots. Everyone wondered why Uncle Spots did not know the words "at ease" or "halt," but insisted on the indelicate command "open your legs." Increasingly, the village folks admired Mrs. Spots.

Everyone knew that the students in the school came from the occupied regions in the northeast and north of China. The homes of many students were burned down. They didn't know whether their family members were still alive.

Mrs. Spots also encouraged the local children to study in the school. If their families were rich, they could donate to the school; if not, the children could study for free.

At this opening ceremony, Mrs. Spots was wearing a particularly beautiful qipao, a dark-red velvet one. Its buttons, like pinpricks of light, were as dazzling as gold. This qipao had long sleeves and a stand-up collar. Its cuffs and neckline were embedded with rabbit fur. On the dark-red background was embroidered a fire dragon, as golden as the buttons. The dragon's head was on her chest, its whiskers on her shoulders, its paws resting on her belly and waist, its shining body and tail clinging to her delicate waistline and plump buttocks. The dragon came to life moving around her. It was the soul and eternal beauty of the Chinese dragon. On that bright and sunny morning, she looked beautiful and charming.

Mrs. Spots had especially planned to wear this particular qipao for the school ceremony. She had asked Uncle Spots to order it for her in Xi'an. What she aimed to tell the students in the school was that the Chinese dragon would never die— the spirit of the Chinese dragon would last forever!

The last event of the opening ceremony was a basketball match. No one in the village had ever seen a basketball game. Neither had Uncle Spots. Seeing ten players running after a ball, Uncle Spots lost his temper at Mrs. Spots and said, "If we could afford a free school, we should afford the balls. Buy one ball for each student and let him play by himself." Before he'd finished, Mrs. Spots started laughing and explained that basketball is played that way, with one ball.

Soon after, Uncle Spots had to leave. Again, Mrs. Spots saw him off at the entrance of the village and touched his face. Again she said, "There is water in man's heart." Uncle Spots turned and left. He went a short distance and turned around again, shouting at Mrs. Spots, "There is blood in man's head."

———

Mrs. Spots managed the school dutifully. The first group of students graduated, and then a new group was admitted. Most of them came from the occupied regions, but naturally, the native children were welcome too. Mrs. Spots visited from household to household and persuaded some parents to support her in holding literacy classes for girls. Girls were being educated for the first time in the long history of Xifu.

Mrs. Spots paid for all the costs—all the students' living expenses and school supplies and the teachers' salaries. In the beginning, she could make ends meet with money Uncle Spots mailed from afar, together with income from his local property. The folks could still see Mrs. Spots pacing in her qipao on her platform in the glow of the sunrise and sunset, but now they rarely saw her smile, sip tea, or play her flute.

The year when the Japanese surrendered, Mrs. Spots was extremely happy for the whole year. That year, her qipao and her smiling face were the brightest spots in the village. In the villagers' memory, Mrs. Spots wore a scarlet-silk qipao with dark peony flowers. That qipao made her face particularly young and fresh. Some folks had a clear memory that Mrs. Spots wore this qipao for just one day—the day that the Japanese surrendered.

After that day, Mrs. Spots put on different qipaos. One day she wore a yellowish silk qipao, the next day another qipao stamped with the Chinese character "happiness," and on another she wore a green one with squares. The qipaos of different colors and styles made Mrs. Spots conspicuous in the village of Xifu—but perhaps there was a reason. Perhaps Uncle Spots had given her these qipaos and it made her happy to wear his gifts. Maybe she changed them frequently for respite from the loneliness, sadness, grievance, and melancholy.

She longed for the homecoming of Uncle Spots, or even for a message. But Uncle Spots was like a drop of water evaporating in the intense heat of sunshine. He neither returned nor sent messages.

Everyone had guesses about his whereabouts. Some thought that he had lost his life; others said that he was being punished by Generalissimo Chiang Kai-shek because he supported the Communist Party. Some people guessed that Uncle Spots had beat the Communist Party on behalf of the generalissimo. There were many guesses, but no one was certain of his whereabouts. The day of the opening ceremony of the school was the last day he was seen in his village.

The expense of the school was now a serious problem, especially after Uncle Spots disappeared. Mrs. Spots's savings were gone. As a result, she had to let some of her servants and guards go. She was no longer receiving rent for the land; all the income was handed directly to the school.

Then the Chinese Civil War broke out.

The school had a hard time surviving. After the Liberation Army fought a war in Fufeng and Meixian Counties, the school had to be closed.

Mrs. Spots did not leave the school. On the contrary, she was still living in her house on the high platform, built in the style of the watery towns of South China. Every day, she put on different qipaos and paced with grace in the glow of the sunrise and sunset. The time came when the work team for land reform was based in the village. Mrs. Spots was taken out of her house, paraded through the streets first, and then tyrannized.

The site chosen to persecute her was the playground where Mrs. Spots had made her speech at the opening ceremony. Her trial began. Folks from the thirteen bands of the village came, and people from neighboring villages flooded there too. There was a sea of faces on the big playground. People even climbed into the tall trees or stood atop walls to watch. Mrs. Spots was still exceptional and attractive. In Xifu, all the women, old and young, wore black or indigo-blue clothing that they'd woven and dyed themselves. Mrs. Spots was different; she had colorful qipaos and rich knowledge.

Two armed gunmen escorted Mrs. Spots onto a platform. They pressed her head down over and over again, but over and over again Mrs. Spots raised her head.

While she was being held captive on the playground, a man was searching her dwelling. Opening her mahogany wardrobes, he stood in amazement: three wardrobes were stuffed full with one qipao after another, every single one delicate and beautiful. He also found a box of jewelry. There were pearls, blue jades—all to match the qipaos. The matching was so perfect that nobody had noticed it before. It spoke of the type of education Mrs. Spots had had. Women without her education might wear silver and golden ornaments, but they could never have known how to wear pearls and blue jades like Mrs. Spots.

Mrs. Spots was still wearing a beautiful qipao when she was tortured mercilessly on the platform. This one was a lily-white qipao, dotted with baby's breath in red on the white background. Mrs. Spots had chosen it intending to justify herself, that she advocated and loved the people's government. When she wore this qipao, a feeling welled up in her heart that the red stars seemed to be infused into her body and blazed forth. Her heart, trembling with excitement, evoked indefinable pangs and flame—the flame of new hope for the future! Her life, Mrs. Spots thought, should be like baby's breath, evoking that new and brilliant light.

However, for people in Xifu, it was unbearable that Mrs. Spots would have new ideas. She was labeled as the mistress of a reactionary warlord. She was called the wife of the despotic landlord. The newly empowered villagers shouted slogans, rushed toward Mrs. Spots, and started to hit and kick her to the ground. The first people who rushed to punch and kick Mrs. Spots were the women of Xifu. They kicked her with their feet, boxed her with their hands, and spat on her. Their spittle, a hail of sticky bullets, shot at Mrs. Spots's head and face and soiled her qipao. Someone twisted off a brick from the wall of the school and smashed her head. Her head was broken, and the bright-red blood flowed out through her hair like a spouting spring.

Mrs. Spots was dead. Her white-silk qipao was stained with her bright-red blood, perfectly coordinating with the baby's-breath embroidery. The qipao was now a bloodstained dress.

On the day Mrs. Spots died, the special commissioner of the newly established people's government of the county rushed to the scene and made an embarrassing announcement: Mrs. Spots was an enlightened democrat.

Undoubtedly, Mrs. Spots was buried in the backyard of her school by the new people's government. Before the Cultural Revolution, I had the good fortune to be accepted by the renamed school and later saw Mrs. Spots's tomb covered with winter jasmine. I had a fantasy that the plentiful winter jasmine became a qipao for Mrs. Spots, a qipao that would not wither as time went by. However, after some time, the ghostly wind of the Cultural Revolution blew more violently. The young students with their red sleeve emblems brought their hoes and shovels and dug the winter jasmine off the tomb, planing it smooth. The gravestone, set up for Mrs. Spots by the new people's government, was overthrown in the Tomb-Planning Movement and broken into two pieces.

Now, if you have a chance to go to Xifu on Guanzhong Plain, all you can see that remains of Mrs. Spots is that high platform. However, people who knew her still speak about the words she left behind. There is blood in man's head. There is water in man's heart.

Translated by Zhang Yating and Hu Zongfeng

Wang Guansheng

Born in Sanyuan County, Shaanxi Province, Wang Guansheng graduated from the Southern Suburbs School of Sanyuan County in 1967. He joined the army in 1969 and worked as a soldier in Unit 505, a staff member of the cultural center of Sanyuan County, a managerial staff member of the Workers' Club of Sanyuan County, and director and associate professor of editorship of the Shaanxi Provincial Writers Association. He made his literary debut in 1982 and joined the Chinese Writers Association in 1993.

18

WANG GUANSHENG

At the Foot of Mount Yanzhi

1

The Elder Zhu was lying idly on the grass. His younger brother, the Younger Zhu, was making letters with stones. The two brothers were on the pasture enclosed with chain-link fence.

"Ain't you jist . . . killin' time?" the Elder Zhu asked without looking at his younger brother. The older brother's gaze passed through the fence to rest on the snow-covered peak of Mount Qilian and then to the gentle slopes of Mount Yanzhi.

The Younger Zhu had finished the two letters *UF* and the third letter had already taken the shape of a *C*. Once a few more stones were added, the huge UFO sign would adorn the vast grassland.

"Those ETs are sharp-eyed. Even if they're standing on the moon they can see a word this big." The Younger Zhu now rose to his feet, talking to himself. He was a good-looking boy of fourteen or fifteen.

"Kin't get a woman, why the fuck did you turn on me?" the Younger Zhu grumbled. He said, "When the ETs come in their UFO to pick me up, I'll go with them an' date a girl on Mars. Will you go with me?"

His elder brother made no reply.

"So you won't? Then you'll die from blue balls," the Younger Zhu said.

The Elder Zhu, still silent, turned over to pillow his head on the right arm so as to see their Shandan horses, which were jujube red and in superb condition—massive and well shaped. Grandpa used to say that tall western horses couldn't be compared with Shandan horses, just like a grandson can't be compared to his grandfather. Every time Grandpa saw Shandan horses, he would repeat this saying.

Tall and sturdily built as Grandpa was, he could in no way dwarf the massive Shandan horse when he rode it. The horse underneath was even sturdier than Grandpa.

One time, on hearing Grandpa's familiar saying, the two grandsons burst out laughing. They said Grandpa wasn't blowing his own horn, but rather he was "tooting his own horse."

Grandpa had laughed, too. He'd squinted his eyes and peered through the misty Shandan grassland, protesting weakly, "You bastards don't believe me, eh? If one rode a Shandan horse an' the other a western horse an' then ran them for t'ree days around the clock . . . and gave them no food or water . . . You'd see!"

The Elder Zhu chimed in: "The Shandan horse would be fine."

"And the western horse would've been beaten out!" the Younger Zhu hurriedly added.

Then the three of them laughed uproariously, tears running down their cheeks.

Now the two Shandan horses, contained by the chain-link fences, had their heads buried in their troughs. The Elder Zhu was gazing, as he had been for half the day, through the horses' legs, at Mount

Qilian. The snow line was perfectly straight; the mountain beneath it was purplish blue and above, snow white. The snow was pleasant to the eyes; it always reminded him of the appealingly white horse milk.

The Elder Zhu turned over again to see his younger brother walking around the letters he had made out of stones, which the older brother could never read. He then rose to his feet and stood in the center of the enclosed pasture. The Elder Zhu was as tall and strongly built as Grandpa and looked much larger than his younger brother, who was able to read English letters. With a sigh, he said to his younger brother, "Get on the horse an' go home!"

"What's the fuckin' rush? The horses are still grazin.'"

Without looking at his younger brother, the Elder Zhu seized the mane of the taller horse, sprang onto its back, and was off with a strike on its rear. The horse, its forelegs soaring up into the air, bounded over the yard-high fence like a floating cloud and landed silently on the soft grass.

The grassland had all turned brownish yellow. Bent over by the recent autumn rain, the grass was smooth and shining like horsehair.

The horse headed east toward Mount Yanzhi.

Grandpa had liked talking about Mount Yanzhi, telling them that the mountain was recorded in quite a number of ancient books. Grandpa said that without Mount Qilian, there wouldn't have been cattle. But he added that without Mount Yanzhi, women wouldn't be good-looking.

Wit'out Mount Qilian,
We wouldn't have cattle so strong-lookin'.
Wit'out Mount Yanzhi,
Our women wouldn't be so good-lookin'.

"Ptew." The Elder Zhu had spit the food he was chewing onto the face of his younger brother, who was sitting across the table. Then, pointing in Grandpa's face, he'd yelled, "Grandpa, you want a woman, don't you?"

The Younger Zhu, face dotted with food bits, chimed in with a wondering tone. "Grandpa's c'rrect. I've jus' learned that at school!"

The Elder Zhu's eyes pointed at his brother, who had rice residue on his face. Despite his elder brother's warning, the Younger Zhu tilted his head and went on earnestly.

"My teacher taught me that an' I recited it ten times on my ride home. Now I kin recite it for you."

The Elder Zhu glared a second time at his younger brother.

The Younger Zhu, head tilted, chanted the nonstandard Mandarin he'd learned at school.

Losin' our Mount Qilian,
Our animals won't breed.
Losin' our Mount Yanzhi,
Our ladies won't be fair.

The Elder Zhu glared at the Younger Zhu for a third time.

The Younger Zhu, not bothering to wipe the rice particles off his face, continued, "'Ladies' means women. Women make wives for men . . ."

Seeing that his younger brother was winning, the Elder Zhu bounded over the table and threw himself on his brother to stop his showing off. The two brawled on the floor.

Grandpa, sitting aside, commented with a satisfied smile, "Gosh, my younger cub's knowledgeable."

Grandpa watched the two brothers wrestle. When the fighting brothers rolled like a ball near him, he gave a kick on each ass to separate them. The two then returned to the table to eat.

Grandpa rose and yelled to the two brothers. "I had a wife!"

"Why ain't we seen her?" the brothers asked earnestly.

"Died of famine years ago." Grandpa yelled, "Eat quick!"

The two brothers hurriedly buried their heads in their bowls. Grandpa lowered his voice. "Wit'out a wife, how could I git you' dad?"

"Why ain't we seen him?" The brothers raised their heads.

Grandpa burst into a roar. "I've told you t'ousand times! That bastard killed you' mom an' was executed by the government."

The two nodded. "No wonder we've ne'er seen him."

———

The Elder Zhu, now astride his horse, curled the corners of his mouth and winked. Only he himself knew what it meant. Effortlessly, the Elder Zhu caught sight of their mud-roofed house, built right at the foot of the mild slope of Mount Yanzhi. Ten feet away from the mud house lay Grandpa's tomb. That morning when the two brothers had awakened, they'd found Grandpa, sleeping between them, ice cold. Grabbing hold of Grandpa's shoulders from both sides, they'd tried to help him up. To their great astonishment, Grandpa had shot up stiff as a ramrod.

Grandpa had never shed tears unless he was happy. Therefore the two brothers likewise shed no tears. With sad faces, they'd dug a grave and buried Grandpa there. Then they had a second thought, realizing they had neglected one thing: Grandpa loved Mount Yanzhi. They should've made the tomb in the shape of Mount Yanzhi. Still with somber expressions, the brothers spent half a day making the tomb into a tent-shaped mound. As night fell, they went to bed, sad-eyed.

By the time the Elder Zhu's horse began to tread on the graveled slope, the older brother heard the Younger Zhu's horse clopping behind. The Elder Zhu had known his younger brother would follow him—for now that Grandpa was dead, the elder grandson became the lead. The Younger Zhu was only a part of him.

2

The educated Younger Zhu apparently did not agree with his elder brother's plan of riding through the Shandan grassland. He insisted that they should've attempted it while Grandpa was alive. Now with Grandpa gone, who would they turn to mock if their Shandan horses died of exhaustion?

Neglecting his educated brother's opposition, the Elder Zhu began to make preparations for the trip. He filled Grandpa's deerskin sack with drinking water.

"Grandpa said give the horses no water," the Younger Zhu reminded his elder brother.

"Won't you need some fuckin' water?" his elder brother replied.

"Why, you're right!"

Elder Zhu then stuffed two feed bags with soybeans and hung one on each horse's neck.

"Grandpa said give the horses no food!" the Younger Zhu reminded again.

"What if Grandpa told you to eat shit?"

"Grandpa ne'er told me to eat shit."

The Elder Zhu didn't want to argue just for the sake of arguing. He walked out of the house and stood by the doorway to piss. The Younger Zhu followed his elder brother out and pissed by his side. Then they mounted their horses and started off for their trip. The Younger Zhu struck his horse hard, and the horse dashed off over the grassland, its mane flying upright in the air like floating seaweed.

The Elder Zhu caught up and grabbed hold of his younger brother's bridle rein. "No rush!"

"Grandpa said the horses could run like the wind," the Younger Zhu said, gazing at his brother.

The Elder Zhu looked away and sighed. "I said no rush."

"OK, I'll slow down." The Younger Zhu let loose his bridle rein. He knew that with Grandpa gone, his elder brother was the decision-making master and he was only a part of the Elder Zhu.

The Younger Zhu's head bobbed from side to side on his shoulders as the horse walked. He was able to fall asleep on horseback at any moment. He was also able to hide himself on one side of a racing horse, making viewers on the other side believe that a riderless horse was passing by. The Elder Zhu could not pull off that trick. He was too massive, and the horse just couldn't hide him.

The horses walked a long distance with the Elder Zhu awake and the Younger Zhu asleep. The brownish-yellow grassland stretched before them equally. In a short distance a yak skull appeared, white all over with black horns protruding, its two eyeholes terribly dark and huge. The Elder Zhu's horse rounded the skull from its left and the Younger Zhu's from the right. A glittering-eyed rat, startled by the clip-clop of hooves, peered out from the nostril of the skull and darted away.

The horses walked another long distance. The Elder Zhu was awake, and the Younger Zhu was still sleeping.

Mount Qilian was approaching nearer and nearer, its snowcap so white as to make a man feel moody. A canal ran into sight, carrying crystal-clear water melted from the white (but not glaring) snow of Mount Qilian. The water was almost invisible to the eye.

The two horses, not needing any guidance, walked to the canal to drink. The Elder Zhu jumped off his horse and grabbed hold of his younger brother's legs to dismount him. Landing flat on the soft grass, the Younger Zhu continued sleeping soundly.

The Elder Zhu fixed a sack of soybeans to each horse's head, leaving them to enjoy their feasts. He produced dried buns and a water sack for himself and his brother. Then he kicked his sleeping brother on the butt.

"Git up to eat!"

The Younger Zhu rose up to sit on the grass, yawning. After looking around for a minute, he sobered up and sniggered. "Yeah, I want solid food."

While the horses chewed soybeans and the two brothers chewed their dried buns, a loud cracking began to resound on the grassland.

The Younger Zhu acted first this time. Jumping onto his horse, he gazed down at his elder brother, who was about to mount his own horse.

"You've got the same trouble as Grandpa had, ain't you?" he yelled at his elder brother.

The Elder Zhu, as if struck by a brick, turned and leaned against his horse, his neck stretched, mouth wide open. He stared dumbly at his younger brother, who now seemed a giant to him up on horseback.

The Younger Zhu, tilting his head, walked his horse around his elder brother, chanting in a stately tone as if reciting an epic. "Ride to the foot of Mount Qilian . . ." The Younger Zhu cleared his throat with a dry cough, which made his elder brother shiver. The Younger Zhu continued walking his horse around in a circle while he drawled out the words. The Elder Zhu followed the Younger Zhu in a circle on the grass, eyes fixed on his younger brother.

"To call on an old man so queer . . ." The Younger Zhu walked his horse in a second circle. His elder brother walked a second circle too.

"Who spares his lovely daughter . . ." The Younger Zhu walked his horse in a third circle. His elder brother followed him in a third circle.

"In exchange for gold and silver." The Younger Zhu was still walking his horse around in a circle; his elder brother had stopped walking. Leaning against his horse, the Elder Zhu dropped his head.

The Younger Zhu walked his horse next to his discouraged elder brother and gave him a light kick on his broad shoulder.

"Gee! Gold and silver you've not got!" he chanted with a giggle.

Now an idea hit the Younger Zhu, who was never short of ideas. He shouted to his elder brother, who looked even stronger than the horse, "Git on the horse and follow me!"

The Younger Zhu, inspired by his idea, was no longer drowsy. He took the lead, riding ahead of his elder brother, who followed, head bowed. The limpid canal was running silently on their left.

The Elder Zhu groped for something in his coat, and at length he produced a handful of paper notes, worn out like straw.

"Here's the money. I'd taken 'em."

The Younger Zhu, hearing the words, turned swiftly and glared at his elder brother, his flaming eyes riveted on the Elder Zhu. "No wonder I couldn't find 'em to pay my tu'tion. You'd stolen 'em!"

With these angry words, the Younger Zhu turned his horse around and headed in the opposite direction. "Git a woman with the money. I'm goin' home!"

The Elder Zhu turned his own horse to stand in his younger brother's way and protested worriedly, the two horses taking the chance to nuzzle each other on the neck. "My dear brot'er, when I get a wife who can take care of the housework for us, you'll go back to school then."

"You bastard!" his younger brother replied with fury.

"I know."

"Do you mean what you said?"

"Yes, sure!" the Elder Zhu confirmed earnestly.

The Younger Zhu turned his horse around again and walked along the limpid canal.

The snowcapped Mount Qilian grew higher, and the Elder Zhu had to raise his head to see his favorite milk-white snow on the top, from which his eyes glided to the purplish hillside and finally rested on the house.

The Elder Zhu brought the horse to a stop and said, "You'll go t'ere and I'll wait for you here!"

"See, the horse's just fine, but you're worn out," the Younger Zhu jeered at his elder brother. "Ain't you a good-for-nothin' bum? You get discouraged on every important occasion!"

Not caring about his younger brother's jeering, the Elder Zhu insisted. "You'll go t'ere and I'll wait for you here!"

"All right!" With a second thought, the Younger Zhu added, "Then wait for me there in the grassy ditch!"

"Good!" replied his elder brother.

3

The old man living in that house was Grandpa's old friend; they used to visit him every now and then. The old man had eight daughters, seven of whom had got married. The youngest daughter was named Plum Maid. Three days before Grandpa died, he and his two grandsons had come to visit his old friend. The four men had sat at the table while Plum Maid served them dinner.

"Marry you' daughter to my elder cub—whaddya say?" Grandpa asked his old friend. Hearing that, the Elder Zhu quickly dropped his head while Plum Maid flushed red and ran out.

The Younger Zhu waited for Plum Maid to serve more food, but the girl did not show up. Leaving the three men sitting wordlessly at the table, the Younger Zhu crept into the kitchen to serve himself. Squatting against the chopping board, he swallowed a huge bowl of rice, wondering why his elder brother wanted Plum Maid, who just couldn't compare to the fair and pretty girls on Mars, with whom he himself was obsessed.

After a long, embarrassing silence, the old man eventually said, "I'll marry her to a rich man."

"How much do you want?" Grandpa asked.

"It's not money. I want her to marry a man holding an office, with guaranteed salary."

The Younger Zhu, who had fed himself more than full, now returned to the table and chimed in with a burp. "We've got a room half-filled with gold and half with silver. Whaddya say?"

The old man stuck out his three-foot-long tobacco pipe to hit the Younger Zhu. The boy dodged nimbly and rushed out of the room, dragging Grandpa out with him. Lifting Grandpa onto the horse, the Younger Zhu struck the horse hard. He raced after the galloping horse for several yards and sprang onto the horse's back, seating himself behind Grandpa. He then turned and yelled at the old friend, who was standing in the doorway, waving his pipe with rage.

"Pooh-pooh!" the old man shouted. "A money-grubber you are, ain't you?"

Later that day, the Elder Zhu, with the old man's spit on his face, returned home to find his grandpa, who was still starving from the unfinished meal at his old friend's house, lying on the mud-brick bed, breathing heavily with indignation. His younger brother, who was one size smaller than he, stood on the earthen floor cursing with resentment. "Damn it! I swear I'll git the bitch for you!"

Now the Younger Zhu's horse, following the limpid canal, ran lightly and rhythmically toward Mount Qilian. He could take on any challenge as long as he was on horseback.

The old man's house came into sight, gray bricks all over with a tiled roof. In the backyard sat a row of kilns, two meters tall, from behind which the limpid canal flowed by.

Right there on top of a kiln was Plum Maid, squatting to add coal to the fire. The Younger Zhu, seeing her fat butt sticking out high as she bent down to do her job, couldn't help sniggering. With a second gaze, he saw at the gateway the girl's father, who was chopping firewood with a broad ax.

With a smile on his face, the Younger Zhu kicked his left foot off the stirrup and turned his body over lightly to hang himself behind the right side of the horse, his right foot holding the stirrup fast. The horse, keeping her normal pace, passed by the old man.

"Whoops, who's lost a horse?" the old man murmured to himself. Hearing this, the Younger Zhu quietly let go one of his hands, with which he was gripping the horse's mane, and covered his mouth so he wouldn't laugh out loud. The horse walked unhurriedly to the kiln, facing the old man with her bare left side. The Younger Zhu was calculating: he was on horseback, and Plum Maid was squatting on the kiln that was two meters above the ground. A slight drag would get the girl onto his horse's back. It would be a piece of cake to him, for he had snatched fat lambs from level ground on his galloping horse. Plum Maid was not as fat—and, more favorably, she was up on the top of the kiln.

Plum Maid was totally oblivious to the approaching horse. The moment the horse walked close to the kiln, the Younger Zhu popped up suddenly to grip the girl's coat from behind. Screaming with fear, Plum Maid fell down right onto the horse, in front of the Younger Zhu. The boy quickly gave a heavy strike on the horse's rump and they set off at a gallop, heading westward like the wind.

When the old man realized what had happened, he began to chase after the racing horse, waving his ax like a storming devil.

High above in the sky, the wheel-big sun was beginning to set, blood red.

Plum Maid had fainted. Leaving her hanging across the horse's back like a bag of grain, the Younger Zhu ran his horse as fast as he could. After running a semicircle of about five miles, he rode near to the canal again.

With a groan, Plum Maid came to and began to struggle hard. The Younger Zhu raised his fist and struck a heavy blow on her butt.

"Better keep quiet!"

Very much frightened, Plum Maid stopped struggling and lay on her stomach on the horseback, weeping and peering at her kidnapper from the corner of her eye.

"Shoot! You know who I am, don't you?" The Younger Zhu shouted threateningly, "I kill pigs, goats, cows, horses, jus' anything!"

Plum Maid was frightened and moved her eyes away, still weeping.

The Younger Zhu then realized he needed to explain the whole thing to the girl. So he tried to speak to her with the refined vocabulary he had learnt at school.

"The reason why I took this action is to help my brother to get a wife."

Stuffing Plum Maid's feet into the stirrups, the Younger Zhu helped the girl up in the saddle where he was sitting. The Younger Zhu now found little room for himself in the saddle.

"See, you' butt's too fat, isn't it?" he complained, moving backward onto the rear end of the horse. "If you agree to marry my elder brother, he promised to work for your father in your family kilns."

"I'm scared!" Plum Maid replied.

"Why scared? I kill pigs, not you!"

"I'm scared. I've never ridden a horse."

"Ha! A useless nut you are, just like my elder brother!" The Younger Zhu immediately regretted that dirty remark, for he realized that "nut" was for men only. He then softened his tone and comforted the girl. "Don't worry, I'll hold you." The Younger Zhu held the girl's waist from behind.

"Too tight!" said the girl.

The Younger Zhu loosened his arms.

"Too loose!" said the girl.

"What a pain in the neck!" the Younger Zhu said impatiently. "I won't hold you, then."

The horse had walked close to the limpid water. The Elder Zhu was nowhere to be seen, nor was his horse.

The Younger Zhu sang cheerfully from his horse. "Elder Zhu, when you have big nuts in your pants, a good-for-nothing git you are! Elder Zhu, when you have small nuts in your pants, a chicken you are!"

Plum Maid wept louder. "I'm scared. I wanna go home!"

Ignoring Plum Maid, the Younger Zhu stopped his horse, searching around for his elder brother—who finally emerged from a grassy ditch not far away, trembling, followed by his horse.

"C'mon! Brot'er! Here's whom you want!" the Younger Zhu yelled.

"You . . . you . . .!" Daring not to look at the girl, the Elder Zhu turned to gaze at his younger brother.

Holding Plum Maid's hand, the Younger Zhu helped her dismount, and then he moved back into the saddle. He had to stay on horseback—otherwise he would achieve nothing.

The Younger Zhu walked his horse in a circle around his elder brother and the girl, instructing them from above.

"You"—he pointed to Plum Maid—"and you"—pointing to his elder brother—"enjoy you' date here. I'll be waitin' for you back home!"

With these words, the Younger Zhu turned his horse about. The horse, following the limpid water, ran into the immense grassland, soon losing itself in the blood-red sunglow.

The jujube-red Shandan horse that the Younger Zhu was riding proved to be superb. She ran like wind, leaving the limpid water behind, leaving the blood-red sunset behind. She galloped on the moonlit grassland and reached the mud house at the foot of Mount Yanzhi, finally stopping in front of Grandpa's tentlike tomb, where she usually slept the night. Her master, the Younger Zhu, had fallen asleep, his limbs dropping to the horse's sides. The Younger Zhu had too much on his mind: the girls on Mars, going back to school, and getting a woman for his brother.

A puff of cool breeze flew down the gentle slope of Mount Yanzhi and set the Younger Zhu to consciousness. He heard the sound of hooves approaching. Against the indigo sky, he saw his elder brother riding on the horse alone.

"Where's my sister-in-law?" the younger brother asked.

"Soon after you left, the old man stormed there, waving his ax in front of me. I hurried on my horse and followed you back."

The Younger Zhu let out a sigh. All of a sudden he burst into loud laughter, which he could not explain himself. The two horses stood close to each other, head to tail, poking at one another's ass and moving in a circle as they smelled each other.

"I thought of something Grandpa used to say," the Younger Zhu said.

"What was that?"

"Born a bachelor with a cock . . ." the Younger Zhu began.

The Elder Zhu recognized what his younger brother was reciting and provided the next line: "You travel to the ends of the earth . . ."

"Catch sight of something and pick it up . . ."

"And raise it up to have a good look."

The two brothers yelled in unison: "A carrot? Oh, no! A cock it was, too!"

Both roared in loud laughter. Astride their horses, they laughed till they felt sick.

Gasping for breath, they both fell down by the side of Grandpa's tomb. They climbed on top of Grandpa's tomb, still laughing.

Translated by Yang Jinmei

Li Chunguang

Li Chunguang, born in 1950, is a member of the Chinese Writers Association, director of Xi'an Writers Association, provisional chairman of Xianyang Writers Association, and honorary chairman of the Institute of Chinese Western Literary Reportage Studies.

His works include *Black Forest, Red Forest, Agent of Love, Luck, Out of the Great Canyon*, and *Red Hot Love*. In his years of writing, he has held up the ideal of equality and created numerous characters with high morals and a great sense of ethics. Though his language tends to be traditional, he is also exploring new avenues and developing new trends. *Agent of Love* won the Xianyang Award for Excellent Literature. *I Hold You, Hong Kong* won the award for Notable Contribution to Chinese Modern Literature.

19

Li Chunguang

Stargazing

With its thousand-mile journey ahead, the majestic river roared past, undisturbed by the passions of the humans whose stories unfolded along its banks.

On the north bank, a winding road traced the river's course up to a bridge.

As night fell, a man in his twenties walked along the road, approaching the bridge. He pushed a pram up the incline, but instead of crossing the bridge, the young man then turned, pointed the pram back downhill, and descended on the other side of the road, where he resumed his unhurried walk.

The man appeared lost in thought, oblivious to the changing scenery. His normally bright, youthful eyes now seemed dull and withdrawn. Occasionally, his eyes would light up as the piping voice of the child in the pram caught his attention, but as the child returned to playing, the man would instantly withdraw again into his inner thoughts.

His inner thoughts, if they could be recorded, would probably sound like this:

Hey, kiddo, can you imagine me performing the duty of a father—giving up everything, every normal enjoyment of a young man my age, just so you can grow up like a normal kid? Yes, that's right. All this for you.

If maternal love is universally known to be the greatest love a person can feel for another human being, then what is paternal love in comparison? And what about a man's love for a baby not even his own?

His heartbeat quickened like a willow leaf stirred by the breath of an evening breeze. Unbidden, the unforgettable scene came back to him: a baby crying its heart out in a basket fastened inside a tire's inner tube, beside which lay the dead bodies of a young couple, stiff on the mudflat left by the flood.

Apparently, in their final moments, the baby's parents had given their beloved son a chance at life.

His silent soliloquy resumed:

Kiddo, luckily you know nothing of hypocrisy. No matter what praises they heaped onto your head, the minute your back was turned you would hear a different tune . . .

On that day, he had taken one look at the crowd that had gathered—pointing, commenting, but no one moving—before he'd gone ahead and picked up the child. The next thing he knew he had the baby in his arms and was an acclaimed hero.

He'd not had the slightest idea of what it took to be a parent. It had all come too suddenly. The only thing that went through his mind was that the child needed care. He had brought the boy back to his bachelors' dormitory, taking his roommates by surprise. Their wonder was soon followed by chants of "Hero!"—but that didn't last. Before the night was over, without exception they'd all decided to move out. A baby screaming through the night was beyond all their knowledge and tolerance.

Hey, kiddo, I knew that a baby needed food and water to grow. But this stupid man was caught by surprise that a baby cries for food delivery! And yes, yes, now I know you also cry for the warm arms of a doting parent.

Despite the talk in the neighborhood, the man decided to keep the kid, feeding, bathing, and looking after him. The man changed the normal pattern of his life accordingly. Now his morning started with baby feeding, followed by arranging a diaper tower—several diapers placed one on top of the other—on which he would place the baby with a fluffy cotton towel for cover; all this on the advice of an experienced mother he knew. And then he would rush off to work. During the noon break, he would come back and change the nappies and then feed the baby before eating his own lunch. The nighttime routine began with the baby's bath and change. Then the man would play with him before the baby dropped off to sleep. Only after that would the man have time to switch on his tape recorder and try to catch up on his missed lessons from his radio correspondence course.

Baby, I have no regrets. Watching you grow each day and hearing you call me Daddy in that sweet, piping voice of yours—it fills my eyes with tears of joy. I'm a ha-a-appy man.

He did not know when or how the course of his life had changed—until one day he was looking in his closet and discovered a pair of training shoes covered in mildew and dust. That brought back the memory of his dorm mates coming running and shouting—and then leaving in disappointment. His determination had wavered at such times. All around him, there was little understanding of all the young bachelor's new worries and troubles. As a last resort, he had picked up the baby and gone to the kindergarten, seeking sympathy from the head teacher.

Being a young man, he should have been living his own life, going on dates with girls. There was no lack of warmhearted would-be matchmakers. They all tried to set him up with lots of pretty girls. However, the kid inevitably put a damper on the women's interest. The occasional girl who managed to get as far as a face-to-face meeting would pull away after less than an hour with the man and his kid, as reality dawned on her: "Wow, how can a little child be so much trouble?"

Kiddo, must I believe your prospective mother is this far away from us? As far as the stars from the earth? Maybe I'll be still sitting here when my hair has turned gray.

In the meantime, he had become inseparable from the kid. If he heard the crying of any child, he'd immediately think it was Little Humble. When his work shift would end, no sooner would he manage to wash the engine oil off his hands and change out of his work clothes than he would hurry over to the kindergarten. When he saw Little Humble tottering and stumbling toward him, those chubby hands waving happily in greeting, the man's steps would quicken. His hands would—as if of their own will—stretch out, ready to catch the child's embrace. When he caught the boy in his grasp, he would plant a warm kiss on the boy's plump cheeks and rub his stubbly beard against the boy's velvet skin, making him giggle, while bringing the child's hands to his own face and feeling their tickly touch. Then he would pick up the boy and stride off at a fast trot.

Yes, he needed to hurry. There were lots of things to do: fry an egg for the kid, heat the milk, try to catch the late-night bus to town and buy a pair of leather boots for the fast-growing little feet.

The river road saw the young man push the kid in the pram, back and forth, year in and year out; to the young man, the years seemed to speed by like shooting stars. Those bittersweet years . . . But no regrets.

She approached from the other side of the road.

The girl had a slender figure that, combined with the high heels and full skirt, gave her a gracefulness, the look of a professional dancer out enjoying a rare moment of leisure. Her large, expressive eyes showed a depth of sensitivity.

A close look at her would reveal the girl searching for something or somebody. Her search was focused on the riverbank in the gathering nightfall. Whenever her steps halted and she moved stealthily into the shadows created by the streetlight, that was the moment the little pram had become visible amid the crowd of pedestrians. She would fix her gaze on the young man pushing the pram and watch him playing peekaboo with the kid.

If she found the man wearing the same clothes for days on end, the kid was never seen in the same shirt for two days running. Her eyes would fix on the man's hair, maybe lingering a bit too long on that thick, black hair, and then move to the oblong face. Oh, the face seemed a shade paler. But the eyes, though weary, were as fascinating as ever.

It was only by coincidence that she knew of the existence of the father and son. She'd been on an outing with a girlfriend; as they stood chatting by a lamppost, her friend had lowered her voice and said, "Look, here they come."

"Who?"

"Look—the young man with the pram."

It sounded like a fairy tale. She stared at the young man and the child, devouring them with her large, clear eyes. Then she and her friend moved stealthily forward, following the course of the pram.

She craned her neck and stole a glance at the kid. He looked healthy, a chubby little boy in a tight-fitting yellow shirt—a child who might have just jumped out of a picture, with both his plump hands in his mouth and a ring of translucent red beads dangling from his neck. She was surprised by a sudden warm feeling and an image of the kid rushing toward her open arms. Her cheeks turned red-hot at the strange feeling.

Her next encounter with the young man occurred a few days later, after the memory of the strange sensation had faded into the background. It was again a coincidence, this time occurring as she walked home from the art school. It was near nightfall, and the crowd was dispersing from the evening market. There he was again with the pram. This time the kid was fast asleep. Everything seemed the same, except she thought the man's feet seemed to fall more wearily on the ground.

As a film student, she decided this was an opportunity to try the technique of transference, imagining herself transferred into the young man's body, trying to feel what he felt: tired, exhausted, ready to cave in at any moment, loneliness gathering around him, no human support from anywhere, and no dear beloved—otherwise his girlfriend would be there with him!

She remembered what her friend had told her. However, she had her own view of him, quite different from what the other girls were saying. They all wondered if he'd now come to regret his decision to keep the kid. After all, it was no mystery that a kid costs energy as well as money.

The river flowed on majestically, following its own course, carrying with it scores of riverboats illuminating the glossy surface of the dark water.

Indifferent to the busy traffic, she followed the young man from behind. She forgot all about the rest of the world—and the fact that she had been heading home—until she heard a low sigh escaping from deep within the young man. That caused her heart to miss a beat. Here was a young man, a good man, compassionate and kindhearted, who gave the kid everything—warmth, happiness, and love—leaving nothing to himself except a deep sigh.

Compassion, an invisible asset, invaluable riches—the essence of life, the spring of creation.

She watched father and son turn down the road, and then she turned toward her home with a knitted brow.

The moment she got home she went straight to bed, burying herself in it. So lost was she in her thoughts that it was only after several calls from her mother that she became aware that she was being summoned. Reluctantly she told her mother the story of the man and the boy.

Her kindhearted mother was moved and said, "This is a very good young man. Very good indeed. Unfortunately, he is so different from us. Otherwise we might be able to offer help."

Amid her mother's prattle, the girl's thoughts went their own way. A story idea had occurred to her and was developing into a dramatic play. With a director's eye, the girl started imagining sets and scenes. If the real characters could be cast in the play, that would make it even better. But did the young man have any talent for acting?

Days went by while her mind dwelled on the same theme. But today something was going to happen.

———

In the morning, she buys a boy's baseball cap, one with green sunglasses. In the afternoon, hidden in a corner away from everybody else, she writes a short letter. She is positive the letter will set the wheels in motion.

Wearing a facade of disinterest, she shadows the father and son from about a dozen meters behind, until the pram comes to a standstill at the railings on the riverbank. The young man starts to point out to the boy various objects on the river. The boy, his face between two poles and his hands on the railing to hold himself upright, turns his head this way and that at his father's prompting. The young man then draws out of his satchel something that he proceeds to put into his ears. He steps forward and leans against the railing, his face taking on an absorbed expression.

He appears to be listening to music or a perhaps a lecture. This is her opportunity. Picking up courage, she approaches. On passing, she drops the baseball cap and the letter into the pram. She takes a few hurried steps farther and finds a spot at the railing, taking a position a short distance from the young man with a couple of young lovers in between them. She waits, biting her lip as her heart thumps away.

Time crawls. Girls and boys stroll in pairs, forming an uncomfortable background. The sunset sparkles on the river in endless variation, but it fails to divert her attention from the young man for even a single moment.

He turns slightly, sending a tremor to her already-heightened senses. But it turns out to be only a readjustment of the earpieces and then a resumption of his total absorption. A long sigh escapes from her. She shuts her eyes, trying to relax.

In this brief pause, a change has taken place. She becomes aware that he has drawn himself up from the railing, removing the earpieces, dropping them back into the satchel, turning to the pram, preparing to go . . .

She stares harder, eyes wide. His own stare is fixed inside the pram in surprise. Seconds pass before he picks up the baseball cap with the letter nestled inside it. Before the young man hesitantly opens the envelope, he casts a sweeping look around him. Now he is absorbed in the letter, reading under the lamppost.

When he finishes reading, he closes his eyes for a moment and then opens them wide, now scanning the riverbank expectantly under the night sky.

Will he find her? Quickly she swings out the fan in her hand and starts fanning herself. Though on the surface she looks calm, inside she's in ecstasy. There is no doubt he can act: she has seen now surprise, doubt, excitement, delight, all finely portrayed and clearly defined. He did not overdo it by walking around too excitedly. Instead, he picked up the boy and put his cheek against the boy's own cheek. If he had let his tears run down onto the boy's face, it would have produced an even better effect.

She's so excited that it almost hurts to watch. She turns away in a hurry.

The next evening, she arrives early at the same spot on the riverbank. Over the last twenty-four hours, she has thought of little else than the new development in the theme. She doesn't know what to expect from the young man, nor what to hope for from his next scene.

All she had wanted was to gather impressions from real life for film directing; she was convinced that scripted acting had had its day and run its course. The future of filmmaking was in real-life acting, acting in situ, for effect. In her experiment she provided neither a script, a briefing of the scenes, nor her intent. She let him try to perform by instinct and act on the spur of the moment.

It's been absolutely wonderful, she tells herself. But if she has raised unrealistic hopes in him and he starts to expect more of her, what will she do?

She's pondering the question as she walks, when a sudden childish cry of "Daddy!" from the curbside snaps her from her reverie. There they are—the boy in a white baseball cap with a pair of sunglasses, not quite appropriate for an evening outing. She lets her eyes follow the pretty hat; admittedly, this is a kind of expression of love. She then lets her eyes go to the young man, who seems to have had a perm, which leaves a strand of wavy hair over his brow. His eyes are shining. The red lips, half-open, seem to carry a permanent smile on a face dominated by a straight nose. He wears light-brown trousers and leather loafers. He looks relaxed and is humming a nursery rhyme to the kid:

There is a star in the sky
Turning the direction of the human eye.
The lonely star across the Milky Way
Is in search of friends far away.

His baritone voice reaches into the depths of her heart. It is like the light rain in the spring that falls on the young shoots in a bamboo forest, creating a hypnotizing staccato. The pleasing rhythm puts the thought of film directing out of her mind.

Stars . . . the star searching for its own kind. What a beautiful metaphor. Yes, if he can choose to take care of the child because he is kind and compassionate, why can't some girl come up and offer to be the kid's mother?

She's struck dumb by the idea. She could bring him up to his role. But she cannot persuade herself that this is acting anymore. She has indeed brought him hope.

She shakes her head, still unconvinced. Then the giggles of a group of teenagers break through her thoughts, like thunder. It strikes her that she is the object of their ridicule, that they're laughing at her: ha, that girl is the mother of the boy!

She shakes her head again, listening harder to what the teens are saying. It turns out they're discussing a rare frame in the Japanese film *A Testimonial of Humanity*.

Why am I bothered by such rubbish? She takes several quick steps and closes the distance between her and the leisurely moving pram.

There is a star in the sky
Turning the direction of the human eye.

The sweet, childish voice carries on, repeating the same lines, drawing indulgent laughter from passersby. The father laughs, too, a natural eruption of joy from within his heart. If she were to walk alongside him, what would the others say? Would an innocent young child change people's perception of her? What is this feeling for the young man who took on the role of fatherhood? Is it only admiration for his courage and goodness?

Her mind goes back to her professional aspirations. Yes, let's be professional. She must try to put the story on the screen. Well, she could try real-life acting too. She is certain she'd be a success.

The pram has stopped by the stone pillar of a signal lamp. This is where the young man and the boy usually pause, perhaps because it's relatively quiet here. Maybe he needs the quiet for his own thoughts—or, more probably, for his lessons. But this time, leaning on the railing, he turns his back to the river and faces the road. He begins to check out each passerby, one by one, carefully. Her heart skips a beat: he must be expecting her!

Shall she approach him and confess to him that it was she, this stranger, who wrote the letter and bought the baseball cap? Or should she take his hand and tell him in earnest that she loves what he represents: love, compassion, and sensitivity? It is easy to love your own children, but not so easy to love a child not your own. You sure challenge the idea that parental love is instinctual and cannot be cultivated. Or will she tell him that she's going to be a film director without an "iron bowl"—that is, without a job contract at a film studio? She is going to study human emotions in situ, in all their real-life manifestations. She wants to portray characters differently from the trite products of the film studios. Everything she has done so far was prompted by curiosity. She must apologize for her experiment with him . . . No, no, no, that is not what she meant. She wants to spend her life with him and together they will search for the meaning of life . . .

Oh, there is no hurry. Better think it over again. Some friend once told her, "Love at first sight only shows immaturity."

"Daddy, I'm hungry." The kid is clawing with his two pawlike hands, trying to climb out of the pram by grabbing the hem of his father's coat. "What do you want to eat?"

"What do you want to eat?" the man asks.

"Ice cream!"

The young man waves a finger back and forth at his son, as if to say no. But the kid shouts, "Bad Daddy! Daddy bad. Not buying me ice cream!"

The young man takes the kid to the ice-cream stand. The kid holds tightly to his father's lapel on their return.

The young woman hears the tender voice again: "Daddy, where is Mommy? Why is Mommy not back? You told me she'd be home soon. I want Mommy . . ."

The young man stares at the kid, looking into the tiny face. This is certainly an unanswerable question. The silence lasts a long time. At last, the young man looks away. He raises his head and, with clear eyes, scans the distant sky. Soon he lowers his head again.

The young woman keeps a close watch on the developing scene, aware that if the young man's melancholy continues, this will end up a tragedy. There's no reason why he shouldn't have a love life of his own, why the kid should have no mother. To be a wife to the young man and a mother to the kid, for a play that has never been and never will be. Besides, she has already lit the fire of love in him. She has no right to let it die again. It's unethical to play with somebody's feelings like that. As for the future, her mother will help them. She is sure of that. Thus she continues with the development of the story . . .

The female lead character is writing a long letter to the male lead, telling him all about herself, beginning with the confession that she is a girl a few years younger than he and, at the moment, a paying student in the city art school studying to be a film director. She loves him because in him she's discovered the qualities for a new generation of human beings. The letter must also mention that in three days' time, at seven thirty in the evening, he should bring the pram and kid to the signal post. He must let the kid know that he is going to see his mommy. At the post, there will be a girl with a toy gun . . .

At the end of the letter, she includes a poem:
There are two stars in the sky
Traveling in the same orbit.
Cold as the sky is,
The stars are journeying to the light.

———

The next three days seem like three years. His mind is alternately gladdened by the apparent coming happiness and troubled by the prospect of possible disappointment. Three days before, he was convinced that the blue light had been snuffed out. Then out of nowhere another light came up right in front of him. He could not believe it. To trust what looks promising at first sight takes purity of heart—or complete lack of experience. Like other normal beings who have not been treated kindly by the world, he could not believe what his heart wanted him to believe. Instead, he was prepared to accept all that the capricious world might deliver.

In the fresh river breeze, under a star-studded sky, the young man sets out, pushing the pram toward the designated spot.

He follows his usual route, expectant and apprehensive at the same time. But sure, he is prepared: behind the child's seat, he has tucked a bunch of flowers bought for the occasion.

The pram creaks and clatters all the way while the kid waves his arms about, his eyes taking in the familiar scene joyfully. Mommy, for whom he has yearned for a long time, is finally back! He has dreamed of his mother, of crying and laughing in her arms, of kissing her lovingly. He can't make up his mind: with his mother at his side, should he become distant from his father?

Maternal love, sacred love.

Now, as the pram approaches the bridge, the boy can't contain his excitement. He starts shouting, "Daddy, fast, faster!" A little later he whispers to himself, "Mommy, I love you."

The kid's happiness touches his father, who has finally let himself go. They are traveling uphill now as they get closer to the bridge. The man is pushing harder than ever when a tall girl with a bag approaches and says to him, "Can I help with the pram?"

"Thanks."

"You're welcome."

The man's mind is all wrapped up with the girl he is going to meet, so he is totally unprepared for the girl by his side, pushing the pram together with him. He has never been so close to a girl before. But not knowing how to refuse the offered help, he has to carry on, though he's fearful of the impression it will make on the girl he is meeting. Well, at the top of the incline there'll be no more need for another pair of hands. Not anymore. Anyway, there are thousands of well-wishers every day.

Thankfully, once atop the incline, the girl lets go. However, instead of taking off, she moves to the side and starts chatting with the man.

"Nice view here."

"Nature's gift."

"Not entirely true. Human effort helped to create the view."

He doesn't know how to reply. Now the man takes the time to have a close look at the girl. Pretty, nicely dressed, certainly fashion conscious—but most unlikely to be his date. The stranger who professes to love him would have to be a plain, homely girl. Not that he cares about that. All that matters is that she has a good heart. At this, his heart and mind start to move toward the signal post.

"It sure is a joy to take the child out on such a lovely evening."

He raises his hand and checks the time on his wristwatch: half past seven already. Without saying good-bye, he strides off toward the signal post, pushing the pram to a run. The kid laughs out loud. Meeting, lovers' meeting. What delight! What joy! As the sight of the signal post comes into view, his heartbeat quickens.

Over the grass lawn, through the throngs of shoppers and pedestrians, he gets through to the meeting place. But there is no girl. Nobody, not the ghost of a person, male or female. He checks the time again. Already five minutes past the appointed time. A sudden dismay overwhelms him. It is all because of that other girl . . . otherwise . . .

He stands motionless. How is he going to explain it to the boy? At such a tender age, the delicate soul can easily be irreparably damaged. Something is drumming in his head, like a train passing over the bridge. No, it's impossible. The boats start to twirl in the river; even the brightly lit bridge and the buildings soaring above the riverbanks seem to be spinning out of control. He feels faint, begins to see stars. The next instant, the stars turn into a tall girl carrying a bag in one hand and a toy gun in the other. It is she. But isn't she the other girl?

"It's you, isn't it?"

His voice is shaking. He picks up the flowers from the pram.

"Yes, of course it's me. Can't you see?" she says with mischief in her eyes.

The boy, seeing the toy gun in her hands, shouts out in excitement, "Mommy, I want the gun! Daddy says the gun is for me!"

With trembling lips she pronounces the words she has been turning over for days. When she gives the gun to the boy, the boy grabs hold of her by the neck and cries out tearfully, "Mommy, you're back! Mommy, hold me."

This heartrending cry from this tiny child was not scripted in her plan. Yet it will leave an indelible impression on the young woman and influence her future occupation. She picks the kid up and starts running her lips all over his sweet little face. Hot tears stream down her cheeks.

"I've done it. The play is a success," she murmurs, wiping tears from her face.

He, too, is crying.

Translated by Liu Yuan

Huang Weiping

Born in 1954 in Haimen, Jiangsu, Huang Weiping graduated from the Party and Government Cadre Higher Education Division, Northwest University, in 1984. He has worked in the countryside and as a well puller in a coal mine; he was also on the editorial staff of the Tongchuan Mining Administration, compiling mining history. He has served as editor in chief, president, and senior reporter of *Tongchuan Daily*. He has been director of the Shaanxi Provincial Writers Association, chairman of the Tongchuan Writers Association, and expert with outstanding contributions in Shaanxi Province. He made his literary debut in 1978 and joined the Chinese Writers Association in 2001.

Huang Weiping's works include the novel *Soul of Dashun Flowers*; the collection of short stories *Magic Tunnel*; essay collections *Sunshine Tour* and *Oriental Ceramic Town*; and the cultural monograph *A Woman Named Meng Jiang*. His work has won the Black Gold Literature Prize given by the Chinese Writers Association and China Coal Mine Federation of Literature and Art. A variety of Huang Weiping's works have been adapted for radio and broadcast in the central and Shaanxi broadcasting stations, and *Blacksmith Liu* won the first-ever National Award for the Best Mini-Novel.

20

Huang Weiping

Wife, or Otherwise

Wu Ran was critically ill.

Wu Ran's illness was incurable. Doctor Shangguan, the authority of the Central Hospital in the coal city, claimed that he had never seen such an unusual case during his medical career of forty years. Wu Ran was thought to have a cancer; when operated on, he was found to have necrosis of internal organs and had to be sewn up again as before. Doctor Shangguan added that man's body has many secrets, one instance of which is spontaneous combustion. Such cases had been found all over the world, yet the reason was still unknown. His implication was that Wu Ran, who had a rare case of illness, would be well known . . . even if not treated.

When the news spread, his department was buzzing and many ideas followed, all of them new. Perhaps this is what we mean when we say, "No final verdict can be pronounced on a man until after his death."

"What a good man! He was once the youngest member of an administrative section in the 1960s."

"That hunchbacked Lao Wu? How could he have that kind of illness? A good person should be rewarded with good!"

Women were talking in whispers too. "He's such a good man, so nice to Caidi . . ."

"Caidi will bear hardships."

"Maybe Lao Wu will free himself instead . . ."

Caidi was indifferent to the heavy blow, as if she had already expected the result. She remained extremely calm; only a little blush appeared over her pale cheeks, a color frequently found on the faces of heart attack patients. At noon, she carried a bowl quietly and went to the canteen as if she were a poor single soul. She had her meal quietly and went out of the gate afterward. As she picked up her feet, she realized she wasn't sure where to go: home or to the hospital? Her legs were rooted to the ground.

Lao Wu was a nice man—at least other women thought so. Before he'd go away on official business, he would be busy buying vegetables, breaking coal, chopping some logs piece by piece for firewood, piling them up afterward for her, and only then leaving at ease.

Never in the past twenty years had she carried a bowl like today, acting like a beggar in the restaurant. On hearing the bad news, she was able to remain extremely calm; wasn't that itself excessive behavior?

It was Lao Wu who'd taught her to remain so calm, directing her to stay calm while writing applications and reading them in the department meetings. He would not criticize her performance today.

He was also the one who'd recommended her for Party membership and served as a guide. In those days, she had been still young and rather naive. He was wooing her—wooing her in a crazy way. Caidi had come to the Northwest from a small town in the South. She had just finished middle school then. Her mum did not want her to go to the barren land where Caidi "could not earn even some pennies," so the woman had locked her daughter in a small room—yet

Mum herself gave a warm send-off with a small flag to those who supported the border areas in the neighborhood. Hearing the deafening sound of gongs and drums, Caidi escaped through the window and ran to the train station in one breath.

Half a month later, she became a tracer in the headquarters of Weibei Coal Construction Base, which was then being built. The people there were all interested in her—her thoughts, her progress, her work, and even her private life. She yearned for a bright future: tranquil, satisfactory, and full of poetic happiness.

At that time, Wu Ran was the section chief of techniques. On a dim, cheerless, moonlit night when she was waiting for someone, Wu Ran came unexpectedly. It happened that the dormitory power was out, or the fuse had blown, and then . . .

Everything had happened.

Everything had not actually happened. Among the section chiefs, Wu Ran was the youngest, most promising, and most likely to be promoted (some section chiefs had already become deputy heads of other departments). He married the most beautiful girl from the South, a girl with an almondlike face, big eyes, and curly hair. A talented young man and a beautiful young woman—they were obviously a well-matched couple, and their marriage was one created by nature. The perfectly fulfilled Wu Ran would smile to everyone he met. Meanwhile, Caidi had a deep hatred inside, and her mind was like the overturned Sichuaner's castor—full of strange tastes. She could not speak the truth, but grinned with bitterness in her heart. He who laughs last laughs best, doesn't he? Just wait and see!

Now Caidi found herself walking back home without even realizing it. The paint on the door had almost peeled off, leaving it stark naked. She dreaded going inside. Since that winter, she always had that peculiar feeling in front of the door.

That winter had looked the same as that dim, cheerless, moonlit night, and it scared her.

One evening there had been a knock at the door; she wondered if it was Wu Ran. Opening the door, she found a man with a large beard.

"Is Gu Caidi living here?"

It was he, her old . . . what? A college friend, a southerner, who had been so earnest to teach her to trace. She hardly recognized him now with his slovenly clothes and unshaved face.

Wu Ran was not at home; he was away on business. Her heart fluttered like a banner gently swaying in the breeze. Her face was suddenly beaming.

She controlled herself.

"Pingping," she called to her neighbor's girl. "Pingping, come and sit here. Have some candy and enjoy it."

She held five-year-old Pingping next to her on the bench.

"Caidi."

"Where have you been, all these years?"

"An accident," he said. "Well, technically. Someone said that I modified the plan without authorization . . . and then . . ."

"But why didn't you send me a message?"

"Xiao Wu said . . . you . . ." The big-bearded man took a careful look at the simple decorations in the room. "You have a happy life."

Caidi's heart thumped and sank instantly. She asked, "Are you . . . married?"

"Well . . ." The big-bearded man smiled reluctantly. "I just left home and was planning to go to Tankegou . . ."

Tankegou was the farthest place away from the city, where the large fault zone was discovered two years ago and the new wells were abandoned.

"Is this . . . your child? So cute." He touched Pingping's chubby hands and then changed the subject.

Pingping was cute. Caidi had always expected to have a child like her. She'd amuse herself by saying, "Pingping, you are my child. I left you with that other family, so that's why your surname is Shangguan." She would joke this way with Pingping and then hug her.

"I don't believe it," Pingping would say, "I don't believe it." Pingping spoke indistinctly because her front teeth were missing. Her "I don't believe it" sounded like "I don't relieve it."

Caidi would parrot: relieve.

Since then, Caidi had taken an icy view toward everything. She was stupefied with the household, her life, and everything, acting like a puppet.

That year, she was pregnant.

That year, she was sick.

She came back to the South where she had not been for many years. When she and Mum saw each other, they wept and smiled, over and over again. She'd returned home with a slender figure and a thin face, yet much fairer.

Wu Ran was eager to have a baby of his own. One time, chatting with her, he claimed he would happily do anything to have a child. To him, a child meant happiness and the family line. He pleaded.

"Since you're so fond of Pingping, we should have a child like Pingping too."

She challenged him coldly: "I am sick. Who forced you to marry me?"

She was sick indeed—mentally sick.

She had not given birth to a child so far.

She started feeling afraid to be alone at home. She would think too much when she was alone. Her mind would wander and she'd think of all her miserable experiences in the past. Recalling what she had suffered, she would always feel bitter inside and would weep.

In public, however, she never showed her true emotions. To her, recalling the past was a sort of intoxication, just as bitter wine could make one intoxicated.

But if she had to be alone at home, then she would fear being bothered. One day Wu Ran went out, saying that he was going to a friend's place for drinks. She didn't hear clearly the name of the friend. Coming home late at night, he was locked out. He knocked and called to her in a soft voice. She didn't answer at all.

Wu Ran never liked to quarrel with her, even at that moment when he knocked so impatiently and she kept silent. Afraid of losing face, he didn't dare knock more loudly. Instead he ran to his office.

However, walls have ears. Many people in the department heard about Wu Ran being locked out. Some even gossiped among themselves: "Hey, poor Lao Wu, his wife must have some hold on him. He's so nice to her, yet still . . ."

"Who knows?"

"God knows!"

Wu Ran lost face, and so he planned to fight with her for the first time in his life.

Caidi, however, had no desire to argue about it. She just insisted firmly, "I was asleep. I didn't hear you."

"You! I've already endured enough."

"Good. You are bound to endure. I've already endured enough, too, but who can I speak to? If I'm forced to lose my temper, I will speak the truth to everyone I meet."

She was always acting like this. Her words were light and simple—yet to him, they were like thorns on a rose. He was afraid, rendered speechless; he didn't dare to go out anymore. If he wanted to see a friend, he had to ask for "leave of absence." If not allowed it, he would stay at home; if permitted, he would leave at once and come back as soon as possible.

He used to enjoy drinking. One who can't drink cannot serve as a coal official, he believed. But from then on, his drinking companions were estranged from him, and insider information became hard to come by. He was gradually forgotten by his peers.

Whenever his name did come up, people would say, "He got tied up by his wife."

Caidi heard the gossip as well, but she paid no attention. She observed that he hated to be neglected or overlooked; the truth, she said, was merely that he didn't earn many opportunities.

One day, he cooked a very fine meal and was behaving especially warmly toward her. She knew he must have something up his sleeve, and she waited to hear what he had to say.

"Tonight, I have to visit the section chief of our department," he told her. "You'd better come with me."

"Why?"

"The office is making some adjustments . . . in the leadership of the various departments."

"Well, if you wanted to be the section chief of the department," Caidi sneered, "why didn't you marry a kind and devoted wife?"

"Look at our house," he pleaded, "not only old but also small."

"Two people have already been ruined because of you. Why aren't you satisfied?"

Caidi's sneering was the plague of his life. He knew it well:

He had not really made it.

He was still a clerical worker.

They still lived in their old house.

——

The house was always deserted. Without him, it seemed more spacious. She trembled with fear.

"Pingping!" she called. Pingping was going to be a mother soon, coming back to her parents' home to give birth. Soon there would be another generation.

Not a sound was heard next door.

She needed something to drink. The faucet rumbled with noise, offering no water. If Lao Wu had been there, he'd have taken care of it. He was like a stone that had once had edges and corners, newly dislodged from the bottom of a well, but had worn away in the water, year after year, until it was good and round.

"Now, wash the bowls. Now, wash the clothes. Now, buy some vegetables." "Now" became his nickname. Occasionally, when she wanted to complain about certain matters, she would intentionally call him "Section Chief." Since the headquarters had been changed into bureaus, the sections had been eliminated. Since then, those words—section chief—caused him fear, as if that was not his history but a debt that he owed.

He would run as quickly as possible to please her.

Sometimes, if he did not come running fast enough, she would glare angrily, loudly calling him Section Chief. She had a talisman—hence she never needed to shout abuses in the street like a shrew.

Seeing that Wu Ran was scared out of his wits at her unbridled bitterness, she would feel satisfied. At those times, everything was as peaceful as a wind that stills and waves that subside.

But once everything was peaceful, she would feel pain. She often thought that she was not a woman. In her mind, women and girls were different: a woman's charm was different from that of a girl, and a woman's affection toward men was different from that of a girl as well. To be a woman was to be a mature person, while to be a girl was to be a dried flower forever.

She was a woman. But she was not a woman. She had neither a woman's charm nor her affection and happiness. Standing in front of other women, Caidi always felt the lack of something. She felt shorter than them and imbued with a sense of nameless melancholy.

As if she belonged to a different species.

In general, she was restless with anxiety. However, once Wu Ran was beside her, she would maintain a hysterical hatred. She would think of that dim, cheerless, moonlit night and that powerless, pitch-dark time as the beginnings of her misery. How could she muster up any passion? Anxiety and suffering still haunted her like an invisible hand trying to strangle her. She would try to resist it. She'd stretch out her own hand to push away the invisible force. She'd reach out her hand to touch, to grab, and to scratch at her own body as if the outer form were not hers, instead belonging to someone else; as if the hand were there expressly for her to fight and give vent to her resentment. Gradually it started to give her a sense of satisfaction. She'd had to make herself drop the habit.

As time passed, she became more like a woman. She never stood in front of men, nor did she sit down or chat before them. Wherever other women assembled, she would seldom seek their company. The house became her whole world.

Life was going round and round and again round and round.

Enemies are bound to meet on a narrow road; they must accept each other, become accustomed to each other. Once in a while, he would try to please her and bring some harmony to their home. She recognized those times.

One day, Wu Ran reported some news he'd heard: "Big-Beard was promoted from Tankegou Coal Mine to the bureau. He did well there and produced some papers, too."

As a matter of fact, she'd already known about it.

He carefully asked, "How about asking him . . . over for a meal?"

Caidi kept silent and waited to see what he would say next.

She asked Pingping to visit Big-Beard. Pingping told her afterward, "The big-bearded uncle wished to be remembered to you!"

"Will he come?"

"He won't come. He said that he had too much work to deal with and there would be more chances later on. And just then Lao Wu came to call on him. They are old colleagues, you know."

"What else did he say?"

"He said, 'You are Pingping? That year when I saw you, you were not taller than the table. Aunt Gu loved you so much that I thought you were her child. I wondered if Aunt Gu could love me instead!'"

Perhaps because he merely wanted to have a chat with Big-Beard, Wu Ran had not invited the man over.

Big-Beard had not been to their home since then.

Year in, year out, they both had grown some gray hair without noticing it. God knows whether the gray hair was the result of torment or anxiety.

One day, Wu Ran brought back an inscribed plaque, awarded for successful relations with neighbors, and presented it to Caidi, discreet in word and deed.

She did not take it. "What rare thing is this?" she sneered.

"The Five-Good . . . Family Award."

"The Five-Good Family Award?" she snapped with biting sarcasm. "Must it be hung?"

"It's up to you."

"Change 'Family' to 'Husband,' then hang it."

Caidi had hit her target. His colleagues awarded Wu Ran the Five-Good Family Award just for his individual performance; but what did he know about family?

He threw the inscribed plaque on the top of the double-doored cupboard. Caidi felt that was not enough, so she smashed it behind his back.

Was she callous to him? She made a careful survey of herself. She knew what people said—that he had a cruel fate, for he'd married a wife who was beautiful yet useless and a chronic invalid. Who was the one suffering? Or were they both suffering? Who paid the highest price?

She thought about the meaning of a smile. Perhaps she could no longer smile sincerely.

There was a knock at the door. Someone asked loudly, "Is Lao Wu's wife in?"

At the door stood Big-Beard, whom she hadn't seen since that first visit. He looked old and grizzled.

Caidi did not hold a job because she had to recuperate at home. The newer neighbors did not even know her real name; they just called her "Lao Wu's wife." Unexpectedly, Big-Beard also greeted her that way.

"Oh, are you here to see Lao Wu? You should go to the hospital!" said Caidi, who had already become eccentric.

"I was just passing by. Since Lao Wu is critically ill, I thought I'd see whether you need, uh, any help at home . . ."

"Please come in."

"You are Lao Wu's wife, so take care of yourself and stay calm in front of him. You shouldn't provoke . . ."

Big-Beard's continually calling her "Lao Wu's wife" severely upset Caidi. She didn't hear what he said next, merely felt her body tense with anger. She unconsciously reached out her hand for something to support her and knocked over the thermos by accident. She pulled herself together, coming to terms with the absence of Lao Wu and the emptiness inside her.

"Pingping, Pingping!"

"Don't bother anyone," he protested. "I don't need any water."

"No, I was going to call her anyway. Pingping!" she called earnestly.

Pingping rushed over, her hands across her pregnant belly. "Aunt Gu, you called me?"

"Keep me company, Pingping. Were you just going out?"

"I heard you calling . . . but I'm suffering from labor pains. I'm at home by myself."

Hearing this, Caidi was more nervous than Pingping—but she seemed quite experienced, asking the young woman, "Is it time to have the baby? Hurry, call the hospital and ask for an ambulance."

"Well . . . yes . . ."

Big-Beard stepped in to help. "Allow me—I'll go call for an ambulance. You wait."

Gazing at Big-Beard's receding figure, Caidi remained steady and calm. She helped Pingping sit down and then hurried to wash her own hands. Her hands were already fair and clean, without any dirt, but she carefully covered them with soap and scrubbed, as if they were the ones that had ruined her life and the ones she'd had to depend upon to meet all her needs.

Thoroughly scrubbed, she sat down near Pingping, waiting quietly. She felt a burning maternal desire, stronger than any she'd felt before. Maybe it was simply because she was accompanying a soon-to-be mother.

Later she would go to the hospital, sending Pingping off into motherhood and looking after Lao Wu. Suddenly she had a powerful realization: She was Wu Ran's wife. If he died, she was still his wife. Even if she married again, she would always have been his wife. This was his family and also hers; it belonged to them both. What could she do with it?

God provided. But she knew with certainty that she could do no more with it!

Translated by Guo Yingjie